REESE'S BRIDE

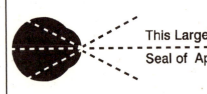

This Large Print Book carries the
Seal of Approval of N.A.V.H.

THE BRIDE TRILOGY, BOOK TWO

REESE'S BRIDE

KAT MARTIN

THORNDIKE PRESS
A part of Gale, Cengage Learning

GALE
CENGAGE Learning·

Detroit • New York • San Francisco • New Haven, Conn • Waterville, Maine • London

GALE
CENGAGE Learning

Thorndike Press® Large Print Basic.
The text of this Large Print edition is unabridged.
Other aspects of the book may vary from the original edition.
Set in 16 pt. Plantin.
Printed on permanent paper.

LIBRARY OF CONGRESS CATALOGING-IN-PUBLICATION DATA

Martin, Kat.
  Reese's bride / by Kat Martin.
    p. cm. — (The bride trilogy ; 2) (Thorndike Press large print
basic)
  ISBN-13: 978 1 4104-2418-1 (alk. paper)
  ISBN-10: 1-4104-2418-9 (alk. paper)
  1. Large type books. I. Title.
  PS3563.A7246R44 2010
  813'.54—dc22   2009046317

Published in 2010 by arrangement with Harlequin Books S.A.

Printed in the United States of America
1 2 3 4 5 6 7 14 13 12 11 10

To my friends in Bakersfield.
Thanks for the great memories.

ONE

England
September, 1855

The crisp black taffeta skirt of her mourning gown rustled as she walked out of the dress shop a few doors in front of him.

Reese Dewar froze where he stood, the silver-headed cane in his hand forgotten, along with the ache in his leg. Rage took its place, dense and heavy, hot and seething.

Sooner or later, he had known he would see her. He had told himself it wouldn't matter, that seeing her again wouldn't affect him. She meant nothing to him, not anymore, not for nearly eight years.

But as she stepped off the wooden walkway, a ray of autumn sunlight gleamed against the jet-black curls on her shoulders and anger boiled up inside him, fury unlike he had known in years.

He watched her continue toward her sleek black four-horse carriage, the crossed-saber

Aldridge crest glinting in gold on the side. She paused for a moment as one of the footmen hurried to open the door and he realized she wasn't alone. A small, dark-haired boy, nearly hidden in the voluminous folds of her skirt, hurried along beside her. She urged him up the iron steps and the child disappeared inside the elegant coach.

Instead of climbing the stairs herself, the woman turned and looked at him over her shoulder, her gray eyes finding him with unerring accuracy, as if she could feel his cold stare stabbing into the back of her neck. She gasped when she realized who it was, though she must have known, in a village as small as Swansdowne, one day their paths would cross.

Surely she had heard the gossip, heard of his return to Briarwood, the estate he had inherited from his maternal grandfather.

The estate he had meant to share with *her.*

Their eyes locked, hers troubled, filled with some emotion he could not read. His own gaze held the bitterness and anger he made no effort to hide. He loathed her for what she had done, hated her with every ounce of his being.

It shocked him.

He had thought those feelings long past. For most of the last eight years, he had been away from England, a major in the British cavalry. He had fought in foreign wars, commanded men, sent some of them to their deaths. He had been wounded and nearly died himself.

He was home now, his injured leg making him no longer fit to serve. That and the vow he had made to his dying father. One day he would come back to Briarwood. He would make the estate his home as he had once intended.

Reese would rather have stayed in the army. He didn't belong in the country. He wasn't sure *where* he belonged anymore and he loathed his feelings of uncertainty nearly as much as he loathed Elizabeth.

She swallowed, seemed to sway a little on her feet as she turned away, climbed the steps and settled herself inside the carriage. She hadn't changed. With her raven hair, fine pale features, and petite, voluptuous figure, Elizabeth Clemens Holloway, Countess of Aldridge, was as beautiful at six-and-twenty as she had been at eighteen.

As she had been when she had declared her love and accepted his proposal of marriage.

His gaze followed the coach as it rolled off toward Aldridge Park, the palatial estate that had belonged to her late husband, Edmund

Holloway, Earl of Aldridge. Aldridge had died last year at the age of thirty-three, leaving his wife a widow, leaving her with a son.

Reese spat into the dirt at his feet. Just the thought of Aldridge in Elizabeth's bed made him sick to his stomach.

Five years his senior, Edmund was already an earl when he had competed with Reese for Elizabeth's affections. She had been amused by the attentions of the handsome, sophisticated aristocrat, but she had been in love with Reese.

Or so she had said.

The carriage disappeared round a bend in the road and Reese's racing pulse began to slow. He was amazed at the enmity he still felt toward her. He was a man who had taught himself control and that control rarely abandoned him. He would not allow it to happen again.

Leaning heavily on his cane, the ache in his leg beginning to reach through the fury that had momentarily consumed him, he made his way to his own conveyance and slowly climbed aboard. Aldridge's widow and her son had no place in his life. Elizabeth was dead to him and had been for nearly eight years.

As dead as her husband, the man she had betrayed Reese to marry.

And he would never forgive her.

Elizabeth leaned against the tufted red velvet seat of her carriage. Her heart was hammering, battering against the wall of her chest. *Dear God, Reese.*

She had known she would see him. She had prayed it would happen at some distant time in the future. Sometime after she had come to grips with the fact that he was living in the house they had once meant to share.

Dear God, Reese. There was a day she thought never to see him again. Rumors had surfaced. Reese, a major in the cavalry, was missing in action somewhere in the Crimea. There were whispers he was dead. Then he had returned and the news had swept the countryside.

He was back at Briarwood, wounded in the war and retired from the army. He was home, living just a few miles from Aldridge Park. She should have been prepared and yet seeing him today . . . seeing the hatred in his brilliant blue eyes, made her chest squeeze with guilt and regret.

She knew how much he hated her. If she hadn't already been certain, she would have seen it in his icy stare today. Every pore in his sun-bronzed face exuded loathing. Every angry thought seemed to reach her across the distance between them. She hadn't seen him since that day nearly eight years ago that he had come home on leave and discovered she had wed another man.

Not since the day he had called her a whore and vowed that one day she would pay for her lies and deceit.

She had paid. Dear God, she had paid every day since she had married Edmund Holloway. She had done as her father demanded and wed a man not of her choosing.

But she had never stopped loving Reese.

Her heart squeezed. She thought of his hard, handsome features, so masculine, so incredibly attractive. In some ways, he looked the same as he had as a young man of twenty, tall and black-haired, his body hard-muscled and lean, his features sharply defined.

And yet he was a completely different man. He had been a little shy in his courtship of her, a little uncertain. Now he wore his masculinity like a comfortable shirt; it was clear in his unwavering stare, the way his gaze too boldly assessed her. There was a harshness in his features that hadn't been there when he was young, and a confidence and raw sense of authority that only made him more attractive.

"Mama . . . ?"

Jared's small voice reached her from across the carriage. "Yes, sweetheart?" A headache had begun to form behind her eyes and she rubbed her temple against the pain.

"Who was that man?" Her son sat quietly on the opposite seat, his voice little more than a whisper. He wouldn't be talking at all, she knew, if he hadn't sensed her distress.

She forced herself to smile and patted the seat beside her. Jared scooted next to her and she settled an arm around his small shoulders.

"Major Dewar is an old friend, sweetheart." A complete and utter falsehood. The man loathed her and she didn't blame him. "He just got out of the army and he is returned to his home."

Jared just looked at her. He didn't ask more, simply gazed at her with his deep-set brown eyes, soulful eyes, she thought. Eyes far too worldly for a child so young, and far too full of loneliness.

Managing a smile, she began to point out the sights along the road as the carriage moved down the lane that cut through the rolling fields. It was mid-September, the leaves turning orange, gold and red. Two small boys played along the roadside tossing a ball back and forth, and Elizabeth pointed them out to Jared.

"Doesn't that look like fun? You like to play ball. Perhaps one of Mrs. Clausen's sons will play with you this afternoon." Mrs. Clausen was the housekeeper, a dear woman raising her daughter's orphaned grandsons, boys eight and nine years old. They liked Jared, but because of his shyness, rarely sought him out. "Why don't you ask them when we get home?"

Jared said nothing, but his gaze remained on the boys and the look in his eyes made a lump rise in her throat. As long as he remained at Aldridge Park, Jared would never come out of the shell he had built to protect himself. It was one more reason she had to leave.

Not *leave,* Elizabeth silently corrected. *Escape.*

As long as her brother-in-law and his wife, Mason and Frances Holloway, lived at Aldridge Park, she was a prisoner in her own home.

Her headache continued to worsen, pounding away inside her skull as it often did these days. She was afraid of Mason. He was the sort of man who stood a little too close, touched her a little too often. She needed to leave, but she was certain he would simply come after her. She had no idea how far he would go to keep her and Jared — now the Earl of Aldridge — under his control. But she was certain there was little he would not do.

She was frightened. Not only for herself but for her son.

An image arose of Reese Dewar, strong, capable, a veteran of the war, the sort of man who would protect his family no matter the cost.

But Reese wasn't her husband and never would be.

And she had no one to blame but herself.

Reese returned to Briarwood, his mood dark and brooding. He tried not to think of Elizabeth but he couldn't seem to get her out of his head. What was there about her? How had she managed to keep a stranglehold over him for so many years? Why had no other woman been able to pierce the wall of his heart as she had done?

His manservant, Timothy Daniels, a brawny young corporal who had served with him for several years before being injured and sent home, arrived in the study just then.

"You are returned," Daniels said. "Is there anything you need, sir?" Tim had been out of work and hungry when he had appeared at Reese's door. In a few short weeks, he had become dedicated to Reese's welfare. With this damnable leg slowing him down, Reese was glad to have a man he could count on.

"I'm fine, Tim."

"Let me know if you need me."

Reese scowled. "I imagine I can survive a few hours studying these bloody damned ledgers." Though in truth, he hated paperwork and would far rather be out of doors, which Timothy, being a military man, seemed to understand.

"Aye, sir. Like I said —"

"That will be all, corporal." Growing tired of the young man's overprotectiveness, Reese snapped out the words in his firmest military voice.

"Aye, sir." The door closed quietly, leaving Reese alone in the wood-paneled room. The study was his sanctuary, a comfortable chamber lined with books, a warm, inviting, masculine place where a fire blazed in the hearth and he could insulate himself from the memories that crept into other parts of the house.

In the days of their courtship, Elizabeth

had been to Briarwood more than once. She loved the ivy that covered the white plaster walls of the manor and hung from the porch outside the front door, she had said. She loved the steep slate roof with its whimsical chimney pots that made the house look like a fairy tale dwelling.

She had made plans to paint the drawing room a pale shade of rose and add lace curtains, to hang flowered silk wallpaper behind the sofa. She loved the master's suite, she told him, loved how sunny it was, the way it looked out over the garden. She couldn't wait to share his big four-poster bed, a gift his grandfather had commissioned for his bride-to-be.

That thought led to one he didn't wish to recall and his loins began to fill. Bloody hell. All these years and seeing her once made him want her again. He forced himself to remember the way she had told him how much she loved him and how happy she would be to live at Briarwood as his wife.

Lies. All of them.

Just weeks after he had left for his assignment in London, she had broken her promise to marry him. Instead she had wed an earl, a man of untold wealth, and abandoned the younger son of a duke, a man who could provide a pleasant home and sufficient income but would never be extravagantly rich.

Reese ground his jaw. Since his return, thoughts of Elizabeth had begun to haunt him, memories he had buried years ago. Two days after he had discovered the news of her marriage, he had left Wiltshire County for good, gone back to London and asked to serve in the cavalry, knowing he would be assigned to duty somewhere far from English shores.

If he hadn't been wounded, if he hadn't promised his father, he would be there still.

His hand fisted on the top of the desk. Reese dragged in a deep breath and forced his mind back to the present. The ledgers sat open in front of him. He forced himself to concentrate and began to skim the pages. He would have to conquer his painful past and concentrate on the future if he meant to fulfill his obligations and make the fallow fields of Briarwood productive again.

Reese intended to see it done.

With her young son, Jared, walking close beside her, Elizabeth entered the magnificent entry of the huge Georgian mansion, Aldridge Park, her late husband's country estate. The property and all others entailed to the earldom, along with Edmund's vast fortune, now belonged to Jared, the recently titled seventh Earl of Aldridge.

The sound of footsteps echoing on the black-and-white marble floor drew her attention and Elizabeth looked up to see her sister-in-law, Frances Holloway, also dressed in black, float into the entry to greet them.

Frances's lips flattened out in disapproval. "I expected you home hours ago. Where have you been?" She was a thin woman, with high cheekbones and a long, narrow nose. Her greatest asset was her strength of will. Frances managed to turn things to suit her purpose no matter how difficult they might be, probably the reason her husband, Mason, had married her.

"I told you Jared and I were going into the village." Elizabeth had given up any attempt at being civil to Frances some months back. The woman disliked her and had since the day she had delivered Edmund a son, making it impossible for Mason to inherit the title. "I had some shopping to do. It took longer than I expected." And lately she hadn't been feeling quite well. It felt good to be out in the fresh air, out of the house.

But that, like the length of time she had spent, was none of Frances's business.

"Jared's tutor has been looking for him. We don't want him getting behind in his lessons."

Elizabeth's arm went protectively around her small son's shoulders. "He's going outside to play for a while. Then he can do his lessons."

Jared looked up at her, his eyes big and dark. "I'll do them now, Mama. Marcus and Benny prob'ly won't want to play with me, anyway."

"But —"

Frances swept in like a tall black raven and scooped Jared off toward the stairs. Elizabeth wanted to tell her little boys needed to do more than just study, but her head was pounding and she couldn't seem to get her thoughts in order. And her son was already climbing the sweeping staircase, Frances right beside him. She watched them ascend a second set of stairs and disappear into the schoolroom.

"So you're home." Mason Holloway's voice snaked across the entry and Elizabeth turned. "I hope you enjoyed your shopping."

Just a year younger than Edmund, Mason was a tall, formidable man, heavy through the chest and shoulders, with brown hair and a thick mustache. Not unattractive and yet there was a coarseness about him, and a tone of false sincerity that made her distrust him. A little shiver crept down her spine as his eyes ran over the swell of her breasts and unconsciously she took a step back.

"All in all, it was quite a pleasant outing," she replied, forcing herself to smile. "A lovely little dress shop just opened. Mrs. O'Neal has some very fine fabrics."

"You should have told me you wished to go. I would have given you an escort."

Having Mason anywhere near her was the last thing she wanted. She had suffered Edmund's company far too long, and her brother-in-law was even more loathsome. Mason Holloway had squandered every dollar he had inherited. He would have been destitute had Edmund not provided for him.

But her husband was nothing if not loyal. In his will, he had left Mason and Frances a life estate on their rooms in the east wing of the mansion, as well as permission to stay in his town house in London. Mason and Frances were there, whether she liked it or not, and there was no way to get rid of them.

"I appreciate the offer," she told Mason, "but I had Jared to keep me company."

He scoffed. "Jared is only a boy. A woman of your position shouldn't be traveling alone."

She hoisted her chin, but the motion made her dizzy. She reached out to catch hold of the stair rail, hoping Mason wouldn't notice. "I was scarcely alone. I had a coachman and a pair of footmen with me."

"That may be true, but next time, I shall accompany you."

Not if she could prevent it, but Mason was a difficult man to oppose and lately she couldn't seem to find the will to fight him. She had begun to feel unwell some weeks back, suffering from headaches and nausea and an occasional bout of dizziness.

It was part of the reason she hadn't moved into Holiday House, the mansion on the outskirts of London she had inherited from her father, along with the rest of the fortune he had provided for her. She had wanted to leave but she was uncertain of her health and sure her in-laws would follow. If she tossed them out, she and Jared would suffer the scandal.

Still, a scandal was better than what might happen if she stayed.

As she stared at Mason, the suspicion that had begun to build over the past few months expanded inside her. If she was out of the way, Mason and Frances would become Jared's guardians. They would control the vast Aldridge fortune.

The thought of her young son left alone and vulnerable and growing even more withdrawn made her stomach roll with nausea. She was all that stood between Jared and the ruthless people who cared nothing for him and only wanted his money.

Sooner or later, she had to do something.

Her headache worsened, pounded viciously against her skull, and again the dizziness struck. "I am afraid you will have to excuse me. I discover I am not feeling all that well."

Beneath his mustache, a sympathetic smile curved Mason's lips. "Perhaps a nap will help."

Turning away from him, she started up the staircase, but Mason caught up easily and fell in beside her, taking her arm to guide her toward the landing.

"I hope you're feeling better by supper," he said as they reached the door to her suite.

"I'm certain I will be." But she wasn't sure at all.

Fear for her son returned. As soon as she felt better, she would make plans to leave. She closed the door and prayed she could see it done.

Two

Jared sat in a carved, high-back chair at the head of the long, polished mahogany table in the state dining room. Elizabeth sat to his right in one of the other twenty-six chairs, Mason and Frances to his left. Tall candles burned in the huge, gaslit, crystal chandelier hanging above the table, and the gold-rimmed plates were of finest Sevres porcelain.

It was too formal a setting for a shy little boy like Jared. But Frances had insisted, since it was his seventh birthday, and the issue didn't seem important enough to Elizabeth to suffer an argument.

The meal was as lavish as the setting: a rich vermicelli soup, roasted partridge with pecan stuffing, lobster in cream sauce, an array of vegetables and fresh baked breads. Dessert was an assortment of cakes and tarts and a fancy custard in the shape of a swan.

It should have been a horse, Elizabeth thought. Jared had always loved horses.

"All right, boy. Time to open your presents." Mason snapped his fingers at the pair of footmen who stood along the wall. They rushed forward, gifts in hand, and set them on the table in front of her son.

Jared looked at the gifts and beamed at Elizabeth. "They're all so beautiful, Mama." It was like her son to appreciate the packages as much as the gifts inside. A lovely silver-wrapped box with a huge blue satin bow sat on top of a larger gift covered in bright red velvet-flocked paper decorated with a red feathered bird. Her own gift was the smallest, but beautifully wrapped in dark brown silk with a simple gold ribbon.

"Which one should I open first?" he asked, looking up at her.

"How about this one?" Mason shoved the red velvet package in front of him, the crimson stuffed bird jiggling with the motion.

Jared pulled the bird off the top and smoothed a hand over its feathers. "I wish it still could fly."

He was a gentle-natured child. He loved animals of any sort, even stuffed ones.

"Open your gift, boy." Mason pushed the box even closer and as Jared reached for it,

25

nearly knocked it off the table.

The smile died on his lips. "I'm . . . I'm sorry, Uncle Mason."

"It's all right, boy. Here, let me help you."

Elizabeth gritted her teeth as Mason pulled the box to his side of the table and ripped off the red flocked paper. He tore open the box then shoved it back to Jared and she saw that it was filled with an army of miniature soldiers.

Each wooden soldier was intricately carved and beautifully painted, half the army wearing the red-and-white uniforms of the British, Napoleon's blue-coated soldiers forming the opposing force. They were the sort of thing a little boy would love and Jared's brown eyes gleamed with appreciation.

Elizabeth shivered. All she could think of Reese and how the army had torn them apart. A memory arose of him striding unannounced into the entry of Aldridge Park dressed in his scarlet uniform, so handsome her heart hurt just to look at him. He had discovered her betrayal and her hasty marriage to the earl. He had called her a liar and a whore and left her standing there shaking, her heart shattered into a thousand pieces.

Elizabeth shook herself, forcing away the

image. Her head was beginning to throb and her mouth felt dry. She watched Jared open the second gift, a woolen jacket that Frances had bought him. He thanked her very properly and reached for the last of his gifts.

He looked up at her and smiled, knowing the gift was from her.

"I hope you like it," Elizabeth said. She was feeling terribly weary. She hoped it didn't show.

Jared carefully untied the gold ribbon, gently eased off the brown silk wrapping and set it aside, then lifted the lid off the box. Inside on a bed of tissue rested a small silver unicorn. It stood five inches high, its thick neck bowed, its powerful front legs dancing in the air.

Jared reached into the box, carefully removed the horse and held it up with reverence.

"A unicorn," he said, his small fingers skimming over the shining horse that gleamed in the light of the candalabra in the center of the table. "He's wonderful, Mama."

Jared had a collection of four other unicorns. He loved horses of every shape and size and especially the mystical creature with the magic horn in the middle of its forehead. "I'm going to name him Beauty."

Mason carefully wiped his mustache with his napkin and shoved back his chair. He had little patience with children and that patience was clearly at an end. "It's getting late. Now that your birthday is over for another year, it is past time you went to bed."

Anger penetrated her lethargy and the pounding that had started in her head.

Elizabeth came to her feet. "Jared is my son, not yours. I will be the one to tell him when it's time for bed." She felt a tug on the skirt of her blue silk dinner gown. Her head was spinning. She hadn't realized Jared had gotten up from his chair.

"It's all right, Mama. Mrs. Garvey will be waiting for me." Mrs. Garvey was his nanny, a kind, gray-haired woman whose own children were grown.

Elizabeth knelt and pulled her son into her arms. "Happy birthday, sweetheart. I'll have the footmen bring your gifts up to your room." She smoothed back an errant lock of his thick dark hair. "I'll see you in the morning."

Jared looked over at Mason, caught his scowl, and eased out of her embrace. "Good night, Mama."

Elizabeth's heart squeezed. "Good night,

sweetheart."

Clutching the silver unicorn against his small chest, Jared turned and raced out of the dining room.

An hour later, Elizabeth sat on the tapestry stool in front of the mirror above her dressing table. It was late. Most of the household was abed. She had napped before supper and yet still felt tired. Lately she couldn't seem to get enough sleep.

She yawned behind her hand, wondering if she had the energy to read, when the doorknob turned, the door swung silently open, and Mason Holloway walked into her bedroom.

Elizabeth shot up from the stool. She was wearing only a white cotton nightgown, hardly proper attire to receive male visitors.

"What are you doing in here?" She reached for the quilted wrapper lying on the bureau, but Mason picked it up before she could reach it.

"I saw the light under your door. I thought you might be in the mood for company."

"What . . . what are you talking about? It's late, Mason. Your wife will be wondering where you are."

"My wife has no say in where I spend my evenings." Instead of leaving, he tossed the robe aside and walked behind her, settled his big hands on her shoulders and began a crude massage.

Elizabeth's stomach tightened with revulsion. She knocked his hands away and whirled to face him, the movement making her dizzy, and she swayed a little on her feet.

Mason caught her arm to steady her. "Still feeling poorly?"

Elizabeth managed to pull free. "Get out," she said, but her head was pounding and the words came out with little force.

Mason leaned toward her, bent his head and pressed his mouth against the side of her neck. His mustache brushed against her skin and her stomach rolled with nausea.

"You don't want me to leave," he said, his voice husky. "You need me, Elizabeth. You need what I can give you."

Her stomach churned. "I'll scream. If you don't leave this minute, I swear I shall scream the house down."

Mason laughed softly. In the light of the lamp on the bedside table, his eyes glinted with sexual heat. "Perhaps the time is not yet right. Soon though. Soon I'll come and you will welcome me, Elizabeth. You won't have any other choice."

You won't have any other choice. Dear God, the words rang with a certainty that

30

made the hair rise at the back of her neck. "Get out!"

Mason just smiled. "Sleep well, my dear. I shall see you in the morning."

Elizabeth stood frozen as he left the bedroom and quietly closed the door. Her head throbbed and the dizziness had returned. Sinking back down on the stool, she fought to steady herself and clear her head. She thought of Jared and the danger he was in and her eyes filled with tears.

She wasn't safe in the house anymore and neither was her son. The time had come. She had to leave.

Ignoring the pounding in her skull, summoning her strength, as well as a shot of courage, she rose from the stool and hurried toward the bellpull to ring for Sophie, her ladies' maid. A search beneath the bed made her nauseous, but yielded a heavy leather satchel she hefted up on the feather mattress.

A sleepy-eyed Sophie, dark hair sticking out all over her head, walked into the bedroom yawning. "You rang for me, my lady?"

"I need your help, Sophie. I'm leaving."

The girl's green eyes widened. "Now? It's the middle of the night, my lady."

"I need you to go upstairs and wake Mrs.

31

Garvey. Tell her to get dressed. Tell her we are leaving straightaway and she needs to pack a bag for herself and one for Jared. Tell her to meet me downstairs at the door leading out to the carriage house."

Beginning to pick up on Elizabeth's urgency, Sophie straightened. "As you wish, my lady."

"As soon as you've finished, go out to the stable and tell Mr. Hobbs to ready my carriage — the small one. Tell him not to come round front. Tell him I'll come to him where he is."

Sophie whirled to leave.

"And don't tell anyone else I'm going."

The little maid understood. Though she had never said so, she didn't like Mason Holloway, either. She bobbed a curtsey and rushed out the door.

Ignoring a wave of dizziness, Elizabeth returned to her packing. By the time Sophie returned, she was dressed in a simple black woolen gown, her hair pulled into a tight chignon at the back of her neck, a crisp black bonnet tied beneath her chin.

"I need help with the last of the buttons," she said to her maid, turning her back so that Sophie could do them up. As soon as the task was completed, Elizabeth grabbed her black wool cloak off the hook beside the door and whirled it round her shoulders. She swayed a little with the effort.

Sophie rushed forward, alarmed. "My lady!"

"I'm all right. Just promise you will keep silent until morning."

"Of course. You can trust me, my lady. Please be careful."

Elizabeth smiled, grateful for the young girl's loyalty. "I'll be careful."

Heading down the servants' stairs, satchel in hand, it didn't take long to reach the door leading out to the stable. Holding two small bags, Mrs. Garvey stood next to Jared, who looked up at Elizabeth with big, worried brown eyes.

"Where are we going, Mama?"

Until that very moment, she hadn't been completely certain. Now she looked at her son, felt a rush of dizziness, and knew what she had to do.

"To see an old friend," she said, and dear God, she prayed that somewhere in the darkest part of his heart, he would find that in some small measure, it was still true.

THREE

Reese awakened from sleep to a banging at his door. Frowning, he swung his legs to the side of the high four-poster bed and shoved himself to his feet. The pounding started again as he dragged on his dark blue silk dressing gown.

Grumbling, he grabbed his cane, crossed the bedroom and jerked open the door to find Timothy Daniels standing in the hall-way.

"For God's sake, man, what is it? Keep that up and you'll wake the whole house."

Timothy's flaming red hair glinted in the light of the whale oil lamp he held in his hand. "It's an emergency, sir. There's a woman. She's downstairs, sir. She says she needs to speak to you. She says the matter is urgent."

"It is well past midnight. Why the devil would a woman wish to see me at this bloody hour of the night?"

"Can't say, sir. But she's here with her son and she seems overly distressed."

Apprehension trickled down his spine. He had seen Elizabeth and her son two days ago. Surely this had nothing to do with her. Then again, he had never been a man who believed in coincidence. "Tell her I'll be down as soon as I can put on some clothes."

"Aye, sir."

Timothy disappeared and Reese made his way over to the wardrobe. Unconsciously rubbing his leg, he jerked out a pair of black trousers and a white lawn shirt, sat down and pulled them on. As he tucked in his shirt, pain shot down his leg. Since he'd taken a chunk of grapeshot at Inkerman, it was stiff, but not completely. Once he began to walk on it, it usually loosened up. At this hour the blasted thing felt like a lead rod connected to his body.

Reese ignored it. As soon as he was dressed, he headed downstairs, wondering what sort of problem awaited him at this hour of the night.

Leaning on his cane, he took the stairs as fast as he could, reached the bottom, and looked up to find his tall, skinny, very dignified butler standing next to a woman dressed in black.

Time seemed to slow. He knew those

finely etched features, the pale skin and raven-black hair, the perfectly shaped eyebrows and lips the color of roses. Images assailed him. Elizabeth in the garden of her home, laughing as she raced him to the gazebo. Elizabeth in his arms as they whirled around the ballroom. Elizabeth out on the terrace, her fingers sliding through his hair, her mouth soft and welcoming under his.

He straightened, met her gaze squarely. "You are not welcome here."

She was trembling, he saw as she walked toward him, her movements as graceful and feminine as he recalled, a small woman, though she had never seemed so. "I must speak to you, my lord. It is urgent."

He wasn't used to the title. Major suited him far more, and it jarred him a little. He might have told her he had no time for a woman of such low character as she, but then he saw that she wasn't alone. A gray-haired woman stood in the shadows next to the boy he had seen in the village, the boy who was Elizabeth's son.

"Please, my lord."

"This way." He moved off toward the drawing room, limping only a little, hoping his harsh tone of voice would compel her to turn and leave. He walked into the drawing room and waited as Elizabeth moved past him, her full black skirts brushing against his legs. He closed the sliding door, making them private, but didn't offer her a seat nor take one himself.

"It's the middle of the night. What is it you want?"

She lifted her chin and he noticed her complexion was far paler than it should have been. She was fighting for composure and the realization filled him with satisfaction.

"I — I know you what you think of me. I know how much you hate me."

He laughed without mirth. "You couldn't begin to know."

She bit her bottom lip. It was as full and tempting as he remembered and the muscles across his abdomen contracted. *Damn her. Damn her to bloody hell.*

"I came here to plead for your help. My father is dead. I have no brothers or sisters, no true friends. You are a man of honor, a veteran of the war. I am here because I believe you are not the sort of man to turn away a desperate woman and her child — no matter your personal feelings." She swayed a little and beads of perspiration appeared on her temple.

Reese frowned. "Are you unwell?"

"I . . . I am not certain. I have been feeling ill of late. That is part of the reason I am here. Should my condition worsen, I am concerned for what might happen to Jared."

"Jared? That is your son's name?"

"Yes."

She swayed again and he started toward her, using his cane only once as he crossed to where she stood and caught her arm to steady her. He was a gentleman, no matter how difficult at times that might be. "Sit down before you fall down."

She moved forward, sank unsteadily onto the burgundy sofa, her black silk reticule falling into her lap. She reached a trembling hand to her temple, then looked up at him with the beautiful, haunting gray eyes that invaded his dreams. The memory of a thousand sleepless nights hardened his jaw and fortified his resolve against her.

"I am not the help you need."

"There is no one else I can turn to."

"You're the Countess of Aldridge. Surely there is someone."

Her hands gripped the reticule in her lap. "I intended to go to London. I might have tried to make it tonight if I hadn't been feeling so unwell." She looked at him with those beseeching gray eyes. "I believe my in-laws may be doing something to my food or drink. If my condition continues to worsen, my son may be in grave danger."

His jaw tightened. "You're speaking of Mason and Frances Holloway?"

"Yes. I'm afraid that even should I reach London safely, my brother-in-law will arrive within days. I'm afraid he'll find a means of forcing my return to Aldridge Park. Once I am there . . ." She shook her head. "I am frightened, my lord. I am here because I don't know where else to go."

"What do you expect from me?"

"I suppose I expect that your honor will dictate you must help me. You're a strong man, the sort who can protect my son. I suppose I am hoping that no matter what I have done, you will not be able to turn me out of your home."

Anger simmered just below the surface. She knew how much he valued his honor. She knew more about him than any other person in the world. He worked to calm the angry pounding of his heart.

"I am afraid, *Countess,* you ask too much." Purposely, he used her title, a reminder of all that had transpired between them.

"Elizabeth . . ." she softly corrected. "We are too well acquainted for anything more formal."

A hard smile surfaced. "I suppose you

could say we are well acquainted. Very well acquainted, indeed."

For an instant, a flush rose in her cheeks, erasing the pallor, but she did not glance away. "Will you help me?"

He began to shake his head. He couldn't do it. He couldn't bear having her in his house, under his roof. He couldn't stand the painful memories.

She came up from the sofa, so close he could measure the incredible length of her thick black lashes.

A black-gloved hand settled gently on his arm. "Please, my lord. I beg you not to refuse. My son needs you. I need you. You are the only person in the world who can help us . . . the only person I trust."

The words hit him hard. She trusted him. Once he had trusted her. Reese stared at the beautiful woman standing in front of him. He had loved her once. Fiercely and without reserve. Now he hated her with the same unrelenting passion.

Still, he could read her desperation, her fear. As she had said, he was a man who valued his honor. She had come to him for help. How could he turn her away?

"I'll have Hopkins show you and your party upstairs." A harsh smile curved his lips. "I believe you remember where to find the guest rooms."

She glanced away but relief washed over her features. "Thank you, my lord. I swear I shall find a way to repay the great debt I owe you."

And then she collapsed at his feet.

"Corporal Daniels!"

Elizabeth stirred as Reese lifted her into his arms. Her mind was foggy, blurred. She blinked up at him, into the hard, carved lines of his face. "I . . . I'm all right. You don't have to —"

"Daniels!" he shouted again and a brawny, red-haired young man appeared beside him. "Yes, sir?"

Reese dumped her unceremoniously into the younger man's arms. "I can't carry her up the stairs — not with this damnable leg."

Corporal Daniels looked down at her and smiled. "Rest easy, ma'am. I'll get you there in a jiff."

She had no time to protest as the young man swept her out of the drawing room.

"Mama!" Jared rushed forward as they entered the hall and grabbed frantically onto her skirts.

"I am fine, sweetheart. Just a little dizzy, is all. Bring Mrs. Garvey and come upstairs."

Jared turned and raced back to where the

older woman stood waiting and grabbed hold of her hand. The butler led the pair a few steps behind as the corporal carted her up the stairs. He carried her into one of the guest rooms and settled her carefully on the bed.

"I'll fetch Gilda to attend you, ma'am. She's the chambermaid."

She didn't protest. She still felt light-headed though the spinning had begun to slow. She rested her head on the pillow and looked up at the ceiling. It was white while the walls were a soft yellow, pretty though the room could use a fresh coat of paint. The curtains were yellow silk damask, the furniture rosewood, recently dusted but in need of a dose of lemon oil.

She was staying at Briarwood. Reese had agreed to help her. She could hardly believe it.

And yet, in her heart, she had been certain, no matter his personal feelings, he would not turn her away.

He walked into the room a few minutes later, tall and masculine, the image of authority and strength. For an instant, she caught the glint of silver on the head of his ebony cane. She knew he had been injured. She didn't know how badly he was hurt.

Icy blue eyes fixed on her face. "You are

here — at least for the moment — and you are safe. I'll have Corporal Daniels fetch the physician —"

"There is no need for that. I just need to sleep. Perhaps tomorrow . . ."

"You're certain?"

She wasn't the least bit certain, but she had already put him to enough trouble for one night. "Yes."

"All right, we'll wait until the morrow."

"Thank you."

"In the morning I'll expect you to tell me exactly what is going on."

She struggled to sit up, eased back until her shoulders rested against the carved wooden headboard. Reese made no attempt to help her.

"Tomorrow my brother-in-law will discover Jared and I are missing. Sooner or later, he'll find out where we are."

"As I said, as long as you are here, you are safe. Get some sleep. Your Mrs. Garvey is with the boy. We'll talk in the morning." Turning, he left the bedroom and Elizabeth realized how rapidly her heart was beating. Dear God, until that moment, she hadn't realized how painful it would be to hear the sound of his voice. How difficult it would be to suffer Reese's bitter dislike of her.

She hadn't realized the feelings she had

believed so deeply buried remained just beneath the surface.

She had to guard them, keep them carefully hidden away. If she failed, if she allowed the slightest crack in her heart, the pain would simply be too awful to bear.

The light of a crisp fall day streamed into the house as Reese made his way down the hall toward the breakfast room, a sunny chamber that overlooked the garden. With its creamy yellow walls and the chairs at the table upholstered in soft moss green, it was a room he enjoyed sitting in to read his daily newspaper and eat his morning meal.

Not today.

Today his mood was grim and had been since he had awakened from a restless night of sleep. As was his habit, he had been up for several hours, working in his study for a while then going out to check on his livestock.

Besides his big black gelding, Warrior — like Reese, a veteran of the war — he had, since his return, purchased several mares and a blooded Thoroughbred stallion. With his damnable stiff leg, he wasn't sure he would ever be able to sit a saddle again, but he had been working to stretch and retrain his muscles, and even if he couldn't ride, he refused to give up his horses.

His latest purchase, the stallion, Alexander the Great, came from prize racing stock. Reese had seen him run and he believed the horse would sire colts capable of winning at Ascot and Epson Downs.

Still making his way down the hall, a noise inside the breakfast room drew his attention. As he walked inside, he saw Elizabeth and her son seated at the table, and his chest tightened at the sight of them there in his house.

He took a deep breath and released it slowly, and continued into the sunny room. The pair were enjoying a meal of sausages, creamed herring, and eggs, though Elizabeth didn't seem to actually be eating, just moving the food round on her plate. She looked up at him just then and the gratitude in her eyes made his chest tighten even more.

It was merely his dislike of her, he told himself, and anger than she had embroiled him in whatever turmoil her marriage to Aldridge had created.

"Jared usually eats with his nanny in the schoolroom," she explained a bit nervously, "but since the house is new to him, I brought him downstairs to breakfast with me. I hope you don't mind."

He looked at the boy, whose eyes were dark and round and clearly uncertain. He perched on the edge of his chair as if he might run. A small silver horse, a unicorn, Reese saw, sat on the table in front of him.

"I don't mind." He turned away from the child. It was hard to look at Aldridge's heir and not feel jealous. The boy should have been his. Elizabeth should have been his.

But money and power had been more important than the promises she had made or her declarations of love.

Then again, perhaps she had never felt the least affection for him. Perhaps it had all been pretense.

"I'm done, Mama," the boy said. "May I be excused?"

The child had stopped eating the moment Reese had appeared in the doorway. Elizabeth seemed to sense his distress and managed to smile. She looked paler than she should have and now he noticed her eyes seemed a duller gray than they usually were, without the faint blue undertones that made them so appealing.

"You may go," she said to the boy. "I'll be up in a little while." Her gaze found Reese's across the table, a little out of focus, he thought. "Perhaps his lordship will allow us to take a walk round the grounds. The trees are lovely this time of year."

Reese merely nodded. He didn't intend to punish the boy for the sins his mother had committed.

The child slid down from his chair, grabbed the unicorn, and hurried out of the breakfast room. Reese walked over and poured himself a cup of coffee from the silver urn on the sideboard. He'd been hungry when he walked in. Seeing Elizabeth there, looking like the wife he had once imagined, his appetite had fled.

As a footman picked up her half-full plate and whisked it away, he pulled out a chair and sat down across from her, leaning his cane against the edge of the table.

Elizabeth was staring out the window into the garden, which was completely overgrown, the plants sprawling over their low brick enclosures into the pathways, fallen leaves covering the ground. The gardener had quit before Reese's arrival. There hadn't been time since his return to hire another one but he vowed he would soon see it done.

"How are you feeling?" he asked.

"A little better. I still have a headache but it is milder this morning."

"Explain to me again why it is that you are here."

She lifted the porcelain teacup with a

trembling hand and carefully took a sip, giving herself time to formulate an answer. She set the cup a bit unsteadily back down in its saucer.

"I know your penchant for honesty so I shall not mince words. I can't be certain, of course, since I have no sort of proof, but I believe Mason and Frances Holloway are giving me something to purposely make me ill. My son is heir to the Aldridge fortune. Should something happen to me, his guardianship would fall into their hands. My brother-in-law and his wife are ruthless in the extreme. I believe they are after Jared's money."

He had never liked Edmund or his brother, Mason. Edmund was arrogant and overbearing, and Mason was worthless and greedy. It wasn't too far a stretch to believe the younger Holloway would go after his dead brother's fortune.

"Go on," he said simply.

She seemed to be fighting to concentrate, though he couldn't actually be sure. "Several months ago, I began feeling slightly unwell. It wasn't . . . wasn't much at first, just headaches and a slight dizziness once in a while. Over the past few weeks, the symptoms have worsened. My memory has become affected. Sometimes things seem hazy, somehow out of focus. I believe my brother-in-law hopes, eventually, that I shall lose all sense of reality. I think he hopes I will withdraw completely."

She lifted the linen napkin in her lap, straightened it nervously, and spread it once more across her full black skirt. "More and more, he tries to take control. He has even begun to . . . to behave . . . in a . . . a manner improper to his dead brother's wife."

Reese tensed. "Are you saying Mason Holloway has made unwanted advances?"

She swallowed. "Yes . . ." The sound whispered out as if she hoped no one would hear.

Anger flashed through him. Fury at Mason Holloway.

Reese was stunned. It was impossible he could be jealous. Ridiculous after all of these years. He took a deep breath, shoving the unexpected emotions away.

Elizabeth looked up at him. "I think Mason is trying to gain control of my mind and my body and in doing so, gain control of my son and his fortune."

He replayed the things she had told him. He had no idea how much of what she was saying was true, but the way she had fainted dead away last night made him believe it was possible.

"Assuming what you're telling me is true, how do you believe Mason is managing all of this?"

"I don't . . . I don't know. Some sort of drug, perhaps, laced into my food. I tried not eating for a while, but I began to feel weak and since I wasn't certain if food was the problem or if I was wrong entirely, I gave up the notion."

"And you never saw a physician?"

She swallowed, took a sip of her tea as if it fortified her somehow. She set the cup back down on the table, moving tendrils of curly black hair, loose from the knot at the nape of her neck, against her pale cheek. Beneath the table, his body stirred to life. His groin began to fill and Reese swore a silent oath.

He needed a woman, he told himself. A single trip to Madame Lafon's exclusive London bordello had not been enough to ease a man's needs after so many months.

"Mason brought someone in to see me," Elizabeth continued, returning his mind to the subject. "A doctor named Smithson. He said I would be fine. I didn't know him. I'm not certain he was a doctor at all."

"My brother's physician is reliable. I'll have him here as soon as it can be arranged." Reese waited to see if she would agree or if her purported illness was some sort of ruse.

"I think that is a good idea. I'll be happy to pay him, of course."

A thread of anger trickled through him. "You might be rich, Countess, but you are a guest here and as such under my care. I am hardly a pauper. Though I suppose compared to an earl it might seem so to you."

"I didn't mean —"

He rose from his chair, the legs grating on the polished wooden floor. Reaching down, he picked up his cane. "I have things to do. I believe your son is expecting you."

Elizabeth said nothing, just sat there staring up at him with big gray wounded eyes. Reese turned away, determined to ignore the twinge of guilt he felt at his harsh words.

He owed Elizabeth nothing. Less than nothing, he told himself as made his way out of the breakfast room.

FOUR

Reese sent a note to his brother, Royal, that morning, asking him the name of his physician, a doctor who lived near Swansdowne, but leaving out the reason why. He knew all bloody hell would break loose if Royal found out Elizabeth was staying in Reese's house.

She wouldn't be there for long, he assured himself. He would see her off to London, perhaps as soon as tomorrow.

The doctor arrived earlier than he expected. At two o'clock that afternoon, a reed-thin, silver-haired gentleman named Richard Long walked into the foyer. Pleading another headache, Elizabeth had returned upstairs to bed. Reese escorted Dr. Long upstairs to examine her, introduced him to the wan-looking woman beneath the covers, then went down to his study to await the doctor's verdict.

Reese tried to concentrate on the ledgers

still lying on his desk, but as usual, his attention continued to stray. He told himself he wasn't worried about Elizabeth, just anxious for her to get well enough to leave his house.

He was staring down at the numbers written on the page in front of him when a light knock sounded, noting the physician's arrival. Reese beckoned him in and Dr. Long sat down in a brown leather chair on the opposite side of Reese's big oak desk.

"How is she?" he asked, a question he couldn't have imagined posing even a few days ago.

"Not well, I'm afraid. Lady Aldridge is extremely fatigued. She has started to perspire and I believe she may soon start vomiting. I left one of the maids upstairs with her."

He ignored a thread of concern. At least she hadn't been lying. She was ill, as she had said.

"The countess was quite candid with me," Long continued. "She told me she believes someone has been drugging her and I believe she is correct in that assumption."

Reese's hand unconsciously fisted.

"I can't say how the drug got into her system," the doctor continued. "But her ladyship appears to be suffering from the effects of a continual use of laudanum."

Laudanum. He understood the effects of the drug often administered to relieve pain. He had been given fairly large doses before and after the grapeshot was cut out of his leg.

"Little by little, she was slowly becoming addicted," Long said. "Today she didn't get whatever dose she usually receives, an amount her body has begun to crave. Until the drug is completely flushed from her system, she will have to endure the effects of the withdrawal."

He fought to contain his temper. Elizabeth was being drugged and she had accused the man who was supposed to be her protector. Reese suppressed an urge to retrieve his saber and run it through Mason Holloway's heart.

Of course he had no proof that Holloway was responsible. For all he knew, she could have been dosing herself. People often became addicted to the feeling of euphoria that accompanied the drug, which also relieved stress and pain — for a while.

"How much time will it take?"

"A few days, is my guess. From the symptoms she described, I would say the dosage has been small."

"Probably why she couldn't figure out

how they were giving it to her."

"Will you go to the authorities?"

"As you say, there is no way to know how the drug got into her system. Even Lady Aldridge can't be certain who might be responsible."

"You are aware that overuse of the drug can cause mind alterations and even death?"

"I am."

"May I presume you will be aiding the countess in her recovery?"

He could barely force out the word. "Yes."

"Then you will provide a safe haven until the matter is resolved." The doctor's dark eyes assessed him. Clearly the man was concerned.

Elizabeth would have to stay, but unless her visit was chaperoned, eventually word would leak out and the scandal of her living in a bachelor household would be enormous. For himself, he didn't care, but there was the boy to think of.

"I'll send word to my aunt. I'm sure she'll agree to a visit while Elizabeth is recovering."

Although he wasn't completely certain. His great aunt Agatha, dowager Countess of Tavistock, had fiercely disapproved of Elizabeth marrying the Earl of Aldridge. Since she had no children of her own, she was wildly protective of her three nephews. And she knew how badly Reese had been hurt.

Still, he believed she would come, if for no other reason than to protect him from the woman she saw as the viper who had destroyed his life.

He might have smiled at the notion of needing to be saved from one small, dark-haired woman if he hadn't remembered his body's reaction to Elizabeth only that morning. Even now, as he recalled her lying in bed last night, his arousal pulsed to life.

He needed a woman, he told himself again, vowing to seek out female companionship as soon as it could be arranged.

In the meantime, he would do a little digging, see what he could find out about Mason and Frances Holloway and something of the life Elizabeth had shared with her husband.

It was the last thing Reese wanted to do.

Elizabeth lay trembling, her body bathed in sweat. Twice she had retched into the chamber pot the little maid, Gilda, had placed beside her bed. *Laudanum,* the doctor had said. He had told her she was suffering a withdrawal from the drug she had probably been receiving on a daily basis but that in a matter of days, she should be fine.

She had guessed it was something like that, though she still couldn't figure out how they had been giving it to her. Probably lacing the fine white powder into her food. She had been right to leave, she thought as her stomach rolled, threatening to erupt again.

She was safe here, no matter Reese's dislike of her.

She tried not to think how handsome he had looked that morning when he had walked into the breakfast room, tried not to remember the way her heart had madly started beating. She couldn't help wondering if the lightheadedness she had felt in that moment had been the drug or merely Reese's presence.

From the instant she had met him all those years ago, he'd had that sort of effect on her. His aunt, Lady Tavistock, had made the introductions at a ball given in honor of Elizabeth's seventeenth birthday. Her father, Charles Clemens, third son of a marquess, had hoped Reese's older brother, Royal, heir to a dukedom, would become her suitor. But it was Reese who attracted her, the dark-haired, blue-eyed Dewar who unaccountably sensitive and even a little bit shy in the presence of a marriageable young woman.

Another wave of nausea struck and Elizabeth reached for the chamber pot. If Edmund were alive and hadn't eventually turned to other women to satisfy his urges, she might have believed she was pregnant, suffering morning sickness as she had when she had carried Jared. She wasn't with child — she had been drugged, just as she had feared.

She fixed her mind on her son and how much he needed her and told herself she could survive the next few days.

Silently, she thanked Reese for setting aside his feelings and taking her and her son into his home.

The house no longer seemed too quiet, the way it had before Elizabeth's arrival. In fact, lately, the place was overrun with people.

Along with Elizabeth and her son and the doctor who had returned several times, another visitor had arrived early that morning. Captain Travis Greer, formerly of the 1st Royal Dragoons, had once served under Reese's command. At the battle of Balaklava, Greer had saved his life when Reese's horse had been shot from beneath him and he had been left unconscious on the battlefield.

Captain Greer had, at great risk to himself,

carried his superior officer to safety.

In the course of his actions, the captain had lost his left arm.

Reese owed him.

On top of that, they had become extremely close friends and he was damned glad to see him.

"Come in, man." Reese welcomed Travis into the study, feeling the pull of a smile for the first time in days. "It's good to see you."

"You, as well, Major." Travis had sandy brown hair and a square jaw, a muscular man whose features were softened by the small gold spectacles perched on his nose. He was an interesting, well-educated man, his mother a Russian ballerina, his father, the son of the late Sir Arthur Greer, a professor at Oxford University.

"I hope you don't mind my stopping by this way," Trav said. "I was heading back to London. I'd heard you were here. Thought I'd see how you fared."

The men shook hands. Travis's left coat sleeve was empty from several inches above the elbow. Reese suppressed a feeling of guilt. The injury wasn't his fault. War was war. Men were injured. Travis had lost his arm. Reese had injured his leg. Both of them were lucky to be among the living.

"Would you like a cup of coffee or tea? Or

perhaps you'd prefer some brandy." Reese headed for the sideboard. He'd been working on the Briarwood ledgers for the last two hours. He deserved to take a break.

"Brandy sounds like a fine idea."

Reese filled two crystal goblets and carried one over to his friend. "I thought you were living in Dorset. What takes you to London?"

Travis grinned. "Believe it or not, a job. I've been offered a column in the *London Times*. I'll be doing a series of articles on soldiering and the war."

"Which one?" Reese said dryly, since it seemed as if there was always at least one war going on.

Travis smiled. "Mostly the one we just fought, but also my thoughts on war in general."

"Sounds like something right up your alley. You always wanted to be a journalist. Looks like you've finally got the chance." Reese lifted his glass in a toast. "Congratulations."

Travis lifted his. "Thanks."

The butler, Hopkins, knocked just then.

"What is it?" Reese asked as the door swung open.

"A man named Holloway is here to see you, my lord."

Reese's jaw hardened. He'd been expecting Mason Holloway, sooner or later. "Show him into the drawing room. Tell him I'll be right there." He set his brandy glass down on top of his desk. "I'm afraid you'll have to excuse me. This shouldn't take long."

Not bloody long, indeed, he thought as he grabbed hold of his cane and started out the door.

Mason Holloway stood up from the sofa as Reese entered the drawing room, a comfortable chamber though it needed a bit of care.

"My lord." Holloway was a big man, tall, with a dark brown mustache and a slightly oily smile.

"Holloway."

"I hope you will pardon my unexpected appearance in your home. I only just received word that my dear sister-in-law might be here at Briarwood."

"She's here. She and the boy."

He gave up a sigh of relief. "Thank God. I had seriously begun to worry. It is not like Elizabeth to hie herself off the way she did. But she has been feeling unwell of late. At times, her thoughts seemed a bit jumbled, but I — that is my wife and I — neither of us expected anything like this."

"Lady Aldridge was feeling a bit under

61

the weather when she arrived, but I assure you she is now on the mend. In fact, she is feeling well enough to stay for a visit with my aunt."

"Your aunt?" Mason repeated as if the words stuck in his throat.

"That's right. Lady Tavistock is currently on her way to Briarwood and looking forward to seeing Lady Aldridge again after so many years." That was a load of rot. Aunt Aggie's note had been curt and to the point.

What could you possibly be thinking to allow that woman into your house? I shall arrive with all haste.

Your aunt Agatha

The phony smile slid from Holloway's face. "Lady Aldridge and her son are best cared for at home. I have brought the traveling coach so that they may ride in comfort the short trip back to the house. Now if I may just speak to her . . ."

Reese flashed a feral smile, exposing the white of his teeth. "I'm afraid she's asked that she not be disturbed."

"That is ridiculous. I'm her brother-in-law and as such — now that her husband is gone — head of the family. I'm here to take her home. Please have one of your servants

62

tell her to prepare herself to leave."

Reese's hand tightened around the silver head of his cane. "Elizabeth isn't going anywhere with you, Holloway. Not unless that is what she wants to do. Neither you nor your wife are welcome here. Please take your leave."

Any trace of civility left Mason's features. "She belongs at home, Dewar. Sooner or later, I intend to fetch her back there — whether you like it or not."

Reese thought of the six-inch blade concealed in his cane and his fingers itched to trip the button exposing it. He imagined using it to carve a warning into the flesh over Holloway's black heart.

"Get out." His glance strayed toward the stairway and he spotted his manservant, brawny Timothy Daniels, hovering protectively nearby.

"You'll be sorry for this, Dewar," Holloway threatened. "Take my word for it."

Reese turned toward the stairs. "See Mr. Holloway out, will you, Corporal?"

"Aye, sir." Timothy started toward him and Holloway turned and headed for the door.

"I'll be back," Mason said over one thick shoulder, and then he was gone.

"If you see him around here, Tim, be sure

to let me know."

"Aye, that I will, Major."

Leaving Timothy to insure Mason's departure, Reese returned to the study. Travis was still standing next to the desk when Reese walked back into the room.

"I couldn't help overhearing," Trav said. "You have a lady houseguest, I gather."

Reese nodded. "The Countess of Aldridge and her son. That was her brother-in-law, Mason Holloway. Elizabeth's afraid of him. She's asked me for sanctuary. I couldn't turn her away."

"Elizabeth . . . That wouldn't be the same Elizabeth you used to curse in your sleep? I seem to recall she married a man named Holloway."

A muscle flexed in his cheek. "That's her."

One of Travis's sandy brown eyebrows went up. "I see."

"No, you don't. You couldn't possibly because I can't figure it out myself. I only know she preyed on my honor as a soldier and I couldn't refuse her request. She's here until I can figure out what to do with her, then she's on her way. It couldn't happen soon enough for me."

Travis looked as if he might say *I see* again, but wisely refrained. "Female problems. They're always the worst."

Reese lifted his crystal goblet and took a deep swallow of brandy. "You can say that again."

FIVE

Several days later

Beginning to feel more her old self again, Elizabeth made her way up to the third floor where Mrs. Garvey and Jared shared adjoining bedrooms. The withdrawal symptoms had faded completely and though she still felt a little tired, she was ready to get out of the house, at least for a while.

She listened at the door a moment, then turned the handle and silently pushed it open. The bedrooms connected to a third room, a lovely little nursery she had admired when she had come to the house with Reese years ago.

At the time, she had imagined seeing their baby lying in the white-ruffled bassinet that still sat empty in the corner. When he had shown her the room, she had smiled up at him and told him what a wonderful father he would make.

The notion twisted her heart. If only her

son had been raised by Reese. If only he'd had a loving father instead of one who was distant, even cruel. Jared had yearned for a father's love, but Edmund had pushed the child away, treating him little better than one of his servants.

If only she had known what her life would be.

But her father had admired the young earl and he had been determined she have a title. *Edmund will make you a countess. He won't exile you to a life in the country while he goes off adventuring with the army.*

It was only one of dozens of speeches he had made. In the beginning, she had simply ignored them, certain that in time she could convince her father to accept the man she loved, the man she had chosen to marry.

In the end, she had succumbed to his words, his dire predictions, and finally his unbending edict, and agreed to his demands. By special license, just a little over two months after Reese had left for London, she had married the Earl of Aldridge.

She closed her mind to what came next, looked across the nursery to where Mrs. Garvey read to Jared. He loved listening to stories and was becoming a very good reader himself.

"Mama!" He rose when he saw her and

raced toward her.

Elizabeth lifted him into her arms. "Good morning, sweetheart." She pressed a kiss on his forehead. "You're getting so big. Soon I won't be able to lift you."

He smiled as she set him back down on his feet, always happy when she mentioned how big he was getting. She thought that in time he would grow into a tall, strong man, but at seven, he was small for his age, and withdrawing into himself as he often did made him appear even smaller.

"So what are you two reading?"

Jared looked over at his silver-haired nanny for an answer.

"It's called *Peter Wilson's Journey,*" Mrs. Garvey said with a smile.

"What is the story about?" she asked Jared, forcing him to speak when he would have kept silent.

"It's about . . . about a little boy who finds treasure in his garden."

Elizabeth smiled. "That sounds marvelous." She glanced out the window. "I know how much you love stories but it's so nice outside. Wouldn't you like to come with me for a walk? I'm sure Mrs. Garvey would be willing to finish the story a little later."

Jared's solemn brown eyes looked up at her. "You aren't still sick?"

"I'm feeling better every day. Come on, let's go." She reached out a hand and Jared clasped it.

"Have a good time," Mrs. Garvey called to them, waving as they walked out the door.

They headed along the hall and down the back stairs. For the past few days while she convalesced, Elizabeth had been able to avoid seeing Reese. Every servant in the household knew of the confrontation Reese had had with Mason Holloway. Sooner or later she would have to thank him for his protection.

And his generosity in giving her asylum. Elizabeth wasn't sure how much longer she could accept his grudging hospitality, but sooner or later, she would have to leave.

The thought sent a chill down her spine. She was stronger now, more able to deal with Mason and Frances, but also she knew that she had been right and that she and her son were still in danger.

Elizabeth pushed through the back door, out into the September sunshine. A soft breeze blew over the barren fields, but they were no longer empty as they had been for years. Men worked hoeing weeds and, in an old abandoned orchard, another group worked pruning trees.

Clearly, Reese meant to ready the place

for spring planting. She knew he had been forced to leave the army because of his injury. Still, he had never been interested in farming. She couldn't help wondering if he would actually stay.

She felt a tug on her hand and realized Jared was urging her toward the stable. Her son so loved horses. She let him lead her in that direction, pulling her into the cooling shade of the barn.

One of the horses nickered softly and Jared hurried toward the sound. A pretty sorrel mare stuck her nose above the door of the stall.

"Isn't she beautiful?" he said with awe, careful to keep his distance. He'd been forbidden to go near any of the horses at Aldridge Park, but he often went out to watch them running across the fields.

"She's lovely."

"Look, Mama, she has a star on her fore-head."

Neither she nor Jared noticed that Reese and another man stood in the shadows until they started forward.

"I see you're feeling better," Reese said, stopping a few feet away.

A little knot of tension curled in her stomach. She prayed he wouldn't make her leave, not until she was fully recovered.

"Much better, thank you. I thought we might come out for a breath of fresh air."

"This is my good friend, Captain Greer," he said, making the introduction. "We served together for several years." He was a man of medium height, square-jawed, with sandy brown hair and wearing a pair of gold spectacles.

"It's a pleasure to meet you, Captain Greer."

"You, as well, my lady. The major mentioned you and your son were guests here."

"Lord Reese has been extremely kind."

Reese's jaw tightened. He turned his attention to Jared, who stood statue-still in front of the little mare's stall.

"You like horses, Jared?" Reese asked.

The boy merely nodded.

"Her name is Starlight. She's a Thoroughbred. She's going to be a mother."

Jared's eyes rounded. "She's going to have a baby?"

"A colt, yes. The stallion, Alexander, is the sire. He's that big red horse with the black mane and tail. You've probably seen him out in the fields."

The boy nodded. "He can run really fast."

"Yes, he can. Someday I hope to race the colts he sires."

Reese returned his attention to Elizabeth.

He had already said more to Jared than Edmund had said to him in the entire six months before the accident that killed him.

Reese's brilliant blue eyes fixed on her face and her nervousness kicked up. "I — I didn't realize you were out here. I hope we aren't in the way. Jared loves horses. I didn't think you would mind."

He looked at the boy, who still watched the mare. There was such a look of yearning on Jared's face, Elizabeth's heart constricted.

Reese must have noticed. "She's very gentle-natured. Would you like to pet her?"

Jared looked at him as if he were a god. "Could I?"

Reese took the child's hand and led him closer. Reaching up, Reese rubbed the star on the horse's forehead and softly stroked her nose. Then he lifted Jared up so that he could do the same.

The little boy very carefully stroked the mare's head and nose. When Reese set him back on his feet, he smiled in a way Elizabeth had never seen before and a lump rose in her throat.

She hid a secret. A terrible secret she meant to carry to her grave. In that moment, she was no longer certain she could.

Jared raced back to her. "Did you see me,

Mama? I petted her and she liked it."

"I saw you, sweetheart." She looked up at Reese and couldn't stop a sudden mist of tears. "Thank you."

Reese glanced away, his jaw hard once more. "I have work to do. If you will excuse us . . ."

"Nice to meet you, Lady Aldridge," the captain said.

"You, as well, Captain Greer."

She watched the men walk out of the barn, saw her son staring after Reese, and in that moment, she realized what a terrible sin she had committed.

Reese and Travis walked the fields. The first of October, he planned to do some plowing, just to churn up the soil and continue preparations for planting. In the spring he would plow again, then fertilize the soil, get it ready for seeding in April.

He meant to plant barley. His brother, Royal, was making wagonloads of money with Swansdowne Ale, which was rapidly becoming famous. The brewery sat not far from Bransford Castle, his brother's home, on a piece of property at the edge of the village, and Royal was already making plans to build a second plant closer to London.

His brother needed barley to increase his

production. Whatever Reese produced was certain to sell.

The thought did nothing to lift his mood. He had never wanted to be a gentleman farmer. He was only there now because he had promised his dying father he would come back and work the land he had inherited.

It was a promise he meant to keep, even if he hated every bloody minute.

So far, if he was honest with himself, being a member of the landed gentry hadn't been so bad. In fact, he had begun to enjoy the peace and quiet of the Wiltshire countryside. No waking up to the sound of cannon fire. No riding for endless hours until he fell exhausted into his cot at night.

Watching the leaves turn red and gold and hearing the wind sighing through the trees instead of watching the men in his command dying in pools of their own blood.

Still, he missed the camaraderie, missed traveling to faraway places, missed his friends. He was glad Travis had stopped for a visit.

It kept his mind off Elizabeth and her son.

"Your Elizabeth . . . she's extremely beautiful," Trav said, pulling his thought back in that direction.

Reese's stomach instantly knotted. He

looked over at his friend. "She is hardly *my Elizabeth.* We are barely civil to one another. I told you, she is only here because she asked for my protection."

"But she *is* beautiful."

He gave up a sigh. "More beautiful, I think, than she was as a girl."

They turned away from the fields and headed back toward the house. Reese made it a point to walk every day to exercise the muscles in his stiff leg. One day he meant to climb into a saddle, though he grudgingly admitted he wasn't up to it yet.

"So what do you plan to do? About the woman, I mean?"

As they reached the top of a rise and looked down on the whitewashed, slate-roofed manor draped with ivy, he blew out a breath.

"I wish I knew. She isn't completely recovered. Once she is, I imagine she'll go on to London. She was her father's only heir. When he died, he intended she would inherit his fortune, including the family mansion, Holiday House. As I recall, it's quite a place."

"Will she be safe there?" Travis asked.

It was a question he didn't want to consider. An unwanted kernel of worry swelled in his chest. "I've sent a letter to an investigator named Morgan. Royal has used his services in the past. I've asked him to find out what he can about Edmund Holloway and his brother, Mason. Once Elizabeth returns to London, I'll have him arrange some kind of security for her protection."

"But still you are worried. I can see it in your face."

He smoothed his features into blandness, but he and Trav had been friends too long to play games.

"Jared is still just a boy. Elizabeth is frightened for him. After my run-in with Holloway, I don't blame her."

"Perhaps they are better off here."

His stomach tightened. Having Elizabeth there was the last thing he wanted. "For the time being, they are. My aunt is due to arrive any day. At least that will staunch any possible gossip."

Travis smiled. "I've met your aunt. Lady Tavistock is quite something."

The edge of his mouth curved. "She is definitely a force to be reckoned with. I don't envy Elizabeth. Aunt Aggie considers her little better than a harlot."

Travis chuckled. "It's a definite coil. I'm glad I'll be leaving before your aunt arrives."

Reese tossed him a glance. "Coward."

Travis just laughed.

They walked along in silence, Reese pondering his good friend's words. Elizabeth and her son were in danger. Of that he had no doubt. He couldn't stop thinking of the boy. Seeing him there in the stable gazing with reverence at the mare, he could have been Reese's own son.

The notion had occurred to him, of course. There had been that single night, a fumbling, desperate coupling between two people who hadn't meant for things to go so far. Looking back on it, he was sorry Elizabeth had suffered his amateurish efforts. She deserved a better initiation, not a bumbling attempt by a novice to the act himself.

He wasn't that green lad anymore. During his years as a soldier, he'd had dozens of women. He had learned from skilled courtesans how to pleasure a woman and in doing so gain more pleasure for himself.

But that single night with Elizabeth, he hadn't even spilled his seed inside her. He had known that much, at least. He had been determined to protect her, and his brother had unwittingly told him the way.

Jared wasn't his, he was sure. His hair wasn't black but a dark chocolate brown, the same deep color as his eyes. His features were softer, less carved than his own. His manner was different, as well. He was extremely withdrawn. Reese had been a little shy as a boy, but neither he nor any of the Dewar brothers had been anything like Jared.

The boy belonged to Edmund Holloway and Reese couldn't help wondering how soon after Reese had left for London, the earl had enjoyed the woman Reese had already made his.

Travis left the following morning, an hour before Aunt Aggie's carriage pulled up in front of the manor. The weather had turned blustery and cold and his frail aunt leaned against him, the wind whipping her skirts, as Reese led her along the brick walkway toward the front porch.

She sighed as they entered the house out of the weather and Hopkins closed the front door. Shoving the hood of her cloak back from her gleaming silver hair, she smiled, resilient as always.

"You're looking well, nephew, if perhaps a little strained."

More than a little, he thought, with Elizabeth under his roof. "It's good to see you, Aunt Agatha."

She cast him a glance. He usually called her Aunt Aggie — much to her distress. "That desperate, are you? It's a good thing

I have come."

He smiled as he settled her on the sofa in the drawing room, thinking how good it was to have her there, though he wished she couldn't read him quite so well. "Thank you for coming, Auntie. As I said in my letter, Lady Aldridge has a son. It's important her reputation be protected."

His aunt merely grunted. "She didn't seem to mind the scandal when she tossed you over for that no-good Aldridge."

He tried not to smile. His aunt had always been prejudiced in her nephews' favor and far too outspoken, even if he did agree.

"She and the boy are in danger. She asked for my protection and I couldn't turn her away."

She harrumphed this time, but didn't argue. Though she might disapprove of the woman in his house, she would have expected no less of him.

"You must be tired from your journey," he said. "Why don't you go up and have a rest? Hopkins has already seen to your baggage. The housekeeper put you in one of the rooms overlooking the garden, though the grounds are a bit ragged yet."

She released a tired breath. "I'm sure you will see to it soon, and yes, I believe a rest would suit me very well."

Afraid he might not be able to see her safely upstairs, hampered as he was by his damnable leg, he glanced round for Timothy and spotted him hovering in the hall.

"See her ladyship up to her room, will you, Tim? The housekeeper knows which one it is."

"Aye, Major."

"What did you just call him?" Aunt Aggie lifted a silver eyebrow and Tim began to stutter.

"I — I meant to say, aye, your lordship."

"That is far better."

Reese just smiled. Things would be different while his aunt was around. As much as he liked her and looked forward to her visit, he would be glad when both women were gone.

"I'll see you at supper," he called up to her as she made her way toward the top of the stairs, leaning on Tim's solid arm. Reese wasn't worried about her. Tim would risk life and limb before he would let the old woman fall.

He smiled again. It felt good. He hadn't smiled much since he had awakened in an army hospital bed, his leg hurting like blazes — unable to remember his name.

Then he spotted Elizabeth coming down the hall and his smile slid away.

Elizabeth jerked to a stop in the middle of the hallway. Traveling the opposite direction, Reese walked toward her, his blue eyes icy cold and fixed on her face.

"Good . . . good morning, my lord."

"It's closer to noon, but I'm sure that's still early for you."

She had been up for hours, but she didn't say so. It didn't matter what he thought as long as he let her stay. To that end, she had worked every day to stay out of his way.

"I was . . . I was wondering . . . I noticed your piano, the one sitting in the music room at the far end of the house. Would you mind terribly if I played it? I feel rather useless just sitting round here doing nothing. At Aldridge Park, I had begun giving Jared piano lessons. I thought perhaps I could continue."

He just scowled. "Do what you wish." Brushing past her, he headed down the hall to his study, where he usually squirreled himself away.

Unconsciously, Elizabeth's hand came up to her heart. It was racing, she realized. *Ridiculous.* The man despised her. She had no reason to feel any sort of attraction to him.

Unfortunately, he had every reason to dislike *her* while she had no reason at all to dislike *him*. In fact, the more she was around him, the more she realized the terrible mistake she had made.

She had loved him so much.

If only she had been stronger. If only she hadn't been so young.

But the past could not be changed. And her time here at Briarwood was limited. Soon she would have to leave for London.

At least in that regard, she had decided on a course of action. She would send Mason Holloway a letter, telling him she knew that he and Frances had been drugging her with laudanum in an effort to gain control of Jared and his fortune. She would tell him he was not welcome at Holiday House, her home outside London. Then she would hire guards to keep watch, to make certain Mason did not bully his way inside.

Once she had taken those actions, there was little more she could do. She thought that perhaps she would document the events that had occurred and what she had done to protect her son — just in case something happened to her.

Perhaps then, Mason and Frances would

not be granted custody.

A shiver went through her. It was a worry that had no end.

Six

Reese heard melodic sounds coming from the music room at the far end of the house. Earlier, the jarring notes from the keyboard had been the clumsy efforts of a little boy. Now the enchanting melodies of Beethoven floated along the hall, pulling him like an inexorable force.

He reached the door and stood transfixed. In a room where most of the furniture was still hidden beneath white cotton covers, Elizabeth sat on the bench in front of the Streicher Vienna grand piano his grandfather had purchased, played, and loved.

It was built of flame mahogany, the legs ornate and partially gilded. Elizabeth's eyes were closed as her pale fingers skimmed over the ivory keys. The boy was gone and she played for herself alone, played as if her heart filled every note. He remembered her playing for him all of those years ago, how the first time he had heard her play, he had fallen in love with her.

The rich chords of Beethoven held him immobile. He couldn't have moved if the house had caught fire. She was smiling when she reached the end of the piece — until she opened her eyes and saw him.

Her features paled. Long seconds passed and neither of them spoke. Yet the air crackled between them, charged with an energy that heightened his pulse and made his breath quicken. The atmosphere grew dense and heavy, seemed to vibrate between them. His body stirred to life and arousal pulsed through his veins.

Her mourning dress was less formal, simple black bombazine with an inset of black crepe reaching all the way to her throat. Her raven hair was unpinned, clipped back on the sides but falling in dense curls down her back.

She was beautiful. More desirable than she had been as a girl.

His loins filled. Need poured through him. Inside his trousers, he was hard as a stone. He wanted to go to her, take her in his arms and kiss her. Wanted to drag her down on the thick Persian carpet and tear off her clothes, fill his gaze with the lush curves of her body.

Though they had made love that one time,

it had been a quick, unsatisfactory coupling. He had never seen her naked as he longed to do now.

"Reese . . . ?"

The sound came out low and throaty. She had called him by his first name as she hadn't done before. His arousal strengthened. He found himself moving toward her, his bad leg cooperating for once.

"You play as well as ever," he said as he reached where she sat. She rose from the bench, so close he caught the scent of her floral perfume, so near he could bend his head and capture her lips.

His brain warned him not to.

His erection throbbed, urging him to take what he wanted.

Her mouth was a dark rosebud pink, her lips full, perfectly curved and deliciously tempting. When she looked up at him and whispered his name once more, he was lost.

Bending his head, he captured her mouth and felt the warm press of her lips. They trembled slightly and he thought she might pull away, but instead those full lips softened, parted and he took her with his tongue. A soft mew escaped, half fear, half yearning. It stirred him even more and he deepened the kiss, took her without restraint.

He owed her nothing. If she accepted his advances, he would hold nothing back. He would show her the pleasure he hadn't known how to give her before.

He caught her against him, pulled her close enough to feel his heavy erection. He felt her tremble, felt her weaken and sway against him the instant before she broke away.

Her eyes were big and round, more blue than gray, as if what had happened completely astonished her. She reached up and touched her kiss-swollen lips.

"You never . . . never kissed me that way before."

He scoffed. "There are lots of things I didn't do before. I was young and green and I was fool enough to believe we would learn those things together. I'm a different man now, Elizabeth."

She swallowed. "Yes . . ."

"I'll be happy to show you what I didn't know before. I guarantee you will enjoy it."

She paled. "I — I didn't mean for that to happen. I just . . . I don't know . . . somehow it just did."

"You're a widow. I'm sure you have needs. As I said, I'll be happy to oblige you in any way you wish."

Her chin went up. He had pushed her too far.

"I'm afraid you will have to excuse me, my lord. I need to check on Jared."

He made no effort to stop her. In most ways he was grateful she was leaving. Silently, he cursed himself for his momentary lapse of judgment. What the hell had come over him? He knew better than to get involved with Elizabeth again.

Turning, he made his way out of the music room, trying not to think how much he wanted to kiss her again.

And so much more.

Elizabeth raced down the hall, willing her heartbeat to slow. Dear God, when she had come here, she had never imagined that Reese would want her. When they had been together, he'd been shy where women were concerned. He would never have pressed her for even a kiss if she hadn't encouraged him.

That night in the carriage when they had made love, she had been the one to urge him on, the one who didn't want to stop.

How could she not have realized he was a man now, no longer a boy? That he would want her the way a man wants a woman, no matter his dislike of her. And yet he had not forced her. He had done little more than kiss her.

And dear God, she had enjoyed it!

Just as before, she hadn't wanted the kiss to end. Until those few heated moments, she had forgotten what it was to desire a man. Those yearnings had disappeared the day Reese had ridden off to London.

She had felt nothing for Edmund. Nothing but disgust.

Edmund had claimed his husbandly rights by force. It never occurred to him that a woman should take pleasure in the act. On their wedding night, Edmund had merely climbed on top of her, lifted her nightgown and thrust himself inside her. Their sporadic couplings had been painful and humiliating. She had grown to hate the sound of his footfalls in the room next door, the sound of the doorknob turning.

She had never thought to enjoy a man's touch again, but today . . . today she had discovered that she was still a woman, and she was still vulnerable to Reese. That he could arouse the same forbidden desires he had before seemed impossible until today.

Now she knew the truth and it was terrifying.

Elizabeth lifted the black skirts of her simple mourning gown and hurried up the stairs. Last night she had avoided supper with Reese and his aunt, Lady Tavistock, who had arrived late that afternoon.

But the dowager countess had sent a request for Elizabeth and her son to join her for afternoon tea, a summons Elizabeth could not refuse. Her hand trembled as she opened the door to her bedroom. Her lips still carried the memory of Reese's mouth moving hotly over hers.

Her heart still thrummed as she stepped into her room, closed the door behind her, and leaned against it for support. Thank God, she had time to collect her wits before the encounter with his aunt. An hour or so to erase Reese from her thoughts, which at the moment, seemed an impossible task.

She would manage somehow, she knew, use the hours ahead to regain control and begin making preparations for her journey to London.

After what had happened in the music room, the time had come.

Elizabeth had to leave.

Two hours later, dressed in a crisp black taffeta tea gown, Elizabeth held on to her young son's hand as they made their way down the hall to a drawing room in the east wing of the manor. It was done in pale gray and white and Lady Tavistock, gowned in a blue silk gown trimmed with Belgian lace, sat on a yellow floral sofa across from the white marble-manteled hearth. A fire blazed there, taking the chill from the room.

The old woman made a slight nod of her head in greeting as Elizabeth and Jared walked into the chamber.

"Lady Aldridge," the dowager said. "So kind of you to join me." There was a bite to the words Elizabeth couldn't miss. She had known this meeting would not be pleasant. The woman protected her nephews like the mother they never knew. She loved Reese, and Elizabeth had betrayed him. Lady Tavistock had every right to hate her.

Elizabeth dropped into a curtsey. "Good afternoon, my lady." Next to her, Jared made the very formal bow he had been taught by his tutor. "May I present my son, Jared, Earl of Aldridge."

The old woman's watery blue eyes fixed on the boy. One of her silver eyebrows winged up as she assessed him. "Good afternoon, Lord Aldridge."

Jared made the reply he had been taught. "Good afternoon . . . my lady."

The dowager returned her attention to Elizabeth. "Why don't you pour for us, Lady Aldridge?"

Elizabeth did as she was bade, pouring tea into cups while Jared perched nervously on one of the matching floral overstuffed chairs. She passed a cup to Lady Tavistock, then handed her son a small glass of fruit punch and a white linen napkin.

"There's some sweet cakes there," Lady Tavistock told him. "You like cake, don't you, boy?"

He nodded, but didn't reach for a sweet. Elizabeth placed several on a porcelain plate and set it down on the table beside his chair. A small hand reached out and grabbed one of the decorated cakes and he ate it in several polite-sized bites.

"He doesn't talk much, does he?"

"He's a little shy, is all. In time, he'll grow out of it." Though Elizabeth wasn't truly sure. Jared wasn't merely shy, he was deeply withdrawn, and she was worried about him.

Lady Tavistock looked as if she knew. She pinned him with a probing stare. "What do you like to do, boy? When you aren't busy with your studies."

The last bite he had taken seemed to stick in Jared's throat. He swallowed and looked over at Elizabeth for help.

"Jared likes to —"

"I didn't ask you — I asked the boy."

Jared's face reddened, and her heart went

out to him. Lady Tavistock's brittle voice softened. "I bet you like horses, don't you?"

Jared looked up at her, caught her smile, and his shyness seemed to fall away. "I love horses. Lord Reese has the most beautiful horse out in the stable. Her name is Starlight and she has a star on her forehead and she is going to have a baby."

Elizabeth could hardly believe her ears. Jared never said that much and certainly not to a stranger.

"Is that so?" the dowager said. "Maybe we'll have time tomorrow to go out there and you can show me Lord Reese's horse."

"He has a lot of them," Jared went on. "He has a big red stallion. He can really run fast."

Lady Tavistock flicked Elizabeth a glance. "You're a good boy, Jared." Little more was said until Jared finished his cakes and fruit punch and asked to be excused. Lady Tavistock gave him permission. When he had left the room, Elizabeth looked over to see tears in the old woman's eyes.

"I thought you heartless for hurting my nephew the way you did. Now I find you truly despicable."

The color drained from Elizabeth's face.

"Do you ever intend to tell him?"

Elizabeth couldn't quite catch her breath.

"I don't . . . I don't know what you mean."

"You know exactly what I mean. The boy is my nephew's son. I knew it the moment I laid eyes on him."

Her heart thundered. "You're . . . you're mistaken."

"How old is he?"

She wanted to lie. She could say Jared was six. He was small for his age; she was certain Reese thought he was younger than he was.

"How old?" the countess demanded.

"Seven . . ." Her voice trembled as the word whispered out.

"I knew it."

She only shook her head. "H-he isn't Reese's son. He looks nothing at all like Reese."

"Not in a way everyone would notice. His features are softer, his hair more brown than black. The thing is, except for the color of his eyes, Jared is the spitting image of Reese's father when he was a boy."

A buzzing started in her ears. Her throat felt too tight to swallow. She had kept the secret for so many years. Had planned to keep it forever.

"I think our tea is finished," the old woman said, rising from her chair.

Elizabeth rose, as well, her knees trembling beneath her full skirts. "What . . . what do you intend to do?"

The dowager cast her a drilling glance. "For the moment, nothing." She started forward, stopped and turned. "But I warn you, the time will come. When it does, I shall do whatever is best for my nephew and his son."

Elizabeth just stood there. For an instant her vision narrowed to almost black and she thought she might actually faint.

She steeled herself. The old woman knew. If she told Reese, Elizabeth could deny it and perhaps Reese would believe her.

One thing was clear. She had to stay at Briarwood at least a little longer. She needed time to think things through, decide what action to take. She needed to pull herself together before she faced the dowager again.

Fear crept through her. The truth would have to be told. The old woman knew her secret. Elizabeth could no longer keep silent. The old woman could destroy Jared's life and Elizabeth's own.

Sooner or later, she would have to tell Reese.

But dear God, not now. The room spun again and she made her way over to the sofa and sat down. Reese hated her already. She couldn't bear the way he would look at her once he knew the true depth of her betrayal.

Somehow she had to convince the old woman to give her time to formulate some sort of plan, time to find the courage to speak to Reese.

Somehow she had to find a way.

He shouldn't have kissed her. He had damned well known better. But he couldn't have guessed the way it would feel to hold her again, to have her respond to him in the exact same manner she had all those years ago.

As if she belonged to him. As if she loved him still.

Reese swore foully. He had never known the extent of her cunning until now. She cared nothing for him, likely never had. She was using him, nothing more. She needed his protection. And though he had already given her that, he couldn't help wondering how far she would be willing to go in order to keep it.

Crossing the room without his cane, more determined than ever to stretch and retrain the muscles that had been injured and inactive for so long, he yanked on the bellpull, summoning Timothy Daniels to help him dress for supper.

At least the evening should prove interesting, if more than a little taxing. Elizabeth and his aunt had taken tea together that afternoon. He would have liked to have been a fly on the wall during that conversation.

At least the ice had been broken. Perhaps supper would be a tolerable affair.

Dressed in black for the evening, Reese grabbed his cane and made his way past Timothy, who held open the bedroom door. He was the first to arrive in the anteroom leading into the formal dining room, where a table seating twelve had been set for three and a fire blazed in the huge, open hearth along the wall.

His aunt was the first to arrive, decked out in sapphire-blue silk, a strand of diamonds at her throat, looking every inch the dowager countess she was.

The old woman paused in front of him. "My, you do look handsome, even without that scarlet uniform the women so favored."

He smiled. "Thank you, Aunt Aggie." She frowned at the use of the name but he knew that secretly she was pleased. "You're looking beautiful, as always."

She waved her hand at the flattery. "Just like your father and brothers, you are. Full of the devil when it comes to the ladies."

He laughed. He had forgotten how good she was at making him laugh.

Elizabeth arrived a few minutes later, gowned in crisp black taffeta, a circle of black pearls at her throat. Only a glimpse of her pale breasts showed above the modest neckline.

Reese thought how much he hated her in black.

"I hope I'm not late," she said, her gaze going to the grandfather clock in the corner, returning to him then quickly darting away. Faint color rose in her cheeks and he knew she was thinking of those moments in the music room.

"You're here just in time," Reese said. "Shall we go in?"

Elizabeth cast a glance at his aunt, who drilled her with a glare down the length of her short, powdered nose. He offered Aunt Aggie his arm and she rested her small gloved hand on the sleeve of his coat for the short walk into the dining room.

He seated both women, his leg holding up amazingly well, then sat down in the high-back chair at the head of the table.

The first course was served, a nice hot rice and plover soup.

"So, what did you think of Lady Aldridge's son?" he asked, hoping to ease some of the tension in the room and begin a semblance of conversation. The women's eyes shot to each other across the table.

"He's too shy," Aunt Aggie said sharply. "Needs a man's influence to give him some gumption."

Elizabeth's hand shook as she lifted her soup spoon, but she made no reply.

Reese fixed his gaze on her face. "Perhaps one day Lady Aldridge will remarry."

She lowered the spoon back into her bowl. "That is never going to happen. One husband was more than enough."

Aunt Aggie's silver eyebrows shot up. "Is that so? Then you must have loved him greatly."

Elizabeth's pretty lips thinned. "Loved him? Marriage is one step away from bondage and I will never allow myself to be put in that position again."

Aunt Aggie eyed her shrewdly. Very carefully, she wiped her mouth on the linen napkin.

"I see," she said, and Reese couldn't help wondering what exactly it was the old woman did see. One thing he knew, his aunt had an uncanny ability where people were concerned. In a single brief conversation, she understood more about a person than anyone he had ever met.

The meal progressed a little easier after that. During dessert, egg custard with a delicious raspberry sauce, he mentioned to his aunt that his best friend, Travis Greer, had stopped by for a visit and that he would be writing for the *London Times.*

"I only met him a couple of times," Aunt Aggie said. "Before his dreadful injury, of course. Always seemed a nice enough sort."

"He's become a very good friend," Reese said, not mentioning the man had once saved his life. The war wasn't one of his favorite topics.

"He was very nice to Jared," Elizabeth added, doing her best to hold up her end of the conversation.

"The boy craves a man's attention. Any fool can see that."

Elizabeth looked into her dessert bowl as if there were something of interest in the bottom. Reese gave her credit. Clearly, Aunt Aggie was at her irascible best. As soon as dessert was over, Reese led the ladies into the drawing room for an after-dinner drink and both of them seemed relieved.

"How about a sherry, Aunt Aggie?"

"Not tonight. I believe I'll go on up to bed. Where is that strapping young man who helped me before?"

Timothy, of course, appeared right on cue.

"May I be of assistance, my lady?" He had adopted his formal demeanor and Reese almost smiled.

"Yes, thank you, Mr. Daniels."

"Good night, my lady," Elizabeth said softly, and received a brusque "good night" in return. Timothy led the dowager out of the drawing room toward the staircase, leaving Reese alone with Elizabeth, an occurrence he hadn't expected.

Reese thought of the kiss they had shared in the drawing room and couldn't help wondering what the balance of the evening might bring.

SEVEN

Seated on the sofa across from Reese, Elizabeth nervously sipped a glass of sherry. She still hadn't figured out how she had wound up alone with Reese. During supper, she had mentioned the possibility of leaving Briarwood, but the dowager had staunched the notion with a warning glance.

If she left without telling Reese the truth about Jared, she was certain Lady Tavistock would see it done immediately.

She had to stay. At least for the moment.

Oddly, the decision stirred a feeling of relief.

"Another sherry?" Reese asked, and she realized she had drained her glass entirely.

"Thank you, no. I believe it is past time I retired upstairs." She rose from her place on the rose velvet sofa, set the empty glass down on the table beside it.

"You seemed to have reached some sort of truce with my aunt," Reese said, rising and setting his own empty glass on the table.

Hardly. Currently the old woman had Elizabeth entirely under her thumb, but of course she couldn't say that. "Perhaps she has decided to keep an open mind. In time, perhaps she will see there are two sides to every story."

Elizabeth prayed it was so. She intended to speak to the dowager on the morrow, try to explain what had happened all of those years ago.

Reese's fierce blue gaze bored into her. "Are there two sides, Elizabeth?"

He was asking her to explain. She doubted he would understand. She didn't entirely understand herself.

"My father refused to let us marry, Reese. He insisted I marry the earl."

"Funny, I seem to remember you saying that you would gain his approval and you would marry me."

She tried not to flinch beneath his cold regard. "We were never officially engaged. In time, I thought my father would give us his blessing. He refused. After you were gone, it wasn't so easy to fight him. I wasn't as strong as I am now."

And I was pregnant and frightened and only eighteen. But she could hardly say that.

"And there was Aldridge," he said darkly,

103

"right there knocking on your door. Writing you poetry, always solicitous, always full of flattery."

"He was nothing at all what he seemed. He fooled my father completely. At first he even fooled me."

"Still, you are a countess, your son an earl."

She looked down at her empty glass, wishing she had more sherry, wishing she had let him pour her some more. "I am wealthy in my own right. My father left his fortune to me. It is returned to me now that Aldridge is dead."

"Lucky for you." He had moved closer, she realized, and now stood right behind her. She could feel his warm breath on the nape of her neck. "Have you thought about what happened in the music room?"

She swallowed. She could scarcely get those moments out of her head. Slowly, she turned to face him. "I've thought about it. I've never been kissed in that way."

He frowned. "Surely Aldridge proved a satisfactory lover."

Her stomach rolled. She couldn't bear to think of the nights Edmund had pressed himself on her. "Please, I would rather not discuss my late husband."

His hands came to rest at her waist.

"You're right, of course. I would rather discuss what might be arranged between the two of us." She stiffened as he bent toward her, pressed his lips against the side of her neck. Gooseflesh raced over her skin and her heart set up a clatter.

"What . . . what are you doing?"

"I am kissing you, Elizabeth." And then he did, his mouth claiming hers as if he had every right. He took her with abandon, a deep, drugging, possessive kiss that should have frightened her but instead left her lightheaded and yearning.

The kiss deepened, grew more fierce. His tongue was hot and slick over hers and he tasted of the brandy he had been drinking. She couldn't think, could barely stay on her feet. Her hands slid up the lapels of his black dinner jacket and she clung to him, breathed him in.

"You wanted me before, Elizabeth," he whispered against her ear. "Apparently, you still do. And believe me, I want you."

He held her so closely she could feel his powerful erection pressing against her. She should have been repulsed but she wasn't. His body was lean and fit, his chest wide and hard, and the feel of his arms around her made her knees feel weak.

She forced herself to pull away. "You

don't . . . don't even like me."

He shrugged those broad shoulders. "Like has little to do with desire." He leaned toward her, bent his dark head and kissed the place below her ear, and her stomach quivered.

"It's obvious the attraction between us remains," he went on. "You're a widow. We could please each other, Elizabeth."

She moved a little away, desperate to save herself. He didn't like her, but he desired her. He was a man, after all, no different from any other. "I'm not . . . not interested in some illicit affair. I have a son to consider. And I refuse to be the victim of another man's lust."

One of his sleek black eyebrows went up. "That's all there was? Edmund and his lust?"

Tears burned behind her eyes. She blinked them away before he could see. "I don't want to think about it. Please, Reese . . ."

At the sound of his name and the plea in her voice, he straightened. He studied her a moment and she wished she knew what he was thinking.

"All right, if that is the way you want it. Just remember, the offer remains open. Think about it, Elizabeth. I can give you the pleasure he couldn't."

She only shook her head. She enjoyed Reese's kisses, the featherlight touches that made her feel like the woman she had once been, but the thought of making love was utterly unbearable.

"I — I'll be leaving here soon," she said. "I haven't got the arrangements entirely worked out, but I'm certain I'll be able to see it done very shortly."

Reese said nothing.

Elizabeth moistened her lips. "Good night, my lord." His blue eyes darkened for an instant, before she turned away. Elizabeth hurried out of the drawing room, headed upstairs. She couldn't wait to reach her bedroom.

And she couldn't understand why Reese's offer made the blood pump so furiously through her veins.

Reese paced the floor of his bedroom. The scene in the withdrawing room had been completely unplanned. But sometime during the course of the evening, watching Elizabeth beneath the glow of the candles, admiring the gleam of her raven hair, the pale smoothness of her skin, the subtle rise and fall of her breasts, desire had begun to burn inside him, along with the notion of having her in his bed.

He kept thinking of the kisses they had shared, remembering the way she had responded. He wanted her and apparently she wanted him.

He owed her nothing.

If he wanted her, why shouldn't he have her?

Discovering how little she knew of passion made his desire for her even greater. Clearly, Edmund Holloway had been an inept lover. The sort of husband who took his pleasure and gave nothing in return. As Reese looked back on the kiss in the music room, he had sensed an innocence he hadn't expected. It was there in her untutored kisses tonight.

He could teach her, give her the pleasure she had missed in the course of her marriage. And in doing so, relieve his need for a woman, unsatisfied since his arrival at Briarwood.

In a way, taking Elizabeth as his temporary mistress would be gaining an odd sort of revenge. He didn't love her. Not anymore. But he desired her. More, perhaps, because he'd had her only once and had never gotten his fill.

He wanted her and she wanted him and only Elizabeth's conscience stood in the way.

A hard smile lifted the corners of his mouth. Considering the ease with which she had jilted him for another man, whatever minor amount of conscience she possessed shouldn't be much of a problem.

Shrugging out of his coat, Reese tossed it onto the bed. His leg throbbed as he walked over to the bellpull to summon Timothy and began to plan his strategy. He'd been an officer in the army. He knew how to mount a campaign.

With very little effort, Reese believed, he would have Elizabeth Holloway in his bed.

Elizabeth sent a note to Lady Tavistock, requesting a meeting at her earliest convenience. The dowager's reply suggested they meet in the garden at two o'clock that afternoon.

Elizabeth paced nervously back and forth across her bedroom, wishing the time would pass. At one o'clock, she summoned Gilda to help her change into a walking dress and coif her dark hair. The chambermaid acting as her temporary ladies' maid was tall and thin, with very curly blond hair. The girl didn't know much about a lady's toilette, but she was willing to do whatever Elizabeth asked.

Gilda opened the door of the armoire.

"Which one, milady?"

Elizabeth bit her lip. Several days ago, she had sent Gilda to Aldridge Park with instructions to get Sophie's help in packing more of Elizabeth's clothes. Once she reached London, she would send for Sophie, who had been her maid for years. Until then, she needed a few more things to wear than she had been able to carry in the satchel with which she had escaped.

She studied the gowns in the armoire. All of them were black, of course, but at least the styles were different.

"Perhaps the one with the pagoda sleeves." She shook her head. "No, I think the silk and crepe with the bodice that buttons up the front would be less formal."

The girl laid the gown out on the bed, walked over and tightened Elizabeth's stays, which had been loosened while she rested after lunch. Gilda helped her into the several layers of black petticoats that held out her full skirts, then helped her fasten the black silk buttons on the front of the gown.

Elizabeth turned toward the mirror. She wasn't as pale as she had been when she had arrived, but it didn't really matter. She hated the way she looked in black.

One more bad mark against Edmund for

dying and forcing her into mourning.

One good mark that he was finally gone from her life.

She sat down in front of the dresser and Gilda worked to smooth her heavy curls into a tight chignon at the nape of her neck. Satisfied she looked proper enough to face Reese's aunt, she rose and started for the door.

"Thank you, Gilda. I shall not need you until an hour or so before supper." At which time, she would put on a different black shroud, one that at least allowed a portion of her bosom to show and displayed a bit of femininity.

She tried not to wonder if Reese would look at her as he had last night after supper. She could still feel the heat of his gaze as it settled on the hint of cleavage between her full breasts. She had never been slender, not even as a girl, but after birthing Jared, her bosom was fuller, her hips more curvy. Reese seemed not to mind.

The thought made her skin feel moist and a trickle of warmth slid into her stomach. She had to stop thinking of him, she told herself as she made her way down the staircase, had to stop thinking what it might be like to let him kiss her again, hold her in his arms.

Instead, she focused on her meeting with the dowager countess. Her greatest concern was her son. She had to find a way to protect him.

Elizabeth crossed the brick terrace and descended the few steps into the garden, which was heavily overgrown. The entire house needed a good thorough cleaning and overall polish. But Reese was a bachelor, and caring for the charming old manor house was a task only a woman could see fully accomplished.

For the next ten minutes, she wandered the gravel pathways, her slippers crunching on a colorful array of fallen leaves. Another set of footsteps sounded on the path behind her, slower, more hesitant, and she knew the dowager countess had arrived.

Elizabeth turned to see the old woman in a gown of apricot silk warmed by a light, matching pelisse moving slowly along the path, leaning heavily on her cane. Without thinking she hurried to help her.

"Why don't we sit right here?" she suggested, easing the old woman down on a wrought iron bench.

"Thank you," Lady Tavistock said stiffly.

"I appreciate your seeing me." Elizabeth took a seat on the opposite end of the bench. The air was crisp and cool but not cold, the wind not more than a whisper.

"It would seem we have a good deal to discuss."

"Yes . . ."

"I rarely make mistakes in judgment, you know. And yet I made one with you. I knew my nephew was in love with you. There was a time I believed you were deeply in love with him. I was wrong. If you had loved him, you never would have hurt him the way you did."

Elizabeth's heart clenched. How could she possibly explain? "I understand the way you feel, my lady. You think I abandoned Reese and married Aldridge for his money and title. It wasn't so. I loved Reese. I wanted to marry him more than anything in the world."

She stared at her lap, the sun beating down on the heavy black folds of her skirt. She looked up at the dowager countess. "Then I found out I was going to have a baby." She swallowed against the memory. "I was terrified. When my father found out, he was beyond furious."

"I remember your father had a temper. I never thought he would hurt you."

"Oh, no, I didn't mean that. He never struck me. He simply . . . my father ruled me. Mother was dead. I did whatever my

113

father commanded. I can't remember a time I ever disobeyed his wishes."

"Is that why you didn't tell Reese about the child?"

Even now the memory was painful. "Father forbade me to have any further contact with Reese. He said he had dishonored me and he was never to come near me again. I wasn't as strong as I am now. I wasn't able to fight him. I did what he told me to do."

The older woman looked at her askance. "And Aldridge's charm played no part in your decision."

"Not his charm, no. Perhaps the safety he offered in giving my unborn child his name. He was older, more settled, and he was there, not off somewhere adventuring. The decision itself was never truly mine. I married Aldridge, as my father insisted. And I regretted it every day of my life."

The countess leaned back against the iron bench. Beneath her shrewd regard, Elizabeth fought not to squirm.

"My nephew says you came here because you feared for yourself and your child, but perhaps you had a different motive."

"What do you mean?"

"Perhaps you came here to resume your relationship with Reese. Do you intend to lure my nephew back into your clutches?"

"No! I came here because I was desperate. I knew my son was in danger. My family is all gone. Reese was the only person I could trust."

"Because he is Jared's father?"

"Because he is a man of honor and strength and I believed he would not turn us away."

The countess seemed to weigh Elizabeth's words. "When will you tell him?"

Elizabeth stared off into the distance. She had no idea how to tell Reese a secret so profound. A secret that would turn his dislike of her to hate.

"I need time. I don't know what he'll do. I don't know what will happen to my son once Reese knows the truth." Tears collected in her eyes. "Jared is already so withdrawn. He is too young yet to understand his true parentage. I'm afraid if the information is handled wrong, it could destroy him completely."

The dowager said nothing for the longest time. "The boy's well-being is the most important concern. This wasn't my business until you came here. Now it is. I'll give you the time you need. I'll give you a chance to figure out the best way to handle the matter, but I won't let you deceive Reese forever."

Her stomach tightened. She couldn't imagine the enmity Reese would feel once she told him the truth.

A lump rose in Elizabeth's throat. "In my heart I knew when I saw them together that sooner or later I would have to tell him. I give you my word that I will. Until then, you have my heartfelt gratitude for giving me the time I need to try to make this right."

The old woman rose shakily from the bench. "As I said, for now, you may do as you wish. But I warn you, do not test my patience too long." Leaning heavily on her cane, Lady Tavistock made her way along the gravel path, up the brick steps and across the terrace. She disappeared inside the house and Elizabeth sank back down on the bench.

For now she had the old woman's co-operation. But dear God, how long would it last?

And how could she explain to a little boy that she had lied to him about the man who was his father?

EIGHT

Wearing only a white lawn shirt and a pair of riding breeches, Reese sat on a wooden bench in the stable, working his injured leg. He and Timothy Daniels had begun to follow the same routine daily.

"Pull harder," Reese said, ignoring the sharp pain that traveled up his calf and along his thigh. He needed to stretch the stiff muscles, find a way to make them limber and useful again. "Now the other way."

Timothy pulled and Reese gritted his teeth at the agony screaming up his leg. He could do this, by God. He would learn to walk without his damnable cane. In time, perhaps he would even be able to ride again.

"Harder, dammit. You're as strong as a bull. Put that strength to use."

Timothy looked dubiously at the sweat popping out on Reese's forehead, but he was a soldier and a soldier followed his superior's commands. "Aye, Major."

Reese caught hold of the wooden contraption they had constructed above the bench and Timothy threw his weight against the leg.

Pain shot through him. "Keep going."

Timothy kept pulling until something made a popping sound and Reese hissed in pain. "Dammit!"

Timothy hovered worriedly above him. "How bad is it, Major? What did I do?"

"You did exactly what I told you to do, nothing more." Very slowly, he forced his knee to bend, which hurt like the very devil. "I'll be all right. But I think we've done enough for today."

"Yes, sir."

"That'll be all, Tim."

"Maybe I'd better stay and help you back to the —"

"I said that would be all, Corporal Daniels."

"Aye, sir." Timothy snapped to attention, turned and left the barn. Reese caught the glint of the young man's red hair as he passed in front of the window on his way back to the house.

That was when he spotted the boy.

"Jared," Reese growled, his leg still throbbing. "I thought you were inside with your mother."

The boy stood frozen, terrified that he had been caught in the barn. Reese frowned. The boy's shyness went far beyond normal. He couldn't help wondering what had happened to make him the way he was.

"It's all right," he said more gently, pulling his riding boots back on. "My leg is hurting, is all. Makes me grumpy as a bear."

The boy said nothing, just stood there transfixed, as if he wanted to turn and run but was afraid of what would happen if he did.

"You pet the mare today?"

Jared started shaking his head. "No, sir, I — I didn't touch her. I swear."

"It's all right. You can pet her anytime you want. As long as you don't go into the stall, you'll be perfectly safe."

Jared didn't move.

"Why don't you go on over there and give her this?" Reese pulled a lump of sugar out of the pocket of his riding breeches. "Just put it in the flat of your hand and hold it out to her. Come on, I'll show you."

Jared inched forward until he came up beside Reese. The two of them made their way to the stall where the mare stood watching.

"Hold out your hand," Reese said. Jared

didn't hesitate. Clearly he wasn't afraid of horses, only men.

Reese set the lump of sugar in the middle of the child's small palm, then lifted him up so that he could feed the sugar to the mare.

She took it with a soft nicker that made the boy grin. "She likes it!"

"Yes, she does," Reese said gruffly, setting the child back on his feet. He could still feel the imprint of the boy's small body against his chest, smell the clean soapy fragrance of his hair. There was a time he had yearned for children of his own. Holding the boy stirred all those forgotten emotions.

Silently, he damned Elizabeth to hell for returning to his life and bringing her young son with her.

"Does your mother know you're out here?" he asked, focusing once more on the boy.

Jared shook his head.

"Then I think you had better go back in."

Jared just nodded. Turning, the little boy dashed out of the barn and ran like fire all the way back to the manor.

Reese watched him until he disappeared. He looked up at the sound of Timothy's voice.

"Sorry to bother you, Major, but Mr. Hopkins said to fetch you. He said to tell you your brother and his wife have arrived."

Reese inwardly groaned. Royal and Lily were there. His brother disliked Elizabeth almost as much as Aunt Aggie. He had known they would come as soon as they discovered Elizabeth's presence. He had only hoped it wouldn't be this soon.

Reese made his way into the drawing room where Royal and his wife, Lily, sat on a deep rose velvet sofa. Even without the improvements he and Elizabeth had once planned to make, the room was comfortable and attractive, done in shades of rose and gold, with rosewood furniture, fringed pillows on the sofas, and Persian rugs over the wide-planked wooden floors. A pair of ancient Chinese vases sat on the mahogany mantle above the hearth, which blazed at the far end of the drawing room.

Royal stood and strode toward him as Reese walked through the open door. Hopkins closed the sliders solidly behind them, making them private. An inch taller, not quite so lean, blond-haired and with the tawny eyes of a lion, Royal fixed him with a glare.

"Have you lost your mind, brother?"

"Apparently so. At least that is the way it seems to our beloved aunt."

Some of Royal's tension eased. "I heard Aunt Agatha was here. That is one of the reasons we came."

"I hope that means you'll be staying for supper at the very least." He looked to his brother's pretty blond wife for confirmation. Gowned in sky-blue silk, Lily's silver-blond hair was far lighter than Royal's dark gold, her eyes a pale shade of green. Being of a much milder temperament than his domineering brother, a man raised to be a duke, Lily was the perfect match for Royal.

"I told him we should send word ahead," she said, "see if our visit would be convenient, but he refused to wait."

"You don't need an invitation. You're always welcome here. Besides, Aunt Aggie has been hoping you would stop by. She sent a note to Bransford just this morning. I know she's eager to see you."

Lily smiled. "Then of course, we shall stay."

Royal flicked a glance at the snugly closed doors. "All right, enough of the idle chitchat. What in blazes is Elizabeth Holloway doing in your house?"

Reese's mouth faintly curved. "She dropped by for a neighborly visit. She's just here for a couple of weeks, is all. You don't think it's a good idea?"

Royal's eyebrows shot up. "Good idea? The woman jilted you for another man! She deceived you and broke her promise to marry you — to say nothing of your heart. Now she is here? Have you gone mad?"

Reese laughed. He couldn't help it. Royal heard the sound and looked as if his brother truly had taken leave of his senses. "You're laughing. You don't laugh, Reese. At least you haven't in years."

He grinned. "I'm sorry. If only you knew how you sounded. Why don't we all sit down and I'll explain as best I can why Elizabeth and her son are here. Then we'll send word up to our aunt to join us."

As Royal crossed to the sofa and sat down next to Lily, he cast Reese an assessing glance.

Was his laughter really so rare? Perhaps his return to the country had been good for him, as his father had always believed.

Or perhaps it was the challenge he had undertaken, his determination to seduce Elizabeth into his bed.

He remembered their heated kisses, remembered Elizabeth staring up at him in wonder after the kiss was over, and whatever humor remained slipped away. Elizabeth was there in his house until her problems were resolved. In the meantime, he intended to make the best of a bad situation, perhaps gain a bit of justice for the way she had treated him.

But bedding her was as far as it would go. He had no intention of letting the woman get to him the way she had all those years ago.

There wasn't a chance that would happen.

Not a chance in the world.

"Go ahead," Royal said, regaining Reese's attention. "This is a story I can't wait to hear."

Reese just sighed. Even he wasn't sure exactly how best to explain.

Elizabeth suffered through the sumptuous meal served in the dining room that night, six courses that included a haunch of roasted beef accompanied by a robust Yorkshire pudding. Though the food was delicious, she could barely force herself to eat.

All evening, her gaze met hostile stares from around the table. Only Her Grace, Lily Dewar, Duchess of Bransford, was the least bit hospitable. Elizabeth had a feeling the young woman understood what it was like to be the outcast in the room.

Perhaps that was the reason the duchess had suggested they meet for tea the following afternoon in an intimate drawing room at the back of the manor that overlooked the garden.

Gowned in a pale green silk gown embroidered with tiny roses, the duchess rose as Elizabeth walked in. "I am so glad you could join me."

"Thank you for inviting me," Elizabeth replied. "I'm happy to have a chance for a bit of female companionship. Though I must admit, I'm surprised your husband would approve."

The duchess smiled. "Royal may be a duke but he doesn't always get his way."

Elizabeth found herself smiling in return.

"Why don't we sit down?" the duchess suggested.

Elizabeth seated herself in a chair upholstered in floral blue chintz across from the matching sofa. The room had white molded ceilings and a mix of blue and white furniture that blended nicely with the garden outside the window.

Lily leaned over and began pouring tea into porcelain cups. "Reese explained why you and your son are here. I know what it's like to feel as if there is no one you can turn to."

"Do you?"

"One lump or two?" the duchess asked.

125

"One is enough, thank you."

The duchess stirred in a lump and handed the cup and saucer to Elizabeth. "My parents died when I was twelve. If my uncle hadn't taken me in, I shudder to think what might have happened. As it was, we had a hard life, but at least I was raised by someone who loved me."

"My mother died when I was five. My father raised me. He passed away four years ago."

The duchess stirred her tea. "I've heard the stories . . . I know you and Reese were supposed to wed and that instead you married another man. It must have taken a great deal of courage for you to come to Reese for help."

Elizabeth carefully rested the saucer in her lap. "As Reese explained, there was no one else I could turn to."

"No one you could trust. That is what you mean, is it not?"

"Yes."

"You must think very highly of Lord Reese."

"I've always admired him greatly."

"Did you love him?"

Her hand shook as she lifted the delicate cup and she almost spilled her tea. She set the cup back down in its saucer. "I loved him. Sometimes things just happen."

The duchess watched her closely. "Sometimes wrongs have a way of righting themselves."

Elizabeth smiled sadly. "Not this time, I'm afraid."

"Why not?"

"Reese feels nothing for me but dislike." *Except, perhaps, for lust.* "Even if his feelings were different, after what I did to him, he would never be able to trust me again."

The duchess sipped her tea. She turned to look out the window into the garden. "The weather is pleasant today. Perhaps we should have taken a stroll out of doors." She continued to gaze in that direction. "The garden is a bit run-down. Lovely though, even as it is."

Elizabeth followed her gaze, grateful for the change of subject. Talking about the past was painful at best. Unfortunately, the future didn't look much better.

"There is something about this place," she said. "It's always been so warm and inviting. I used to dream of living here with Reese."

"Did you?"

She wished she hadn't given away so much. She still knew little of the duchess. "It was a long time ago."

127

"Yes . . ." the duchess agreed. "And yet not so long a'tall."

No, now that she was staying in the house, those days with Reese seemed as if they had happened only yesterday.

They spoke of mundane things after that and Elizabeth was relieved. Eventually, the hour came to an end and both of them rose from their seats.

"I enjoyed our conversation very much, Your Grace."

"I have few women friends," the duchess said. "Those I have I value greatly. I have a feeling we may become good friends. I would like it very much if you called me Lily."

A tightness swelled in Elizabeth's chest. Over the years, Edmund had destroyed the friendships she had cherished. Frances was petty and jealous. Elizabeth would dearly love to have the friendship of a woman she admired.

"I would be honored. And I hope you will call me Elizabeth."

And so the pact was made. The duke might not approve. She knew Reese wouldn't like it. Still, Lily Dewar didn't seem to care, and Elizabeth would always be grateful for the effort the woman had made.

If she went to London, she would be free of Mason and Frances, free to begin making a life for herself, making new friends. Perhaps Lily Dewar would be the first among them.

She almost smiled, might have if she hadn't thought of Reese and the secret she had to tell him and how he would make her feel.

Dear God, how much longer would she have to suffer for the mistakes she had made as a girl?

Royal and Lily had not yet returned to Bransford Castle. The carriage ride from Briarwood took only a little over an hour, but Reese hadn't seen his brother in several weeks and he was enjoying the chance to visit.

Besides, Royal and Lily put a buffer between him and Aunt Aggie, and more importantly between him and Elizabeth.

His brother and his wife would be leaving after luncheon, but this morning, another visitor had arrived. Chase Morgan, the investigator Reese had hired, the same man Royal had employed some months back to help him find out who had swindled their father out of the Bransford fortune.

Morgan brought news of Edmund Holloway and since Royal had worked with the investigator before, Reese asked him to join the two of them in the study.

Morgan, a man in his early thirties, tall and dark and whipcord lean, made the appropriate greetings then sat down in the chair Reese indicated next to the one Royal occupied, and Reese took a seat behind his big oak desk.

"So what have you discovered?" Reese asked, never one to waste time.

Morgan removed a file from his leather satchel and opened it on his lap. He glanced down at the notes he had made. "Edmund Holloway, sixth Earl of Aldridge, died on July ninth, a little over a year ago. There were a number of rumors concerning his death, gossip that perhaps an excess of drinking was involved." He glanced up. "Apparently the man had developed quite a taste for brandy or whatever else happened to be in his glass at the time."

Reese was a little surprised. Back in the days when the men were competing for Elizabeth's affections, Edmund had never overindulged. But the earl had been a great deal younger then. He had more money than he could spend in a lifetime. Perhaps boredom had taken its toll.

Reese had a hard time imagining ever being bored with Elizabeth as his wife. And there was the son she had given the earl. Did Edmund care nothing for the boy?

"Go on," he simply said.

"Along with being an earl and wealthy in the extreme, Holloway led a secret life. After the first few years of his marriage, he began seeking the company of prostitutes. He had a reputation for cruelty, especially when he drank. The women didn't like him and he was banned from several places."

Something stirred inside him. What sort of life had Elizabeth led? How badly had Edmund treated her? Reese warned himself not to feel pity.

"What about Elizabeth? Were you able to discover anything about her relationship with Aldridge?"

"From what I learned, the earl and his wife did not get along. Over the years, his drinking became worse and worse. Their fights were loud and vocal. The servants said Lady Aldridge often argued with her husband about the boy."

He didn't like where this was headed. "What else?"

"Not much. Just that when Mason and Frances moved into the house three years ago, things got markedly worse. Edmund set himself against his wife and now he had the support of his brother and sister-in-law. Life must have been hell for Lady Aldridge."

Reese glanced over at his brother, whose jaw looked hard. No matter what Elizabeth had done, neither of them believed in treating a woman the way Aldridge had treated Elizabeth.

For the first time, Royal entered the conversation. "You're aware Lady Aldridge believes Mason and Frances were drugging her in an effort to gain control of the boy and his fortune."

"Lord Reese told me."

"Is there a way we might be able to prove it?" Royal asked.

Morgan's long fingers came up to rub his chin. "I can do a little more digging. Maybe one of the servants knows something, but the odds aren't good. I doubt anyone but the Holloways knows how it was being done and they sure as hell aren't talking."

"Give it a try," Reese said, rising from behind his desk. "The boy must be protected. If we can prove the Holloways were drugging Jared's mother, there's no way they could ever get custody."

Morgan came to his feet, as well. "I'll give it a try, my lord. Maybe something will turn up."

Morgan left the study and Reese sat back

down across from Royal.

"What a coil," Reese grumbled, running a hand through his wavy black hair.

"Lily likes her," Royal said.

Reese just grunted. "Your wife is the sort who brings home stray animals. Is there anyone she doesn't like?"

Royal laughed. "Point taken."

Reese managed a smile, but it gradually slipped away. "The boy . . . Jared. He had a real bastard for a father. I wonder if he was mistreated."

Royal leaned back in his chair. "Hard to say. He seems a nice enough lad, awfully quiet though. I have a feeling he's better off with his father gone."

And so was Elizabeth. Reese wished it didn't bother him to think of all the years she had been forced to live with the drunken earl.

Then again, as his father always said, "Lie down with dogs and you will get up with fleas." Elizabeth's drive for wealth and position was to blame for the life she had suffered.

The man she had married had been of her own choosing.

NINE

Dinner that night was strained. Now that the duke and duchess were returned to Bransford Castle, only Elizabeth, Reese and Lady Tavistock dined at the supper table.

The dowager had excused herself early, saying she suffered a bit of indigestion, and brawny young Corporal Daniels had escorted her upstairs. Reese suggested a glass of sherry in the drawing room, but thinking what had occurred the last time they had been alone together, Elizabeth had declined.

Now she was upstairs in her bedroom, the household mostly retired for the night, and she discovered she could not sleep.

Instead, she sat reading before the fire, only a single lamp burning to light the pages. An autumn storm had begun to build and she could hear the wind whistling through the leafless branches of the big sycamore outside her window. Before retiring, she had gone upstairs to check on

Jared, but found him already fast asleep.

She looked down at the book she was reading, *Hide and Seek,* a mystery by a prominent author named Wilkie Collins, but the print began to blur. She was tired, but not sleepy, tense and edgy and worried. She set the book aside, thinking that perhaps if she climbed into bed she might fall asleep. She turned in that direction and heard a light knock at her door.

Surely Gilda wasn't up at this late hour of the evening.

A trickle of fear went through her. Perhaps it was Mrs. Garvey. Dear God, had something happened to Jared?

Elizabeth hurried to the door, her white cotton nightgown billowing out behind her. She stepped back in shock as Reese walked into the bedroom.

"What is it? Has something happened? Is Jared all right?"

"Everyone is fine as far as I know."

Relief trickled through her, followed by a shot of uncertainty. "What do you want?"

His incredible blue eyes made a leisurely perusal of her body, from the top of her head to the bare feet peeking out from beneath her white nightgown.

"It's good to see you in something other than black. Though I would prefer you in violet or perhaps a bright sapphire-blue."

She looked down at herself, realized the thin cotton fabric clung to every curve, and heat roared into her cheeks. Turning, she reached for her blue silk wrapper, but Reese caught the fabric and drew it gently from her hand.

"You don't need that. I saw your lovely breasts years ago, as you recall. But I'd rather see you in nothing at all."

Elizabeth stood motionless, trapped by the heat in his gaze, the faint tilt of amusement at the corner of his mouth. Her breathing quickened. Her pulse kicked up. She watched in wicked fascination as he bent toward her and gently captured her lips.

She wasn't sure how it happened, how, suddenly, she was there in his arms. She only knew that he was kissing her, his mouth claiming hers in a leisurely manner she hadn't expected, as if he had all the time in the world, as if he meant for the kiss to go on forever.

Sensation poured through her, heat and dampness and a rapidly building need. His lips melded perfectly with hers, softer than they appeared, warming her as they took control, taking and giving all at once. They alternately coaxed and then demanded, took possession then retreated, insisted she open to allow him entrance until she seemed to have no choice. His tongue slid erotically into her mouth, tasting her, claiming her, forcing a response.

Elizabeth whimpered. She told herself to stop him, to insist he leave her bedroom. Instead her arms slipped around his neck and her fingers curled into his silky black hair. He wore only a pair of fitted black trousers and a full-sleeved shirt. Through her thin cotton nightgown, she could feel the strength of his lean, hard body, the muscles across his chest, the ladder of sinew that banded his flat stomach, and the powerful erection that told her what he wanted.

She should have been frightened. Might have been if there had been anything the least bit threatening in his manner. But there were only tender kisses, sweet and coaxing, and deep, saturating kisses that made her head spin. There was only the heat of their bodies and the fierce attraction she had always felt for him.

She moaned as she pressed herself against him, let her head fall back to give him better access as his mouth traveled leisurely along her throat and he took an earlobe between his teeth. Gooseflesh washed over her skin and desire burned like fire through her veins.

"Reese . . ."

Sun-browned fingers worked the buttons on the front of her nightgown. He parted the fabric and his mouth moved to her shoulder. A moist trail of kisses scorched over the flesh he bared. Her skin seemed to catch fire wherever he touched, and her body wept with desire for him.

She gasped as the gown slid lower, baring one of her breasts, and he took her nipple into his mouth. He suckled the fullness, bit down on the end, and her knees went weak. He caught her before she could fall, his arm like a band of steel around her waist.

"Easy . . ." he whispered softly.

Elizabeth clung to him, her heart pounding wildly. "Dear God, Reese . . ."

Kissing her deeply, he skillfully ministered to each of her naked breasts, stirring the flames that scorched through her body, and she realized he had maneuvered her over to the side of the bed. The nightgown slipped down to her waist and he palmed her breasts, lifted and caressed each one. He cupped her bottom and pulled her into the vee between his long legs, forcing her more fully against his erection, letting her feel how big and hard he was.

Her heart was hammering, trying to tear through her chest. Her body was on fire.

She had to stop him. She knew what would happen next. Memories arose, ugly recollections of humiliation and pain.

"Stop!" she cried out, trying to pull away. "Stop it, Reese! Let me go!"

She wasn't certain he would. He was a man, after all, and men took what they wanted. He was breathing hard, his eyes as blue and hot as the tip of a flame. Little by little, he brought himself under control.

"You want this, Elizabeth. Just as much as I do."

She trembled as she pulled her nightgown back into place, covering her breasts once more. "You're wrong. This . . . this isn't what I want. Whatever . . . whatever feelings we once shared are over. Please, I am asking you to leave."

His jaw hardened. "You're a woman, Elizabeth. That hasn't changed. You can deny your body's needs, but that won't make them go away."

Elizabeth bit her lip. Even if he was right, it didn't matter. "Good night, Reese."

His icy blue gaze made a last lingering perusal of her body and his mouth curved harshly. He made a mocking bow. "Good night, *my lady.*"

And then he was gone.

Elizabeth stared at the place he had been.

Her skin still burned where he had touched her, kissed her naked flesh. Her breasts felt heavy and achy, imprinted with the heat of his mouth. Her body still pulsed with desire for him.

What he'd said was the truth. Even after all of these years, she desired him.

But too much had happened. The terrible memories of Edmund and his cruelty would never go away.

Still, she wondered. . . . Was it possible that with Reese it would be different?

Even her awkward first time that night in the carriage with Reese had been better than anything that had ever happened with Edmund.

And yet she dared not risk it.

Sooner or later, she would have to tell him the truth.

Reese would hate her.

And he would never forgive her.

Reese closed the door of the master's suite, willing himself not to slam it as hard as he could.

Goddammit!

Tonight he had only meant to make the first assault in his campaign. Unable to sleep, he had wandered down to his study for a while, then as he returned upstairs several hours later, he had seen the light beneath Elizabeth's door.

Guessing she was unable to sleep, as he had been, he had knocked, thinking to do little more than kiss her. He hadn't meant to press her for more, wouldn't have if she hadn't responded so passionately.

But even when Elizabeth was young and entirely innocent, she'd had a passionate nature. That fire remained, but now it was buried so deeply he wasn't sure he could completely unearth it. He had only meant to stir her desire for him, but his lust for Elizabeth was nearly uncontrollable. For an instant when she tried to stop him, he wasn't certain he could.

He'd wanted to ravish her, tear off her flimsy nightgown and bury himself inside her.

He wanted her as he never had another woman.

He might have pushed harder, demanded more, if she hadn't looked up at him with those big gray wounded eyes. There was something there he didn't understand. Something that made him want to protect her — even from himself.

Bloody hell.

It didn't change things. He still meant to have her. He knew what she wanted, what she needed, even if she didn't. And he intended to give it to her.

It was just going to take a little longer than he had planned.

Reese sighed into the dim light of his bedroom, lit only by the single lamp burning on the table beside the bed. His leg ached like blue blazes. He had purposely left his cane, forcing his muscles to work. Now he was paying the price.

He grabbed the silver-headed length of ebony to steady himself and made his way over to the big four-poster bed. By now, Timothy would be sleeping. Reese wasn't about to wake him. Leaning against the bedpost for support, he managed to strip off his clothes then climb beneath the covers.

He leg throbbed all the way to his groin. He wished he had a dose of laudanum, but he'd become far too dependent when he had been in the hospital, and recalling Elizabeth's recent bout with the drug, he refrained.

Elizabeth.

He wished she would leave and he would never have to see her again.

He wanted her to stay.

He just flat wanted her. He prayed that in time, she would come to him, let him satisfy both of their needs.

As he stared up at the gold silk bed hangings unable to fall asleep, he wondered if Elizabeth was as tightly strung and as restless as he.

Elizabeth was still awake when the first purple-gray light began to filter through the windows. It would be chilly outside this early, but she loved the out-of-doors and she needed time to think. Years ago, she and Reese had ridden the fields of her home, Clemens Abbey, and once, those at Briarwood. Of course, they had always been properly chaperoned.

Always — except for the single night he had wound up escorting her home from a party at Squire Donovan's house.

The night that they had made love.

Elizabeth shook her head. She was tired of thinking of Reese and exhausted from her sleepless night. Managing to put on her black velvet riding habit without the assistance of her still-sleeping maid, she headed downstairs and out to the stable.

One of the grooms was stirring, beginning his daily routine. Elizabeth headed in his direction.

"I'm sorry to bother you so early, but I am in need of a horse. I'm a fairly decent rider, but it's been a while. Can you find me a suitable mount?"

Realizing he was in the presence of the lady who was staying at the house, the groom jerked off his cap. "The major — I mean Lord Reese — 'e's got a fine eye for livestock. Got several nice geldings what would suit." He glanced around, a little uncertain. "It's awful early, ma'am. Are ye sure —"

"What's your name?"

"Morris, ma'am." He gripped his cap and she noticed an ugly scar on the back of his hand that traveled past his wrist and disappeared inside the sleeve of his work shirt. Another of Reese's veterans, no doubt.

"I wonder, Morris, if the sidesaddle I used many years ago might still be somewhere about. Everything around here seems pretty much the way it was before Lord Reese went into the army."

"Yes, ma'am, there's one 'ere and it's in fine condition. Me and the boys, we take real good care o' the major's stock and equipment."

"Fine, then saddle a horse for me and I'll be on my way."

Morris shook his head, dislodging some of the shaggy brown hair that had been hidden by his cap. "No, ma'am, 'fraid I cain't do that. Not unless I go with ye. Lord Reese — why, he'd have me hide I let a lady ride off all alone."

Perhaps he was right. Aldridge Park wasn't that far away and she hadn't forgot that Mason wanted custody of Jared and control of the Aldridge fortune. She didn't believe her brother-in-law would give up so easily.

"All right, then, a horse for you and one for me. And hurry. I am eager to get out into the fresh morning air."

"Aye, ma'am. I won't be a minute."

Reese rose early. He'd had a hellish night, probably well deserved. For the past two hours, he had been in his study, reading *Advice on Improved Farming Methods* by a man name Ulysses Markham. It was slow going at best.

And he was getting hungry. Checking the clock, he headed down the hall toward the breakfast room. Cook knew his habits. She would have coddled eggs and sausage warming in the silver chafing dishes on the sideboard. He could smell the rich aroma of Arabian coffee even before he got there.

"My lord!"

He looked up to see Hopkins rapidly approaching, his long, thin legs moving with purpose across the floor, a silver salver gripped in a white-gloved hand.

"This just came, my lord. Arrived only moments ago — from London, it seems. The messenger who delivered it said it was urgent."

Reese took the note and popped the wax seal, saw it was a letter from Travis Greer.

Major —
Sorry to bother you as I know you have problems of your own. But it appears I am in some trouble and in need of your help. I would come to you and explain but I have been warned not to leave London. I am hoping there is a way you might come to me.

> Your friend,
> Travis Greer

Reese reread the letter. Travis was in trouble. He couldn't imagine what that trouble might be, but his friend had never asked him for any sort of favor. Whatever was wrong, it had to be important, and Reese intended to do whatever it was Travis needed done.

He had to go to London. Unfortunately, that meant leaving Elizabeth and Jared at Briarwood. The notion did not sit well. Mason Holloway was a ruthless man and he wanted control of Elizabeth's son. He might make another attempt while Reese was away in the city.

He considered, for a moment, sending her to Bransford Castle, leaving her and the boy in the care of his brother.

But it wasn't Royal's problem, it was Reese's.

He ran over his options. He needed to keep Elizabeth and her son safe and he had good men in his employ, men he trusted. He would have Timothy hire a couple of the men Reese knew in the village, enough to protect Elizabeth while he was away.

His decision made, he ordered Hopkins to see his breakfast packed for traveling and his carriage brought round front. He went upstairs and instructed Timothy to pack a valise for each of them, then went in search of Elizabeth.

"I'm afraid she ain't in her room, milord," her maid, Gilda, informed him. "Maybe ye'll find her downstairs."

He nodded, headed in that direction. He needed to speak to her, tell her his plans. He had just reached the bottom of the stairs when the front door burst open and one of his grooms, former sergeant Morris Dexter, rushed in without knocking.

"Major! Thank God I found ye! It's 'er

ladyship, Major. We was ridin' this morning, just on our way back to the house and almost 'ere when a poacher's shot went wrong."

Reese's heart jerked.

"She's lying out there, Major — just behind the stable!"

He was already moving, ignoring his cane and gritting his teeth against the extra strain on his leg. Elizabeth had been shot. Even now she might be dying.

Might already be dead.

His insides tightened into a knot. Morris raced toward the stable, Reese beside him, moving as fast as his damnable leg would allow.

Both of them rounded the corner of the barn to see Elizabeth limping as she walked toward the house. Relief hit him so hard he felt shaky.

"I'm all right," she said, holding her narrow-brimmed, black silk hat in her hand. "Twisted my ankle when I fell, is all. Truly, I am fine."

But she didn't look fine. Leaves and twigs clung to her full black riding skirt and the pins had come loose from her hair. Heavy black strands framed her face, which looked paler than it should have, and long curly tendrils tumbled down around her shoulders.

"Morris says someone took a shot at you. Are you certain you weren't hit?"

She held out her arm. There was a hole in the puffed, upper portion of the sleeve before it tightened at the elbow. "My horse spooked at the sound of the shot. I wasn't prepared. I haven't ridden for a while."

His gaze ran over her, searching for any sign of injury, but aside from her dishevelment and slightly pale face, she appeared to be all right. "Morris thinks it was a poacher. Do you believe that?"

She glanced away. Clearly, she did not.

"Neither do I." He turned to tell the groom to fetch the gig for the short ride up to the house, but Timothy appeared just then and scooped Elizabeth into his brawny arms.

"I got her, sir."

He just nodded. It annoyed him that another man had to perform the tasks that he could not. Still, getting Elizabeth safely into the house was all that really mattered.

That and protecting her.

He thought of Travis. His friend was in trouble. Travis needed his help. So did Elizabeth and Jared.

What the hell was he going to do?

■ ■ ■ ■

Reese didn't leave for London that day. Neither did he go that night down to the dining room for supper. He had too much on his mind. He had to go to London, but he was afraid if he left, something would happen to Elizabeth. He was fairly certain the gunshot wasn't an accident. Someone had been watching the house. Someone Mason Holloway had paid to finish the job he had started.

If Mason couldn't control Elizabeth, Reese believed, he would simply have to kill her.

Worry trickled through him. More men had already been hired, men from the village, men he trusted. They had searched for the shooter, but found no sign of him. Round the clock, they would be guarding the house and keeping watch for anyone who might be there without permission.

Anger burned through him. This was his home, by God. Anyone here should be safe.

He stayed up late that night, pacing the floor of his bedroom, going over his options. Which were few and far between.

He refused to abandon his friend, a man he owed his life.

And whatever had happened in the past between him and Elizabeth, he could not stand by and let someone hurt her or her son.

Another hour slipped past. The clock chimed as he brooded in front of the fire, the flames in the grate burning low. Outside the window, it was as black as one of Elizabeth's dismal mourning gowns. Reese swirled the brandy in his glass and took a sip.

One thing was becoming crystal clear. If he went to London, Elizabeth and Jared would have to go with him.

He took another drink of brandy, the notion he had been contemplating for the past several hours nagging him, as it had for most of the evening. There was a way the boy would be safe. A way he could have what he wanted from Elizabeth.

It was the solution he searched for and yet he resisted. He could never trust Elizabeth, not after the promises she had made and broken. But perhaps it didn't matter. As long as his heart was not involved, the arrangement would merely be a matter of expediency.

He would have Elizabeth in his bed, satisfy the lust for her he had suffered for nearly eight years, and be able to protect her and the boy from her ruthless, greedy in-laws.

That she was an heiress added an extra benefit to the equation. He didn't really need her money, but by English law it would come to him just the same.

The more he pondered, the more the notion made sense.

Elizabeth needed his protection. He needed a woman in his bed.

And not just any woman, he had discovered.

He wanted Elizabeth and he knew exactly the way he could have her.

TEN

Elizabeth slept little again that night. There were decisions to make, matters of life-threatening importance that would affect her and Jared, but after the shot that had narrowly missed killing her, she was even less certain the right course of action to take.

She rose a little later than she intended, rang for Gilda, dressed and headed upstairs to the nursery. Mrs. Garvey was helping Jared read from a book of children's stories.

Elizabeth watched them a moment, thinking how well he was learning to recognize the words, thinking that her son needed to resume his education. She had never really liked Mr. Horton, his tutor, but Mason had hired him and at the time, she had not been up to the challenge of fighting about it. Once she was in the city, she would hire someone she liked and trusted.

Jared looked up and spotted her just then,

jumped to his feet and raced toward her. "Mama!" He clung to her skirts, burying his small face in the heavy black folds.

Elizabeth smoothed back his thick dark hair. "You're reading. That's wonderful."

"Jared is a very fast learner," Mrs. Garvey said proudly, as if the boy were her own. Elizabeth felt a surge of gratitude to have Mrs. Garvey in her employ.

"He has always loved learning. Once we are at Holiday House, I shall find him a suitable tutor to begin his studies again."

"When are we leaving, my lady?" Mrs. Garvey asked.

"I — I am not quite certain. Soon, I hope." In the meantime, she would have to tell Reese the truth about Jared.

Dread churned through her. Her hand trembled as she smoothed her son's hair. *Her son and Reese's,* she silently amended. She was grateful for the distraction of a soft rapping at the door.

Hopkins, the butler, stood in the hallway. "His lordship would like a word, my lady, at your earliest convenience. He awaits you in the blue drawing room."

Elizabeth just nodded. Reese wanted to see her. He hadn't been at supper last night. It was insane to wonder where he had been. Insane to have missed his presence.

"I have to go, sweetheart," she said, tipping Jared's face up so that she could kiss his cheek. "Perhaps we could go out to the stable a little later and feed Starlight a lump of sugar."

Jared beamed. "Oh, I would like that ever so much."

Elizabeth smiled. He was such a sweet little boy. "It is settled, then. I shall return for you a bit later."

Her heart was pounding as she made her way downstairs. Was it nervousness or anticipation?

Reese was waiting in the drawing room, sitting on the comfortable blue chintz sofa, his cane resting beside him. He stood as she walked in, tall and dark and utterly masculine, looking entirely out of place in the feminine room that overlooked the garden.

"Thank you for coming," he said very formally, which only made her more nervous.

"You have been very kind in providing a safe haven for my son and for me. I presume that is the matter you wish to discuss."

"It is."

Elizabeth steeled herself as she made her way toward one of the blue-flowered chairs near the sofa. As soon as she sat down, Reese returned to his seat. He sat very erect, a legacy of his military years. He was incredibly handsome, not in the usual sense but in a far more male, more virile, more striking way.

It occurred to her that the hard, tough man he had become was far more attractive than the handsome young man he had been.

He settled back on the sofa. "After the shooting yesterday, I spent a good bit of time mulling over your circumstances. Considering you could have been killed, it is clear the danger you face is far greater than either of us realized. Mason Holloway wants your son and his money. Apparently, he is willing to commit murder in order to get what he wants."

A shudder rippled through her. "I agree it seems likely, but we can't be entirely certain."

"No, we can't. But we can't afford to assume anything less, not and assure your safety."

Reese was right. They had to assume the worst in order to be prepared.

"The reason I asked you here is that my friend, Captain Greer, also has a problem. You recall meeting him?"

"Why, yes. He seemed quite a pleasant man."

"Travis once saved my life. The gesture

cost him the loss of his arm. Which makes me extremely indebted to him. I have to leave for London and I need to do it soon."

Fear shivered down her spine. Reese had to leave, which meant she had to go, as well. "Of course, you must leave. It is past time I departed at any rate. I've been thinking of returning to Holiday House. I shall begin making preparations immediately." She rose to leave, but Reese's deep voice held her immobile.

"I didn't ask you here because I wanted you to leave. I asked you to come because I think I may have figured out a way to protect your son."

She sank back down in her chair. "How, if may I ask?"

"If I were to adopt the boy, give him my name, even if something happened to you, Holloway wouldn't be able to gain custody. Jared would remain safely in my care. Of course it goes without saying that in order for you to continue to raise your son — as I am sure you wish to do — we would have to marry."

She could feel the color draining from her face. "You are not asking me —"

"Holloway is no fool. He'll understand the ramifications of our marriage and Jared's adoption — which, since my brother is a duke, should be a matter easily resolved. Jared would be completely out of Holloway's grasp. Killing you would no longer serve his purpose."

She only shook her head. There was no way she would ever marry again and certainly not a man who would rather punish her than love her.

"No," she said flatly.

"That is your answer? You don't even want to think about it?"

"I told you before I have no interest in becoming a wife. I will never put myself in that position again."

Fierce blue eyes bored into her. "Not even to save your son?"

Elizabeth's heart squeezed. Jared meant everything to her. *Everything*. And should he fall into Mason's hands, his life would never be his own. To say nothing of the cruelty, even danger, he might face in living with a man as ruthless as his uncle.

"You realize there is something else you haven't considered."

"What . . . what is that?"

"If your son were to die, Holloway would be next in line for the title."

Elizabeth sat up straighter in her chair. "I know that. As ruthless as Mason is, I don't believe he would stoop so low as to kill a little boy."

"But he would have no qualms in killing the little boy's mother."

Elizabeth trembled. She hadn't considered Mason would go so far as to have someone shoot her. Yesterday had shown her how wrong she could be. Would he be equally willing to kill Jared? With the little boy dead, there would be nothing in his way. Mason would become the Earl of Aldridge, with all the money and power the title conveyed.

"With a special license," Reese pressed, "we can be wed in a matter of days. I'll start adoption proceedings immediately thereafter."

Elizabeth shook her head. "I couldn't . . . couldn't possibly marry you." She didn't want to marry anyone. And especially not Reese.

"I'm a military man, Elizabeth. I know what needs to be done to protect you and your son. You'll be safe with me, and I think you know it. That is the reason you came here in the first place."

"Yes, but —" She cut herself off. She *couldn't* marry Reese. Dear God, once she told him the truth about his son, he would despise her. One bitter, vengeful husband was enough.

And with that thought, the answer struck.

He wouldn't marry her if he knew the truth. He would loathe her with every part of his being. And he would do anything to protect his own son.

"I don't expect you to give me your answer now," Reese was saying as he rose to his feet. "Tonight will be soon enough. I leave for London on the morrow. You and your son can go with me. Marry me, Elizabeth, and I'll keep you and Jared safe. On that you have my solemn vow."

Reese's honor meant everything to him. She knew he would not pledge himself if he did not mean to keep his word.

She sat there, her heart clamoring with a mixture of dread and fear, watching as Reese picked up his cane and walked out of the drawing room.

She had to tell him. She would do it tonight. In the morning, she would leave for London.

Twenty minutes later, she still sat in the drawing room trying to imagine what she was going to say to Reese, how she would try to explain. A knock sounded and she turned to see tall, regal Hopkins standing in the doorway.

"I am sorry to disturb you, my lady, but Lady Tavistock wishes to see you."

Frail and hunched, leaning heavily on her

cane, the old woman brushed past the butler into the drawing room.

Elizabeth shot to her feet. "Lady Tavistock."

"Sit down, girl. We need to talk."

She sat down obediently. "Yes, my lady," she said, feeling much as she had eight years ago whenever she had been in the old woman's presence.

The dowager sat down shakily on the sofa. "My nephew has spoken to me. He tells me he has asked you to marry him. He has explained that he wishes to offer you and the boy his protection."

Elizabeth tried to smile but failed. "It . . . it was kind of him to make such an offer. But marriage is too high a price for him to pay. I intend to refuse his proposal. Tonight I will tell him the truth about Jared."

The dowager's silver eyebrows shot up. "Indeed, you will not!"

"What?"

"You will marry the man as he has asked."

"You . . . you can't possibly mean you *want* me to marry him."

"I have never meant anything more. You will marry Reese as soon as possible. You will do what you should have done when you realized you carried his child."

"B-but I can't. Don't you see? Sooner or

later I will have to tell him the truth about Jared. Once he knows, he will hate me forever."

"Perhaps not. After you are married, you will have the time you need to make him understand why you acted in the manner you did. Keep in mind, Reese is not an innocent party in all of this. You were young and naive and he seduced you. In time I believe he will see that the fault in all of this is not yours alone to bear."

If only she could believe that. In truth, she had been the seducer, not Reese. And in his world, there was only black and white, right and wrong. The child was his. She should have married him.

Dear God, if only she had.

The dowager's reedy voice softened. "I have watched the two of you together. I believe you still care for my nephew. I don't believe he would have considered a marriage between the two of you unless he still retained some feelings for you as well, however deeply buried they might be."

"He wants me. He has made that clear. That is his only interest in me."

"It doesn't really matter. You must think of the boy. Reese is a strong, capable man. He will find a way to protect you and Jared."

Elizabeth's fingers tightened around a fold

in her black taffeta skirt. "Please, my lady, you don't understand. You mustn't ask this of me."

"I am not asking. I am telling you that this time you are going to do what is right. You are going to do it because you owe Reese. And because you love your son."

Elizabeth's eyes welled. She thought of Reese and the pain she had caused him all of those years ago. She thought of the years he had missed raising his son, the terrible years the boy had spent with Edmund and the way Edmund had treated him.

Edmund had known the truth from the start. Her father had insisted on telling him. But her dowry was huge, her inheritance even larger.

He had married her.

But he had made her pay every day they were together.

Now Reese was giving her the chance to make things right. Jared would be his, as he should have been from the start. In time, she would find a way to tell him the truth. In time, perhaps he would forgive her.

She swallowed, brushed away the wetness on her cheeks. "I'll do as you ask, my lady."

The old woman nodded. "I knew you would. You were always a good girl, Elizabeth. Somehow you just lost your way."

Her heart squeezed. She *had* lost her way and even *she* wasn't certain how it had happened.

Perhaps in marrying Reese and giving him back his son, she would find a way to make amends for the wrong that she had done.

Leaning back in a deep leather chair, Reese sat before the fire in his study trying to finish the book he had been reading, waiting for Elizabeth to come to him with her answer. It was past ten o'clock. Elizabeth had declined to join him and his aunt for supper. He imagined her thoughts were in turmoil — as were his own.

He wondered if she would refuse his proposal of marriage. She was a countess, a wealthy, independent woman. She was different now than she had been as a girl. Stronger, braver, far more determined.

She was also a mother who clearly loved her son.

Reese had offered his name as protection for the boy, which would prevent Holloway from ever gaining custody. He hoped Elizabeth was right and Holloway would not go so far as to try to murder the boy. Even should he make the attempt, Reese intended to put round-the-clock security in place and begin looking for ways to end the threat

Holloway posed.

Reese would protect mother and child no matter the cost and he believed Elizabeth knew him well enough to trust that he could see it done. He believed she would put aside her doubts and accept his proposal, choosing safety for her child.

Still, he couldn't be completely certain. He glanced at the ormolu clock on the mantel. As the minutes ticked past, he realized how much he hoped she would agree. He told himself it was simply a matter of desire, tempered by concern for the boy. He wanted Elizabeth in his bed and he had begun to feel a certain affection for her son. The notion of Holloway hurting the child made his blood boil.

He glanced down at the book in his lap, trying to concentrate on the agricultural tips on the page, then looked up to see Elizabeth standing in the open doorway.

Setting the book aside, he rose and beckoned her into his domain. "I was beginning to think you would not come."

"I meant to come sooner. I hope I haven't kept you up too late."

"I rarely retire before midnight."

"I have formed that habit myself."

He motioned her toward the brown leather sofa, watched as she crossed the room. The last eight years had been good to her. Her curly hair was still as black as her dismal mourning gown, her skin as smooth as cream. Her figure was more voluptuous, her breasts a little fuller, making her even more womanly and desirable.

His groin tightened at the thought that if she agreed, she would soon be in his bed.

She toyed with a fold of her skirt as she sat down in one of the two brown leather chairs. She was nervous, he could tell, but then so was he. He had only made a marriage proposal one other time in his life — and it had been made to the same woman.

"I presume you have reached a decision," he said, anxious to hear her answer. He had never been a particularly patient man and that had not changed.

"I have." She took a deep breath and slowly released it. "I have decided to accept your proposal — under certain conditions."

He cocked a brow at the unexpected parry. "Which are?"

"The marriage shall exist in name only. A marriage of convenience."

Reese just laughed. "I'm a man, Elizabeth. A man has needs. Since the day I first had you in the seat of the carriage I've wanted to have you again. I've imagined it for nearly eight years. I won't agree to this marriage unless you become my wife in every way."

Her cheeks flushed, making her look like the young girl she had been when he had first met her. "A number of years have passed. We scarcely know each other anymore. You are asking a very great deal."

"And I am offering a very great deal."

She glanced away, bit down on her lush bottom lip. Desire slipped through him. He could still recall the taste of her, the feel of her soft curves pressing against him, the way her nipples had tightened in his hand.

"If . . . if I agree, I'll need some time," she said. "I need to get to know you better before . . . before . . ."

He frowned. "You are not some simpering virgin, Elizabeth. You've been married. You've borne a child. You understand what happens between a man and a woman. Aside from that, there is the not so small matter that you desire me, perhaps as much as I desire you."

Her cheeks pinkened. "I enjoyed your kisses, yes, but I . . . I . . ."

"You what? You didn't like the way I touched you, caressed you? Don't lie to yourself, Elizabeth." She opened her mouth to argue and he shook his head in defeat. Arguing would not get him what he wanted.

"All right, I'll give you a week from the

day we marry before I claim my husbandly rights."

She glanced away and her chin wobbled. Rising to her feet, she walked over to the hearth, spent several long moments staring into the flames. Having learned how much she valued her independence, he had known the decision would not be easy, but it bothered him to think that she would deny his suit if she could.

Her head came up as she turned to face him. There was something in her eyes, something tenuous and fearful that made his stomach tighten.

Elizabeth squared her shoulders. "I'll agree to your terms, but . . . even if you are my husband, I — I won't let you hurt me."

His chest squeezed. God's blood, what had Aldridge done? He had never liked the man but surely her husband hadn't physically harmed her.

Reese moved toward her. He had never meant to frighten her. "I won't force you, Elizabeth," he said in a gentler voice. "For God's sake, I've never forced a woman in my life. I don't intend to start with you."

She looked up at him and her lovely gray eyes filled with tears. Reese felt her pain as if it were his own.

"I don't know, Reese . . . I don't . . . I

don't know if I can do it."

He reached for her, eased her gently into his arms. What had happened in the years after he left? Was her life with Aldridge truly that unbearable? He felt her trembling and a tiny crack formed in the wall he had built around his heart.

Reese steeled himself against it. He couldn't afford to show weakness, not when it came to Elizabeth. Still, he didn't let her go.

"We'll take it slowly, get to know each other again, discover each other's likes and dislikes. I won't do anything you don't want me to." He tipped her chin up. "On the other hand, I'll expect your cooperation. I won't be denied forever."

She looked up at him, blinked, and the tears in her eyes rolled down her cheeks. He wished she wouldn't cry. She had never cried, not even once, when they had been together. Reese brushed away the wetness with the pad of his thumb.

"Say yes, Elizabeth. Let me protect you and your boy."

Her gaze remained on his face, deep pools of gray filled with unfathomable emotion. Elizabeth slowly nodded. "All right, Reese, I'll marry you."

Something unfolded inside him. Something sweet and yearning. He ruthlessly crushed it down.

Bending his head, he very gently kissed her. He could feel her soft mouth trembling under his and knew this was not the time to press for more.

"There is one last thing," he said as he eased away.

She eyed him warily. "What is it?"

"Once we reach London, you will abandon those dreadful black dresses. You will dress as my wife, not another man's widow."

For an instant, he thought she might argue. Instead, she almost smiled. "As you wish, my lord."

"Then we are agreed. Tomorrow I'll begin making arrangements. By the end of the week, we'll be married."

Elizabeth just nodded. Her shoulders began to droop and her bravado seemed to fade. "I hope you don't mind, but I find I am suddenly tired. If you will excuse me, I believe I shall go on up to my room."

"Of course."

Turning away from him, Elizabeth walked out of the study.

Reese released a deep breath. In a few days' time, they would be wed. He would be marrying a woman who had betrayed him, a woman he did not trust. A woman who still appealed to him far more than he ever would have imagined.

Reese prayed he was doing the right thing.

ELEVEN

Flat gray storm clouds hung over Briarwood Manor. A fierce October wind blew a bitter chill across the barren fields as Elizabeth stood next to Reese in the main drawing room of the house. In deference to Reese and because he refused to let Gilda return to Aldridge Park for more of Elizabeth's clothes, she wore a gown of lavender silk with an overskirt of shot silver tulle, a garment made for her by the Duchess of Bransford, deftly sewn by the lady herself.

Standing next to Elizabeth in a velvet-collared, navy blue tailcoat and dark gray trousers, Reese's hard-carved features, darkly forbidding appearance, and fierce blue eyes didn't lessen his masculine appeal.

And yet she dreaded to think that soon she would be his wife.

Elizabeth steeled herself against the chill that swept down her spine and forced her attention back to the man in white satin robes in front of them, a thin, gray-haired, man with a sallow complexion. His voice droned on as he spoke the sacred vows of marriage, words Elizabeth barely heard.

The guests were few. Reese's brother, Royal, stood to his right, while the duke's pretty blond wife, Lily, stood next to Elizabeth. Sheridan Knowles, Viscount Wellesley, a longtime friend of the Dewar brothers who lived on a nearby estate was there, a charming, sophisticated man Elizabeth had met on several occasions. A few feet away, her small son sat in a chair next to Reese's aunt Agatha, Jared's dark eyes solemn and uncertain.

Elizabeth had tried to explain to him what was going to happen today, that she and Reese would be married, that Lord Reese would be living with them from now on.

"Is he going to be my father?" Jared had asked, making Elizabeth's stomach churn.

"Why, yes, I suppose he is."

"What should I call him?"

Dear God, when she had accepted Reese's proposal, she hadn't considered how to handle any of this. "For now, why don't you just keep calling him Lord Reese?"

Jared had looked up at her and simply nodded. As was often the case, she had no idea what he was thinking.

The vicar's use of Reese's name dragged her back to the moment.

"Wilt thou, Reese, take this woman, Elizabeth, to be thy wedded wife, to live together in God's holy estate of marriage? Wilt thou love her, comfort her, honor and keep her in sickness and in health and forsaking all others, for as long as you both shall live?"

Reese's deep voice said firmly, "I will."

"And wilt thou, Elizabeth, take this man, Reese, to be your wedded husband, to love him, comfort him, honor and keep him in sickness and in health and forsaking all others, for as long as you both shall live?"

Elizabeth's voice trembled. "I will."

Reese clasped her icy hand and slipped a heavy gold ring embedded with rubies on her third left finger. The ring was old and beautiful and she wondered what significance it held. Placing her shaking hand on the sleeve of his coat, he turned once more to the vicar.

"By the giving of a ring and having consented together in holy wedlock, therefore, in the name of the Father, the Son, and the Holy Ghost, I pronounce you husband and wife. What God has joined together, let no man put asunder." He smiled. "You may kiss your bride, my lord."

Reese leaned toward her and Elizabeth closed her eyes. Very softly, he settled his lips over hers. She didn't expect the jolt of heat that flared inside her, or the feel of a warm blush rising in her cheeks. She didn't expect that when the kiss should have ended, Reese deepened it, claiming her in some fashion before he let her go.

Reaching toward her, he touched the heightened rose in her cheeks. "Everything is going to be all right," he said softly, and dear God, she wanted to believe it.

"Your aunt, Lady Tavistock, has arranged a wedding breakfast in your honor," the vicar said with a smile. "I for one am quite looking forward to it."

"As am I," Reese's frail aunt said, rising shakily to her feet, "and I am certain this young man is hungry, too."

Jared grinned, and all of them laughed, grateful for the break in the tension. They were on their way to the dining room when the front door burst open. On a gust of wind, Rule Dewar strode into the entry.

"Sorry I'm late," he said, sweeping off his greatcoat. "Damned roads were a bloody —" he coughed behind his hand "— muddy nightmare."

"Rule!" Reese smiled and moved toward him, leaning a little on his cane. Elizabeth had noticed he hadn't used it during the ceremony. She wondered how much it had cost him. "I didn't expect you to travel all the way from London on such short notice."

Rule, the youngest and perhaps the most handsome of all three Dewar men, enveloped his brother in a hug.

"Are you mad?" Rule said. "My brother is getting married. Did you think I wouldn't want to be here?"

Reese smiled, obviously pleased. "You're a little late for the actual event but I am damn — extremely glad to see you. Thank you for coming, little brother."

Rule turned toward Elizabeth. "Welcome to the family, my lady." He had the same blue eyes as Reese and as they perused her head to foot, she caught the gleam of male appreciation. "It appears my brother has as fine an eye for women as he's always had for horses."

Elizabeth laughed at the lopsided compliment, certain she was going to like the youngest Dewar brother. "I hope you will call me Elizabeth. We are, as you say, family now."

Rule had been just fourteen when she and Reese had first meant to wed. She remembered seeing him only once, when he had been home on a visit from boarding school.

Perhaps his youth was the reason he seemed less resentful of her, more inclined to give her the benefit of the doubt.

Whatever the reason, she was grateful to have one less problem to deal with.

She motioned for Jared to come forward, then rested her hand reassuringly on his small shoulder. "I would like to introduce my son, Jared."

"Handsome boy," Rule said, then went down on one knee in front of the child. "I'm your uncle Rule. It's nice to meet you, Jared." Rule stuck out his hand and the little boy shook it.

"You're my uncle?"

"That's right. You have two of us now." Rule grinned and dimples appeared in his cheeks. "Your uncle Royal is right over there."

Royal waved at the boy, accepting his role without question and Elizabeth's heart pinched. Reese's family was clearly ready to accept the child, even without knowing the truth of whom he was. This was what Jared had missed. A loving family.

In that moment, Elizabeth realized she had made the right decision. The Dewars would protect one of their own no matter the cost, and Jared had just become one of them.

Her eyes welled. She felt Reese's solid presence beside her. "Are you all right?"

She nodded. "I just . . ." She looked over at Rule, still talking to her son. "Thank you."

Reese's gaze followed hers and he seemed to understand. "I won't let anything happen to him, Elizabeth."

Elizabeth managed a smile. "I know you won't."

"I'm starving," Rule said, rising and taking hold of Jared's small hand. "At least I made it in time for the food."

All of them laughed and everyone headed for the dining room, eager to sample the sumptuous buffet.

The wedding breakfast was a small but elegant affair, orchestrated by Lady Tavistock. Well wishes were given and received. Toasts were made, one by each of the brothers, one by their friend, Sheridan Knowles.

"I know this day has been a long time coming," the viscount said, raising his champagne glass. "But the best things in life are often worth the wait. To the bride and groom. May they find many years of happiness together."

"Hear, hear!" the small group agreed.

By twelve o'clock, Reese's coach-and-four had been loaded and brought round to the front of the manor in preparation for the journey to London. Goodbyes were said to Aunt Agatha, who was also departing; as well as both brothers, the duchess, and the rest of the wedding guests.

Elizabeth's carriage had also been readied for the trip. Mrs. Garvey and Jared, Timothy Daniels and Gilda, along with the baggage they would be transporting to Holiday House, would be riding aboard the second conveyance.

She was married. She and her husband would be traveling to London.

Once again, her life had drastically changed.

Reese sat across from Elizabeth as the traveling coach rolled over the muddy, rutted road toward London. The wind had calmed, but the temperature had dropped, making the inside of the carriage bone-freezing cold.

Across from him, Elizabeth rode with a horsehair lap robe draped over her heavy skirts, her feet propped on the warm brick he had provided. Her face was a little pale but he figured it was more from the unsettling change in her life than the chilly early October air.

He still found the happenstance hard to

believe. He was married. Wed to the last woman on earth he would have considered taking to wife.

At least not since the day she had jilted him for another man.

How was it, he wondered, the hatred he had once nurtured had changed into something else entirely? Aside from a healthy dose of lust, he wasn't even sure what that emotion was.

One thing was clear. Whatever his feelings, he had to keep a safe distance between them. They could rub on together quite well, he was sure, without the burdensome emotion of love.

Elizabeth shifted on the tufted velvet cushion, drawing his gaze back to her, though his thoughts hadn't strayed far since the moment the vicar had pronounced them man and wife.

Heat settled low in his groin. She belonged to him now. Soon he would consummate the marriage. Reese ground his jaw. Unfortunately it wouldn't be tonight.

Elizabeth drew off a kidskin glove and held up her hand to study the heavy gold-and-ruby ring she wore on her third left finger. "It's beautiful, Reese. You had so little time I wasn't sure there would be a wedding ring at all, and certainly not one so lovely."

He smiled, oddly pleased that she approved. "It belonged to my grandmother on my mother's side. Since Royal was heir to the dukedom, my grandparents felt it their duty to look out for Rule and me."

"If I remember, your mother died when you were six."

"Yours at five, I recall."

She nodded.

"With their own offspring deceased, Rule and I became my grandparents' heirs." He thought of the problems Royal had faced that Reese had only recently discovered. "As it turned out, Royal was the one who wound up with the gravest need for money. Fortunately, that is a problem he seems to have solved."

"You're speaking of your brother's business interests."

"Yes. Royal was always clever. He inherited a penniless dukedom instead of the fortune that was meant for him. Thankfully, the Swansdowne Brewery, Royal's notion of how to set things right, turned out to be a great success."

"I've read in the newspapers how popular the ale is becoming."

"He's doing very well."

"He certainly seems happy."

"I think he is."

"The duchess says they plan to remain mostly in the country."

He nodded. "Bransford is a very large estate and Royal likes the challenge of running it. And he married a woman who enjoys a simpler life." *Unlike you,* he couldn't help thinking. Lily had known Royal was in desperate financial straits. Unlike Elizabeth, who valued wealth and position above all things, Lily had married Royal because she loved him.

"What about you?" Elizabeth asked, breaking into his thoughts. "What are you planning to do now that you are retired from the army?"

It was a question that once had haunted him. Now his future had been settled. "Farm the lands at Briarwood. Royal needs all the barley the land can produce. It shouldn't be such a difficult task."

"But you never liked farming," she reminded him.

Reese shrugged his shoulders. "It was my father's dying wish."

Elizabeth studied him closely. "And now you are married and responsible for a family, giving you even less choice in the matter."

He frowned. She had always been able to read him too well. "I'll get used to it. Besides, life in the country isn't nearly as bad as I once believed."

Elizabeth turned her soft gray gaze toward the window where a light mist hung over the rolling hills. "Briarwood is lovely. There is something special about it."

The notion pleased him, though he didn't really see anything unique about the old manor house that had been built in the seventeen-hundreds. It was just a house and nothing at all as lavish as any of Aldridge's luxurious residences.

An image arose of the handsome, incredibly wealthy man Elizabeth had married and a bitter taste rose in his mouth. Tonight was his wedding night, but because of Aldridge, he wouldn't be enjoying his beautiful bride's luscious body. He consoled himself with the thought that he had been the man Elizabeth had gifted with her innocence, not Aldridge, no matter that the earl had been the one she had chosen to wed.

"What about your friend, Captain Greer?" she asked. "Have you heard from him?"

"I sent Travis a letter telling him we would soon be arriving in the city. I'm hoping whatever trouble he is in will be more easily resolved than he seems to believe."

And he had also set up a meeting with Chase Morgan, the investigator his brother had recommended, to discuss security for Holiday House, where they intended to take up residence, as well as personal security for Elizabeth and Jared.

"Captain Greer is lucky to have a friend like you."

"I was lucky to have a friend like him. I wouldn't be here if he hadn't risked his life to save me."

Her gaze drifted down to his leg, which had stiffened in the cold. He straightened it even more, trying to ease the ache that had begun there.

"I heard you were injured," she said. "For a while I wasn't certain if . . . that is, I thought you might have been killed."

He couldn't help wondering, now that he had practically forced her to marry him, if his death would have been a relief.

"For a while when I was in the hospital, I wished I had been. But I've recovered for the most part and I'm determined to improve the condition of my leg."

"I'm sure you will, if that is your wish. Just as I'm certain you'll be able to help your friend. You were always good at coming up with solutions."

"Like our marriage?"

She glanced down at her lap, picked up her glove and tugged it back on. "I suppose that remains to be seen." She lapsed into silence and so did he, which gave him the chance to study her.

Beneath her simple black wool traveling gown, her breasts rose invitingly, though the bodice was buttoned to the neck and a warm woolen pelisse draped over her shoulders. Her waist was small and though he had never seen the sweet curves below, he imagined they would be as tempting as the rest of her.

His body clenched and his loins began to fill. Bloody hell, tonight was going to be torture of the very worst sort. He had given Elizabeth a week to get used to the idea that he would be her husband in every way, and though it was killing him to wait, he would not break his word.

Still, he intended to spend the night in her bed. Rooms had been reserved for their party at the Roving Bull Inn, including the one they would share. Tonight would set the tone for the way he meant to go on and that meant starting with the upper hand.

Elizabeth was a passionate woman, even if she didn't know it. Tonight he would give her a glimpse of what the future held in store for them.

He leaned back against the velvet seat, tilted his head back against the cushions and watched her from beneath half-closed lids. He imagined himself pulling the pins from her glossy black curls and running his hands through her hair. He remembered the lush feel of her breasts and he wanted to put his mouth there, to suckle and taste them until she begged him to take her.

His arousal stirred, pressed painfully against the front of his trousers. Tonight would challenge his strength of will, and yet there would be certain . . . rewards.

Reese looked over at Elizabeth, thought of the goal he had set for himself, and vowed to see it done.

TWELVE

The Roving Bull Inn on the road to London was a welcome respite from the long, cold journey. Whenever Elizabeth had traveled to town with Edmund, he had insisted on making the exhausting trip in a single day.

Instead, Reese had taken measures to insure her and Jared's comfort, stopping several times along the route and arranging an overnight stay at an inn. It was amazingly clean and well appointed, she discovered as she walked next to her son and Reese into the whitewashed, thatch-roofed building. Low-beamed ceilings hung over the taproom, and a warm fire blazed in the hearth along the wall.

While Reese went to see to their quarters for the night, the rest of their small group of weary travelers huddled around the fire, warming their chilled hands and feet.

Reese returned a few minutes later. "They've got our rooms nearly ready. In the meantime, they've a nice kidney pie for supper. Or there is roasted quail." He looked down at Jared, who shrank back only a little. Her son was still adjusting to the change, uncertain what all of it meant, and her heart went out to him. She waited for Reese to send him off to dine with his nanny as Aldridge would have done, but he surprised her, as he had so many times in the past few days.

"Why don't you have supper with us tonight, Jared? Your mother has been deprived of your company all day. I think she would enjoy the chance to see how you fared on the journey."

Jared looked up at him with wide, soulful brown eyes. "All right," he agreed, as if he actually had a choice.

Reese clamped him on the shoulder. "Fine, then, let's see if we can manage to get ourselves something to eat."

He ushered Elizabeth and Jared into the dining room and seated them in a private alcove he had previously arranged. The others took tables in the main part of the taproom.

"The food is quite good," Elizabeth said, halfway through the meal. She looked down at her son. "Don't you think so, Jared?"

He smiled and nodded, tucked back into

his kidney pie. Several times Reese had tried to draw him out, but mostly he had given simple yes or no answers. Elizabeth prayed Reese wouldn't get annoyed with him as Edmund would have done.

Jared was just finishing his last bites of food when Mrs. Garvey arrived at the table. "The innkeeper says our room is ready. With your permission, my lord, I think it is time I took Jared upstairs and got him into bed."

Elizabeth leaned toward him as he rose from the wooden bench where he had been sitting. "Ask his lordship if you might be excused."

Jared obediently complied. "May I be excused, Lord Reese?"

Reese frowned. Elizabeth wasn't sure why. But Jared took a step backward, might have gone even further if he hadn't been blocked by Mrs. Garvey's enormous skirts.

"It's all right," Reese said gently. "You've finished eating. Of course you may be excused. Sleep well, Jared."

"Good night, sweetheart," Elizabeth said, smoothing back an errant strand of his dark hair. "I'll be up to say good-night in just a few minutes."

Mrs. Garvey led Jared out of the dining room and the two of them headed upstairs.

"What was it Jared said that upset you?

He tries so hard to do everything just right."

"It wasn't Jared. I just . . . soon he is going to become my son. Perhaps once he is, we can discuss the matter of how he should address me."

"He asked me what to call you. I — I wasn't exactly sure."

Reese rose from his chair, picked up his ebony walking stick, and drew her to her feet. "This is all going to work out, Elizabeth. We just need to take our time."

Her throat tightened. He sounded so certain. And yet tonight was his wedding night and she was denying him. She wondered just how much patience he had.

Reese led Elizabeth upstairs, following the swaying hips of a buxom chambermaid.

" 'Ere we are, milord. The grandest room in the 'ouse. Nice fresh linens. Water's in the pitcher next to the basin on the dresser. Fire's a-blazin' in the hearth. If there's anythin' else ye need, just let me know." She gave him a saucy wink. "There's a bellpull right there in the corner."

"Thank you, Molly," Reese said.

" 'Tis me pleasure, milord." She flashed him a glance that promised she meant what she said. If he needed anything — anything at all — Molly would be happy to give it to him.

Reese clenched his jaw. He needed a woman — and badly, but the only one he wanted refused him the comfort of her body.

"I presume this room is yours," Elizabeth said, nervously glancing around. "Where . . . where am I to sleep?"

The time had come. Reese led her farther into the room and firmly closed the door. "I told you I would give you a week and I intend to keep my word. I also said I expected your cooperation."

"Yes, but —"

"We are married, Elizabeth. This is our wedding night. I intend for us to share a bed."

Her breathing grew shallow and faster. He could see the fear creeping into her pretty gray eyes.

"Listen to me, Elizabeth. I am not going to force you in any way. I gave you my word and I don't intend to break it. Now turn round so that I may help you undress."

She only shook her head.

"We're married, Elizabeth. I'm your husband and I want to see your beautiful body. At least you can grant me that much."

For several long moments, she just stood there. Finally, she nodded. "All right, if that

191

is your wish. But I need to call Gilda."

"You won't need the girl tonight. Tonight I'll act as your ladies' maid."

More seconds passed and she made no move, just kept her gaze on his face. Then she squared her shoulders and turned her back to him so that he could unfasten her buttons.

Relief filtered through him. Tonight was only a first step, but it was a very important one. "I'm going to undress you completely. I've already seen a good bit of your delectable body so there is no need for you to be embarrassed."

She started to tremble.

His jaw tightened. In the past, she had longed for his touch, often been the one to initiate their passionate kisses. He wondered what had happened to the woman she had been.

Aldridge, he thought bitterly, and pity welled inside him. Reese turned her to face him and eased her into his arms.

"We're going to do this together, Elizabeth. I'm going to help you get over your fears. You trusted me enough to come to me at Briarwood. Trust me in this."

She inhaled a steadying breath and some of her trembling eased. "I do trust you, Reese."

It was true. Elizabeth trusted Reese as she never had another man. There was something about him that had always made her feel sheltered and protected. And he had given his word.

She released the breath she had been holding. They were married. He deserved a wife who pleased him in bed. She would do her best to give him what he deserved.

Instead of hurrying to undress her as she had imagined, Reese bent his head and kissed her, a tender, gentle kiss meant only to ease her fears. But liquid heat poured into her stomach and a kernel of desire bloomed inside her.

Moving of their own volition, her arms slid around his neck and she leaned toward him. Reese's arms went around her and the kiss turned hot and fierce.

Elizabeth trembled but not with fear. She opened to him, parting her lips to allow him entrance, and his tongue swept in to taste her. Inside her corset, her nipples hardened, rasping erotically every time she moved.

He had shed his jacket and waistcoat, and she could feel the lean slabs of muscle moving beneath his shirt. Wavy black hair, always a little too long, curled round the tips of her fingers.

"Reese . . ." she whispered, pressing herself more fully against him. She nearly stumbled when Reese pulled away.

Tenderly, he cupped her cheek. "You see? This isn't going to be nearly as hard as you think."

Not as hard? The word had her glancing down. Reese was fully aroused, and from what she had felt through her skirts, obviously far larger than Edmund. She shivered.

"Turn round, sweeting. Let me help you with your clothes."

The endearment washed over her. He had called her that when she was a girl. She obeyed his command, her lips still burning from his kisses, her nipples still erect. She stood unmoving as he eased her wrinkled traveling gown off her shoulders, then unfastened the tabs holding up her heavy black skirts.

Soon she would be wearing bright colors again. Reese had no idea the favor he had done her.

"Come, let me help you."

Taking her hand, he urged her out of the heavy pile created by her petticoats and full silk skirt. He lifted her corset cover over her head and started on her corset, amazing her how expertly he dealt with the strings then dispatched her whalebone stays. She tried not to think how many women he must have made love to over the years.

"Sit down on the stool and I'll take off your shoes."

She wore only her undergarments, garters and stockings, and a pair of soft black leather half boots. Beginning to grow uncertain again, she perched on the edge of the stool and Reese slowly bent his stiff leg to kneel in front of her. He removed each low-heeled boot, then unfastened her pink satin garters and rolled down her black silk stockings.

When he looked up at her, the heat burning in his eyes made her breath catch. No man had ever looked at her the way he was, not even the young Reese she had once known.

"Stand up so I can take off your chemise," he said gruffly, his voice thick and husky.

Beneath the thin lawn fabric, her breasts swelled and her nipples tightened almost painfully. Moisture settled in the place between her legs. It occurred to her nothing like that had happened since Reese had made love to her all those years ago.

She stood up slowly, breathing too fast, wanting him to touch her. Afraid of what would happen if he did. Reese moved behind her, began to pull the pins from her hair, allowing the ink-black curls to tumble round her shoulders. His suntanned fingers combed through the curly strands and he lifted a curl and inhaled the scent.

"Like roses," he said. "I remember you always smelled like roses."

Her stomach contracted. He remembered that about her, remembered the scent of the rosewater she bathed in. But then she had remembered things about him, as well. The way the edge of his mouth curved when he smiled, the small indentation in his chin, the rich sound of his laughter that once had come so easily to him.

Reaching up, she slipped the straps of her chemise off her shoulders, let the garment slide down to her waist. Her breasts were full and round, the areolas a dusty rose. His gaze fastened there, took in the plump shape and diamond-hard nipples, and his eyes turned a fierce shade of blue. Her heart was pounding, hammering away inside her chest. Her body thrummed with heat.

Reaching down, Reese pulled the string on her drawers, then slid them along with her chemise down over her hips. Though she tried not to be embarrassed, she could feel a flush burning into her face, spreading down her neck and across her shoulders. No man had ever seen her naked, not even Edmund.

"Beautiful," Reese said gruffly, his gaze as hot as the tip of a flame. Bending his dark head, he kissed the side of her neck, kissed her shoulders, trailed scorching kisses down to her breasts. It felt so good. So hot and sweet. She had forgotten how good his touch could feel.

Reese cupped her breast, lowered his head and took the fullness into his mouth, and a wave of desire tore through her. Elizabeth found herself clutching his shoulders, arching her back to give him better access. The shadow of his evening beard abraded her skin and her stomach quivered.

Reese turned his attention to her other breast, thumbed an aching nipple, then ministered to it, as well. Heat and moisture slid into her core. An ache began there and her legs became unsteady. Reese kissed her deeply, stirring the flames, drawing her into the passion. She forgot to be frightened, thought only of his kisses, his magical caresses — until his hand cupped her mound, parted the soft folds of her sex, and a finger slid inside her.

Elizabeth bit back a cry of sheer terror and jerked away. She stumbled against the stool in front of the dresser, trembling all over, fear clawing at her insides.

"Easy," Reese said, as if he were gentling one of his mares. "Everything's all right. I want you, but it isn't going to happen until you're ready. I promise you that, Elizabeth."

Her throat tightened. She wanted him, too, she had just discovered, and yet she was afraid. Grabbing her chemise off the floor, she held it protectively in front of her, still trying to control her trembling limbs. Reese swore softly, walked over and opened her satchel, drew out her warm blue quilted wrapper. Limping slightly, he returned to where she stood and draped the garment round her shoulders.

"I promised we'd go slowly. I didn't mean to rush you. Now get into bed. I'll join you there as soon as I finish undressing."

Elizabeth released the breath she had been holding, hurried to the bed and climbed up on the mattress. Snuggling beneath the fluffy covers, she felt the warmth of a brick beneath the sheets and sighed in sheer pleasure.

"As you see, the bed is warm. Now take off that damnable robe."

Her eyes flew wide. "But I —"

"Do it, Elizabeth. Remember you made promises, too."

She had promised to cooperate, but it wasn't that easy. Wishing she had been less amenable to his terms when she had agreed to the marriage, she shed the robe. She wasn't truly afraid of him. At least not at the moment.

Comfortable in the big feather bed, determined to gain something for herself tonight, Elizabeth watched in fascination as Reese began to disrobe, removing each of his garments with military precision, draping them over the back of a wooden chair.

She told herself to close her eyes, that it wasn't proper to stare. But as he stripped off his shirt, leaving him naked to the waist, her gaze remained riveted on the lean bands of muscle across his wide chest, the thatch of curly black chest hair that narrowed to a thin line down his flat stomach, his solid arms and powerful biceps. He removed his trousers and she admired his long, sinewy legs, noticed the scar running from his left knee up his thigh, disappearing inside his drawers.

The sympathy she was feeling changed to something else as Reese turned his back to her and shoved down his drawers. If she had expected him to sleep in his undergarments, she should have known better. Instead he stood gloriously naked, his back smooth and broad, his buttocks narrow and tight. When he turned, she gasped at the heavy erection rising up against his flat belly. Interest mingled with an electrifying awareness she never thought to feel, and as he strode toward her, sinfully aroused, it occurred to her the price he was paying to keep his word.

Her gaze remained fixed on the hard length of his shaft, a sight she had never seen before. Edmund had come to her in the darkness, taken his pleasure, then left her.

"You are staring, Elizabeth. And you are making me harder than I am already."

Elizabeth looked up at him, hoping he wouldn't notice the color in her cheeks. "I've never seen a man's . . . private parts."

His features tightened. She thought it betrayed an even greater dislike of Edmund.

"Since that is the case, then perhaps we are beginning exactly as we should." Naked and unembarrassed, Reese stopped beside the bed, allowing her to look her fill. She had the strangest urge to touch him, see if his heavy member was really as hard as it looked.

Embarrassment kept her hand where it was. She moved over a little as he settled himself on the mattress and drew the covers up over his chest.

"Come here," he said softly.

When she made no move to join him, he reached for her, slid an arm beneath her waist and dragged her solidly against him. She could feel the heat of his body, the solid ridges of muscle meshing with her own soft curves. Accidentally, she brushed his arousal and Reese hissed in a breath.

"Go to sleep, Beth," he said gruffly, tucking her against his side.

The name washed over her, bringing a fresh flood of memories. How could she have forgotten how good it had been between them? How had she ever been convinced to marry any other man?

But she had, and once he knew the truth about his son, Reese would demand penance for what she had done.

Elizabeth closed her eyes, certain she wouldn't be able to sleep. But the warmth of Reese's body seeped into her weary bones, along with an unexpected feeling of security, and in minutes she drifted into a peaceful sleep.

She slumbered soundly for a while, but during the night her pleasant dreams turned into nightmares of Reese and Jared. Elizabeth began to toss and turn, her mind filled with thoughts of the grim, uncertain future that lay ahead of her.

THIRTEEN

Night sounds began to creep in, a dog barking somewhere down the lane, the hoot of an owl in the rafters above the stable, crickets chirping in the grass around the perimeter of the inn. Reese had barely slept and now lay awake, listening to Elizabeth's deep breathing.

It was impossible to sleep with his beautiful bride nestled in his arms and his body on fire for her. During the past long hours, he had replayed his first glimpse of her curvaceous, womanly body, the full, rose-tipped breasts and the sweet roundness of her bottom. Her legs were shapely, her feet small and her ankles trim.

God, he had never seen a more desirable creature. And he had not mistaken her passionate nature. Her innocent responses set his blood on fire. Still, her encounters with Aldridge had clearly been unpleasant. The bloody fool had used her with no thought to her pleasure.

She turned on the mattress and soft black curls teased his shoulder. Beneath the sheets, his erection stirred to life. Dammit to bloody hell, he'd been hard as granite most of the night.

He rolled away from her and closed his eyes, exhausted and hoping for at least an hour or two of sleep. When that time had passed and he still lay awake, he slid to the edge of the bed. His leg was always a little stiff in the mornings. Forcing his muscles to move, he stifled a groan, bent and straightened his knee several times, loosening the joints and sinews, then dressed quietly and left the room.

A bit of breakfast would improve his mood, he was sure, and after a hearty plate of sausage and eggs, discovered that it actually had.

It was time to rouse Elizabeth. Reese found himself looking forward to waking his bride with a kiss.

Unfortunately, when he climbed the stairs and opened the door, Elizabeth was already out of bed preparing to dress, standing naked in the middle of the room. She looked tousled and delectable and his arousal returned for what seemed the hundredth time.

"Reese!" Coloring with embarrassment, she rushed to the dresser and scooped up her blue silk wrapper.

The edge of his mouth faintly curved. "It's all right, I saw you naked last night, remember?"

Her blush deepened as she turned her lovely backside in his direction and hurried to put on the robe. Reese frowned at the scar near her elbow he hadn't seen in the faint glow of lamplight the night before.

"What happened to your arm?"

She drew the robe together and tied the sash, then turned to face him. Unconsciously, she rubbed the place where the jagged five-inch line cut into her flesh.

"I broke it. The bone pushed through the skin." She glanced away, but not before he caught the flash of memory in her eyes, a look he had seen before.

"How did it happen?" he pressed, afraid to hear the answer.

"I fell. I hit the edge of the dresser when I went down."

"You fell."

She lifted her chin. "That's right."

"Aldridge is dead. I'm your husband, Elizabeth, and I want the truth. Did that bastard break your arm?"

Her lovely gray eyes brightened with a

sheen of tears. "I'd rather not talk about it."

"Yes or no."

She glanced away. "Yes."

Reese's jaw hardened. "What about the boy? Did he mistreat his son, as well?"

"Edmund never . . . never struck Jared."

"Just you, then. He only hurt you." Fighting down his anger, he strode toward her, gently drew her into his arms. "If Aldridge wasn't dead already, I swear I'd kill him myself."

Instead of pushing him away as Reese feared she might, Elizabeth turned into his embrace. "I hated him," she said softly. "I never want to think of him again."

Reese's hold tightened. For God's sake, no wonder she was afraid of him. He pressed a kiss on the top of her head. "You're safe now, Elizabeth, and no one is ever going to hurt you again."

She looked up at him and he could read the turbulence in her expression, the uncertainty. There was something more, he could tell. He wished he knew what it was.

"It's getting late," she said, moving out of his arms. "I need to dress so that we can leave."

Reese just nodded. "I'll send Gilda in to help you." Grabbing his silver-headed cane, he left the room, silently raging at Aldridge

206

all the way downstairs. Elizabeth no longer had anything to fear from the earl.

It was the earl's brother, Mason, who threatened her now.

Reese silently cursed.

Mason Holloway stood in the long gallery at Aldridge Park, staring at a wall of gilt-framed portraits of his ancestors. His brother Edmund's picture was the most recent addition, hanging next to a family portrait that included Mason's father and mother, Edmund, and himself.

"We have to do something." Frances sat across from him in a carved wooden chair at a small round table draped with a fringed, red-velvet cloth. "We can't just sit here and let that woman ruin our lives."

Mason shook his head. "I can't believe she married him. It's been little more than a year since Edmund died and already she is sleeping in another man's bed."

Mason had heard about the hurried nuptials that had taken place at Briarwood Manor. After the failed attempt against Elizabeth that would have taken care of the problem caused by her sudden departure, Reese Dewar had posted guards around his property. But money had away of breaching barriers, and one of the kitchen maids had been more than willing to report any unusual activity in the house.

In time, Mason was sure, another opportunity would arise. Once Elizabeth was out of the way and Mason and Frances became Jared's legal guardians, Edmund's fortune would fall rightfully into their hands.

Mason swore foully. He hadn't expected Elizabeth would go so far as to marry Dewar in order to thwart him.

"If things had gone as we'd planned," Frances said, voicing his earlier thoughts, "Elizabeth wouldn't be a problem. She would be upstairs in her room, grieving the death of her husband as she should be."

"And we would be in control, as my brother would have wanted." He still couldn't believe Edmund had married the chit, a decision he had regretted within months after the wedding.

But Edmund was infertile, or so he believed, having suffered a severe case of measles as a child, which their parents alleged was the cause. The girl, Edmund had confessed to Mason, had come to him pregnant, which gave him the chance for an heir. Unfortunately, the young woman had proved a disappointment in bed and the child had been nothing at all like Edmund.

His dislike of them both had grown, along with his regret. He had intended to change his will, leave all of his unentailed properties and the bulk of his fortune to Mason. They had spoken of the matter often, but Edmund was a young man, still, and his death had been completely unexpected.

A night of heavy drinking and a misstep on the terrace had led to a broken neck. The future had arrived in an instant and Edmund had not been prepared.

"Perhaps it isn't too late," Mason said. "Until the adoption is final, we can still set the matter to rights."

Frances made a sound in her throat. She was a thin, pale woman, not the least attractive, and yet he had never regretted marrying her. She was intelligent and cunning, and she understood his male needs. If he wanted a woman, his wife merely looked the other way.

"Even if the girl was dead," she pointed out, "Dewar would likely seek custody of the boy, and his brother *is* a duke. As the lad's stepfather, there is a good chance he might win guardianship of Jared."

Mason ground his jaw. Frances had always been astute. And ruthless in getting what she wanted. It was a quality he admired and one of the reasons he had married her. "So what do you suggest?"

"I say we go to London. According to your informant, Elizabeth is staying at Holiday House. We can take up residence in Edmund's town house — at least your brother provided for that."

Edmund's will, unchanged before his death, provided at least some comfort. Mason had a respectable annual income and life estates in apartments in each of his brother's numerous properties.

Still, Edmund had intended they inherit far more.

Mason intended to see that they got what they deserved.

"Once we are in the city," Frances went on, "we'll set a man to watch them. Sooner or later, the opportunity we're seeking will arise."

One of his thick brown eyebrows went up. "You aren't saying . . ."

"I am saying what we both know is the truth. The boy isn't even Edmund's son. You should have been earl, not some other man's by-blow."

Edmund had never revealed the name of Jared's real father and Mason didn't care. The law was the law and Jared had inherited. There was no evidence of his true parentage and Edmund was married to the boy's mother at the time of his birth. Frances, as usual, was correct.

Edmund had utterly regretted that the son who wasn't even his and was so completely unlike him would one day inherit the earldom, but it was too late.

Mason stroked the ends of his mustache. Though he hated the notion of disposing of a child so young, perhaps he would simply be righting an injustice.

Mason walked over to the table and took hold of his wife's thin hand, urging her to her feet. "Pack your things, Frannie. We are leaving for the city."

Frances looked up at him and her narrow face broke into a smile.

The streets of London glistened from an early morning rain. A damp mist hung in the air and the sky was a flat, leaden gray as Reese's carriage rolled toward the town house occupied by his friend, Travis Greer.

Yesterday, Reese had settled his newly acquired family at Holiday House, Elizabeth's luxurious residence near Hampstead Heath, which, as her husband, now belonged to him. He wasn't quite certain how he felt about that, but since their future was linked together, he didn't suppose it really mattered.

It was her safety that was important. Before he'd left for the city, an hour's ride away, he had sent a letter to the investigator, Chase Morgan, updating him on events, including the attempt on Elizabeth's life, his marriage, and their upcoming visit to London. He'd asked Morgan to hire enough men to secure the house and grounds twenty-four hours a day.

On their arrival at Holiday House, Reese discovered Morgan had done his usual efficient job. Six men were responsible for guarding the exterior of the house and grounds. Every visitor was checked as he arrived and two men stood watch inside the house.

Still Reese hated to leave. By now Mason Holloway was certain to have discovered Elizabeth's hasty marriage. Until Jared's adoption was finalized, she was still in danger.

They both were.

With the wealth of an earldom at stake, Reese wasn't nearly as convinced as Elizabeth that Mason would not harm the boy. But his friend's needs were also important. He had to know what sort of trouble Travis was facing.

The carriage rolled to a stop at the side of the street and Reese climbed down with the unwelcome help of his cane. He intended that he and Timothy should continue working his injured leg at Holiday House, and Reese felt certain the limb would continue to improve.

The huge estate backed up to Hampstead Heath, which, with its hundreds of acres of rambling green hills, duck-filled ponds, and ancient woodlands, provided plenty of open space for riding. Since the house sported a nicely kept stable and a dozen saddle horses, he had sent Timothy back to retrieve his big black gelding, Warrior. It was past time he mounted a horse again, and though he might suffer a few cuts and bruises in the process, he was determined to ride once more.

Reese looked up at Travis's town house, a three-story, white-trimmed brick building just off Berkley Square, a pricey neighborhood for an ex-military man. The location might have surprised him if he hadn't known Travis had inherited a goodly sum of money on the death of his ballerina mother.

According to Travis — told to Reese on a night of hard drinking in a tavern in the Crimea near Varna — Katarina Markolov was descended from Russian royalty. As Reese followed his friend's white-haired butler into an elegant drawing room and surveyed the velvet curtains and rich ruby sofas, he smiled to think the story appeared to be true.

Travis arrived in the drawing room a few minutes after the butler departed. Sliding his small gold spectacles up on his nose, he closed the paneled doors behind him, making them private.

"Nice place," Reese said, reaching out a hand Travis accepted. The empty left sleeve of his coat was a bitter reminder of what Travis had suffered because of him.

"The house belonged to my mother," Trav explained. "I kept it leased while I was in the army. Once I knew I was coming back to London, my solicitor gave the tenants notice so I could move in."

Reese glanced around, noting the slightly feminine décor that didn't really suit the hard, fighting soldier he knew Travis Greer to be.

"I guess I should make some changes," Trav said, raking back his sandy brown hair, reading Reese's thoughts. "Then again, I may not be living here all that long."

Reese squared his shoulders. "All right, I think it's time you told tell me what's going on."

Travis nodded. "Would you like a brandy or something?"

"No, thanks." Reese sat down on the ruby sofa and Travis took a chair across from him. Travis blew out a breath. "It all started with the journal. You remember I was writing one when we were in the Crimea?"

"I remember." An image arose of his friend sitting for hours with the leatherbound volume propped open in his lap as he penned his reflections on what was happening around them.

"When I was first released from the army," Travis continued, "I came back to London for a while. I interviewed for several newspaper jobs but didn't get hired. Not until later, when I got the offer from the *Times*. At any rate, while I was here, I . . . Suffice it to say, the Countess of Sandhurst had certain charms I couldn't resist. I knew better, of course, but . . . well . . . things just happened."

"You'd been gone a damned long time. If the lady offered, it only seems logical you would accept."

"I suppose so. Caroline's husband mostly ignored her. She was looking for male companionship and I was in need of a woman. We saw each other for a while and on several occasions I mentioned the journal."

"So?" He couldn't see where this was

leading. So Travis kept a journal. So what?

"So her husband came home early one day and caught us together. He was furious. I guess he must have overheard me talking about the journal. The affair ended, but Sandhurst wasn't satisfied. He started digging into my past, found out my mother was Russian. He knew I spoke the language and that I was stationed in the Crimea. The earl went to the authorities suggesting I might well be a spy."

Reese grunted. "A spy? That's ridiculous. You fought like a demon over there. You lost your arm at Balaklava fighting to save my life. Surely that alone was enough to prove you were innocent of any such charges."

"I thought my record would speak for itself. Apparently I was wrong."

Reese fell silent. If there was one thing he knew for sure it was that Travis was a loyal Englishman. "What happened to the journal?"

Trav released a breath. "That's the worst part. Last week, men from the Foreign Office came to the house. They searched the place. The journal was sitting on the desk in my study. It never occurred to me to hide it. The men took it with them."

Reese looked at him hard. "Tell me there was nothing in the journal that shouldn't have been there."

Travis glanced away. He shoved his small gold spectacles up on his nose. "Everything I saw over there, everything I knew, I wrote down on those pages. I wanted to be a journalist. I thought it would help me remember what war was like once I got back home."

"Bloody hell."

"They think I might be guilty of treason, Reese. That's the reason I didn't want to put all this in a letter. And why I need your help."

Clearly Travis needed all the help he could get. "Who's in charge of the investigation?"

"Colonel Malcolm Thomas of the Foreign Office. Apparently he and Lord Sandhurst are friends."

"This just gets worse and worse."

Trav's shoulders tightened. "I know."

"Anything else you can tell me?"

"Not at the moment."

Reese stood up from the sofa. "My wife and I —"

"Your *wife?*" Travis shot up from his chair. "You got married?"

Reese managed a nod. "I believe you met Elizabeth while you were at Briarwood."

"Yes, you told me about her no-good brother-in-law, but I thought you —"

"It's a long story. As you said, things happen. At any rate, we are in residence at a place called Holiday House. It's near the village of Highgate on Hampstead Heath. If you need to reach me, send word there."

Travis actually grinned. "So you married her. I always figured you were still in love with her. You have to have strong feelings for someone to hate them for that many years."

Reese just grunted. "There were extenuating circumstances. Holloway is still a threat. I'd promised to protect her. I had no other choice."

A slight, knowing curve remained on Travis's lips. Wisely he didn't say what he was thinking. "Congratulations."

Reese made no reply. He didn't tell his friend the marriage had yet to be consummated. He didn't say he had been counting the days till the end of the week. Or that though there were only a few days left, each night lying next to her felt like an eternity.

"I'll start digging," Reese said, "see what I can find out. I can't imagine Sandhurst's accusations alone would be enough to cause all this commotion. There has to be something more."

"I wish there was something I could do. I gave them my word I wouldn't leave the house until this was settled. Apparently, my word isn't good enough — they've got men posted across the street round the clock."

Reese didn't like what that meant. He clamped his friend on the shoulder. "I'll let you know what I come up with."

As he left the house and climbed aboard his carriage, he pondered his friend's situation and wished he could read the journal. They hanged traitors. Reese was determined not to let that happen to his friend.

From Travis's house, Reese headed to his appointment in Threadneedle Street, at the office of the investigator, Chase Morgan. Since the attempt on Elizabeth's life, Morgan had beefed up his efforts to uncover what he could about Mason and Frances Holloway. A meeting had been arranged to discuss his findings.

"Any problems with security at the house?" the investigator asked as Reese took a seat across from his desk.

"None so far. I assume these are men you trust."

"I've known most of those men for a number of years. Each has been extremely reliable. One of the inside men, my head of security, Jack Montague, is particularly good at his job."

Reese nodded. "I talked to him before I left the house. I wouldn't have gone if I thought he couldn't do the job." He shifted in his chair, studied Morgan with a probing glance. "So what about Holloway? What more have you found out?"

"Not much, unfortunately. A couple of the servants at Aldridge Park said they thought something might be going on with Lady Aldridge, but they didn't know exactly what it was. And they had no idea who might be responsible."

"In other words, we still have no proof."

"Not yet." Morgan sat back in his chair. "I also spoke to the late Lord Aldridge's solicitor, Milton Bryce. Apparently, the earl was planning to change his will, leave everything not entailed to the earldom to his brother."

Reese frowned. "Jared is his heir. Why would he do that?"

"According to Bryce, Aldridge and his wife were barely speaking. The son she gave him was a bitter disappointment. And Mason and Frances were devoted. I suppose in his mind it made sense."

Reese glanced down, surprised to see one of his hands had fisted. The boy was gentle and sweet, and behind the barrier of his shyness, appeared to be extremely intelligent.

Reese couldn't see how such a child could be a disappointment.

"No wonder Mason is after the boy's fortune," he said. "He believes it should have been his."

"The law disagrees. The will wasn't changed. The boy inherits everything. It's as simple as that."

"Not for long if Mason has his way."

Morgan made no reply. It was his company's job to protect Elizabeth and her son, but Morgan and Reese both knew there was always a chance Holloway would succeed.

"He's in town, by the way. He and his wife arrived just this morning. They're staying at Aldridge's town house. Apparently they have the legal right."

Reese swore under his breath.

"I've got a man on it. We'll know what they're doing before they do."

"Good. That's good." He had considered asking Morgan to investigate the case being built against Travis, but Elizabeth's situation was too uncertain. He didn't want to divert Morgan's attention from the more important task of keeping Elizabeth and Jared safe.

And he had an idea where he might find even better help for that sort of problem. Royal would be arriving on brewery busi-

221

ness in just a few days. He and his friends moved effortlessly through the highest circles of society. They might be able to find out what Reese needed to know.

In the meantime, he wanted to talk to Colonel Thomas of the War Office, discover how bad Travis's situation actually was.

Reese rose from his chair. "Keep in touch," he said to Morgan, reaching for his cane.

"Count on it," said Morgan.

FOURTEEN

Elizabeth hummed merrily as she worked with two of the chambermaids, freshening the upstairs bedrooms at Holiday House. She hadn't been to the estate since her father died. For a time, it held too many sad memories.

Since her return, she had discovered those memories could be pleasant, reminders of the life she had led as a girl. Her mother had been alive some of those early years and though her father had been dictatorial and often overbearing, she had loved him and he had loved her.

This morning after Reese had left for London, she had made a cursory examination of the mansion. The housekeeper, Mrs. McDonald, had been in charge for as long as Elizabeth could recall, but in the past few years, the woman had grown old and sickly and was barely able to leave her quarters. Tasks she used to oversee with such skill had become more than she could handle.

The house needed a good thorough cleaning and Elizabeth had decided to take on the task. She had been working since early that morning and amazingly, she was enjoying herself.

"The rugs in the east wing guest rooms all need to be beaten, Fanny." Lovely Persian carpets in every color whose bright hues would surely return with a little care. "Take one of the footmen along to help you."

"Yes, my lady." The chambermaid scurried away, and Elizabeth turned to another task.

"Betty, you strip the sheets and take them down to be laundered. We'll tackle the drapes in the morning."

"Aye, milady."

Elizabeth headed down the corridor, catching a glimpse of herself in one of the big gilded mirrors on the wall. She had stuffed her heavy curls beneath a mob cap, tied an apron over her skirts and set to work. She looked a bit of a fright, to be sure, but since Reese wasn't due back for several more hours, it didn't really matter.

Descending the sweeping marble staircase, she moved purposely toward the butler's pantry to check on the progress being made with the silver polishing. As she reached the bottom stair, she saw Reese standing in the entry staring up at her.

"Since when does the lady of the house have to do servants' work?" Amusement laced his deep voice. She hadn't expected him back so soon, but even with guards inside and outside the house, she knew he was concerned for her and Jared's safety.

She thought of the dust on her skirts, the curls escaping from her cap, and a blush rose in her cheeks.

"Mrs. McDonald has grown quite old," she said a bit defensively. "Until I find a suitable replacement, I've decided to take care of things myself."

He looked surprised. "Are you certain? Surely you can find someone to do it for you."

"I'll find someone, sooner or later. In the meantime . . ."

The shuffle of small feet drew her attention as Jared appeared in the entry. "Mama likes to clean. It makes her smile."

Elizabeth looked at her son and felt a rush of love for him. Jared was extremely perceptive and he was right. She had been smiling all morning.

"So it does," Reese agreed, the corner of

his mouth tilting up.

At Aldridge Park she'd done nothing but sit round all day embroidering or reading. It wasn't proper for a countess to work in any sort of fashion, Edmund had said. She had ridden occasionally, but never without a groom and even then, Edmund disapproved.

After his death, worry for her son and later the drugs Mason and Frances had been giving her had sapped most of her energy. She glanced at the banister, polished to a high, glossy sheen. It felt good to be accomplishing something again.

"See?" Jared pointed up at her. "She's doing it again."

Reese laughed. It was such a rare occurrence and it made him look so handsome her breath caught.

"A countess who likes to dust. Who would have guessed?"

Her chin inched up. "I am hardly doing it alone. I've put half a dozen servants to work this morning."

Reese chuckled and she felt an odd little lift in her heart. Every night since their wedding, she had slept beside him. Each night he demanded a little more, and yet he was always careful not to press her too hard, demand too much.

The last few evenings, she found herself

looking forward to his kisses, his skillful caresses. So much so that when he stopped, turned onto his side and pulled her against him, she felt edgy and restless, desperate for him to continue. Tomorrow night, he would claim his husbandly rights. She should be frightened but every time he looked at her the way he was now, all she felt was anticipation.

Elizabeth took a deep breath, fighting the urge to go up on her toes and kiss him. She wondered what he would do if she did. It wasn't going to happen with Jared standing right beside her.

"How was your meeting with Captain Greer?" she asked instead.

Reese's smile slowly faded. "I'll tell you about it when you're finished." He glanced down at his son. Though she knew how dangerous it was, she could no longer think of Jared any other way.

Reaching out to the boy, he ran a gentle hand over his hair, smoothing back a wayward dark strand. "In the meantime, why don't you and I go out and take a look at the horses? I hear your grandfather kept a very nice string."

Jared's big dark eyes widened. "Oh, that would be ever so grand!"

"I sent Corporal Daniels back to Briarwood. He should be back soon with Warrior."

Jared looked up at him. "Do you ever ride him?"

"When I was in the army, I rode him all the time. Eventually, I'm going to ride him again."

Worry flared in the pit of her stomach. She wanted Reese's leg to improve but sitting a horse without the balance he needed could prove extremely dangerous.

"I'll see you in a bit," he said, flashing her a grin and a last long glance that said he would like to see her the way he did each night — naked and responding to his kisses. A look that had nothing at all to do with Captain Travis Greer.

"All right," she replied a little breathlessly. "Enjoy your outing," she said to Jared, who hesitated only a moment before falling in beside Reese.

Watching father and son walk away, Reese's hand resting protectively on the little boy's shoulder, her heart squeezed. She considered telling Reese the truth and wished with all her being that she could.

Not yet, a little voice warned. *Not until you become his wife in more than just name.*

Not until he comes to care for you. But she wasn't sure how much he would ever truly care. And even if he did, that care would disappear — once he knew what she had done.

Waiting for Elizabeth to join him, Reese sat on the sofa in front of the fire in the library, a huge, two-story chamber with a row of mullioned windows along the wall near the ceiling to let in light. Except for a comfortable seating area built around a marble hearth, the room was lined with walnut shelves filled with hundreds of leather-bound books.

It was an interesting room, Reese thought, one he had taken over to use as a study until the actual study could be refurbished. He and Charles Clemens, Elizabeth's father, had little in common. Reese wanted the bric-a-brac removed, the leather sofas cleaned, and the room repainted to remove any lingering traces of Lord Charles's cigars.

Reese had asked Elizabeth's permission, of course, and she had readily agreed. The past was over. It was time to look toward the future.

"How was your trip to the stable?" she asked as she appeared in the doorway then crossed the room to where he stood waiting. He motioned for her to take a seat on the sofa in front of the fire then sat down beside her, trying to ignore the scent of roses that drifted up from her hair.

"It's past time your son learned to ride," he said. "The way he loves horses, I'm surprised Edmund didn't insist on giving him lessons."

Elizabeth glanced away. "Edmund spent very little time with Jared. Their likes and dislikes were very dissimilar. Edmund owned a number of fine, blooded horses, but he never enjoyed riding himself."

"Unlike you." He remembered how much she had loved to ride. Had done so at Briarwood as soon as her health had returned.

"Edmund and I . . . we also had little in common."

"I see." But he didn't really understand at all. What had drawn her to a man with whom she enjoyed so few interests? A man who gave her not the least amount of pleasure in bed?

The word *pleasure* stirred a jolt of heat that shot straight into his groin. An image arose of Elizabeth last night, kissing him with wild abandon, whimpering as he caressed her lovely breasts. Tomorrow night, her week would be up. He would take her, satisfy this lust that rode him like a demon every minute of the day.

His gaze ran over the curve of her voluptuous breasts. He knew exactly the fullness, the dusky hue of her nipples. He knew exactly the way they tasted, the way they tightened into firm little buds beneath his tongue. His erection pulsed. He needed her, dammit. He needed to assuage this constant lust he felt for her.

"I have business in the city again on the morrow," he said. "I plan to take you with me. I'm tired of seeing you in those damnable black dresses. And as much as I would like to, I can't keep you cooped up inside forever."

And two of Morgan's men would go with them. He figured with the three of them to protect her, she would be safe.

Elizabeth's features brightened, then the rose in her cheeks slowly faded. "What about Jared?"

"He'll be safe right here. Jack Montague is a professional. He's an ex-soldier. Served in the 62nd Foot, and from what I can tell, extremely capable. He'll stick with Jared every minute until we get home."

She nibbled her lush bottom lip and his loins began to stir. He had already made up his mind he wouldn't be sleeping with her tonight. The next time he came to her bed, he would claim her. Until then, the physical toll was simply too great.

"Perhaps we could stop by the newspaper office and place an ad for a tutor," she suggested. "Jared's education has been postponed too long already."

"We'll have to be extremely thorough in our investigation of whomever we hire, but you're right. The boy is intelligent and rapidly growing bored. He needs to be learning."

"Thank you."

Reese ignored the soft smile that stirred his hunger. "You asked me earlier about Captain Greer."

"Is the trouble he is in truly as bad as he believes?"

"Worse. He hasn't been charged yet, but there is a very good chance he will be. There are people in the foreign office who believe Travis is a spy."

Elizabeth's gray eyes widened. Reese went on to explain about the journal and Travis's Russian background, and her concern deepened.

"But Captain Greer is a journalist," she said. "Surely writing his memoirs of the war isn't enough to convict him of treason."

"That's what I've been thinking. I'm trying to get an appointment with Colonel Thomas at the Foreign Office, see what else might be going on. Apparently the colonel is out of town on business and won't be back for a couple of days."

"What will you say to him?"

"I'll speak for Travis and explain about the journal. Greer is a bloody hero, for God's sake, not a criminal."

"Surely there is some sort of misunderstanding."

"If that's all it is, they're going to a great deal of trouble. Travis is confined to his house and watched twenty-four hours a day."

Elizabeth rested a hand on his arm. "You'll make them understand, I know you will."

"I'll do my very best."

Rising from the sofa, he drew her up against him. His gaze met hers, his dark with hunger, letting her know how much he wanted her.

"Tomorrow night, Elizabeth. Tomorrow night, you're mine."

Her breathing quickened. Nervously, she moistened her lips and he couldn't resist lowering his head to taste them. The kiss deepened, lengthened.

Elizabeth didn't fight him. Instead her arms went around his neck. Desire tore through him, gripped him like an unseen force. He cupped her bottom and pulled her against his arousal, letting her feel how hard he was. Elizabeth gave up a little whimper as he claimed her mouth again. He could feel her rapid heartbeat against his chest and his need swelled along with his erection. Close to the breaking point and afraid he might take her right there, he let her go.

"Tomorrow," he reminded her softly.

Elizabeth raised a trembling hand to her kiss-swollen lips, turned and fled the library.

Reese sighed. Tomorrow seemed an eternity away.

London bustled with activity. Freight wagons, carriages, and hansom cabs clogged the cobbled streets. Pedestrians dodged horses and tradesmen hawking their wares, making travel difficult, to say the least.

Two of Chase Morgan's men, heavily armed, rode at the back of Reese's carriage. Though he didn't expect trouble so soon after Holloway's arrival, he carried a five-shot pocket pistol, and of course, the vicious little dagger concealed in his cane.

Their first stop was the solicitor's office. Mr. Edward Pinkard was a man trusted by all three Dewar brothers. Pinkard, who had worked for Reese's father, had tried to protect the late duke from the terrible swindle that had drained most of Royal's inheritance.

Fortunately, Royal was rebuilding the dukedom and replenishing the Bransford fortune. With Lily's help and support, he appeared to be doing a damned fine job.

Pinkard, with his pale blue eyes and a leonine mane of silver hair, walked toward them. "It's good to see you, my lord." He smiled at Elizabeth. "A pleasure to meet you, my lady." Pinkard bowed formally over Elizabeth's hand. "I wondered if this young rascal would ever be brought to heel."

Reese almost smiled. He was hardly young anymore and lately felt even older than his twenty-eight years. But Pinkard, Reese's father's age, had known him as a boy and some things just didn't change.

"You're aware of my recent marriage," Reese said. "As I said in my letter, I'd like to start proceedings to adopt Elizabeth's son. Now that Elizabeth and I are married, I want to give him my name."

Without too many details, Reese made certain Pinkard understood who Jared was and the urgent need to see the matter accomplished. When he had finished, he leaned over the solicitor's desk.

"We need this done with all haste. My brother has agreed to help in any way he can. Suffice it to say, the boy needs the protection of my name."

The solicitor frowned but knew better than to press for more. "A hearing will be required. There may be certain stipulations — the boy is an earl, after all. But unless the adoption is contested, it will only be a matter of formality. I'll let you know as soon as the date is set."

"Thank you."

"You have my word I'll see this done as quickly as possible."

They left the office and returned to the carriage, Reese settling back against the tufted velvet seat.

"You don't think Mason will protest the adoption?" Elizabeth asked.

"I don't think he has grounds. You're Jared's mother. His father is dead and your husband is a member of the aristocracy."

Elizabeth didn't say more. Both of them knew it was impossible to predict what Mason and Frances might do.

The *London Times* was the next stop on their agenda. It didn't take long to place an ad for a qualified tutor. When they climbed back aboard the coach, Elizabeth looked relieved.

"I worry about him. Jared is so incredibly shy. I need to find someone who can get through to him, win his trust."

Reese's gaze found hers. "Jared is more than just shy, Elizabeth. The boy is extremely withdrawn. What happened to make him the way he is? Was it Aldridge?"

She blinked several times. In the light streaming in through the windows, he caught the faint sheen of tears.

"I don't know exactly what happened. Edmund never physically hurt him. He just . . . he always made Jared feel as if he had done something wrong. Jared did everything he could to please him but it was never enough."

Reese silently cursed. The bastard was lucky he was dead.

"Once Edmund realized that Jared was never going to be the kind of son he imagined, he turned away from him completely. Jared grew more and more distant, more and more insecure."

She looked up at him and the tears brimming in her eyes slipped over onto her cheeks. "I'm glad Edmund is dead. God forgive me, I am glad."

Reese drew her into his arms. "Hush," he soothed, feeling the wetness against his cheek. "Aldridge is gone from your life. You and the boy are safe. Sooner or later, Jared will realize his life has changed for the better and he'll come out of his shell."

Elizabeth gave him a tentative nod and managed a watery smile. She wiped the tears from her cheek. "I'm sorry for the way I treated you all those years ago. Sometimes when Aldridge hit me, I thought it was punishment for what I did to you."

Reese's chest squeezed. "Whatever happened between us, Beth, Aldridge had no right to hurt you. Never believe he did."

Elizabeth stared at her lap, and Reese clamped down on the ache he felt for her.

She had suffered so much.

And yet he couldn't allow himself to feel pity. Once her betrayal had nearly destroyed him.

Elizabeth was back in his life, but he couldn't allow her back in his heart.

FIFTEEN

The carriage rolled at a fast clip toward Bond Street. Elizabeth hadn't meant to tell Reese about Aldridge's cruelty to Jared, but now that he knew, she felt a sense of relief.

Whatever the future held, he deserved to know the truth — all of it. And soon she intended to tell him.

Soon — but not today.

"We're almost there," Reese said. "I want you out of those black rags and properly clothed as my wife."

Elizabeth fought not to smile. "They are hardly rags. Mourning clothes are very expensive." A little spark of mischief had her sighing. "But I suppose I have no choice. I did agree, after all."

The corner of Reese's mouth edged up as if he knew she was getting exactly what she wanted. He looked so handsome her stomach fluttered.

Tonight they would make love. She could

barely remember the night she had made love with Reese in the back of the carriage, but she knew she had enjoyed it.

Trepidation warred with excitement. She wanted this to happen, wanted the chance to become a normal, healthy woman.

The carriage rolled to a halt. *Madame Brumaire, The Bond Street Modiste* read the sign above the door of Elizabeth's chosen destination. Word had been sent ahead and they were greeted by Madame herself, a thin woman with silver-streaked dark hair and a slightly pointed chin. She ushered them to the rear of the shop, an elegant salon furnished with thick carpets, crystal-prismed lamps, and richly textured fabrics at the windows. A burgundy brocade sofa sat next to a matching chair in front of the design platform.

"Why don't you sit here, my lord," the older woman offered, guiding him in that direction. Reese sat down, looking not the least uncomfortable in his utterly feminine surroundings. Elizabeth couldn't help comparing this man of confidence and authority to the shy youth he had once been. The man she had married was a far different person and despite her fears, she felt far more drawn to him now than she ever had before.

For the next several hours, Reese assisted

her in her selections, all the while being pampered by a bevy of females who catered to his every need. All in an effort to divest him of as much of his money as possible.

Reese didn't seem to mind. Leaning back on the comfortable sofa, he sipped a cup of thick, Turkish coffee, watching as she paraded in front of him scantily dressed in one sinuous fabric after another.

She'd always had good taste, if a bit on the conservative side, something Reese seemed determined to change. Insisting on a number of evening gowns in brilliant colors — a gleaming sapphire taffeta, a rich scarlet velvet, a lush emerald-green satin, he gave specific instructions as to how he wanted them made.

"I'd like to see the bodice cut a little lower," he told Madame. "My wife has a lovely bosom. I enjoy looking at it whenever possible."

He tossed Elizabeth a heated glance that reminded her he would be doing far more than looking tonight. He would be caressing her breasts, touching her in ways that set her on fire, joining their bodies together and making them one.

Reese shifted on the sofa, his look hot and hungry, raking over her as she stood on the platform in front of him, her undergarments covered by little more than a swatch of pale blue silk. The fabric swirled round her hips and swept up over her breasts, but clearly there wasn't nearly enough.

If she touched him, that hot look said, he would cross the distance between them, drag her out of the salon and straight to the nearest bed.

Her breathing quickened. With his dark, chiseled features, wavy black hair, and incredible blue eyes, Reese Dewar was one of the most attractive men she had ever seen. A memory arose of his tapered fingers cupping her breasts, his mouth settling there, sucking gently, making her squirm with pleasure.

For the first time, she realized how badly she wanted *him.*

"I believe we have enough for the moment," Reese said to Madame Brumaire, drawing Elizabeth's thoughts from the embarrassing path they had taken. He turned that fierce blue gaze in her direction and she could feel the heat of it even from six feet away. "Is there anything else you need before we leave?"

I need you, she thought and realized to her horror it was true. Dear God, she couldn't afford to need him. She had taught herself to depend on no one. She couldn't afford to fall under Reese's spell. Not with the lies that still stood between them.

She managed a shaky smile. "Gloves and hats," she said, thinking he would probably be disinclined to indulge her in shopping any further and she could escape back to the safety of the house.

Reese was hardly a patient man.

Amazingly, he smiled. "Get dressed. We're here. Let's see it done."

Returning to the changing area, she put on a simple dark green woolen gown Madame's helpers had altered for her, one another woman had ordered but never picked up. Gaining a promise from the dressmaker to have at least half the new gowns completed within the next three days, she made her way out of the shop on Reese's arm.

She wasn't sorry to have abandoned the expensive clothes in storage at Aldridge Park. She wanted nothing to do with Edmund or anything that might remind her of him.

Making their way along Bond Street, Elizabeth led Reese into J. D. Smith well where she purchased several pairs of kidskin gloves and left swatches of material for long evening gloves to match the ball gowns she had ordered.

They were passing by the front window of a glass blower's shop when he paused.

"What is it?" Elizabeth's gaze followed his through the window.

"I see something I want to buy. Come on, I'll show you."

He escorted her inside and she watched as he made his way to a shelf that held lovely, hand-blown crystal animals. A unicorn stood on a glass shelf with one of its front legs lifted and its neck bowed.

"You think he'll like it?" Reese asked.

Elizabeth's heart swelled as she realized he meant to buy it for Jared. "It's beautiful. He'll love it, Reese."

He bought the horse, and the owner boxed it up and tied it with a bright blue bow. Reese carried the box as they made their way along the street on their way to the Lily Pad, the millinery shop owned by Lily Dewar, Reese's sister-in-law.

"Lily rarely works in the shop anymore," Reese told her as they stepped inside. "She still makes hats, but mostly she works out of her home. Her assistant takes care of things here at the shop."

And the girl, Tilly Perkins, slender with carrot-red hair, was extremely efficient. With her help, Elizabeth ordered feathered and beaded hairbands for evening, along with an array of bonnets and caps for other occasions.

"Just let me know what else ye need," Tilly said as they headed out the door. "We'll get 'em for ye straightaway."

Elizabeth smiled. "Thank you, Tilly."

"Just one more stop," Reese said as they made their way back toward the carriage, their arms full of packages.

"I think I have everything. Do you need something?"

"No, you do." Tugging her through the door of a narrow shop with mullioned windows, they passed frilly silk drawers, pink whale-boned corsets, silk stockings of every color, and a rack that held an array of expensive French nightgowns and negligees. She wanted to ask him how he knew the shop was there, but didn't.

Reese was a man, not a boy. She thought again of the night ahead and hoped that she could please him. The idea of him turning to other women left a sick feeling in her stomach.

Reese held up a lavender nightgown, no more than a scrap of satin trimmed with lace that would barely cover her bottom.

"Tonight I'd like to see you in this."

Her cheeks burned. "But I couldn't possibly . . ."

"You needn't worry, love. You won't have it on that long."

Embarrassment washed through her. She couldn't imagine herself in something so wanton. And yet she was his wife. If it pleased him, what difference did it make? And as she looked at the very naughty nightgown and several others he purchased, along with a frilly corset of the new style that closed up the front, she couldn't help feeling a little thrill at the thought of wearing them for Reese.

Her cheeks were still warm as they left the shop, and as he handed her up into the coach, a little thread of heat settled low in her belly. Was it desire? She knew that it was and it thrilled her. Perhaps tonight wouldn't be frightening, it would be magical.

Elizabeth held the thought in her heart as Reese settled himself beside her in the seat.

Several hours later, Reese sat at a wide, carved walnut table in the library. Outside the row of windows near the ceiling, dense gray clouds said a storm had begun moving in. Distant lightning occasionally brightened the panes, but it was too far away to hear thunder.

In front of him sat the box that held the

crystal horse for Jared, a gift yet to be presented. He had suggested Elizabeth give it to him, but she had refused.

"It's your gift. You should be the one to give it to him."

Perhaps she was right. The boy needed a father and though he had never anticipated such an occurrence, Reese had taken on the job.

Lying next to the box were messages he had received that afternoon from London, notes that had been waiting when he had returned to Holiday House. One had come from Colonel Thomas suggesting a meeting at eleven o'clock in the morning. The other came from Royal, saying he and Lily had arrived in London and would be staying at the Bransford town house.

Reese had immediately replied, informing both men he would be in London on the morrow.

A noise overhead drew his attention. Reese glanced up at the ceiling as if he could see into the rooms above. Supper was over. Elizabeth had gone upstairs to bid good-night to Jared, then retired to her room. All Reese could think of was joining her.

He knew Elizabeth was ready. All day she had worn the look of a woman in need of a man, and tonight he intended to give her exactly what she needed.

Still, he was nervous. He wanted to make it good for her, wanted to be the man Aldridge never had been.

He had given her the week she had asked for. It was long past time their marriage was consummated. Tonight he meant to see it done.

He reached for his cane, rose a little stiffly to his feet. He and Timothy had been working his leg each morning, stretching the muscles and tendons. He was making progress, but it was a slow process. Tim had returned with Warrior, and Reese was determined to ride the horse again.

In the meantime, he had a far more satisfying ride ahead of him. A faint smile curved his lips as Reese left the library and headed for the stairs.

Dressed in the lavender silk nightgown Reese had purchased for her, Elizabeth stood in front of the cheval glass in her bedroom. She surveyed her full figure, grateful she had weathered her pregnancy so well. Just a few faint stretch marks and slightly fuller breasts. Her waist was small again, her stomach flat.

She looked good in the skimpy scrap of

lavender, exactly the wanton Reese had wanted her to appear. With her black hair curling down her back and her legs bare, she felt feminine and womanly and desirable.

Her nipples hardened at the thought of his impending arrival. Her skin felt sensitive. The rasp of lavender lace felt erotic against her flesh. Soon Reese would join her, take what she had denied him, what she was now more than willing to give.

As she stared at her reflection, she trembled. She wanted this to be right for him, wanted to please him as a wife should.

She turned at the sound of the door opening between their bedrooms, saw Reese step into the room. He was wearing a dark blue dressing gown, a portion of his wide chest exposed in the V above his narrow waist. His bare feet sank into the thick Persian carpet and she could see a portion of his long legs.

He stopped just inside the doorway, his gaze scorching as he surveyed the lavender nightgown that barely covered her body. Heat rolled through her. And the strange yearning she had felt before.

"You look beautiful," he said gruffly. "God, I want you." He started toward her, limping only slightly, reached out and pulled her into his arms.

His mouth came down over hers, gently at first, but the heat was there and the banked fires flamed to life. The kiss turned hot and fierce, claiming her, devouring her, and heat roared through her body.

She felt dizzy and weak. Gripping the lapels of his dressing robe, she fought to stay on her feet. Her mind was reeling, her body on fire.

"Reese . . ." she whispered when he brushed her hair aside and began to kiss the side of her neck.

His answer was to slide his long fingers beneath the rough lace of the gown and curve them around her breast. Desire flared inside her. And a need so strong she swayed toward him.

"Reese . . ." she whispered again, surprised at the desperation she heard in her voice.

"Easy," he whispered between nibbling kisses. "We're going to take this nice and slow — even if it kills me."

Amusement eased some of her tension, but when he slid the straps of the nightgown off her shoulders, pulled it down and lowered his mouth to capture the fullness of her breast, her whole body tightened and she pressed herself against him, arching her back to give him better access.

Reese suckled and tasted, gently bit the end, and heat roared through her.

She had to touch him, feel the texture of his skin. Untying the sash on his robe, she drew it open then slid her palms over the hard slabs of muscle, ran her fingers through his curly black hair on his chest.

She didn't realize the nightgown had disappeared until she felt his hands cupping her bottom, drawing her into the V between his legs, letting her feel how hard he was. He returned to her lips, plundering them, taking her deeply and relentlessly.

Her nipples tightened and began to throb. She shifted restlessly, ran her fingers through his hair, felt the erotic rub of her breasts against his chest. Her body felt hot and tight; her heart pounded madly. She was wet, she realized as his hand moved lower and he slid a finger inside her.

Instead of pulling away, she helplessly pressed herself into his hand, wanting more, aching for something just out of reach.

Reese stroked and caressed her, kissed her and kissed her and kissed her. She hardly noticed when he lifted her up and carried her the few feet to the bed. Settling her there on the mattress, he suckled her breasts, laved and tasted until she was squirming.

Deep drugging kisses followed as he came up over her, and Elizabeth returned each one. She wanted this, wanted to become his wife in every way.

One of his hands found her breast while the other slid lower, back to the nub that had given her pleasure before. She could feel the heavy weight of him settling on top of her, pressing her down as he covered her with his tall, powerful body. She could feel the thickness of his shaft as he spread her legs and positioned himself between them, prepared himself to take her.

Her breathing quickened, but the pleasure began to fade. Images of Edmund filled her mind and icy dread washed over her.

It's Reese, it's Reese, she tried to tell herself, but all she could see was Edmund holding her down, suffocating her with his thick body, forcing her to take him inside her.

A scream rose in her throat. She choked back a sob and bit down on her lip to keep from crying out. She tasted the coppery flavor of blood and her eyes filled with tears.

He eased her legs even farther apart and she felt his hardness beginning to push inside her. A scream rent the air, then another. The heavy weight jerked off her and Reese recoiled in horror.

"Elizabeth! For God's sake!"

She bit down on her lip to stifle another cry, trembling all over, fighting to pull herself together.

"I'm sorry," she whispered brokenly. "I'm so sorry."

The past continued to fade and reality returned as Reese left the bed and strode naked over to the window. Outside the storm had finally reached the house and a flash of lightning reflected the sheen of perspiration glistening on his broad back and narrow buttocks.

"I'm sorry," she said again. "I wanted . . . I wanted this so much. I tried to warn you. I was afraid this would happen."

And then the sobs began, deep racking sobs she couldn't seem to stop. She felt the mattress dip with Reese's weight, then he was gathering her up, pulling her across his body, wrapping his arms around her.

"Don't cry, sweetheart," he said, his hand stroking over her hair. It tumbled around her face and stuck to the wide, damp chest that pillowed her cheek. "This is his fault, not yours."

But the sobbing didn't stop and all the while Reese held her. She had failed him. Failed herself. And she was certain that she had lost him.

She wasn't sure how long they lay together. Long enough that her crying ceased and a strange lethargy filled her. With it came a restless stirring. As she lay across his tall, solid body, her arms around his neck, her nipples pressed into lean bands of muscle, his hand ran gently up and down her back, soothing her, and a coil of heat began to unfurl in the pit of her stomach.

She could smell the salty tang of his skin, the warmth of his body under hers. Her gaze fixed on the heavy rod lying against his flat belly, unsatisfied as he had been all week. He was big and hard, ready to give her the pleasure he had promised.

If only she were brave enough.

Her body stirred. Desire slithered though her. Her breasts ached. The place between her legs throbbed with need. She wanted to taste him, to know the smooth feel of his skin. Pressing her lips there, she curled her tongue around a flat copper nipple, suckled gently, and heard him groan.

"Beth . . . please, love . . . I can't . . . I don't want to hurt you."

Moisture slid through her, settled in her core. She lifted her head to look at him. "I want this, Reese. I need you. I don't know what to do. Help me . . . please."

His eyes found hers, fierce and burning.

For an instant, he didn't say a word and she could read his indecision. Then he was lifting her up and setting her astride him. Reaching behind her neck, he dragged her mouth down to his for a long, burning kiss.

Lightning flashed outside the window and thunder rumbled, shaking the house. Elizabeth battled the storm raging inside her.

"You decide, Beth. Take what you want. Find your pleasure. You decide when you're ready."

She could feel his thick shaft beneath her, straining upward, rising toward the place between her legs. As she looked into his handsome face, she saw Reese, not Edmund. Reese, the man she had loved.

The man she loved still.

She blocked the words, concentrated on the need scorching through her. "Show me," she said softly. "Help me, Reese."

His mouth found hers one last time. His hands cupped her breasts, caressed and teased until she was squirming. Then he lifted her, slid her down his hardened length.

Dear God, it felt so good. So good.

"Tell me what to do," she whispered, afraid to move, uncertain how to proceed.

Big hands wrapped around her waist and he lifted her a little, let her sink down, then lifted her again, showing her the movements that would give her the ease she so desperately needed.

"That's right," he said roughly as Elizabeth began to understand, began to feel the pleasure. "Take me inside you, Beth. All of me. Let me give you what you need."

She sank down again, driving him deeper, feeling the hot rush of sensation. She cried out as his hard length stretched and filled her, coaxing her body to accept his heavy size and length. For an instant, Reese stilled, worried he had frightened her again.

"Don't stop," Elizabeth begged. "Oh, God, Reese, please don't stop."

A groan tore from his throat and then he was moving, holding her in place for his deep, penetrating thrusts, stoking the fires in her body, drowning her in pleasure.

"More," she pleaded, her head falling back as he drove into her, carried her higher. "Oh, God, please, Reese."

"Let yourself go, Beth. You're mine now. Do it for me."

And she did, her slick passage tightening around him as pleasure flooded through her, her mind spinning away. In an instant, she broke free, shattering into a million pieces, soaring to a place she had never been before.

Reese thrust deeply again and again, and

once more the pleasure filled her, swept her away. Reese soon followed, a growl low in his throat, his muscles clenching, his seed spilling hotly inside her.

Elizabeth slumped onto his chest, every part of her alive with sensation. She had never guessed, never imagined what it could be like.

She clung to Reese and started to sob again. But this time she wept tears of joy.

Sixteen

Following a fair-haired young lieutenant, Reese walked down the hall toward the chambers occupied by Colonel Malcolm Thomas of the Foreign Office.

"If you will just have a seat, my lord," said the lieutenant, the colonel's aide. "I'm sure he'll be right with you."

"Thank you, Lieutenant." Reese sat down in a straight-backed wooden chair in front of the colonel's desk, making a cursory surveillance of the office. Spartan, immaculately clean. Nothing that spoke of family. The colonel would be all business, and not prone to emotion.

Colonel Thomas walked into the room a few minutes later, average height, ruddy-complexioned with medium brown hair. Nothing extraordinary about him. Except for the sheer determination that glinted in his steely dark eyes.

Thomas wouldn't be an easy opponent.

Greetings were exchanged. Both men took their seats.

"You wished to see me on behalf of your friend, Travis Greer," the colonel began.

"Captain Travis Greer, yes."

"Captain Travis Aleksei Markolov Greer, should you wish to make a point of it."

Reese took a breath. He could see this wasn't going to be easy. "It is well known that Captain Greer's mother was a Russian ballerina. He speaks the language, which made him useful while he was stationed in the Crimea."

"That was certainly the army's intention in sending him there."

"The man risked his life to save mine, Colonel. That is how he lost his arm. Captain Greer is a patriot, sir, not a spy."

"I can understand why you might feel that way. You owe the man a considerable debt. However, certain information has come into our possession that is extremely condemning."

Reese shifted in his seat. "You're talking about Captain Greer's journal. Undoubtedly, you're aware that the captain was eventually hoping to become a journalist. He kept his memoirs in order to document his experiences during the war. In fact, he is presently employed by the *London Times* to do just that."

"As I am well aware. Unfortunately, the journal he kept goes far beyond a memoir. The book contains information on British troop movements, meetings with top-ranking officials, and even campaign strategies. Dates and times are listed — all information of infinite value to the Russians."

"The thing is, sir. He didn't give the journal to the Russians. As you said, you have it in your possession."

"That is true enough. And it would, perhaps, be a credible explanation — if not for the trip the captain made across enemy lines."

Reese's insides tightened. He fought not to show his surprise — or the subtle anger that Travis had not told him.

"I can see by the set of your jaw that you were unaware of this, Major."

"I presume you have some sort of proof."

The older man nodded. "During the investigation, a sergeant in the captain's regiment mentioned the night he left camp. Greer said he wanted to visit a relative who lived near the village. Under questioning, several other men confirmed the story."

"What did the captain have to say in his defense?"

"We are still collecting data. Currently he is under house arrest, as I'm certain you know."

"There's an explanation, Colonel. Captain Greer is as loyal a soldier as I've ever known. I need to speak to him, find out what happened that night."

The colonel made a faint nod of his head. "You may ask him whatever you wish. Our investigation will continue. We are building a case against the captain and I warn you, Major, once we have the evidence we need, we shall not hesitate to prosecute to the fullest measure."

Reese left the office feeling a mixture of anger and dread. He headed straight for Travis's Brook Street town house. Trav had lied to him — a lie of omission at the very least.

As the carriage rolled up in front of the house, Reese caught sight of the watchdog standing guard beneath the street lamp. Undoubtedly another man kept an eye on the rear of the building. Reese made his way up the walk and pounded on the door, and only seconds later, Travis pulled it open. His sandy brown hair was disheveled as if he had been running his hands through it and the eyes peering out through his spectacles were bloodshot and grim.

261

"You look like hell," Reese said, pushing past him into the entry. "What'd you do, climb into a brandy bottle last night?"

Travis sighed. "I drank more than I should have. I'm about to tear down the walls being trapped inside for so long."

"Yes, well, you may find yourself trapped inside a far worse place than this — that is if you don't hang."

Travis straightened. "You spoke to Colonel Thomas?"

"That's right. I just left his office."

Travis tipped his head toward the drawing room where they could speak in private and both men walked in that direction.

Travis slid closed the doors. "What happened?"

"To begin with, you might want to tell me why you didn't mention the not-so-insignificant fact that you left camp without permission. That while you were absent without leave, you crossed into enemy territory."

Travis deflated like a punctured balloon. He sank down on the sofa. "I should have known they would find out."

Reese sat down across from him. "What the hell were you thinking?"

Trav shoved his gold-rimmed spectacles up on his nose. "I went to see my aunt —

my mother's sister. I'd never met her, but I knew where she lived. It wasn't that far away. I figured I could make it there and be back before morning. I don't have any family left, just my aunt and a couple of distant cousins. I had to go. I couldn't resist."

Reese shook his head. It was a really stupid thing to do, but over there, loneliness preyed on a soldier's mind and the notion of family that close . . .

"How did they find out?" Travis asked.

"They questioned men in your regiment. You must have told some of them what you were going to do." The incident had happened nearly a year ago, before the battle at Balaklava and the fighting that had taken Trav's arm.

He released a slow breath. "They were men I knew pretty well. I told them I wanted to see my aunt and I needed their help to get away. It was kind of a lark to them at the time, and they understood why I wanted to go. Or at least I thought they did."

"It's damning, Trav, I can tell you. Colonel Thomas isn't going to stop until he has enough evidence to convict you."

Travis shot up from the sofa. "He'll never have enough evidence. I didn't help the Russians in any way. I'm not a spy, Major. I swear it."

Reese rose, too. "I believe you. The trick is to find a way to make Colonel Thomas believe you."

"What should I do?"

Reese glanced round the town house, inhaling the scent of stale pipe tobacco. Trav was not a man to be kept indoors.

"Sit tight a little longer. I'm on my way to see my brother. He knows everyone in this damnable town. I'm hoping he'll be able to use his connections to find out why Thomas is so determined to prove you guilty."

The look of misery on Travis's face was enough to speed Reese's departure.

"I appreciate it," was all Trav said.

From Brook Street, Reese headed to his brother's town house, only a few blocks away.

The day was cloudy, but not too cold as Reese rapped on the door. "Good afternoon, Rutgers," he said to the longtime family butler, who stepped back so that he could make his way inside.

"Good afternoon, my lord."

"I assume my brother is here. He should be expecting me."

The aging, silver-haired man gave a faint nod of his head. "Yes, sir. His Grace is in the study. He said to send you in as soon as you arrived."

Reese started past him. "No need to show me the way." He knew the house, had stayed there with his father and brothers when he was a boy. Heading down the hall, he rapped on the study door, turned the knob and pushed it open.

With his dark blond hair and golden brown eyes, Royal sat behind his big desk like a tall golden lion. His best friend, Sheridan Knowles, Viscount Wellesley, sat across from him.

"I didn't realize you had company," Reese said.

"Sherry's not company," Royal said. "He's part of the furniture."

Sheridan laughed, a slender, elegant man whose wit and charm made him popular with the ladies and a welcome addition to any society function. Now that Reese thought about it, Sherry's help might prove extremely useful.

"If you'd like to speak privately . . ." Sherry said, beginning to rise from his chair.

"Actually, I'd appreciate your input on this. Perhaps you might be able to help."

Sherry sat back down and Reese took a seat, as well.

"How's married life?" Royal asked.

Reese thought of the hours he had spent

in Elizabeth's bed last night, thought of her terrible fear and the way she had so bravely conquered those fears. He thought of her passionate responses, and heat slid into his groin. "A helluva lot better today than it was last week."

Royal laughed. He knew the terms of Reese's marriage. Clearly, he was glad things were progressing in a more normal manner.

"No problems with the Holloways?" Royal asked. "No more trouble for Elizabeth or Jared?"

"None so far, but Mason and Frances are now in the city. I don't believe in coincidence. They're here for a reason and whatever it is, it isn't good."

Royal frowned. "You've got Morgan helping, right?"

"His men are guarding the house. Elizabeth and the boy don't go anywhere without them. I still don't like it."

"Then you'll be glad to know the solicitor, Mr. Pinkard, was here. He asked for a letter expressing my support of Jared's adoption. I'm sending it over this afternoon."

"Thank you."

"You really think that will help?"

"It removes the boy from their control.

266

Elizabeth will no longer be in danger, since harming her would gain them nothing, but I'm not sure it will protect the boy."

"You believe they might actually try to kill him?" Sherry asked.

"Elizabeth doesn't think so. But the Aldridge title and incredible wealth is at stake. Greed drives people to do all sorts of things."

"As Lily and I know only too well," Royal said. Greed had cost their father most of the family fortune. It had nearly cost Royal and Lily their lives.

"I appreciate your help with Jared," Reese said. "Unfortunately, there is something else I need from you."

Royal sat forward in his chair. "You know I'll do whatever I can."

"A friend of mine is in trouble. I believe you may remember him, Captain Travis Greer?" For the next half hour, Reese filled Royal and Sherry in on the unofficial charges being made against Travis and the evidence being assembled against him. Both men knew him fairly well, since he had accompanied Reese several times when he had been on leave in London.

"Trav isn't a spy," Reese said. "I'd stake my life on it." He explained how the man had lost his arm hauling Reese to safety during the battle at Balaklava. "He fought like a tiger. I wouldn't be alive if it weren't for him. Trav did a couple of stupid things and now he's paying for it. What I need to know is why the authorities are so determined he has done treason."

Reese glanced from Royal to Sherry. "Both of you move easily in society. I'm hoping you might be able to pick up some sort of information that might be useful."

Sherry cast a look at Royal. "We need more ears than just ours. Why don't we send word to The Oarsmen?"

Royal grinned. "I haven't seen those fellows in far too long. Let's call a meeting at the club. With all of us working, we ought to be able to figure out what's going on."

Reese sat back in his chair, relieved at the first ray of hope he had felt since he had left the colonel's office. He was no longer in this alone. With all of them working together, maybe they could find a way to clear Travis's name.

Elizabeth was shaking. She held Jared tightly in her arms, her cheek pressed to his to convince herself he was safe.

"I am sorry, milady. It won't happen again, I promise ye."

"I'm all right, Mama," Jared said, pulling

back a little as her gaze went to the stocky guard standing a few feet away in the entry. "We were only just playing. The man didn't hurt me."

"What's happened?" Reese stormed into the house like a man on fire. "The guards are prowling the fields and the grooms are in a tither. What the hell is going on?"

Elizabeth swallowed. She didn't approve of Reese's occasional bad language, but he was, after all, a military man and clearly he was upset. "A man tried to kidnap Jared."

Reese's gaze swung toward to the boy. "He isn't hurt? Jared's all right?"

"He is fine. I'm the one who is upset."

Jared squirmed to be free and Elizabeth reluctantly set him on his feet, forcing herself not to reach out and grab onto his hand.

"Tell me what happened," Reese demanded. She could almost feel the anger pumping through him, his concern.

"Charlie and Jared were playing outside and —"

"Charlie? Who the devil is Charlie?"

"He is Mr. and Mrs. Brody's son — the couple who live in the gatekeeper's cottage. They're in charge of outside maintenance."

"All right, go on."

"Charlie's father made him a little toy

sailboat and the boys went down to the pond to try it out on the water."

"And . . . ?" Reese prodded.

"And a man came out of the bushes and tried to carry Jared off with him. If it hadn't been for Mr. Gillespie, he might well have succeeded."

Reese turned his hard gaze on the security man who worked inside with Montague. "Your job is to prevent this kind of thing. Dammit — how did the fellow get so close to the house?"

"The pond sits at the edge of the forest, milord. I shouldn't have let the boys go down there in the first place, but things have been so quiet and they really wanted to sail their boat. It won't happen again."

"You can bloody well count on that." Jack Montague strode into the entry, a big, barrel-chested man with thinning dark brown hair. "You're fired, Gillespie."

Gillespie blanched. He was shorter than Reese or Montague, but powerfully built and, up until now, seemed competent in the extreme.

"I put you in charge of protecting the boy," Montague went on. "That is what you should have done. Now get out."

"I don't mean to interfere in your business, Mr. Montague," Elizabeth said, notic-

270

ing how pale Jared had grown. "But it seems to me that Mr. Gillespie *did* do his job. He fought the man and rescued my son." She flicked the guard a glance, caught the regret and determination in his face. "I believe if you let him remain, he will do everything in his power to keep Jared safe."

Jared and Sean Gillespie were becoming fast friends and since Jared rarely trusted adults, she was hoping that friendship might continue.

"What happened to the man?" Reese asked Gillespie.

"Got away, milord." He rubbed his jaw, where a purple bruise was beginning to form. "I was more interested in gettin' the boy to safety. You let me stay, I'll see nothin' happens to 'im. Ye have me word on that."

"Mr. Montague?" Reese asked, looking to Morgan's head of security for the final word.

"Gillespie's always been one of our best. I suppose a man's entitled to one mistake — long as it doesn't happen again."

"No, sir, Mr. Montague, it won't."

"Your men are searching for the attacker?"

"Aye, but odds are they won't find him. He likely had his escape route well planned."

A muscle flexed in Reese's jaw. "Hire a couple of extra men to patrol the perimeter.

I don't want any more intruders."

"Aye, sir," Montague agreed.

Reese took a calming breath, reached down and took hold of Jared's hand. "Come on, son. I've got something to show you."

As the security men returned to their duties, Reese tugged Jared along the corridor toward the library. Elizabeth fell in behind them, not ready yet to let her son out of her sight.

She had been wrong about her-brother-in-law. Mason wanted Jared's inheritance and he would go to any length to get it. A shudder rippled through her. Dear God, if she hadn't married Edmund, her son would not now be in danger.

She released a deep breath as she reached the open library door and peered inside. Reese had set Jared on the edge of the table he was using as a desk and handed him the gift he had purchased in Bond Street.

The little boy hurriedly pulled the blue ribbon and opened the box, carefully parted the tissue and peeked inside.

"Go ahead, take it out," Reese urged.

Jared reached a small hand into the box and pulled out the crystal unicorn. It glinted in the sunshine streaming in through the high paned windows.

Jared's eyes widened. "Oh, he is grand,

my lord! The most beautiful horse I have ever seen!"

Reese smiled with pleasure and Elizabeth's heart squeezed. The older Jared got, the more she noticed the similarities between father and son. She ached to tell Reese the child was his. If only she had the courage.

She wondered if Reese would come to her bed tonight and if he did, if she could summon the courage she had found last night or if memories of Edmund would return to haunt her.

"Thank you, ever so much," Jared said. "It is such a marvelous present."

Reese ruffled the little boy's dark hair and set him on his feet. "From now on, you stay close to Mr. Gillespie, all right?"

"Yes, sir, I will." Jared looked down at the crystal unicorn. "I am going to name him Rainbow. For all the colors that sparkle inside him."

Reese smiled. "*Rainbow* . . . that's a very good name."

"Is it all right if I go and show Charlie?"

"As long as you take Mr. Gillespie with you."

Jared nodded, turned and raced out of the library. He ran past Elizabeth without even noticing she was there.

273

"You were wonderful with him," she said as she made her way into the library. "Thank you, Reese."

"He's a good boy. I'm sorry about what happened today. I'll speak to the men, make sure they keep a closer watch on him." His jaw hardened. "Holloway has gone too far. I'm not about to let him harm my family. I intend to make him understand that."

"How do we stop him, Reese? Mason is determined to become earl. He'll always be a threat. How do we keep Jared safe?"

"If Gillespie had been able to bring down Jared's attacker, we would have had something to take to the authorities. As it is, I'm going to make an official report. I'm also going to report the shooting that occurred at Briarwood and the suspicion that you were being drugged."

"None of it proves Mason and Frances are involved."

"I know. If I had my way, I'd shoot the bastard and be done with it, but that would still leave Frances to deal with and I have a feeling she's as ruthless as her husband."

"Worse." Elizabeth walked toward him and he drew her into his arms. "I'm frightened, Reese. Frightened for Jared."

His hold tightened around her. "In time, we'll find a way out of this. Until that happens, we'll keep him safe."

Trusting him to do everything in his power to keep his word, Elizabeth looked up at him. With his dark skin and brilliant blue eyes, he was unbearably handsome. Her heart began beating overly fast and her breath seemed to stall. Neither of them moved. In the next instant, he was kissing her, softly at first, then more deeply.

A flame began to burn inside her, spreading out through her limbs. Her body softened against him and her fingers curled into the lapels of his coat.

"Do you know how much I want you?" he whispered as he kissed the side of her neck.

She knew. She could feel his heavy arousal even through her skirts, demanding and at the same time, promising.

"I want to have you a dozen different ways," he said, "but I'm not going to rush you."

Elizabeth's pulse kicked up. Last night, after her fear had receded, their lovemaking had been wonderful.

And yet she remained uncertain. The old fears lurked just beneath the surface. She had no notion what small thing might set them off.

Reese kissed her again, his hand moving over the fabric of her gown to cup a breast, and her nipple tightened. Last night, he had shown her the pleasure he could give her and she wanted that pleasure now, right there in the library. She arched toward him and a soft moan slipped from her throat.

A noise in the hall alerted them, reminded them where they were. Elizabeth flushed as the butler, Mr. Longacre, very tall with black, slicked-back hair, appeared in the open doorway. Reese faintly cursed.

"I am sorry to disturb you, my lord. But her ladyship asked me to let her know when Mr. Benson, the tutor, arrived for his interview."

"Oh, yes, yes, I'd quite forgot." Elizabeth smoothed a loose curl back into the coil at the nape of her neck and hoped the blush would fade from her cheeks. Flicking a glance at Reese, she preceded the butler out of the library and headed down the hall to the green drawing room, where Mr. Benson, the second potential tutor who had answered her ad, sat waiting to be interviewed.

She tried not to think of Jared, forced herself not to go outside and find him, make certain he was safe. Dear God, it was her fault her son was in danger. If only she could turn back time and somehow change the past.

But the past could not be changed. She prayed the price she would pay for her mistakes would not be the life of her son.

Seventeen

Mason Holloway slammed the door to the study so hard the cinnabar vase on the mantel fell over and crashed onto the floor.

"Bloody damn incompetent fool!"

Frances rose from the chair beside the fire where she had been sitting. Dusk grayed the streets outside the window. A heavy fog had begun to settle over the town house. "Perhaps he'll have better luck next time."

"There won't be a next time — at least not for him. The fool was nearly caught. He'd be recognized the instant he showed his face anywhere near the house."

"So you sent him away?"

"I paid him half what I promised, though it galled me to do so. He didn't get the job done. He didn't deserve as much as he got."

"They can't prove anything," Frances said. "We were miles away at the time of the attempt."

"Dewar won't let it pass. He'll know we're

behind it. I'll be lucky if he doesn't call me out."

"Dueling is against the law and if he harmed you in any way, I would see him arrested and severely punished. Dewar is smart enough to know that."

Mason sighed. "We need the boy out of the way."

"Exactly. Once that happens, you will be the Earl of Aldridge. Without proof of your involvement, there won't be anything Dewar can do."

"Except kill me. Let us not forget, the man was a major in the army. He is tough and determined and not the sort to be trifled with."

Frances walked over to the hearth, stared down into the low-burning flames. Firelight reflected on her pale skin and the long, narrow length of her nose. "We failed to get control of the boy. Trying to kidnap the child didn't work. There has to be a better solution."

Mason sighed. "That is what I have been thinking. We need to hire someone inside the house, someone we pay well enough to keep us informed and do exactly what we tell them."

Frances turned. "One of the servants?"

"Perhaps. Or maybe one of the guards."

"We must choose very carefully. If we don't, we will fail."

Mason clenched his jaw. "We have failed enough already. We are risking a very great deal. Failure can no longer be tolerated."

Frances walked over to where he stood. "The strain you've been under lately is taking its toll. Perhaps tonight you deserve a bit of . . . pleasure."

Mason reached out and touched her cheek. "You are a very special woman, Frances. You understand a man's needs." He smiled. "And I believe you may be right. I think I shall go out for a while this evening. Don't expect me back until late."

Frances looked up at him. "Enjoy yourself, dear heart. Tomorrow will surely be a better day for both of us."

Mason thought of the evening he meant to spend at Madame Lafon's exclusive bordello. Tomorrow he would return to the task they had set for themselves. Tonight, he would enjoy a night of sensual pleasure.

Notes of a grand piano drifted along the corridor, coming from the music room in the opposite wing of the huge brick mansion. Supper was over. Though Reese had wanted to cart his wife straight upstairs to bed, he had forced himself to wait until a more respectable hour and instead had gone into the library to work for a while.

Tomorrow he would move into the refurbished study that had been painted and made ready for his use. Like Briarwood, Holiday House was beginning to feel like home, an odd concept for a man who had spent much of his life on the road. The army shuffled him from place to place and he had convinced himself it was the life he wanted. The life he would always want. Now, as he thought of the woman upstairs and the child in the nursery, a feeling of home and family settled over him and he was no longer so sure.

The music drew him, an intriguing Brahms concerto. Rising from his chair, he made his way down the hall in the direction from which the sounds were coming.

When he reached the music room, he stood in the doorway listening. Elizabeth sat on a wooden bench, her back to him, unaware of his presence. He enjoyed her playing for a few moments more, but he was a man of strong appetites and Elizabeth attracted him greatly.

He closed the door softly and moved toward her, recalling her response to him earlier in the library. After last night, he understood her physical needs far better than she did herself. He knew that Aldridge had merely come to her, pressed her down in the mattress, and taken what he wanted.

, He understood that it was the suffocating, punishing brutality she feared, and until she trusted him completely, he would not make love to her in any way that remotely resembled what Aldridge had done.

Inwardly he smiled. He would keep Elizabeth's fears at bay by making love to her in far more inventive ways, a notion that pleased him greatly.

Reese silently crossed the room, stopped when he came up behind her and rested his palms lightly on her shoulders. Bending his head, he gently pressed his lips against the nape of her neck.

Elizabeth fumbled over a key, quickly brought herself under control and continued to play. Reese's lips brushed lightly over her skin, raising little goose bumps wherever they touched.

She could feel his powerful presence behind her, the strength of his desire holding her like a tangible force. The fire in the hearth had been stoked to a golden blaze. The blue velvet draperies had been closed to keep out the chill. Only a single lamp burned, giving the room a soft yellow glow.

Reese had closed the doors, making them private.

A little shiver went through her. He was here and he wanted her. And Elizabeth wanted him.

She felt his mouth like a brand on the side of her neck, the scrape of his straight white teeth nibbling the lobe of an ear. Long dark fingers pulled the pins from her hair, combed through the thick black strands, then he lifted the heavy curls aside and kissed her bare shoulder.

Her stomach floated up and Elizabeth's playing ceased. It was difficult to think, impossible to make her fingers move over the ivory keys.

"Don't stop," Reese whispered softly. "I love hearing you play."

She took a shaky breath, closed her eyes, and did as he commanded, letting the music take over. The chords matched the thrumming of her heart, heated the desire pulsing through her veins.

Working the buttons of the back of her gown, he eased the fabric off her shoulders and his mouth moved there, across her bare back, his hands slipping inside her corset to cup her breasts. They swelled into his palms, her nipples tightening almost painfully.

Her playing abruptly ceased, the music in

her head stifled by her building desire. As she came up off the stool, Reese captured her face in his hands and kissed her, a long, wet, scorching kiss that had her mind spinning and soft heat tugging low in her belly. His tongue slid into her mouth, taking her deeply, and she caught the faint flavor of the chocolate he had sampled for dessert.

His erection pressed against her, thick and heavy and throbbing. She inhaled the scent of starch and man, and need poured through her. Taking her hand, he led her from behind the stool, kissed her, reached down and unfastened the tabs holding up her skirts.

Her glance slid nervously toward the door, but Reese just shook his head.

"No one will bother us here."

A moment of uncertainty slipped through her, but her body was pulsing, her need far greater than her fear of discovery. The heavy folds of her skirt, bodice, and petticoats pooled around her feet as she stepped out of them, leaving her in corset, drawers, and stockings.

His hungry gaze ran over her, hot and fierce, moving slowly, taking in the wanton picture she made. She thought she must look like a Rubens nymph with her lips moist from his kisses and her breasts swelling above the top of the corset.

Reese captured her lips in a deep, probing kiss and she felt his lust, his hunger. It should have frightened her, but it did not.

He kissed her deeply and she could feel the hard length of him against her belly, feel the heat and the power. As he lifted her breasts into his palms and lowered his head to taste them, Elizabeth moaned.

She was trembling, wanting him as she had never thought to want a man.

"Do you trust me not to hurt you?" he asked softly.

She moistened her lips. "I trust you."

Reese kissed her deeply, stirring her passions until she was clinging to him, her hard nipples rubbing erotically against the corset's lacy cups.

He kissed the side of her neck and turned her to face the piano. "Put your palms flat on the bench."

Uncertainty warred with interest.

"Do it, love. I'll make it good for you, I promise."

She did as he asked, flattening her hands on the bench, thrusting her hips into the air. Reese moved behind her. She gasped as he slid down her drawers, trembled as his hand smoothed over the curves of her bare bottom and he began to stroke her. A rush of wetness slid into her core and a jolt of the same hot fire she had known the night before.

Her head fell back and a little whimper escaped. She started to rise, but Reese's firm hand held her in place.

"Part your legs for me, sweeting."

She couldn't seem to catch her breath. Her legs widened of their own accord, making room for him, and she heard the buttons pop open on the front of his trousers.

He stroked her again and again, and heat tore through her. She cried out at the invasion she hadn't quite expected, the slow penetration of his shaft. She was hot. Unbearably so. He captured her hips and continued his deep penetration, and an instant later, Elizabeth simply shattered.

"Dear God!" Release shook her as he drew out then drove himself in, and she heard his low male growl of triumph. Gripping her hips, he took her with heavy driving strokes and Elizabeth came again. Reese didn't stop, just took her and took her until she cried out in a last powerful climax, then he followed her to release.

His arms eased around her waist, drawing her back against him, and for long moments, he just held her.

"Oh, dear God," she said again as he

slipped her undergarments back into place, buttoned his trousers, and turned her into his arms.

"It's good between us, Beth. You see that, don't you? You don't have to be afraid anymore."

Her gaze found his and she fought not to cry. "You aren't him. I know that now. I won't be afraid again."

Reese kissed her deeply, and Elizabeth prayed it would be true.

"Royal has explained the situation," Sherry said. "You all know Captain Greer. Reese is certain of his loyalty. I'm hoping you will be willing to help him."

Four of Royal's best friends sat round a table at White's, his gentlemen's club, discussing the charges against Travis Greer. The men had known each other since Oxford, all of them members of the Oxford sculling team. After winning the famed Oxford-Cambridge Race, the group had dubbed themselves The Oarsmen and been loyal, dedicated friends ever since.

"My sister probably knows Greer better than the rest of us," said Quentin Garret, Viscount March. "She and Greer's sister were once close chums. You remember Greer's sister married young then died in childbirth?"

"I recall something about that," said Benjamin Wyndam, Lord Nightingale, the only married man in the group. "Poor chap. Greer's family all gone, and then there was losing his arm the way he did. I'll be happy to do what I can. Of course, if I find something that proves him guilty, I won't hesitate to inform the authorities. I won't countenance spying, no matter the justification he might give."

"That is hardly too much to ask," said Dillon St. Michaels, who lounged back in his chair. St. Michaels was a big man with a dry sense of humor that sometimes bordered on rude. "Though I daresay, I trust Reese's judgment, particularly in military matters, and if he says Greer is innocent, I imagine he is."

"What about you, Savage?" Royal asked one of London's most notorious rakes. Tall, dark, and dangerous, Jonathan's good looks and wicked reputation drew women like a sale on Bond Street.

"Life's been dull now that you and your lady have managed to stay out of trouble," Savage said to Royal. "A little intrigue might help stir my blood."

"Your blood hardly needs stirring," St. Michaels drawled. "The scent of a starched petticoat is enough to do that."

Savage just laughed.

"Quent?" Royal asked.

"My sister has had a crush on the man for years. She would cut off my ballocks if I refused to help him."

"That's it then," Sherry finished, "we see what we can find out."

The men relaxed in their chairs.

"There is one more thing," Royal added. "You all know my brother was recently married. What some of you may not know is the reason for all the haste."

Savage's dark eyes gleamed with amusement. "I presumed he put the lady in a family way. Your brother, being the honorable sort he is, did the proper thing."

"I wish it were that simple. Unfortunately, that was not the case. I'm sorry to say, the situation is far more complicated." Royal went on to explain about the Holloways, how they tried to gain control of Jared and his fortune by drugging Elizabeth, and the threat they still posed.

"From what's happened," Royal said, "it's clear that Holloway and his wife are willing to do whatever is necessary to gain the Aldridge title. I'm asking that while you are all out there trying to help Greer, you keep your ears open for anything that might be useful in stopping the Holloways from whatever they have in mind for the boy."

The men muttered between them. Royal could sense their tension. Reese was family. They all were. Royal could count on them to do everything in their power to help his brother.

The purple haze of morning lit the sky over Hampstead Heath. A cold October wind whistled through the trees around the big stone house and sliced through Reese's clothing yet perspiration beaded on his forehead.

"One more time, Tim." The stout young man tugged hard on Reese's leg, stretching the stiff muscles then reversing his movements and bending his knee. Reese clamped hard on his jaw until the process finally ended and Timothy released his leg.

A breath of relief whispered out. Reese sat up on the bench and flexed his leg several times. "It's getting better every day. Thanks, Tim."

"You're the one doing all the work."

Reese blotted his forehead with his elbow, wiping away the wetness on the sleeve of his shirt. "Warrior's saddled and ready?"

"He's ready. You sure about this, Major?"

"No, but I have to try it sometime." Timothy left to fetch Reese's big black gelding and returned a few minutes later. The horse had an easy disposition and though Reese hadn't ridden since his injury, the animal was accustomed to the feel of him in the saddle. It was just a matter of getting his leg to cooperate enough to keep him there.

Since mounting from the left was impossible with his injury, he walked over to the mounting block and climbed the steps to the platform. Timothy led the black up to the block and the animal whinnied when he saw Reese waiting.

"We've been through some tough times together, eh, boy?" Reese scratched the horse's ears and the gelding nickered softly. Collecting the reins, Reese swung his good leg over the horse's back and settled himself on the flat leather seat.

Damn, it felt good to be there.

"How're you doing?" Timothy asked.

Reese looked over at the brawny redhead. "There was a time, I felt more comfortable in the saddle than on the ground."

"Not today, I guess."

"Not yet, at any rate." Though he had been able to bend his knee enough to fit his boot into the stirrup, he felt awkward and uneasy. Reaching down, he adjusted his foot until his leg felt more secure.

The problem was his grip. A horseman used his knees and thighs to grip and control the animal and maintain his seat, but the muscles in his injured leg were weak.

"Lead him into the ring," he instructed, giving Warrior time to get the feel of him again, fighting to keep his balance as the horse walked off behind Timothy.

They made their way into the small arena and Warrior began to prance, eager for the exercise. Reese nodded to Timmy. "All right, let's give this a try."

Timothy backed away as Reese set the horse into a walk. They made their way twice around the ring before he nudged Warrior into a trot.

Posting tortured his leg. He forced the muscles up and down in rhythm to the animal's gait, gritting his teeth against the pain. He made two passes round the ring before his knee forced him to kick the animal into a canter. The pain instantly eased.

Slowly, he began to feel a little more relaxed, a little more comfortable in the saddle, though he hadn't nearly the control he'd when he had ridden with the cavalry.

Warrior patiently kept up a steady pace and Reese's leg relaxed even more, allowing him a slightly better seat. He was riding passably well until the stable cat, a big yellow-striped tabby, ran into the arena and darted between Warrior's legs. The horse shied only a little but it was enough to set Reese off balance.

The next thing he knew he was flying through the air, landing in a pile of dirt in the middle of the arena.

"Papa!" Jared's high-pitched, frightened voice reached him from behind the fence, where he and his protector, Mr. Gillespie, had apparently been watching. As Reese pushed to his feet and began to dust off his clothes, he caught sight of the little boy racing through the gate. An instant later, Jared's small body hurled against him, nearly knocking him back in the dirt.

"Hey! Hold on there!" The child was shaking all over, clinging to him fiercely.

"I don't want you to die. Please don't die."

Reese's chest squeezed. He smoothed a hand over the child's tousled hair. "I'm not going to die. I'm fine. It was just a little fall, nothing to worry about." Reese looked down at the boy and smiled. "You called me Papa."

Jared stared up at him, his dark eyes shiny. "Yesterday you said I was your son. I thought . . . I — I thought . . ."

Emotion swelled in Reese's heart. "You

thought that made me your father and you were right." He had used the expression but it never occurred to him the boy would take it literally. He took a calming breath. "I am your papa now. I think it's past time you called me that."

Jared eased back to look at him. "Are you all right, truly? Warrior didn't hurt you?"

Reese managed to smile. "Only my pride, lad." Warrior stood a few feet away, Timothy holding the reins. Turning, Reese swung the little boy up on the saddle and Jared's eyes nearly popped out of his head.

"All right?" Reese asked, careful to keep a hand on the boy to steady him, Timothy doing the same on the opposite side.

Jared just nodded.

"How does it feel?" Reese asked.

The little boy grinned ear to ear. "I'm sitting on a real live horse."

"That's right."

Jared leaned down and patted Warrior's sleek black neck. "He's really big."

"Yes, he is. You need a horse more your size. In the meantime, hang on real tight and Corporal Daniels will give you a turn round the ring."

Jared gripped the front of the saddle, the grin even bigger on his face. Timothy took his cue and led Warrior at a slow pace around the arena.

"Again?" Reese asked when they returned, and Jared nodded enthusiastically.

The ride continued and they reached the starting spot once more. "Can we do it again?" the little boy asked.

"Not today. Soon, though, I promise. Both of us will ride again." Silently, Reese vowed to work on building the muscles on the inside of his thighs — and find a suitable pony for the boy who had just become his son.

EIGHTEEN

"Do you think you're ready to face them?" Reese asked Elizabeth as she descended the wide marble stairs into the magnificent entry of Holiday House.

"I have to — sooner or later. It might as well be now." But the gossip would be brutal. A woman was supposed to wait at least the three-year period of mourning before she took another husband. Some women wore black for the rest of their lives and never remarried.

"We won't stay long. But Lady Annabelle was willing to help by giving this ball and she has managed to get the Holloways to attend. I'd like to make sure they understand we're not going to let them hold us hostage."

Elizabeth adjusted the long blue gloves that matched her sapphire taffeta gown, one of those Reese had ordered with the low-cut bodice.

She cast him an assessing glance. "Lady Annabelle is a friend, is she not? I've never met her, but I hear she is quite a beautiful woman."

Eyes the same brilliant blue as her gown studied her closely. "She is a friend of my family's, a good friend to Royal and Lily. She is also a friend of Travis's, which is why she agreed to hold this ball."

Elizabeth glanced away. "I see."

Reese caught her chin and turned her to face him. "She has never been more than a friend to me, if that is what you are thinking."

Relief trickled through her. She had been wondering that very thing, wondering if perhaps the lovely widow had known Reese as a lover, the way Elizabeth was beginning to know him.

A little thrill went through her. Last night, Reese had made love to her on the thick Persian carpet in front of a blazing fire in his newly refurbished study. The surroundings were so unlike anything she had experienced that memories of Edmund had never entered her mind.

"I believe the carriage is waiting," he said. "We had better be on our way."

She glanced toward the rooms upstairs. "Are you certain Jared will be all right?"

Reese's gaze followed hers and his jaw clenched. "We'll be back as soon as we can. Gillespie and Montague are here and a couple of extra guards are outside. But Jared will never be truly safe until we expose the Holloways and make all of this come to an end."

He was right, of course. After the abduction attempt, they could no longer sit back and do nothing. They had to take action. Reese had already spoken to his brother, who had asked for the help of his friends. Perhaps with all of them working together . . .

Forcing her thoughts in a more pleasant direction, Elizabeth made her way to the door, down the wide porch steps, and Reese handed her into the carriage. She ignored a little twinge of disappointment when he took the seat across from her instead of sitting beside her.

The coach lurched into motion, the driver urging the four-horse team along the circular gravel drive. All the while, Elizabeth's thoughts remained on Reese and what had happened between them in the study. What she hoped would happen again.

"Keep looking at me the way you are and I shall come over there and do exactly what you are thinking about."

Heat rushed into her cheeks. "I wasn't thinking anything."

Reese's mouth edged up. "Yes, you were, and I don't mind in the least. You may look forward to exactly that happenstance on our journey back to the house."

Her insides softened. He meant it. He would take her there in the carriage on their journey back home. He was determined to erase any lingering memories of Edmund's crude attempts at lovemaking and he was doing a very thorough job.

"Until then," he drawled, "I suggest you pull your wrap over those luscious breasts or I shall be forced to take you right now. I imagine we would look quite a sight by the time we arrived at the ball."

"You are outrageous," she said, her cheeks burning brighter. But she loved his fierce masculinity and she was coming to crave his incredible lovemaking. She was a woman of surprising passion, she had begun to discover. Something she never would have guessed.

She settled back on the seat, fluffing her skirts out around her just to have something to do, trying not to look at him, to think how handsome he was. Trying to ignore the anticipation that made her breasts swell inside the cups of her corset.

They spoke little on the journey, their thoughts on the upcoming ball and the difficult evening they faced ahead. It wouldn't be easy, but Reese was the son of a duke and Elizabeth a countess. Along with that, Royal and Lily would be there to lend their support, as well as a number of the duke's influential friends.

And there was the promise of what would happen once the ball was over and they were returning home.

She bit her lip. The two of them were growing closer every day. If only she could tell him the awful secret she kept from him.

But if she did, she would lose him.

Elizabeth forced down the unbearable thought.

The ball, a well-attended affair, was being given at the elegant home of Lady Annabelle Townsend. Annabelle, a widow whose husband had died five years ago, was the daughter of the Earl of Leighton. Quentin Garret, Viscount March, was her brother, Lord Leighton's heir and one of Royal's best friends.

Elizabeth had never met the woman, thanks to Edmund's strict dictates and her rare trips to London. But as she entered the receiving line, she saw that Lady Annabelle was younger than she had imagined, no more than four-and-twenty, and lovely in the extreme. With her honey-brown hair, sky-blue eyes, and slender figure, she drew the eye of a dozen different men. At her warm, welcoming smile, Elizabeth liked her immediately.

And Lady Annabelle seemed to like her.

After their initial introduction and a few brief words, Annabelle had insisted on personally escorting them into the ballroom.

"Come along," she ordered. "His Grace and the rest of his party are awaiting your arrival. They are eager to see you both."

She was lending her support, Elizabeth realized, ignoring the low mutters of disapproval and whispers of speculation as they all walked into the ballroom.

A group of men and women, some of whom Elizabeth recognized, stood waiting to greet them. Among them were the Duke and Duchess of Bransford.

"Good evening, my lady." Tall and golden, Reese's older brother bowed gallantly over her hand.

"Good evening, Your Grace," she replied. "It's good to see you."

Elizabeth and Lily spoke briefly. Lily asked about her son then reached over to squeeze her hand.

"All will be well with your boy," the duchess promised. "Royal and the others will not let you down."

Elizabeth felt the quick sting of tears. It had been so long since she had enjoyed the friendship of another woman. "Thank you, Your Grace."

"Please, it's just Lily. We are family, after all. I thought we were agreed."

Elizabeth smiled brightly. "Family, yes . . . Thank you so much, Lily."

Elizabeth greeted Sheridan Knowles, Viscount Wellesley, as well as Benjamin Wyndam, Lord Nightingale, and his little wife, Maryann. Other of Royal's friends were scattered around the room, sniffing about for various and sundry bits of gossip that might help Travis Greer.

, Annabelle departed to return to her duties as hostess, and Elizabeth turned to greet the latest arrival in the group. Her stomach tightened as Agatha Edgewood, Lady Tavistock, Reese's elderly aunt walked up beside her.

"Good evening, Elizabeth." The frail old woman cast her a glance so piercing she felt light-headed.

"My lady."

The dowager knew her terrible secret. And also that Elizabeth had not yet told Reese the truth about his son. The old woman must have read the fear in her eyes or noticed the sudden pallor of her face.

"Be at ease, my dear," the dowager said. "Your son's life is yet in danger. You must say nothing that would distract Reese from trying to see the threat to Jared ended."

Her eyes filled. "You are very wise, my lady."

"For heaven's sake, girl, don't cry. You must keep your head tonight at all costs."

She blinked rapidly, fighting to regain her composure. "Of course, my lady."

Aunt Agatha patted her arm. "Everything will be all right. Reese will see to it."

But of course there was no way to know for sure.

Reese warmly greeted his aunt, then leaned down and spoke to Elizabeth softly. "Stay here with our friends. There is something I need to do."

Elizabeth nodded as he walked away, his limp barely perceptible. His leg was growing stronger, his determination paying off a little at a time. She followed his progress as he moved across the ballroom toward the door and realized he had spotted his quarry. Mason Holloway was there and heading for the gaming room. She spotted Frances in conversation with a group of women on the

303

opposite side of the ballroom, and fear trickled through her.

Elizabeth suppressed a shiver.

Reese caught up with Holloway just as he started for the door of the gaming room. Reese stepped in front of him, blocking his entrance.

"I think it's time we had a word."

Holloway pushed him away. "I have nothing to say to you, Dewar."

"Unfortunately, I have something to say to you. I can say it here in the hallway where word will spread over half of London by morning or you can open the door on your right and step inside and I can say it in private."

Holloway glanced around, saw several of the guests had begun to watch them. Swearing softly, he opened the door and Reese followed him into an intimate, rarely used drawing room.

"What do you want?" Holloway demanded.

"I think you know exactly what I want. I'm here to warn you, Holloway. I want you to know I've reported each of your attempts against my family to the authorities."

"What attempts? I don't know what you're talking about. You have no proof whatsoever that I've done anything to anyone."

"The authorities need proof," Reese said.

"I don't. You come near my wife or the boy, you harm either of them in any way — you're a dead man."

Mason's thick shoulders tightened. His mustache pulled tight as his lips thinned. "You're threatening me?"

"As I said, I'm warning you. Harm the boy or his mother and you die."

"You think it would be that simple? Even if you succeeded in killing me, you would hang."

"Some things are worth dying for. That's what I believe. How about you? Are you willing to die so your wife can get rich? Because you won't be around to enjoy the money yourself."

Mason said nothing.

"Think it over, Holloway." As Reese left the room, his tension did not ease. He had meant every word, but dispatching justice after Jared was dead wasn't the answer. He had to find a way to end the threat Holloway posed.

And there was Frances to consider.

Perhaps tonight, Royal and the others would uncover something that would help put an end to the problem.

■ ■ ■ ■

Two days later, the small group of friends met in a private room at the Horn and Hoof Tavern on Kentish Town Road. Reese had tried to persuade Elizabeth to stay home but she had refused.

"Jared is my son. The men may have learned something that will help protect him. I want to hear what they have to say."

"They may only have information dealing with Greer."

"And they may have more."

"Dammit, Beth!"

She only smiled. She liked it when he called her that, the way he used to in the days when they were to marry. It didn't happen often. Reese guarded his emotions even more than she guarded her own. Neither of them wanted to suffer the pain they had endured before.

They protected their hearts but not their passions.

In the carriage that night after the ball, Reese had kept his word. He had taken her twice, leaving her sated and limp, then held her while she slept in his arms until they reached home.

The tavern loomed ahead, a squat, slate-

306

roofed stone structure with a stable at the rear. In a simple gray wool gown trimmed with forest green velvet, Elizabeth held onto Reese's arm as he escorted her past the taproom into a small private chamber at the back of the tavern.

The men all rose as Elizabeth walked in: the duke; Sheridan Knowles; Lord Nightingale; Lord March, and Jonathan Savage. Those she hadn't known already she had met at Lady Annabelle's ball. Elizabeth was surprised to see Reese's brother, Rule, among those seated round the table.

Apparently, Reese was also surprised. "What brings you here, little brother? I wasn't sure you were still in London. I didn't see you at Annabelle's ball."

"Unfortunately, I had a previous engagement. I stopped by the next day to see Royal. He brought me up to snuff on what's been going on. I get round a bit. I thought I might be able to learn something that could be useful."

From what Elizabeth had heard, Reese's younger brother *got round* a very good bit. He was a lady's man, an unabashed rogue. Women threw themselves at him, though his reputation was not as black as that of Jonathan Savage, the son of an earl who was barely tolerated by society.

"We appreciate anything you can do," Reese said.

The balance of the greetings were brief and they all took their seats at the wooden table. Mugs of ale sat in front of each man and a serving maid appeared with ale for Reese and a cup of tea for Elizabeth.

"Since Royal called this meeting," Reese said as soon as the serving maid left, "I assume there is something to report."

"Several somethings," Royal said. "Quent, why don't you begin?"

Lord March, a dark-eyed man with handsome, well-defined features, set his mug of ale on the table. "The ball was a good idea. I picked up a few interesting tidbits during the course of the evening." Since his title was merely a courtesy until he inherited the Leighton earldom, he preferred his friends call him Quent.

"So what did you learn?" Reese asked.

"Turns out Greer's nemesis, Lord Sandhurst, had met the captain through a mutual friend several years ago. Sandhurst knew Greer's background, knew he was half-Russian. And the earl and Greer had a run-in over Lady Sandhurst once before."

"Interesting," Reese said.

Royal turned to another of his friends. "Nightingale, I believe you had something to add."

Very dark-haired, solidly built and sophisticated, the Earl of Nightingale was the sort who instantly commanded attention.

"Actually, I didn't have much luck at the ball, but the following day I paid a visit to a friend who works in the Foreign Office. He told me there were already rumors circulating of a spy in the mix before Sandhurst went to the colonel. Field Marshall Lord Raglan believed information was being leaked to the Russians. That was the reason the Russians pulled back at Sevastopol and were gone from their naval base by the time the army arrived."

"In other words, the government was looking for a spy before Sandhurst went to them with Travis's name."

"That is correct."

Reese's jaw hardened, and Elizabeth immediately understood. "You are worried that not only have they got the wrong man, but that they will stop searching for the real spy and he might get away with his crimes."

"Exactly," Reese said.

"Or worse yet," Nightingale added, "he might continue his traitorous activities."

"Trav isn't a spy," Reese said firmly, "which means our soldiers are still in danger."

Sheridan Knowles looked thoughtful. "We need to find out a little more about Lord Sandhurst. Perhaps the earl had more to gain than revenge against Greer. Perhaps the accusation was a means of diverting suspicion from himself."

"Interesting supposition," said Reese, a long finger tapping the side of his pewter mug.

"I know Lady Sandhurst fairly well," Rule put in, drawing the group's attention. No one seemed surprised at his acquaintance with a woman reputed to enjoy a good deal of sexual freedom. "Let me speak to her, see what she might be willing to tell me about her husband."

"Good idea," Reese said.

"And, of course," drawled Savage, the edge of his mouth curving faintly, "there may be certain . . . benefits. The countess is said to be a very talented woman."

Reese flicked him a glance that reminded him there was a lady present.

"Sorry," he said, but he didn't look repentant in the least.

"We need to figure out who else might be a player," suggested Quent. "Someone is selling government secrets. There is big money in that."

"And we need to find out who's buying

them," Savage added.

Reese leaned back in his chair. "That's where Travis could be useful. He speaks Russian. He could move easily within the Russian community. He might be able to find out who is interested in buying secrets."

"Let's talk to Colonel Thomas," Nightingale suggested to Reese. "I'll set up a meeting with the three of us. We'll see if we can convince him to release Greer into our custody then turn him loose among the Russians."

Reese looked hopeful. "It's definitely worth a try."

They discussed Captain Greer's situation for several more minutes. Elizabeth was beginning to lose hope they had found anything that could help Jared when Royal spoke up again.

"All right, we all know what we need to do in regard to Greer — which brings us to an even more important subject."

Royal turned his tawny gaze toward black-haired Jonathan Savage. "I think Elizabeth might like to hear what Jonathan has to say. Savage . . . ?"

He finished the last of his ale and sat forward, his attention fixed on her, no longer playing the role of casual observer as he usually did. Instead, he reminded Eliza-

311

beth of a panther tracking its prey.

"As we all know, trying to prove your former in-laws are hoping to do away with your son will not be easy. It also may not be the answer. With any luck, the way to stop them may be to prove they have already done murder."

"What?" Elizabeth rose half out of her chair.

"I don't have proof — at least not yet. But during the years before they moved into Aldridge House, Holloway and his wife were involved in what appears to be a less than respectable business right here in London."

"I knew they lived here for a time, though they rarely spoke of their days in London."

"That's because they were not in society. Your late husband sent them money enough to live quite comfortably, but Mason wanted to build a fortune of his own. Two weeks before he and Frances left for Aldridge Park, a man was murdered. For a time, they fell under suspicion."

"How did you happen upon this information?" Reese asked.

Savage shrugged his wide shoulders. "I'm in the shipping business. Ansel Van Meer, the man who was killed, was a cargo broker." Jonathan had inherited a failing shipyard from his father, Reese had told Elizabeth, and turned it into one of his highly profitable endeavors.

"Go on," Reese urged.

"One of my employees knew Van Meer. He said the two men were involved in some kind of shady business deal that went bad. Then Van Meer turned up dead and the partnership dissolved. There were no witnesses — or at least none came forward, and the investigation turned up nothing. Holloway and his wife moved away the following week."

"You think you could dig around a little more, see what else you might turn up?" Royal asked.

"That was my intention."

"Why don't I have Chase Morgan look into it?" Reese suggested.

"He's been investigating the Holloways for a while," Royal said. "I'm surprised he didn't come up with the information himself."

"The Holloways were only in the city a very short time," Savage explained, "and they kept a very low profile."

"I'll get hold of Morgan right away," Reese said, "though I'll need a few more particulars before I speak to him."

Elizabeth quietly sipped her tea while Savage filled Reese in, giving him as much information as he had been able to come up with in so short a time.

"We really appreciate your help, Jonathan," Reese said.

Savage glanced away, clearly uncomfortable with any sort of sentiment. He was a hard man, Elizabeth could see, and yet she thought she saw a hint of vulnerability hidden beneath his cool facade.

A few more details were discussed. The meeting was finally adjourned and the small group dispersed. On the carriage ride home, Elizabeth was thoughtful.

If Mason and Frances had committed a crime, perhaps it could be proved.

Perhaps with God's help — and that of The Oarsmen — they would be punished for the crime they had committed if not the one they planned.

NINETEEN

Dressed in a walking gown of rich russet taffeta, her light brown hair pulled into curls that barely showed beneath the wide brim of her bonnet, Annabelle Townsend rapped on the door to number twelve Brook Street just off Grosvenor Square.

From the corner of her eye, she caught sight of a stout man leaning against a lamppost. He straightened at the sound of her knock, clearly interested in who might be visiting Travis Greer.

Anna ignored him. Instead, when the door jerked open and Travis stood in the entry, she looked up at him and simply smiled.

"Good afternoon, Travis."

"What the . . . ?" He looked charmingly disheveled, his sandy brown hair mussed, his jacket and waistcoat missing. She could only imagine how much he hated being kept indoors.

"May I come in or must I stand outside

like some out-of-work chambermaid in search of a position."

Travis's hazel eyes ran over her as he stepped back to let her pass. "You could never be mistaken for a chambermaid, Anna." He raked back his sandy brown hair, which always seemed in need of a trim. "What are you doing here? This is a bachelor household. You shouldn't be here."

"I'm a widow paying a call on a sick friend." She glanced around. "Where is your butler? I'm sure you must have one."

"I couldn't stand him hovering about any longer. I gave him a few days off."

"Well, then, close the door and invite me into the drawing room so that we may speak in private."

"There's a man outside watching the house. What's he going to think when you —"

"I don't care what he thinks." She made her way into the drawing room and settled herself on the plush ruby sofa. The room was cluttered with collectibles and far too feminine for a man as virile as Travis Greer, but as a friend of his late sister, she knew he had inherited the house from his mother.

"I hate to repeat myself, but what do you want?"

"I came to see how you are faring at such

a trying time." Her gaze traveled over his rumpled shirt, one sleeve tied up for lack of an arm, and wrinkled brown trousers. He had never been meticulous, but he had always been neat. "Looking at you, I can see you are doing very poorly."

Travis blew out a breath. For the first time he seemed to relax. "You shouldn't be here, Anna."

She knew that. Even now she was beginning to feel the old attraction, the yearning for Travis to notice her as a woman. But he only saw her as his sister's best friend. She would always be a little girl in his eyes and he would always be the man she had fallen in love with all those years ago.

"Well, I am here, so you may as well try to be cordial." Travis was the reason she had married Gerald Townsend when she was just nineteen, a marriage her father had arranged. Gerald was twenty years older than Anna. He was a patient, doting husband who never made unreasonable demands, and in a way she had come to care for him. But she had agreed to marry him only because she couldn't have Travis.

"Do you want some tea or something? The rest of the servants are still around. I could ring for some refreshment, if you like."

"I am fine." She would love a cup of tea,

317

but her hands were trembling and she didn't want him to notice. It had taken a good deal of courage for her to come here.

"You look different," he said as she pulled off her bonnet and smoothed back her hair.

And you look just as handsome as you always did. It didn't matter that he only had one arm.

"Are you all right, truly?" she asked. "I know you are not a spy. You are a loyal Englishman and always have been."

"I'm glad you think so. Not many do." He sank down wearily in a chair across from her.

"You'd be surprised. You have a number of loyal friends, Trav. Including me."

"I heard you gave a ball so that Reese and his friends might have a chance to pick up some gossip or some information that might help. I appreciate that, Anna."

She glanced away. Though Travis wore small gold spectacles, they had never been able to hide his thoughts. She could read his turmoil and his worry.

"Reese and Nightingale are going to speak to Colonel Thomas. They hope to convince him to let you help in the search for the real spy."

Travis came up from his chair and paced toward her. He was a big man and impres-

318

sively built. Anna's breath caught. She rose so she wouldn't be at such a disadvantage.

"Are you sure?"

She nodded. "They are hoping Colonel Thomas will release you into their custody."

"Does Reese think Thomas might actually agree?"

"We're all hoping."

Travis's gaze ran over her, taking in the swell of her breasts beneath her crisp taffeta day dress, and her very small, corseted waist. When he spoke, his voice sounded husky. "You've turned into a beautiful woman. You've grown up, Anna."

A faint blush colored her cheeks. It was a rare occurrence. She was a widow, after all, and a very sensible woman. "I'm glad you finally noticed. I always hoped you would."

Travis frowned. "You wanted me to notice you?"

"You're a very handsome man. Even before you left to join the army, I always hoped you would notice me."

His sandy brows drew nearly together. "I wouldn't have been right for you back then. I wanted adventure. That's the reason I joined the cavalry."

"I know."

His gaze found hers, held her immobile.

"I noticed you," he said softly. "Even back then."

He was standing so close she had to tilt her head back to look at him. "Did you?" she asked breathlessly.

"You needed a husband. I wasn't ready for marriage. But I noticed."

She kept her gaze on his face. "I've had a husband, Travis. I'm not looking for another."

His eyes seemed to darken, changing from light green to brown. "What *are* you looking for, Anna? Why did you come here?"

She moistened her lips. "I told you. I wanted to see you how you fared."

"I'm in trouble, Anna. Very serious trouble. Coming here wasn't a good idea."

Her heart was beating. Every fantasy she'd ever had about Travis seemed to be blazing through her head. "I want to help you. I'm going to do everything I can to prove your innocence."

He reached out and caught her shoulders and she felt the heat of his hands as if they burned right through her clothes.

"I want you to stay out of this."

"No."

His jaw firmed. "I'm a man, Anna. You can't come here like this."

She read his hunger. He had never looked

at her that way before, or if he had she had
been too young to understand. "Why not,
Travis? Why can't I come here?"

His hold faintly tightened. "Because seeing you again makes me remember the
hundreds of times I've thought of you over
the years. Because when I did, I imagined
us being alone together the way we are now."

Relief at his confession and a wave of
excitement rose inside her. He had thought
about her. As a woman, not a girl.

"I want you to leave," he said.

"I'll leave. All you have to do is kiss me.
Just one kiss and I'll go."

He stood there shaking his head, but his
breathing quickened and his hands still
gripped her shoulders. "I can't. It's wrong,
Anna."

"It isn't wrong in the least, Travis."

His gaze deepened, darkened. Then he
was pulling her into his arms, settling his
mouth over hers. His kiss was fierce, as hot
and exciting as she had always imagined.
He tasted faintly of brandy, and she caught
the masculine scent of soap. Anna swayed
against him. Her breasts pushed into his
muscular chest, and he groaned.

For an instant, he deepened the kiss and
desire burned through her. Then he was
pushing her away, stepping back from her,

sliding his glasses back up on his nose. She could almost feel the tension in his body, the effort it took to stay in control.

"You have to go, Anna. Before something happens both of us will regret."

"I'll go. But I'm not letting you off so easily this time, Travis. I'm a widow. Widows enjoy a certain freedom other women don't. And everyone knows a widow has certain needs."

His eyes widened. "You don't know what you're saying."

"I know exactly what I am saying."

"For God's sake, you're my sister's best friend!"

"And if Beatrice were alive, she would tell me I am doing exactly the right thing."

"But —"

"We're going to find a way to prove your innocence, Trav. Then you and I . . . well, we'll just have to see."

His expression remained one of disbelief as she turned and left him standing there in the drawing room. Annabelle smiled to herself. At last, she had found the courage to do exactly what she had dreamed of doing for as long as she could remember.

She had finally kissed him.

And it had been worth every ounce of courage she'd had to summon in order to do it.

Reese stepped into the entry of Holiday House, his mind on the meeting he'd just had with Chase Morgan.

"This could be our first real break in the case," the investigator had said. "I'll talk to Jonathan Savage, see if I can speak directly to the employee who told him about the murder. I'll also talk to the police. I've got some very good connections in that area. Maybe I'll be able to come up with something useful at last."

Reese had left the office feeling better than he had in days. If a man was capable of murder — and he believed Holloway was — then it wouldn't be surprising to discover he had done it before.

He shoved open the door leading into the entry, shaking the dampness off the cape of his overcoat. A chill wind rustled the branches of the leaves outside and a light mist hung in the air. It felt good to be indoors.

"You're home!"

He looked up to see his wife hurrying toward him down the hall. He tried to ignore the rush of pleasure that filled his chest. "So I am."

"How did it go?"

"Morgan was excited. He thinks this might be the break we've been looking for. I'll tell you all about it later. First I've got something for Jared. Do you know where he is?"

"He's with Mr. Connelly, his new tutor." They had hired the man three days ago. He was the third person to apply for the position, but Elizabeth and Reese had both been impressed with the intelligent fifty-year-old man who seemed dedicated to the job of teaching, as well as his impeccable credentials. And Jared seemed less ill at ease with him than with either of the men before.

"They are upstairs in the nursery," Elizabeth added. "Mr. Connelly wants to convert it to a schoolroom, now that Jared is older."

"I think that's a good idea."

She eyed him curiously. "So you have brought him a gift? What is it?"

Reese smiled and shook his head. "Ask him to come down for a moment and you'll see. It shouldn't take too long, and perhaps it will motivate him to pay attention to his studies."

He could see he had piqued her interest. Turning, she hurried up the stairs and returned a few minutes later with Jared tucked in beside her. The stout security guard, Sean Gillespie, followed a few paces behind.

"Your . . . papa has a gift for you." At the use of the word she looked up at him. Reese thought she was more uncomfortable with the new form of address than he was. "He has brought it with him from the city."

"Actually it came from a farm just down the road. Shall we go out and take a look?"

Jared grinned. "Oh, yes!"

The little boy stood impatiently while the butler fetched his coat, along with Elizabeth's woolen cloak, then the boy ran ahead of them out the door. Reese smiled at the child's excitement as they made their way toward the barn, where Timothy Daniels waited for them, his hand gripping the reins of a dappled gray thirteen-hand pony.

Jared stopped dead in his tracks, his gaze riveted on the small horse with the silver mane and tail.

"His name is Dusty," Reese said.

Jared's gaze remained locked on the horse. "He's beautiful."

"I'm glad you like him because he's yours."

The little boy whirled toward him, his eyes twin pools of dark brown. "Do you mean it?"

"Of course I mean it. I said you needed a

325

horse more your size. Dusty's small but big enough for you to grow into."

Jared stared up at him and Reese caught the faint glint of tears. "Thank you. No one has given me such a wonderful gift." And then he was running toward Timothy, stopping in front of the pony, reaching out tentatively to pet the small horse's neck.

When Reese turned, Elizabeth was crying.

"What's the matter? You don't think it's a good idea?"

"I think it's a wonderful idea. Edmund never gave Jared any sort of gift. I used to buy them for him and say they came from his father, but I think Jared knew it wasn't true."

Reese eased her into his arms. "We'll make it up to him. We'll see he gets lots of presents."

Elizabeth managed a wobbly smile and nodded.

Ignoring the unexpected squeezing in his chest, Reese led Elizabeth toward the little boy and his new horse.

"I've hired an instructor," Reese said. "Mr. Montague is checking his credentials. Once we are certain everything is completely aboveboard, he is going to start giving you lessons every afternoon. Pretty soon you'll be riding Dusty as fast as the wind."

Jared grinned up at him. "And you can ride Warrior. We can go riding together."

Reese thought of the work he had been doing on his leg and vowed to make another attempt with the big black gelding. Still, they would have to stay close to the house until the threat to Jared was over.

"You have to get your schoolwork done first," Reese said. "After that, you can have your lesson. Once you get good enough, we'll ride together."

Jared looked up at him as if he were a god. "You're the very best papa I've ever had."

Reese smiled grimly, not doubting it for a moment.

Leaving Jared and Reese in the stable, Elizabeth returned to the house. She was in trouble. Frightening, terrible trouble.

Today, when she had watched Reese with his son, when she had seen his kindness and concern for a boy he didn't even know was his own, something inside her had crumbled and the glaring truth revealed.

She had done the unthinkable. She had fallen deeply in love with Reese.

Her heart squeezed. She had seen it coming. She had done her best to guard her heart, but since the night he had allowed her and Jared into his home, since the moment he had set aside his ill will and lent them his protection, she had been falling more and more under his spell.

She was in love with him. Hopelessly and eternally. In love with him far more deeply than she had been as a girl. In love not with the boy he once was, but the man he had become.

And when she told him the truth about Jared, when he looked at her with disgust and loathing, it was going to break her heart.

Elizabeth took a steadying breath, fighting the tears that threatened. There was no use crying. She had known from the start she would have to tell him and that once she did, her hopes and dreams would all turn to dust.

Until that day, she meant to enjoy every moment she had with him.

The butler was waiting when she walked back into the house. Elizabeth looked into his somber face. "What is it, Longacre?"

"A letter, my lady. It arrived just a moment ago from London. One of the security people intercepted the messenger at the gate and brought it to the house himself."

"They seem to be very efficient."

"Indeed, my lady. The messenger awaits your reply."

She broke the seal on the letter which was

addressed to both her and Reese. It was from Mr. Pinkard, Reese's solicitor. The adoption hearing was set for two weeks hence. They would both need to be there, but Mr. Pinkard was certain the adoption would be approved. It was only a matter of formality.

She hurriedly penned a note, assuring the solicitor they would be there and handed the note to the butler. "Will you see this delivered to the messenger?"

"Of course, my lady."

"Thank you."

The butler made a faint nod of his head and took the note to the guard, who stood waiting on the front porch steps. The man disappeared and Elizabeth made a mental note to tell Reese the date for the hearing had been set.

Soon Jared would legally become his son. Elizabeth felt sick to her stomach. It was past time she told Reese the truth.

TWENTY

Pacing back and forth in the cluttered drawing room of his town house, ignoring the faint smell of old perfume that reminded him of his mother, Travis turned at the sound of a firm rap on his door. He strode to the window, peered outside, and spotted Reese on the porch.

His butler had not yet returned — thank God. Travis wasn't used to being inside for days on end. He needed some space to move about. With a houseful of servants, it wasn't that easy to find.

He strode to the door and pulled it open, relieved his friend had finally come. "I've been eager to see you." He motioned his friend into the house, then led him down the hall to the drawing room. Once they were inside, he slid closed the doors, making them private. "I hope you're bringing good news."

"I suppose that's all in how you look at it.

And how did you know I was coming?"

"Annabelle stopped by. She said you and Nightingale were going to talk to Colonel Thomas. She said something about trying to get me released so that I could help find the real spy."

Reese frowned. "Lady Annabelle Townsend? She came by to see you?"

Travis felt a wave of guilt. She was an unattached female and he didn't want her becoming the subject of gossip. "We've known each other for a number of years. She and my sister, Beatrice, were best chums."

"Her brother mentioned that."

"She stopped by to see how I fared."

Reese nodded. "Annabelle believes strongly in your innocence. She is determined to help you in any way she can."

Travis looked away. She wanted to help him, all right. She hadn't come right out and said it, but it strongly appeared she wanted him to make love to her.

Travis sank down in an overstuffed ruby chair, a memory arising of her mouth under his, her full lips softening, trembling slightly as he took control and deepened the kiss.

His groin tightened. She had only been eighteen when he had joined the army, but she had been a beautiful girl even then and he had imagined kissing her at least a dozen times. None of his musings had compared with the real thing, and thinking of it now, he shifted to relieve the pressure of his hardening shaft.

Travis silently cursed.

"You're sweating," Reese said. "You aren't sick, are you?"

A little lovesick, maybe — God forbid.

Travis sighed. "I've got a problem."

Reese grunted. "You're jesting, right?"

"I mean a different sort of problem." He straightened in the chair, pushing thoughts of Annabelle away. "Tell me what Colonel Thomas said."

"Apparently, Nightingale's information was correct. He discovered the Foreign Office was already looking for a spy when Sandhurst came to Colonel Thomas pointing the finger at you."

"Since I am not a spy, the traitor must still be out there."

"Exactly so. Which is the reason Thomas agreed to release you into our custody. We pointed out to him that if he is wrong about you — which both of us and a number of others are convinced — he is allowing the real spy to continue to betray our country. We convinced him that you were the best man to discover the identity of the traitor, and suggested that since you are Russian, you could easily move about in the Russian community. If anyone can find the traitor, you can. Of course, you will also have to find sufficient proof."

Travis shoved to his feet. "You're telling me I can finally leave this damnable house?"

"I am. As long as what you do when you leave helps us find the man who has betrayed his country."

Travis paced over to the hearth, where a low fire burning against the grate warmed the room. His body thrummed with nervous energy — to say nothing of unsatisfied lust. He had been too long without a woman, he told himself. It wasn't that he desperately wanted this particular female.

"So how do I begin?" he asked.

"Word has been purposely leaked that the authorities believe you may be selling secrets to the Russians. The plan is for you to begin frequenting places and people in the Russian community. Let it be known you are selling information. If we get lucky, someone will be interested in buying it."

Travis nodded. "And once I have a name, we may be able to strong-arm the fellow into telling us who else might be involved."

"Exactly. It's dangerous, so you'll have to be careful."

"I'll be careful. I spent a little time in the neighborhood when my mother was still alive. I met a few people. It shouldn't be hard to renew old acquaintances, make a few new ones."

"That's what I hoped you would say."

Travis paced over to the sideboard. "You ready for a drink?"

"More than ready."

"Brandy all right?"

"Perfect."

Travis unstoppered a crystal snifter and poured them each a drink. He handed a cut-crystal glass to Reese.

"So what's this other problem?" Reese asked, inhaling the aroma, then taking a sip.

"Woman trouble."

"Ahh . . ."

If there was one man in the world he could trust, it was Reese. "I mentioned Lady Annabelle?"

"Yes, I believe you did."

"Well, it seems we share a mutual . . . attraction."

"Is that so?"

"I didn't realize . . . I mean, until she came here that day . . . it never actually occurred to me to . . . The thing of it is, she pointed out that she is a widow. She says

334

everyone knows that widows have special needs."

Reese's eyes widened. "Annabelle said that?"

Travis nodded. "As I said, we've known each other for quite some time."

Reese shrugged his shoulders. "Annabelle's a grown woman. I suppose if the two of you are mutually agreed, an affair wouldn't be —"

Travis was appalled. "I can't do that! Anna was my sister's best friend!"

"And you don't think your sister would approve?"

"It isn't really that. I mean the thing is, Annabelle isn't the sort to have an affair."

"I never thought so until now."

"She's the kind of woman you marry."

"Ahhh. I am beginning to see the problem. On the other hand, now that you mention it, you could certainly do worse."

Travis shook his head. "Not a chance. I'm a dedicated bachelor. I could never settle down."

Reese just smiled. "That's what I used to say. Now that I'm married, it doesn't seem half bad. In fact, I discover there are a number of advantages."

"Name one."

Reese's smile broadened into a grin. "I

don't go around breaking out in a sweat."

Travis laughed for the first time in days. "Yes, I guess there is that."

"Whatever you do, I know you'll make the right decision. In the meantime, keep me posted. And don't go anywhere aside from your house and the Russian district. You do, Thomas is likely to set his bloodhounds on you."

Travis just nodded. He wouldn't do anything to provoke the colonel.

Instead he intended to focus his full attention on finding a spy.

Jared fell ill sometime before midnight. He tossed and turned and began to run a slight fever. Worried the illness might be serious, Mrs. Garvey awakened Elizabeth, which awakened Reese, who was sleeping in her bed.

Elizabeth followed the broad-hipped nanny down the hall, Reese moving purposely along beside her.

"Do you have any idea what could be wrong?" Elizabeth worriedly asked Mrs. Garvey at Jared's bedside.

"I don't know, my lady. You dropped in to see him before he went to sleep. Did you notice anything at the time?"

"Only that he seemed a little tired. I

thought he had simply been playing too hard with his friend, Mrs. Brody's son." The first real friend Jared had ever had.

"It's probably nothing to worry about. Likely he'll be fine by morning."

Elizabeth stared down at him, hoping it was true. But by morning, Jared's temperature had risen alarmingly and Reese summoned a physician. Then Jared's stomach began to rebel and he lost the contents several times.

Frantic with worry, Elizabeth sat next to her little boy's bedside, watching the doctor examine him. Reese paced up and down the hall outside the room, both of them anxiously awaiting the physician's prognosis.

Finally, Elizabeth could stand the waiting no longer. She stood up from her chair. "What is it, Dr. Petersen? He's burning up with fever and he can't keep anything on his stomach. What do you think is wrong?"

"I'm not certain yet. A boy his age . . . it could be any number of things. We'll keep an eye out for any sign of German measles or chicken pox. Or it could be a case of the mumps."

"But he doesn't show signs of any of those things. No rashes. No sore throat."

The doctor leaned over the boy, who had finally sunk into a restless sleep. The man was older than she would have liked, with thinning white hair and a short, straggly beard. She had never met him before but he was the closest physician in the area and he had come to help straightaway.

The white-haired doctor looked up at her. "Is there a chance the boy might have ingested something that didn't agree with him? Something that is causing his upset stomach?"

"Not that I know of. I'll ask Cook if he might have eaten something we don't know about." Her chest constricted. For the first time, it occurred to her that someone in the household might be responsible for Jared's illness. That someone might have given him something that resulted in his illness.

She looked over at Reese, who stood a few feet away. His jaw looked hard as granite. Clearly, he had come to that same conclusion.

Her heart began to clamor. She needed to speak to Cook straightaway.

Then Reese said the words she hadn't had the courage to utter. "Is there any chance, Doctor, that the boy could have been poisoned? Are his symptoms anywhere near the same?"

The older man's gaze flew to Reese's. "You believe there is a possibility that might have happened?"

"There's a chance. I can't tell you how it might have been done, or if anything was given to the boy at all. But yes, there is a chance."

The doctor's thin shoulders straightened. "We should take measures just in case. Since he has already emptied his stomach a number of times, we needn't worry about that." Dr. Petersen reexamined Jared's throat for any sign of blistering or any other indications that some sort of poisoning had occurred.

All the while, Elizabeth stood there with her heart in her throat, barely able to breathe and aching for her son. Had Mason managed to penetrate their defenses? Had he hired someone to harm Jared as she was certain he wished to do? Was there a conspirator in their midst?

"We'll keep a close watch on the boy for the next few hours," the doctor said. "Perhaps some symptom will occur that will give us the answers we need."

Throat aching, Elizabeth gave him a nearly imperceptible nod. This was her fault entirely. She had married a viper and now her son was paying for her mistake. Her legs felt weak. She sank back down in the chair beside the bed.

"I'm going down to the kitchen," Reese said. "I'll speak to Cook and her helpers, see if they noticed anyone prowling about the kitchen who shouldn't have been there."

Elizabeth just nodded.

She felt Reese's hand settle gently on her shoulder. "You mustn't think the worst — not yet. It is not uncommon for boys Jared's age to fall ill with one thing or another. My brothers and I . . . there was rarely a time when one of us wasn't sick with something. We all managed to survive."

She looked up at him. "What if . . . what if it's Mason?"

Reese's jaw turned to stone. "Then he is a dead man." Turning away from her, he left the bedroom and headed downstairs. Elizabeth knew he was as worried as she, and emotion filled her chest. She had a caring husband and a wonderful son. The sort of life she had always imagined.

Dear God, she treasured each day with them.

For the next three hours, Jared slept. Since there was no change in his condition, Dr. Petersen left to visit another patient living nearby with the promise he would return.

During the late afternoon, Jared suffered several more rounds of vomiting and afterward, each time fell into an alarmingly deep slumber. Reese's unlikely valet, Timothy Daniels, stopped by several times during the day to check on the boy and Elizabeth appreciated his concern.

"He's going to be all right, isn't he?" the young corporal asked.

"I'm sure he is," Elizabeth replied, though just saying the words made her throat ache, since she wasn't certain at all. "He'll be fine in a couple of days."

"When he wakes up, tell him I came by to see him, will you?"

She managed a smile. "Of course. Thank you, Timothy."

By the time the doctor returned that evening, Elizabeth was exhausted. Reese tried not to show his worry, but she knew he remained as frightened as she.

The doctor examined Jared as he slept. "His fever hasn't worsened. Is he still vomiting?"

"Not for at least several hours."

Dr. Petersen nodded. "That's good. But be sure to have someone in the room at all times."

"We won't leave him alone." The request was unnecessary. She had no intention of leaving her son's bedside.

"I'll be back first thing in the morning."

"Thank you, Doctor." Elizabeth watched

him leave, praying Jared would be better by the time the doctor returned. Several times during the night, Reese insisted on trading her places and she didn't have the heart to refuse him. Jared was his son — even if he didn't know it.

Still, she couldn't sleep. By the time the sun came up, she was tired clear to the bone. Though Mrs. Garvey had brought up a tray, she couldn't swallow a bite to eat. Her legs felt shaky and her hands trembled.

"His color looks better," Reese said, standing over the child's bedside. "And he hasn't vomited since midnight." Reese hadn't slept either. It was obvious how attached he had become to their son. He rested a hand on Jared's forehead, tenderly smoothed back his perspiration-drenched hair. "His fever is gone this morning. He seems to be sleeping much more peacefully."

Elizabeth leaned over the bed and adjusted the covers over Jared's narrow chest. His forehead did indeed feel cooler to the touch.

"It's too soon to know for sure," Reese said, "but I think he's going to be all right."

"He is definitely improved."

"I don't think he was poisoned."

"I don't think so, either." But there was no way to be certain. And in truth, it no longer mattered.

342

During the long, frightening hours of the night, Elizabeth's terror had forced her to make a decision. Nothing was more important that her little boy's safety.

Not money, not power, not an exalted position in society.

The earldom simply wasn't worth Jared's life.

She looked up at Reese. "Thank you for helping."

"I wasn't much help, I'm afraid, but I'm glad he is so much better." Leaning down, he gently touched the little boy's cheek.

There were smudges beneath Reese's eyes and a shadow of beard darkened the line of his jaw. As he left the room, his expression was hard and Elizabeth was sure he was thinking of Mason Holloway and the threat he continued to pose.

Her own thoughts ran much the same. Crossing the room, she tugged on the bell-pull, summoning Gilda to run an errand for her.

The gangly blond girl appeared a few minutes later and dropped into a curtsey. "Ye rang, milady?"

"I need you to bring my portable writing desk up here, Gilda. I've a letter I wish to post."

"Aye, ma'am." She flicked a glance toward

the bed. "Your son . . . I hope he's feelin' better."

"I think he is. We'll know more once he awakens."

"He is such a sweet little boy. Always nice to everyone. Ye can be proud of him, milady."

Elizabeth's throat closed up. "I am, Gilda. I'm very proud of him."

The girl left the room and returned a few minutes later with the articles Elizabeth needed. Setting the small oak desk on her lap, she placed a sheet of paper on the top, dipped the plumed pen in the inkwell and began to scribe her letter.

Mason,

I believe I have a proposition that will interest you. Meet me at the Horn and Hoof Tavern on Kentish Town Road tomorrow at the hour of noon. Come in through the rear entrance. I promise your journey will be worthwhile.

Elizabeth

Elizabeth sealed the note with a drop of wax. After checking on Jared and summoning Mrs. Garvey to sit with him until her return, she headed downstairs.

"Mr. Longacre, will you please see this

letter reaches London — number three St. George Street." She knew Mason and Frances were in London, which meant they would be staying in the Aldridge town house, as Edmund had given them the right to do. "I would like it to get there as soon as possible."

"Very well, my lady." The butler took the note and went to retrieve a footman to see it delivered.

Tomorrow Reese had an early morning meeting in the city. It was certain to take him most of the day. Elizabeth planned to travel to the tavern with Mr. Montague, then instruct him to wait outside.

She had something to offer Mason.

Something he wanted above all things.

She thought that perhaps Reese would approve her idea, but she couldn't take the chance. She needed to act now, before the adoption was final, while she, as his mother and the Countess of Aldridge, was still Jared's legal guardian.

She would do whatever she had to in order to protect her son.

TWENTY-ONE

Reese stared out the window of his carriage, watching at the passing landscape, a cottage here and a tavern there scattered along the road.

He was returning from his meeting with his solicitor, Edward Pinkard, signing a few more papers pertaining to the adoption, assuring the man that he and Elizabeth would be in London for the hearing.

After Jared's illness and the terrible fear he had managed to keep hidden, Reese had realized adopting the boy was no longer a matter of helping to protect Jared from the Holloways. It was simply a matter of providing the child with a loving home and a father who cared for him, something the boy deserved and had never gotten from Aldridge.

Grudgingly, Reese admitted the little boy had managed to find a way into his well-guarded heart. He loved the child as if he were truly his own and he would protect the boy with his last ounce of breath.

The wheel jolted into a pothole, jarring Reese from his thoughts. He glanced out the window and recognized a portion of the landscape marking the halfway point on his journey home. The Horn and Hoof Tavern loomed ahead.

Reese frowned as the coach drew near and he spotted a familiar carriage out in front bearing the gilded crest that marked it as belonging to the Countess of Aldridge. Worry lanced through him. What in God's name was Elizabeth doing here?

Reese rapped on the ceiling with the silver head of his cane. "Pull over, driver."

Harness jangled as his coach rolled to a stop behind Elizabeth's, and Reese stepped down from inside. As he climbed the stairs to the porch, he caught sight of the security guard, Jack Montague, standing beside the front door.

"Montague! What are you doing here? What in blazes is going on?"

"You needn't worry, sir. I checked the place thoroughly before the countess went inside. All is well."

"What the devil is she doing here?"

"She didn't say, sir. Just that she needed half an hour at the tavern and she wanted me to come along as protection."

Reese's worry only heightened. Turning away from the guard, he walked into the tavern but saw no sign of Elizabeth and headed for the private room in the rear that he and Royal had used for their meeting. The door was closed, but he could hear voices coming from inside, a male and a female. He recognized Elizabeth's voice and his stomach knotted. She was secretly meeting a man.

Fury tightened the muscles across his shoulders. Elizabeth had betrayed him once before. By God, he wouldn't allow her to do it again!

It took iron control to clamp down on his anger. He needed to be certain of what was happening in the room before he lost his temper. Quietly turning the knob, he eased the door open a crack. He could hear the conversation clearly and then he got a glimpse of Mason Holloway.

"I am offering you everything you have ever wanted," Elizabeth said. "In return, I want you to leave Jared alone."

Relief hit him so hard a tremor went through him. She wasn't cheating on him with another man. She was trying to protect her son.

In the wake of relief, anger rose again.

Why the hell hadn't she come to him, told him what she planned? How could she be so foolish as to put herself in danger?

Reese forced himself to stay where he was and listen to the conversation. He needed to know the whole of it before he intervened.

Mason looked stunned. "Are you telling me you will sign the papers forfeiting Jared's claim to the Aldridge title?"

Elizabeth pressed forward. "That is exactly what I am saying." Seeing Mason again reminded her how ruthless he could be and assured her she was doing the right thing. "The lands and money that come with the earldom will also be yours, of course. Jared will not suffer. My father left me extremely well off. And my husband has money of his own."

"Money, perhaps, but not the massive wealth that belongs to your son. Are you certain Dewar will agree?"

"He doesn't have to agree. Until the adoption is final, I am Jared's guardian. I have the power to abdicate the title in his name. I only wish I had thought of it sooner."

Beneath his thick mustache, the edge of Mason's mouth lifted smugly. "Come now, you wanted the boy to be an earl. You wanted him to have the power and wealth that goes with the Aldridge title. Deep down, you are no different than I am."

Her stomach rolled. She was nothing at all like Mason. "I am entirely different from you. I would never contemplate murder, no matter how great the financial reward."

Mason flicked an imaginary piece of lint from the lapel of his coat. He looked up at Elizabeth. "So then, we are agreed. You will take the legal steps necessary to see the abdication made legal and there will no longer be any need to worry about the safety of your son."

Her lips thinned. "Then you admit you planned to kill him."

"Don't be ridiculous." One of his eyebrows arched up. "On the other hand, if some unfortunate accident happened to claim the child's life, leaving me in line for the earldom . . ."

"You are a monster."

Holloway just laughed. "Actually, what you're doing is only setting matters aright. We both know the boy isn't my brother's son."

Her chest squeezed and she struggled to keep her voice steady. "What . . . what are you talking about?"

"You seem surprised I know. Edmund and

I were extremely close. He was sick as a child. My brother was infertile. He told me Jared wasn't his son but he never said who had actually fathered the boy. Whose by-blow is he, by the way?"

Elizabeth was afraid her legs would give way and she would collapse right there on the floor. "That . . . that is none of your concern. Legally Jared is the earl." She stiffened her spine. "As I said, I am offering you everything you've ever wanted."

Mason smiled wolfishly. "You have two weeks. Take the necessary steps and all will be well."

"I am not at all certain I can get the legalities taken care of that fast."

"Oh, I imagine you can." Holloway dragged his overcoat off the back of a chair. As he swung it round his thick shoulders, the door leading in from the tavern burst open.

Elizabeth was stunned to see Reese standing in the doorway. She had never seen anything so terrifying as the look on his face.

"Get out," he said to Mason, his voice low and dark, his iron control making him appear all the more dangerous. "Get out before I kill you right here."

Holloway cast a last glance at Elizabeth,

his message clear. Jared's life was in her hands.

Wordlessly, he strode to the back door, pulled it open, and disappeared out of the tavern. Elizabeth returned her attention to Reese, knowing he would be angry with her for meeting Mason, but his expression was far worse than that.

"Aldridge was infertile," he said. "Jared wasn't his son."

Fear slammed through her. He had been listening! He knew the truth about Jared! God in heaven, why hadn't she told him? Why had she waited so long?

His fierce blue eyes burned into her. "What is the man's name?" he pressed, his jaw so tight he could barely force out the words. "Who is Jared's father?"

But she could tell by the look on his face that he knew. That he had known the moment the words slipped from Mason's mouth. Tears stung her eyes as he moved toward her, reached out and gripped her shoulders so hard she winced. "Who is he?"

She looked into his beloved face and the tears in her eyes rolled down her cheeks. "You're his father. Jared is your son."

A muscle bunched in his lean cheek. He released her so abruptly, she almost fell.

"You were carrying my son when you married Edmund Holloway? You were carrying my child and you didn't tell me?"

The lump in her throat was so thick she couldn't swallow. She moistened her lips, which felt cotton dry. "My father forbid me to tell you. He wanted me . . . to marry Aldridge."

"What kind of woman denies a man his son?"

She shook her head and more tears fell. "You were leaving . . . going off to war. I was pregnant and unmarried and I was . . . I was afraid." She pushed the words past the tightness in her throat. "I didn't want to bear a child alone."

His hands unconsciously fisted. "The baby was mine! The child you carried was mine!"

He was barely hanging on to his temper. His face was distorted with rage and for the first time she was afraid. Images of Edmund arose. She could almost feel his fists slamming into her face.

"I — I should have been stronger," she said. "I should have done what was right. But my father . . . my father convinced me."

He moved closer, towered above her. Elizabeth flinched and backed away.

Reese took a deep, calming breath. "I'm not like Aldridge, Elizabeth. I've never hit a woman and I never will. No matter what she might have done."

A sob welled, escaped from her throat. "I'm so sorry, Reese. I've been sorry every day since the day I married Edmund."

Reese's jaw hardened even more. "Were you ever going to tell me?"

She bit down on her trembling lips. "I wanted to. I planned to tell you before the adoption went through. I should . . . should have done it sooner. I meant to, but I . . . I couldn't find the courage." *And I didn't want to lose you. I love you, Reese.*

"Does anyone else know the truth?"

"Your aunt Agatha. She saw Jared and she knew."

His eyes briefly closed. "I should have seen it myself. I should have figured it out." He shook his head. "I missed all those years with my son. All those years."

"You were in the army. That was the life you wanted."

"He was my son!"

Her eyes brimmed. "I know."

He walked over to the door and she thought that he would leave. But he waited, held the door as she donned her woolen cloak and passed by him, her head bent as she walked toward the front of the tavern.

Jack Montague stepped away from the wall as she made her way out onto the porch. Elizabeth kept walking. She climbed into her carriage and Reese closed the door behind her.

"I was more of a fool than I thought," he said from outside the carriage window. "I don't know how I could actually have believed you loved me."

Elizabeth's heart twisted.

"I'll never forgive you, Elizabeth."

The coach jolted into motion and a sob of anguish caught in her throat. As a girl, she had loved him. She simply hadn't loved him enough.

Dear God, how that had changed.

Reese followed the butler down the hall to the study in Royal's town house. His chest felt as if a stone rode on top. He should be home but he simply wasn't ready to face the boy he now knew was his son.

Instead, when he stepped into Royal's favorite book-lined chamber, he saw his fair-haired brother seated behind his desk, and across from him, his dark-haired younger brother, Rule.

Royal's eyes widened as he spotted Reese and he shot to his feet. "My God, what's happened?"

Rule stood up, too, both of them clearly worried at the grim look on his face.

"It's not the boy?" Rule asked worriedly. "Nothing's happened to Jared?"

Reese shook his head. He walked over to the sideboard and lifted the stopped off a decanter of brandy. "Jared's all right. He was sick for a couple of days. We were both terrified that Holloway had somehow managed to infiltrate our defenses, but that doesn't appear to be the case."

"And he is recovered?" Rule asked.

Reese took a large swallow of brandy, felt the burn of the amber liquid as it trickled into his stomach. "Jared is fine."

"Well, clearly you are not," Royal said. "I want to know what's wrong."

Ever the demanding duke, Reese thought, and another time might have smiled. He raked a hand through his hair. "Jared is my son."

Royal frowned. "I thought the proceedings were still a few weeks away."

Reese just looked at him. "I'm his father, not Edmund Holloway."

"Good God." Royal sank back down in his chair.

"He looks like you," Rule said, also sitting back down. Reese tossed his brother a single dark glance. Everyone seemed to see the resemblance but him.

"Before I left for the army, there was a

night . . . Elizabeth and I . . . well, suffice it to say, Jared was the result of what happened that night."

For several long seconds, silence descended on the study.

"Elizabeth never told you," Royal said darkly.

"No."

"So how did you find out?" Rule asked.

Reese took another swallow of brandy. "A little past noon on my way back to the house, I happened upon her carriage. It was parked in front of the Horn and Hoof. As it turned out, she was there to meet Mason Holloway, though of course I didn't know it until I found them together in the back room. I overheard most of the conversation. She told Holloway she would see that Jared forfeited his rights to the earldom if he would guarantee the boy's safety."

"And . . . ?" Royal pressed.

"And Holloway said it was only fair. He said he deserved the earldom since Jared wasn't Edmund's son."

Rule hissed in a breath.

"And Elizabeth admitted the truth?" Royal pressed.

Reese just nodded. He took another gulp of his drink. He figured if he managed to get at least half drunk then Elizabeth's second, even larger, betrayal wouldn't hurt so badly.

"Why didn't she tell you? The two of you expected to wed. If the child came a few weeks early, it wouldn't have mattered."

"She said her father pushed her to marry Aldridge. The truth is she wanted to marry him."

"She said that?" Rule asked.

"Not in so many words. She said she knew I would be gone and she didn't want to be alone." He finished the last of his drink and returned to the sideboard to refill his glass. "I should have known better than to trust her again. I shouldn't have let down my guard."

"You've always loved her, Reese," Royal said softly. "When she came to you for help, you had no choice but to give her your aid."

Reese carried his glass over to the sofa and sat down wearily. "I don't know what to do. She's my wife and Jared is my son. I can't just leave and I don't know if I can stay."

"Was she ever going to tell you the truth?" Royal asked.

Reese sighed. "I don't know. She said she was planning to. I don't know what to believe anymore. I don't even know if it matters."

What mattered, he realized, was that he loved his son. Had come to love the little boy when everything inside him warned him not to.

What no longer mattered was that he had begun to fall in love with Elizabeth all over again.

Or perhaps, as his brother said, he had never truly stopped loving her.

He let his head fall back on the sofa.

"You can stay here, if you like," Royal offered, "until you figure things out."

Reese shook his head. "I have to go home. I have to make sure the boy is safe."

"If Elizabeth agreed to forfeit Jared's inheritance, Mason has no reason to hurt him."

"I know. If I had known he was my son, I might have suggested it myself — though it galls me to reward that bastard for trying to kill both Elizabeth and the boy. On the other hand, now that I know the truth, I don't want Jared taking anything from Aldridge."

"So you'll tell Elizabeth to go ahead with the abdication?" Royal asked.

"If that is her wish." He sighed. "I've got to go back. I've missed seven years of my son's life. I don't want to miss anymore."

Another lengthy silence descended. Rule

poured himself a drink, as well as one for Royal. He carried his brother's glass over and handed it to him.

"You'll figure all of this out," Rule said. "Just give it a little time." He took a sip of brandy. "I've got a bit of news that might take your mind off your troubles for a while."

Reese straightened. "What is it?"

"I had a meeting with Lady Sandhurst."

One of Reese's black eyebrows arched up. "A meeting? That is what you call it?"

Rule grinned wickedly. "I told you we were acquainted. Her husband is away and the lady was lonely. After our . . . meeting . . . she was pleasantly relaxed. Enough so that when I asked her about her husband, she was willing to talk."

Reese sat forward. "What did she say?"

"She said she was the one who told Sandhurst about the journal. She was angry at Travis for the way he had treated her. I took that to mean putting such an abrupt end to their relationship."

"So Sandhurst didn't just overhear. His wife goaded him into making those accusations."

"Perhaps. But she also told me that until three years ago, Lord Sandhurst was in desperate financial straits. Fortunately, events began to turn in his favor and there hasn't been a problem since."

Reese swirled the brandy in his glass. "There is big money in spying, which means Sandhurst may, in some way, be involved."

"You're thinking he may be the one who is buying and selling secrets," Royal added. "Finding out about the journal was information he could use to his advantage."

"It seems plausible," Reese said. "It would certainly account for his sudden influx of money."

"I agree," Rule said. "Sandhurst has any number of connections. From what I've heard, not all of them are with people of the highest reputation."

Reese pondered that. "I'll get the information to Travis. Maybe he can find a connection between Sandhurst and someone in the Russian community."

"I'll talk to Night and the others," Royal put in, "see what information they might be able to add."

"Once you collect all the facts," Rule said, "perhaps the picture will become clearer."

"In the meantime —" Royal shot a pointed look at Reese "— try to keep a clear picture of what is important to you. Sometimes people make mistakes. I nearly married the wrong woman and for all the wrong reasons."

"Perhaps Elizabeth regrets what happened," Rule added. "Perhaps she was hoping the two of you could make a fresh start."

Reese made no reply.

"Think about it," Royal urged.

Upending his glass, Reese swallowed the last of his brandy, set the crystal snifter down on the table and started for the door.

"Thanks for the information," he said. "And for the advice."

"Take care, brother," Royal called after him as Reese walked out the door.

TWENTY-TWO

At the sound of the butler's voice coming from the door to the drawing room, Lily Dewar set aside the feather-trimmed bonnet she had been sewing.

"What is it, Rutgers?" She and Royal yet remained in London. Royal refused to return to the country as long as his brother needed his help.

"You've a visitor, Your Grace. Lady Annabelle Townsend. Shall I send her in?"

"Why, yes, please do."

Lily felt a stirring of excitement. She and Annabelle had become friends when Anna had helped her and Royal as they worked to regain the fortune that had been swindled from Royal's father.

"Lily!" Annabelle hurried forward, heavy silk skirts rustling as she moved. "It is so good to see you!"

"You as well, Anna." The women briefly embraced. "It has been too long since last we spoke."

"Yes, it has." Lily rang for tea and they chatted pleasantly until the tea cart rattled into the drawing room. Seated on the sofa, Lily filled two gold-rimmed porcelain cups, added lumps of sugar, set two sweet biscuits on each saucer and offered a serving to Annabelle.

"I hope you don't mind my intruding this way," Anna said, stirring her tea and sending the scent of jasmine into the air. "It isn't my usual behavior."

Lily smiled. "Not a'tall. I am grateful for the company. Royal has been busy lately trying to help Reese and his friend, Captain Greer."

Annabelle's cheeks colored faintly. "Actually, that is one of the reasons I am here. As you know, Captain Greer is my friend, as well. I was very close to his sister."

"So I understand."

"Beatrice was a lovely young woman. It broke all of our hearts when she died so young."

"Childbirth, wasn't it?"

Annabelle nodded. "Beatrice was one of the few people who knew my true feelings about her brother."

Lily's interest heightened. "You're speaking of the captain?"

"Yes. I fell in love with Travis when I was just fourteen. He was young and so very handsome. My affections grew over the years. By the time I was eighteen, he was a dashing cavalry officer and even more attractive. Unfortunately, he didn't return the sentiment. He wanted a life of adventure. Until recently, I never knew he had noticed me at all."

Lily sat forward on the sofa, her cup and saucer balanced carefully on her lap. "What happened?"

"I went to see him. Suffice it to say, I believe my attraction to Captain Greer is returned. The question I came here to ask is what I should do about it?"

Lily frowned. "Why are you asking me? I am hardly an expert on matters of the heart."

"I am asking you because you are a married woman whose opinion I trust. You see, I am considering having an affair with Travis."

Lily swallowed the bite of biscuit she had just taken. "I see."

"Normally, I would talk to my close friend, Lady Sabrina Jeffers. But she is younger than I, and the subject of an illicit relationship is hardly a discussion fit for a virgin. Besides, I don't think she could begin to understand."

Lily nodded. "I imagine you are right. Love isn't something you figure out until it happens to you."

Annabelle released a slow breath. "You realize I am speaking of an affair, not marriage. Neither of us has that in mind."

Lily made no reply. She didn't believe for a moment that if Annabelle loved Captain Greer, she would be happy until he loved her in return and they were husband and wife.

"I trust you, Lily," Annabelle continued. "You are one of the bravest women I have ever known. I knew you were in love with Royal the moment I saw the two of you together. Even when he was engaged to marry another woman, you had the courage to follow your heart."

"And now you wish to follow your own."

"Yes. Do you think I'm a fool?"

Lily smiled softly. "Not in the least. A woman has to do what she believes is right — as long as she is willing to face the outcome."

"You mean the heartbreak once the affair is over."

"Exactly."

"Even if I decide that is what I want, Travis won't pursue such an arrangement. He is too worried about my reputation. I shall have to be the one to make the first move."

"He sounds like an honorable man."

Anna smiled. "That is one of the reasons I've always loved him."

Lily brushed a crumb from the skirt of her gown then looked up at her friend. "Do what your heart dictates, Anna. That is my advice to you."

Annabelle set her cup and saucer down on the table in front of the sofa. She leaned over and caught Lily's hand.

"You are a dear friend, Lily. I promise when this is over, I shall not come here to cry on your shoulder."

"I wouldn't mind, Anna. I know what it is to love a man and have your heart broken. I am one of the few who managed to find a happy ending."

Annabelle just nodded. "I'm afraid I must leave. There are plans I must make."

"Remember I am here if you need me."

"Thank you, Lily. I am fortunate to call you friend."

As Annabelle left the house, Lily wondered if she had given her friend the best advice. Perhaps Captain Greer would fall in love with Anna, as Lily and Royal had fallen in love.

But as with any affair of the heart, there

was always the chance there would be no happy ending.

Reese hadn't realized how much he would miss her. Oh, she was there in the house, but they no longer shared meals together, no longer talked after the meal was over. At night, Elizabeth slept in the room next to his but he didn't go to her, didn't make love to her until both of them were sated, their bodies warmly entwined.

He hadn't realized how much he would miss the laughter that no longer echoed through the halls. He hadn't guessed the gnawing lust he had felt for her before would return with such powerful force.

And mingled with all those emotions was the anger that rode him morning to night, the knowledge that she had betrayed him far worse than he had ever imagined.

He had a son. A boy he loved and might never have known existed. And he wasn't even able to tell Jared the truth of his birth. It would be years before the child was old enough to understand the difference between his biological father and the man his mother had married, the father who had not wanted him when Reese wanted him so badly.

Elizabeth had done that. She had kept him

from his son for all of those years. She had married a man who had abused the boy, if only by withholding his love. Just thinking about it brought a renewed surge of anger. Elizabeth had denied him his son.

And yet, as furious as he was, he still wanted her. A moment didn't go by that he didn't lust for Elizabeth. A glimpse of her climbing the stairs made his loins grow thick and heavy. The brush of her skirts as they passed in the hall made him go rock-hard.

He was hard now just thinking of the times they had made love.

His fist slammed down on the desk in his study. She was his wife, dammit! Whatever she had done, she belonged to him. He imagined her naked and responsive, free from the fears Aldridge had instilled in her and once more the passionate creature she had been as a girl. He was her husband. As such, he had the right to her beautiful body.

The day passed and the hour grew late. He had seen her several times during the afternoon but they had not spoken. Still, the lust was there, goading him, driving him to think of her beneath him, her legs spread in welcome. He imagined filling her with his hard length, pounding into her until both of them reached an explosive release.

He wouldn't force her. God's blood, no

matter his need, he wasn't like Aldridge. But these past few days, each time he had seen her, each time they had chanced upon each other in the corridor, he had glimpsed the same need in her lovely gray eyes that burned in his own. She wanted him, just as he wanted her.

Seated behind his desk, Reese looked up at the brass hands of the clock on the mantel. He knew she had gone into the library to read after supper. He had asked Longacre to inform him when she retired upstairs to her room. The butler had done so just moments ago, retreating quietly afterward, silently closing the door.

Reese left his study and headed upstairs. At the sound of his uneven footfalls, Timothy Daniels stepped into the corridor, there to help him undress, but Reese just shook his head and Timothy slipped off toward his own room farther down the hall.

Reese walked past his suite. When he reached his wife's room next door, he didn't knock, simply turned the silver knob and walked into the bedroom. Elizabeth gasped at his unexpected arrival, her eyes going wide and uncertain. She had begun to undress and stood clothed in only her corset and petticoats. Her little maid, Gilda, pulled the last of the pins from her silky black hair.

Reese's groin tightened. Desire hit him like a fist in the stomach and his shaft began to fill.

"That will be all for tonight, Gilda," he said, his voice rough and husky, dismissing the maid, who turned and scurried out of the room.

Elizabeth didn't move, just stood frozen, her gaze locked on his face. Reese moved toward her, reached out and caught a lock of her curly raven hair. It felt silky between his fingers, and heat slid into his groin.

"I've missed you," he said softly, and her eyes filled with tears. He steeled himself. That wasn't the response he wanted. He wasn't there to offer forgiveness. The anger he felt still burned inside him, nearly as hot as his need.

"I've missed you, too," she said.

Reese ignored the unwelcome tightening in his chest. Instead, he bent his head and settled his mouth very softly over hers. He felt her tremble and moved to the side of her neck. "Perhaps I should have said I have missed making love to you."

Elizabeth stiffened. She understood his meaning. Nothing had changed. He hadn't forgiven her. Desire was all he felt. He wanted her and he had come there to have her.

Resting his hands lightly on her shoulders, he lowered his head and kissed her again, began to gently coax away her reluctance, to tease and sample until he felt her body soften, felt her full lips meld into his. On a sigh, she opened to him, giving him access, and his tongue slid into her mouth. She tasted faintly of citrus and he inhaled the fragrance of roses.

His arousal strengthened. His shaft was so hard he ached with each beat of his heart. He wanted release and he intended to have it. In return, he would give her the pleasure he had promised her from the start.

He glanced down at her lovely breasts, swelling above the top of her fancy lace corset, the one he had bought her at the lingerie shop, one of those that closed up the front. He kissed her as he unfastened the hooks all the way to her waist and her breasts spilled forward, into his waiting hands. He lifted each one, bent and took the fullness into his mouth.

A soft moan escaped. Her nipples were like firm, unripened berries, diamond-hard and so sweet his mouth watered at the taste of them. He bit down on the tips and suckled gently, kissed her neck, her shoulders, then returned to her breasts, laving and caressing until she swayed against him and he knew that she was as aroused as he. He wound his fingers into her heavy black curls, and tilted her head back, pressed his mouth against the rapid pulse beating at the base of her throat.

Slow, deep, erotic kisses had her trembling and Reese on the edge of control. Lust nearly blinded him. Desire rode him like a ravenous beast. He began to urge her backward, kissing her all the while, a slow, sensuous journey that brought her shoulders up against the wall.

"Lift your petticoats."

Her gaze found his, her eyelids languid and heavy. She trusted him in this, in making love, trusted him to make it good for her, and he intended that very thing. She caught handfuls of the soft white cotton fabric and hoisted it above her knees.

"Higher," he softly commanded. When the petticoats reached her waist, he kissed her again, deeply and thoroughly. He wanted to be inside her more than he wanted to breathe.

"Don't let go," he instructed, reaching beneath the fluffy fullness to untie her drawers. They whispered down over her hips and pooled at her feet. Elizabeth made a soft little mewling sound, but she didn't let go.

Skimming his hands over her naked flesh,

he circled her navel, moved over the flat spot below, ran a finger through the nest of raven curls between her legs, dipped between the soft folds of her sex.

Her hands were shaking. She was wet and ready. Elizabeth moaned as he began to stroke her and her hips arched toward him. She was hot and slick and it was all he could do not to bury himself to the hilt. Instead, he unfastened the tabs on her petticoats and slid them down to join her drawers, leaving her deliciously bare to the waist, her luscious breasts quivering, spilling from her corset, an offering he couldn't resist.

He suckled each of them, unzipped his trousers and freed himself. Kissing her deeply, he found her core, parted her flesh, and eased himself deeply inside.

Elizabeth moaned. Her fingers dug into his shoulders as he lifted her and wrapped her legs around his waist.

"Easy . . . I've got you." He took her with one penetrating stroke after another, took her and took her while Elizabeth clung to his neck and made soft little incoherent whimpers that nearly drove him over the brink. His control was slipping badly. His body burned with the need to spill his seed. He clamped down on the urge to satisfy his lust and continued the deep penetrations until her body clenched around him and Elizabeth cried out his name.

His control completely snapped. Every muscle in his body clenched, and hot seed spilled from his loins. Satisfaction poured through him, and a rush of pleasure unmatched by anything before.

No other woman could make him feel this way. No other woman but Elizabeth.

The knowledge sobered him. His need of her was too strong, too powerful. He couldn't afford to let it grow even stronger.

And yet, it felt so good to be inside her. So perfectly right.

Once he had loved her.

He couldn't afford to love her again.

Holding onto her waist, he withdrew from her tight, comforting warmth and set her back down on her feet. With her raven hair tousled and her breasts nearly bursting from the corset, she made the most erotic picture he'd ever seen.

Desire rose again, swift and greedy. Refusing to give in to the urge to carry her over to the bed and make love to her again, he began to rearrange his clothes and rebutton his trousers.

He looked up at the feel of her palm against his cheek. "Don't go . . ." she whispered. "Stay here with me."

His throat tightened. He wanted to stay so badly he ached. Then he thought of the night he had arrived home on his first leave only to discover that two days earlier, his future bride had married another man. He remembered the soul-crushing pain, the feeling of unbearable loss. He remembered the years of anger that had followed, changing him into a different man.

Reese removed the gentle hand pressed against his cheek and forced himself to turn away. "Sleep well, Elizabeth."

As he stepped out into the passage, he steeled himself against the sound of Elizabeth's tears, and the urge to return and pull her into his arms.

Elizabeth knelt in the front pew of the tiny chapel at Holiday House. It was a lovely, quiet place, the walls paneled in ornately carved rosewood, the interior brightened by rows of stained glass windows. Her mother had taken her there when she was a little girl, and though she had come several times when she was older, it wasn't the same.

This morning, Elizabeth had felt the need to visit the chapel again, to light the candles on the altar, to kneel in front of the cross and seek forgiveness for her sins.

Once she had believed strongly in God.

After she had married Edmund, her belief in God had faded beneath the pain that no amount of prayer seemed to lessen. Then Edmund had died. Mason and Frances had taken control of her life and again God seemed to have abandoned her and her son.

The night she had fled Aldridge Park, she had prayed to God as she hadn't in years. She had asked for His aid in saving her son, and in His wisdom, He had sent her to Reese. He had given her the chance to make amends to her son and his father, a chance to find the happiness she hadn't known since she had lost Reese all those years ago.

Elizabeth's throat ached. Bending her head, she began to pray, asking again for God's wisdom, asking Him to help her find a way through the muddle she had made of her life, a way back to Reese.

A sob welled in her throat and tears rolled down her cheeks. Dear God, she loved him so much.

She wasn't sure how long she knelt there, but when she rose, her knees ached and the lace shawl she wore over her head had slipped to her shoulders. Her cheeks were wet and her heart felt utterly broken. And yet, she could not give up hope. She loved Reese and perhaps in time she would find a way to make him believe in her love again.

When she turned to start up the aisle, she caught a glimpse of someone leaving the chapel. One of the guards, she was sure.

Reese was still being watchful. He didn't trust Mason, though tomorrow they would travel as a family to London to meet with Reese's solicitor and begin the legalities that would result in Jared's abdication of the Aldridge title. She had convinced Reese to rent a furnished town house for the next few weeks, since the journey back and forth to Holiday House was tiring and they were unsure how long the proceedings might take or even if the courts would grant their petition.

In the meantime, until Mason was earl, Elizabeth, like Reese, would also be watchful.

And she would remain hopeful.

Dear God, help him learn to love me again, she silently prayed as she made her way up the aisle and out of the chapel.

TWENTY-THREE

Reese walked away from the tiny chapel, his chest once more leaden. He had wanted to speak to Elizabeth about their upcoming journey to London. Or perhaps he simply wanted to see her. He had found her there in the chapel, kneeling in prayer. Respecting her privacy, he hadn't intruded.

Reese thought of the years she had denied him his son and wondered if she prayed for forgiveness, though lately he had begun to think that living with Aldridge, suffering his abuse, was penance enough.

It wasn't what he wanted to believe. He wanted to stay angry. To guard himself and remain aloof from the powerful attraction he felt for her. Again and again, he reminded himself of her betrayal eight years ago, the son she had kept from him, the hell he had endured in loving her. Again and again, he told himself he dared not trust her.

As he made his way out to the stable to

see his son, he worked to keep his anger alive, simmering just beneath the surface, but it was getting harder and harder to do.

Spotting Jared in the arena, hard at work with the riding master, Mr. Hobbs, Reese stopped a moment just to watch him. The little boy sat atop the small gray horse, listening to his instructor and grinning from ear to ear.

Emotion swelled in Reese's chest. Jared was the son of his loins, his blood. God had given him the child he had always wanted. Reese saw it now, the likeness he should have seen before. The familiar way the boy's eyebrows winged over his eyes, the small indentation in his chin. Even the curve of his mouth seemed familiar. Reese wondered why he hadn't noticed the resemblance from the start.

But he had been blinded by Elizabeth's claim that the boy belonged to Aldridge. And certain the precautions he had taken that night had been enough to protect her.

In truth, there was no way to be certain. He had been a novice at sex and in love and unsure even what exactly to do.

He looked over at the child in the ring. Jared was a natural rider, just as Reese had been. At seven years old — not six as Reese had believed — he stuck to the saddle like a burr in wool, handling the horse with confidence and ease, undaunted even after yesterday's unexpected tumble. Reese watched him circle the pony round the ring, urging the animal faster.

"Very good, my boy!" said his instructor, a fortyish, slender man with hair as dark as Jared's. "You have a nice manner with Dusty and he is enjoying himself, just as you are."

"Can I jump him?"

Hobbs shook his head. "You are only just a beginner. Walk him over to the fence and let him step over it. Let him get used to the motion."

Jared did as instructed, allowing the pony to examine the low fence, then step over it.

"Now, again."

The boy repeated the action several more times before the lesson came to an end.

Hobbs smiled. "That will be all for today. You did a very good job."

Reluctantly, Jared handed the reins to one of the grooms and ran out of the ring, heading back to the house to resume his studies. He didn't see Reese until he was almost upon him, then the boy slid to a halt and the grin on his face instantly faded.

Reese forced himself to smile, uncertain what this new reticence meant, wishing he could find a way to break through the child's defenses. "You did very well out there today."

Jared said nothing, just stared up at him. Reese could read the turmoil on his face, what seemed to be worry mingled with fear.

"What's the matter, son?" Reese asked, kneeling in front of the boy, beginning to worry himself.

Jared flicked a glance toward the house, looked back at Reese as if there were something important he wished to say but didn't know how to begin.

"Go on, tell me."

"You're angry at my mother."

Reese took a breath. He should have expected something like this. The boy loved his mother. Of course the child would notice the rift between them. "We quarreled. That happens between married people sometimes."

Jared's small jaw jutted forward. Reese noticed his hands unconsciously fisted. "I won't let you hurt her."

His chest knotted with emotion. Regret for the way things were and a yearning for what could not be. "I would never hurt you or your mother. Nothing either of you could do could make me do that."

"It . . . it happened to her before."

Reese chose his words carefully. "You

mean before you came here?"

Jared nodded. His defiant stance did not alter. "I saw him. I saw him hit her. He did it more than once."

"Aldridge?"

Another slow up and down motion.

Reese reached out and cupped the little boy's cheek. "I won't ever hit her. I give you my word on that."

Jared's dark eyes filled with tears. Reese ached to lift him into his arms and give him the assurance he needed. But there was something in his expression, something more the boy needed to say. Reese held his breath, silently urging the child to continue.

Jared looked up at him and his bottom lip trembled. "I should have helped her. I should have tried to make him stop but . . . but I didn't. I was afraid he would hit me, too."

Reese's heart squeezed. "You were just a little boy. You couldn't have stopped him. There was nothing you could do."

The tears in the Jared's eyes rolled down his cheeks. He angrily wiped them away. "I won't let anyone hurt her again."

Reese couldn't breathe. His chest was aching as if someone had punched him with a fist. Scooping the child up in his arms, he held him against his chest. "I'll protect your mother. And I'll protect you. I promise I'll keep both of you safe. You don't ever have to be afraid again."

Jared's small arms went round his neck and the little boy buried his head in Reese's shoulder. Reese's eyes were burning and his throat ached too much to swallow. Jared started to cry in earnest and Reese didn't try to stop him. Just held him gently until his crying eased.

"It's all right," he soothed, the child still tight in his arms. "Everything is going to be fine." He took a steadying breath, trying to rein in his emotions, consigning Edmund Holloway to the depths of hell.

As he started back to the house, his leg hurting less than the ache in his chest, he spoke softly to the child, reassuring him once more that everything would be all right. When he reached the back door, he set the boy on his feet, took out his handkerchief and wiped away the last of his son's tears.

"Ready to go back in?"

Jared nodded. He seemed to stand up a little straighter, as if the burden of his undeserved guilt had been washed away. Reese took hold of his hand and they walked inside together.

"Is everything all right?" With a mother's

instincts, Elizabeth hurried toward them, gazing worriedly at her son.

"Everything is fine."

The boy looked up at him. Reese understood that look and a silent vow passed between them. Whatever they had shared would remain theirs alone.

Elizabeth turned to Jared, a hint of concern still lingering in her voice. "Mr. Connelly is waiting. When you didn't arrive upstairs on time, he began to worry."

"It was my fault," Reese explained. "I kept him overlong at the stable."

Elizabeth managed to smile. "You had better go on upstairs. You don't want to keep Mr. Connelly waiting any longer."

Jared cast Reese a last grateful glance and rushed toward the staircase. Reese watched him all the way to the second set of stairs that led to the newly refashioned nursery that now served as a schoolroom.

Reese turned to Elizabeth. "He worries about you."

Elizabeth gazed up the stairs. "I know."

"I don't want him to worry about you or anyone else."

She managed a shaky smile. "I'll talk to him, tell him I am fine."

Reese gently caught her shoulders. "I told him I would take care of you and I will. I'll take care of you both."

"I never doubted it."

Whatever happened between them, her trust in him never wavered. "We'll get past this, Elizabeth," he found himself saying. "We have to. We have a son to think of, a boy who needs a mother *and* a father."

She swallowed and her eyes brimmed with tears. "I wish I could change the past. We both know I can't. I should have told you the truth as soon as I came to Briarwood. I wanted to, but I . . ."

"But you what? Why did you wait, Elizabeth?"

"I needed time to gather the courage. After . . . after we were married, I wanted a chance for us to get to know each other again. A chance for us to be happy."

Something moved inside him. Reese had wanted that, too.

"I can't undo my mistakes," she went on, "but if you will give me a chance, I promise you, Reese, I'll do everything in my power to be the wife you deserve."

The wife he deserved. The wife she would have been eight years ago when she was just a girl?

Or perhaps something more. Perhaps she could also be the passionate lover and protective, giving mother she had grown into as she matured.

Oddly it seemed this was the woman he truly wanted.

"That's all a man can ask," Reese said a little gruffly. But of course there was more — much more.

Elizabeth could love him.

It surprised him to discover how much he wanted that to happen.

The hour was late, the London streets slick with mist, a heavy fog beginning to settle over this part of the city. Travis could barely make out the sign up ahead, lit by the lamplight spilling out of a nearby window, a tavern called Little Russia, the lettering on the sign printed in the Cyrillic alphabet.

Most of the signs in the neighborhood were printed in English. There was, after all, a war going on, and no one wanted to be singled out for trouble.

Travis passed the entrance to Little Russia, the taproom overflowing with raucous laughter and the sound of heavy glasses clinking together, and continued toward a spot halfway down the next block, a place called Nikolai's.

Travis knew the owner. Nikolai Godunov was married to a distant cousin of his mother's. Since Travis had begun prowling the district, he had made it a point to renew old acquaintances. He had been just a boy when his mother had taken him along with her while she paid calls on friends in the neighborhood, but the Russian community was close-knit, and his mother was well remembered as a famous ballerina.

Travis shoved through the doors and walked into the smoky, low-ceilinged taproom. The bearlike man mopping the bar lifted the towel he was using and waved it in Travis's direction.

"Eh, Aleksei!" the man called out, using Travis's Russian middle name. "Come in and I'll buy you a drink."

Travis forced himself to think in Russian. "It is good to see you, Nikolai." He ambled over to the bar and the big man poured him a shot of vodka and set the glass down in front of him. Travis reached for the glass and tossed it back, downing the liquor in one swallow.

Another shot quickly appeared. Travis let this one sit or another would be forthcoming and he had never been much of a drinking man and clearly a failure by Russian standards.

"So what brings you out on a night like this?" Nikolai asked, his voice as gruff as the bear he looked like.

Travis shrugged. "I don't know many people in London. Now that I'm back, it feels good to hear people speaking my mother's tongue."

Nikolai nodded as if he understood and moved off down the bar to serve another patron. Travis scanned the crowd. As he made his rounds, he would stop by Little Russia and a couple of other places. Word had been leaked that he had secrets to sell. Sooner or later, someone was bound to approach him.

After an hour in Nikolai's, another at Little Russia, and a stop at a place called Troyka, he knew it wouldn't be tonight. Frustrated with so little to show for the efforts he had been making, he hailed a hansom cab at the corner and headed back to his town house.

The place was no longer being watched, or if so only off and on. His servants mostly lived elsewhere and his butler would be retired to his third floor quarters for the night.

Travis found his way easily to the door. Apparently, the old man had left a lamp burning for him downstairs for soft light shone through the window. Travis quietly made his way inside the house and moved toward the drawing room to snuff out the lamp.

In the open doorway, he jerked to a halt. Lying on the plush ruby sofa, Annabelle Townsend lay curled on her side, a book lying open beside her. Her bonnet was missing, her light brown hair slightly mussed, several loose strands teasing her cheek.

Her lashes fluttered and her eyes shot open as he drew near, and she sat up on the sofa.

"Travis . . . you're home. . . ."

"Annabelle. What the devil are you doing here?" Worry crept in. Surely she wouldn't have come unless she needed his help. "Has something happened? Are you all right?"

Annabelle shoved back the stray lock of hair and smiled. Travis remembered she'd always had a lovely smile.

"I am fine. I told the butler it was urgent I see you. He said you had gone out but he didn't think you would be late in returning." She glanced at the clock. "I see he was wrong."

"Why did you need to see me?" He stopped right in front of her, so close he could smell her soft floral perfume.

"What you are going through can't be easy. I came to be certain you are all right. Are you?"

"Of course I'm all right. You shouldn't be here, Anna." But finding her in his drawing room, her blue silk gown slightly rumpled and her cheeks flushed so prettily, he couldn't deny he was glad to see her.

She got up from the sofa and walked toward him, her eyebrows dipping slightly together. "You've been gone a good long while. You weren't with a woman, were you?"

His eyes widened. "Of course not." He frowned. "Not that it would be any of your business if I were."

"I suppose not, but perhaps it would be . . . if we were having an affair."

An affair with Annabelle Townsend. Just the thought made him start to go hard. He clamped down on a surge of lust. "We aren't having an affair, Anna. And we aren't going to."

"Do you deny there is an attraction between us?"

He should. He should tell her she stirred him not in the least. It was difficult to do when his arousal strengthened every time he looked at her.

"Do you?"

"You're a beautiful woman, Anna. I won't deny I feel a certain attraction to you."

She stopped right in front of him. "Do

you want to make love to me, Travis?"

His pulse quickened, began to throb against his temple and in his groin. He couldn't believe he was having this conversation. "You shouldn't be asking me a question like that."

"Tell me, Travis, do you want to kiss me? Do you want to remove my clothes and make wild, passionate love to me? Because that is exactly what I want you to do."

Travis hissed in a breath. "Anna . . ."

"Answer me, Travis. Is that what you want?"

He could count his own heartbeats, so loud they rang in his ears. He had to stop this now, before it was too late.

"You want to know the truth, Anna? The truth is, I'd like to rip off every stitch of clothing you are wearing. I'd like to see you naked. I'd like to lay you down on the sofa, part your pretty legs, and bury myself inside you as deeply as I possibly could. I'd like to take you every way a man can take a woman, make love to you until neither of us has the strength to move. Is that what you want to hear?"

He waited for her shock and repulsion. He imagined her screaming and running from the house. He imagined her never speaking to him again, and though it tortured him to end their friendship in such a manner, it had to be done. He needed to protect her. From him and perhaps even herself.

Anna grinned. "I knew it!" Lifting her skirts and petticoats out of the way, she raced toward him, threw her arms around his neck and kissed him for all she was worth.

Travis groaned. He locked his arm around her waist, pulling her tightly against him, knowing she would feel his powerful erection but no longer able to care. He was rock hard and pulsing, aching for exactly what she offered.

"We can't," he whispered, between soft, nibbling kisses. "We can't do this, Anna." But the kisses turned hotter and deeper and his lust grew until he feared he might burst. "I don't . . . I don't want to ruin your good name."

"I'm a widow," she countered breathlessly, kissing the side of his neck. "And I've never been with a man I desired. I want you, Travis. I need you to make love to me."

"Anna . . ." He reminded himself she was his sister's best friend. He told himself to do what was right, to set her away from him and send her out in the cold. Instead, he kissed her again and again and couldn't seem to stop. Not until she took hold of his hand.

"Take me upstairs, Travis. Show me how good making love can be."

He shook his head but didn't let go of her hand and in the next instant, they were climbing the stairs and he was leading her into his bedroom. It was neat and orderly, Spartan compared to the rest of the house. He was a military man, after all, and when he saw the approval on her face, he felt an odd sort of relief.

"Are you certain, Anna? Are you sure you won't be repulsed by a man with only one arm?"

Anna gave him one of her sweetest smiles. "I don't give a whit about your arm. You are the most masculine man I have ever known and I have never been more certain of anything in my life."

The words filled his heart. It was foolishness. Utter insanity. He wouldn't marry her. He wasn't cut out to be a husband.

But as she lay gloriously naked beneath him, as he came up over her, filled her and began to move inside her, he thought that nothing had ever felt so good as having Anna Townsend in his bed. When he brought her to a stunning release topped only by the power of his own, he couldn't imagine ever letting her go.

Travis bent his head and kissed her, and ignored the unwelcome thought.

TWENTY-FOUR

Royal called a meeting of The Oarsmen. Reese received his brother's request to join them and prepared to meet them at White's that night. All the Dewars were members of the elite London gentlemen's club, though unlike his brothers, Reese rarely visited.

Still, he looked forward to the gathering tonight. He hoped one of the men had gleaned information that might help Travis. Or perhaps there was news of Mason Holloway.

Thoughts of the man made his stomach churn. Holloway was a blight on humanity, a man willing to kill innocents to get what he wanted. Though Reese wanted nothing for his son from the Earl of Aldridge, it galled him to think of the Holloways blackmailing Elizabeth into doing what they wanted.

Unfortunately — except for disposing of the man, a notion Reese found extremely appealing — there was no way to keep his son completely safe. Although he had killed men in war, murder was something altogether different. He wanted his family safe and he wanted a future with his son, and dispensing with Mason Holloway would only get him hanged.

His coach rolled to a stop in front of the big bay window marking the location of the club. Reese stepped down from the carriage and crossed to the door, relying on his cane only occasionally. His injured leg continued to improve, thanks in part to Corporal Daniels. Soon he intended to ride again, as he had vowed to do.

Reese passed a pair of blond footmen holding open the door and stepped into the quiet interior that as a younger man had unnerved him. He'd been too active, too restless for a staid establishment like White's. Now he found the subdued atmosphere oddly soothing.

It occurred to him that he had changed over the past few years. The life of adventure and travel he had once craved appealed to him little now.

He made his way past the main drawing room to a meeting room where the gathering was meant to take place. Seated on both sides of a long mahogany table, Royal,

Sherry Knowles, Quent Garret, and Dillon St. Michaels were already there. Jonathan Savage walked in a few paces behind him.

"Good evening, gentlemen," Jonathan said, seating himself across from Reese. Only his brother, Rule, was missing.

Reese almost smiled.

At three-and-twenty, his younger brother was still sowing his oats and a bit irresponsible. In time, Reese was certain that would change.

The men chatted amiably for a while. Then Royal brought the meeting to order.

"I've asked you all here to exchange the information you've collected. I know several of you have made discoveries. I'm hoping that by sharing them, we might come up with something we can use."

"Indeed," St. Michaels agreed, settling his muscular frame against the back of his chair.

Royal fixed his gaze on his best friend, Viscount Wellesley. "Sherry?"

"Just a bit of gossip, I'm afraid. I heard that Mason Holloway has been running up quite a debt about town. He has purchased an entirely new wardrobe, top to bottom, nothing but the best. His wife is also spending more money than apparently they have. Holloway has been convincing the merchants they will be well taken care of once he comes into the fortune he is owed."

A muscle ticked in Reese's jaw. He forced himself to stay calm. "My wife and I have agreed to abdicate Jared's title as earl. It's the only way to completely insure the boy's safety."

"Aside from eliminating the Holloways," St. Michaels drawled.

"Believe me, I've considered it. Unfortunately, without proof of their intent, killing Holloway would result in my hanging."

Sherry's mouth curved into a smile, exposing several crooked bottom teeth. "Yes, well, there is that."

"As Royal has probably told you," Reese continued, "the boy is mine and not Aldridge's, and I'd just as soon my son take nothing from the bastard who treated him so badly."

Savage's dark eyes swung in Reese's direction. "I can understand your thinking, but you must admit it's a great deal to give up. As he gets older, the boy might resent you for it."

"It's possible, I suppose, though I certainly hope not."

Royal spoke to the group again. "How about you, Quent?"

"Not much. Just that Holloway has been gaming fairly heavily. Word is, his markers will be golden in the very near future."

Reese swore softly.

"What about you, Savage?" Royal asked. "Anything new on the Van Meer murder?"

Jonathan straightened, his lean muscles tightening as he sat up in his chair. "I've been working with Morgan on this. It seems Holloway was Van Meer's silent partner in some sort of shipping swindle. A good deal of money was raised, all of which was supposedly lost to investors before Van Meer was killed. None of the money ever surfaced, but rumor has it the profits were to be split between the two men."

"So you think Holloway killed Van Meer and took the money they made on the swindle," Reese said.

"It's a damned good bet."

"Did you uncover any sort of proof?"

"Morgan's still working on it. He's been canvassing the neighborhood, trying to come up with someone who might know something. Van Meer had a son. Morgan's been trying to find him."

Reese just nodded. It was more than they'd known before, but still not enough.

At the head of the table, Royal turned his attention to St. Michaels, who only shook his head.

"Sorry, but so far I've struck out entirely.

400

I'll keep my ears open, though. Perhaps something will eventually turn up."

"You've done your best," Royal said, turning to the black-haired man who seemed the most solemn of the group. "Nightingale?"

The earl released a breath. "As you know, I've been working to help Captain Greer and I'm afraid my news isn't good. I spoke to my friend in the Foreign Office. Apparently, they believe the defeats the army suffered in June at Redan and Malakoff may have been due to inside information the Russians received. Prior to that time, Captain Greer was in London. They think he may have somehow got hold of the information and seen it delivered into enemy hands."

"That is insane," Reese said. "Just last month, we defeated the Russians at Tchernaya. We're pressing them hard. It's only a matter of time until the war is over."

"That doesn't absolve Greer from the charges," Nightingale said. "On the other hand, the authorities aren't completely convinced or the captain would now be in prison."

Reese sighed. "Then there is time, yet, for Trav to find the man we're looking for."

"For his sake, I hope it happens soon."

Royal stood up from the table and surveyed the group of men. "That's it then. Anyone have anything else?"

Before anyone could speak, the door burst open and Rule strode into the chamber, his black hair wind-tousled and his overcoat flapping against his long legs. "Sorry I'm late."

The others were beginning to stand.

"We're just finished here," Royal said. "I'll fill you in later."

Rule just smiled. "I've got something you might want to hear."

The men eased back down in their chairs.

"What is it?" Reese asked.

"I've discovered Lord Sandhurst isn't quite the man he appears."

"Is that so?" Reese felt the pull of a smile. "I take it you and Lady Sandhurst had another *meeting*."

Rule grinned, digging dimples into his cheeks. "You might say that. And afterward, she confessed something interesting. She said she and her husband had never had a satisfactory marital relationship because her husband . . . well, occasionally, he had affairs with other men."

St. Michaels whistled. "Interesting to say the least."

"Sandhurst is a handsome bastard," Quent

added, "and masculine enough, I always thought. I wouldn't have figured . . ."

"I gather he uses his sexuality in whatever way it serves his purpose. In this case, it makes one wonder what that purpose might be."

"Yes, it does," Reese said, and in that moment, he decided that he would take a personal interest in Philip Keaton, Earl of Sandhurst. He would follow him, see where he went in the evenings, see whom he might be meeting. Travis was sure to be recognized but Reese had never met the man.

He stood up from his chair. "I want to thank you all for what you've done. You've accomplished more than I ever imagined."

Savage stood up, as well. "If we find out anything more, we'll come to you directly."

Reese gave a nod of his head. "Thank you."

But finding out more was unlikely. The men had pressed their connections in society as far as they could. Morgan was still trying to link Holloway to the Van Meer murder, but a good deal of time had passed and the odds of uncovering some sort of evidence weren't good.

On the positive side, once the abdication proceedings were over, Holloway would have what he wanted and Jared would be safe.

Until then, the boy remained heavily guarded. Gillespie and Jack Montague, along with several of Montague's men, were there at the rented town house. The adoption hearing was scheduled for tomorrow. God willing, by the end of the day, Jared would legally be his son.

The notion tightened his chest. He wanted to proclaim the boy his by blood but he wouldn't do that to Elizabeth. It was his fault he had gotten her with child. And she had suffered enough in that regard.

As he bid farewell to Rule, Royal, and Royal's close friends, men who had become his friends as well, he thought of the woman who waited for him at home. He hadn't made love to Elizabeth since the night he had invaded her bedroom.

Not because he didn't want her.

Because he wanted her too much.

His anger was slowly fading, replaced with a need for her that amazed him. And frightened him. He needed to bring his emotions under control, to guard himself against the power she held over him.

In time it will all work out, he told himself, repeating the words he had said to her. Elizabeth was his wife. If he was careful, he could take care of her, make love to her, and yet protect his heart, but it wouldn't be easy to do.

Reese shook his head as he made his way outside the club and went in search of his carriage. He had to stop thinking of Elizabeth and concentrate on Travis. His friend was in the gravest danger now. Prison loomed like a rapidly approaching storm. If something didn't happen soon, Travis might be the one to hang.

Reese had a lead in Sandhurst that might divert the storm and he intended to pursue it. His instincts were telling him the earl, with his insistence that Travis was a spy, his various sexual proclivities, and his recently reinvigorated fortune, was the man to watch.

Reese intended to start tonight.

Three days passed. Every night, Elizabeth lay awake in her bedroom next to Reese's, hoping to hear the sound of her husband's footfalls on the stairs. She knew they would not be forthcoming. Each night he left the house right after supper. An errand, he said, that involved his friend, Captain Greer.

Elizabeth wondered if the betrayal he felt had finally pushed him into the arms of another woman. Had he found solace somewhere else? Found a woman he believed he

405

could trust? The thought drove a dagger into her heart.

At least one good thing had occurred. Jared's adoption hearing had taken place and his adoption formally approved. Unfortunately, Reese's happiness at officially becoming Jared's father only made Elizabeth feel worse.

During the time they were courting, she and Reese had discussed having children. She knew he wanted a family but she hadn't realized how much, or what a marvelous father he would make.

It was amazing how rapidly the bond was growing between Reese and his son, as if some invisible string drew them together. Jared was a Dewar through and through and perhaps it was simply that. Lately, the boy seemed to laugh more often, to talk a little more excitedly, to speak a little less guardedly.

She didn't know what had happened, but she was grateful for whatever it was.

Seated in the drawing room late in the afternoon, Elizabeth worked on her embroidery, trying not to think where Reese might be spending his evenings. Jared was upstairs with his tutor, Mr. Connelly, working on his studies. The security man, Mr. Gillespie, stood guard outside the door.

Reese had been gone all day. With the adoption final, he had turned his attention to the abdication proceeding, attacking the problem with a determination she hadn't expected but should have.

"I want him safe," he had said. "I don't care about Aldridge's fortune. The boy is mine. I'll be the one to see to his future."

Elizabeth completely agreed. If she had married Reese in the first place, her son would have been a Dewar, as he was now, the nephew of a powerful duke. Reese had money enough to provide for Jared's future, and combined with the money from her own inheritance, it was a goodly sum.

Jared didn't need the Aldridge title. Mason could have it. All the title had ever done was to bring her pain.

Taking an embroidery stitch, determined to concentrate, Elizabeth glanced up at the sound of a light knock on the door. Expecting a visitor, she set her embroidery hoop aside and walked toward the entry as the security guard, Jack Montague, answered the knock. She walked into the entry and recognized the silver-blond curls belonging to her sister-in-law, Lily Dewar.

"It's all right, Mr. Montague. This is Her Grace, the Duchess of Bransford. I've been expecting her. Lily, please do come in."

The duchess walked into the house and Montague closed the door. Elizabeth led her into the drawing room, which wasn't as elegant as any of the rooms at Holiday House or even Briarwood, but was immaculately clean and well-cared for. The three-story structure had several drawing rooms, a study, adjoining rooms for her and Reese, as well as rooms on the second and third floors to accommodate Jared and Mrs. Garvey, the servants, and Mr. Montague and his security people.

The women sat down on a burgundy horsehair sofa, which had a matching chair. A warm fire burned in the hearth, taking the first of the November chill out of the air. Elizabeth rang for the downstairs maid, and instructed her to fetch tea and cakes for the two of them.

"I'll see to it, my lady," the slender girl said with a curtsey, then turned and hurried away.

"Royal told me you and Reese were renting a house in town until your business is completed," Lily said. "You know you are more than welcome to stay with us."

"If it were just the three of us, we would love to stay with you. But as you can see, we have brought along a small entourage. It seems half the household has come to

London with us."

Lily glanced toward the entry, where Jack Montague stood watch. "Yes, I see what you mean." The maid returned with a tea tray and set it on the Sheraton table in front of the sofa. Elizabeth poured refreshment for them both.

Lily sipped her tea. "This whole affair must be terribly trying. I'm sure you will be greatly relieved when all of this is over and Jared is finally safe."

"You can't begin to imagine."

"Royal told me the adoption was approved."

"Yes, and we are so very grateful. Reese is a wonderful father. I can already see a world of difference in my son."

Lily smiled wistfully. "I can't wait to be a mother." Her cheeks turned a pretty shade of pink. "In fact, that is one of the reasons I wanted to stop by. You see, I have just discovered I am going to have a baby."

"Oh, my heavens!" Elizabeth felt a rush of gladness that must have shown in her face. "I am so very happy for you!" She set down her cup and saucer, leaned over and gave Lily a hug. "The duke must be ecstatic."

Lily grinned. "The man is walking on air. He is already making plans to refurbish the nursery at Bransford. We've been working on the house, bit by bit, but the nursery was not at the top of the list until now."

"I can't wait to tell Reese he is going to be an uncle."

Lily took a sip of tea and eyed Elizabeth over the rim of her cup. "Perhaps in the future, you will make him a father again."

Some of Elizabeth's joy slipped away. She glanced down at the cup and saucer in her lap. "Perhaps." But she wasn't sure Reese would ever return to her bed. Perhaps he no longer desired her. Or as she feared, had turned to another woman.

She pasted on a smile for her friend. "So what names have the two of you picked out?"

Lily laughed, the sound like the tinkle of water over stones in a brook. "We haven't got quite that far yet. Perhaps we will discuss it tonight."

"I think we ought to go shopping. You are going to need a world of baby clothes."

Lily's smile lit her whole face. "It's going to be so wonderful to have a child."

Elizabeth thought of Jared and how much she loved him. "There is nothing more marvelous than being a mother."

"Except, perhaps, having a husband who loves you."

Sadness overcame Elizabeth. For a moment it was hard to speak. "You're very lucky, Lily."

As if she read Elizabeth's thoughts, Lily's happy smile slid away. "Give him a little time," she said, reaching over to take hold of Elizabeth's hand. "In time, he'll work things out."

But he still hadn't come to her bed and she worried he never would again.

A thick fog shrouded the redbrick buildings and floated snakelike through the narrow, cobbled streets. Reese turned up the collar of his heavy black overcoat and tightened the woolen scarf around his neck.

Philip Keaton, Lord Sandhurst, moved at a brisk pace ahead of him, into an area of middle-class establishments. Four nights in a row, Reese had followed him, waiting outside the earl's expensive Mayfair town house until he left his dwelling, entered his carriage, and the coach rolled off down the street.

Reese had hired an unobtrusive dull black conveyance and ordered the driver to follow at a discreet distance, careful to keep the Sandhurst carriage in sight. The first three nights, the earl had simply made stops at a number of gentlemen's clubs about town, including Brooks, the Carlton, and White's.

Tonight, the Sandhurst coach was heading in a different direction, taking the earl into a far less respectable area of town. It wasn't a rough neighborhood, just not the sort a wealthy, titled gentlemen usually frequented.

When the coach rolled to a stop and Sandhurst departed, leaving instructions for the driver to return three hours hence, Reese waited until he had walked a ways down the block and climbed out of his rented vehicle, advising the coachman to wait. Then he followed at a discreet distance behind the earl, mostly hidden by the dense fog that nearly obscured his quarry.

Sandhurst paused in the doorway of an establishment called the Rose and Thorn, and Reese stepped back into the shadows, flattening himself against a wall. He waited. Sandhurst disappeared inside, but Reese didn't move. Minutes ticked past.

He had just started toward the tavern when a man appeared out of the fog, walking toward the tavern from the opposite direction. He was tall and slenderly built. The hair beneath his stylish beaver hat gleamed like pale gold in the lamplight streaming out of the tavern window.

There was something familiar about him: the recessed chin, the elegant nose and graceful way he moved, and yet Reese couldn't recall where he might have seen him. He stepped out of the shadows as the man disappeared inside the tavern.

He had no fear that Sandhurst would recognize him. Reese hoped the blond man wouldn't know him, either. Making his way along the damp, muddy street, he shoved open the door to the tavern and walked into the taproom.

The place was low-ceilinged and smoky, but quieter than he might have expected. On the far side of the room, he spotted Sandhurst, seated at a table with the slender blond man. Reese moved to a scarred wooden stool at the bar, ordered an ale, and watched them from the corner of his eye.

There was something in the close proximity of the two men, something in the way the blond man's head tilted toward the slightly older, far more masculine man. There was something in the soft smile on the younger man's face when he looked at Sandhurst that put Reese on alert.

As soon as the pair had finished their drinks, they walked toward the stairs leading up to the second floor. There were rooms for hire up there. Rooms available for a night or a week. The men took the stairs side-by-side and as they passed by the lamp that lit the stairwell, Reese got a clear look at the younger man's face.

His jaw hardened. Reese had his answer.

Though he wasn't in his lieutenant's uniform, the man with Sandhurst was Colonel Thomas's young, blond aide.

TWENTY-FIVE

Although he had come home in the late hours last night, Reese was up and dressed and ready to leave before the rest of London had risen from their beds.

Jack Montague's second-shift man stood guard at the front door as Reese approached. He needed to see Travis this morning, to tell him what he had found out last night, see what Trav had discovered that might help their case.

He had almost reached the door when he heard a firm pounding outside. He waved Montague's man away and went to answer the knock himself. When he opened the door, the man he needed to see stood outside on the porch.

"I found him!" Travis said, his hazel eyes gleaming behind the glass in his spectacles. "I know who he is!"

Trav didn't seem the least surprised to find Reese up so early. Both of them were used to army life and Travis knew him well. Reese cocked his head toward the study and both men headed in that direction. Once inside, Travis quietly closed the door.

"His name is Boris Radonyak. He never approached me because someone in the Foreign Office tipped him that I was working undercover for the government."

"How'd you find him?"

"A big Russian named Nikolai Godunov. He knew my mother. He knows just about everything that goes on in the neighborhood. Maybe Radonyak mentioned my name to Nikolai, or maybe to someone else and word got back to him. Nikolai said he brought his family to England to start fresh and that Radonyak was a threat to him and the rest of the community."

"He's damned well right."

"Boris is our guy, but I haven't figured out where he's getting his information."

"I think I know exactly where he's getting it."

"You do?"

"An aide in the colonel's office. A young lieutenant. I saw him last night with your good friend, Sandhurst."

"You think Sandhurst is involved?"

"I'm sure of it. The earl is getting information from the lieutenant, then selling it, apparently to Radonyak, who is delivering it to the Russians."

Travis took a minute to digest the information. "If you're right —"

"It all adds up. Until a couple of years ago, Sandhurst was nearly broke. Then miraculously, his finances changed. He found out about your journal and pointed a finger at you to divert suspicion from himself. All the while, he's lining his pockets by selling out his country. I don't think it'll be all that hard to follow the money he's been getting right back to good ol' Boris."

"Nice work, Major." Travis smiled and Reese slapped him on the shoulder.

"Come on. Let's take what we have to the colonel."

"You think he'll believe us?"

"Thomas is smart. We give him the pieces, it won't take him long to put the puzzle together."

The men left the house, heading for the building that housed the Foreign Office. Thomas would want to verify the facts for himself, but Reese was certain, once he did, that Travis's name would be cleared.

And the young lieutenant, along with the Earl of Sandhurst and Boris Radonyak, would come under investigation for treason.

As they climbed into Travis's carriage, the

burden on Reese's shoulders felt lighter than it had in weeks. At least one of his worries was about to be over.

"So how are you and Annabelle getting along?" he asked, settling himself back in the seat.

Travis's features turned grim. "I'd rather not talk about it."

Reese hiked a brow. "That bad, is it?"

Travis made no reply, just turned to stare out the window.

"At least if you decide you want her, you won't have to worry about hanging."

Trav's attention swung back to Reese. His hazel eyes glinted behind the lenses of his spectacles. "Oh, I want her. Make no mistake about that."

Reese said nothing more. Annabelle Townsend was beautiful and desirable and, fortunately for Reese, she was Travis's concern.

Reese had kept his promise to help his friend.

But he couldn't help wondering what Travis would do about the lady who had, apparently, managed to burrow very deeply under his skin.

The security guard, Jack Montague, answered the knock at the door. Hearing a

418

woman's voice out on the porch, Elizabeth rose from the sofa and started in that direction. Stoop-shouldered and silver-haired, Reese's aunt Agatha made her way into the house.

Elizabeth's heart beat dully. She had known this moment would come. By now, the old woman knew that Reese had discovered the truth about his son. Both his brothers knew and they were not wont to keep secrets from the matriarch of the family.

What would the dowager say when she discovered that Elizabeth had not been able to earn her nephew's forgiveness? That there would be no loving family and no more children, as the dowager seemed to wish? When she found out that Reese had abandoned her — that Elizabeth wasn't able to make him love her?

Fighting to hold back tears, she took a deep breath and pasted on a smile. "Lady Tavistock . . . please do come in."

Leaning heavily on her cane, the frail old woman looked her over from head to foot, and her thin silver eyebrows pulled nearly together. "You look puny, my girl. Are you sick?"

Sick at heart, Elizabeth wanted to say. Though Reese had brought good news yesterday about Captain Greer, believing his friend's name would soon be cleared of any suspicion, he had spoken with her only briefly then left her alone.

He had spent several hours with Jared, accompanying him and Mr. Gillespie on a walk to the stable in the park. He had not come that night to her bed. He was keeping his distance, she knew, determined not to risk himself again.

Elizabeth led the dowager into the drawing room, a journey that took a little extra time with the older woman's slower pace.

"Why don't we have some tea?" Elizabeth suggested as Lady Tavistock seated herself on the burgundy sofa. She started for the bellpull but the dowager shook her head.

"Had enough tea already. Want to know what is going on between you and my nephew."

Elizabeth bit back an urge to tell the old woman it was none of her business, but of course in a way it was. Aunt Agatha loved all three of her nephews like the sons she never had. She had a right to worry about Reese.

Elizabeth steeled herself and sat down on the opposite end of the sofa. "He knows Jared is his son. I presume you're aware of that."

"Of course I am. We don't keep secrets in

this family." *Not like you,* were the unspoken words.

"I should have told him myself. I shouldn't have waited."

"You should have told him eight years ago. But that is water under the bridge. The important thing is that the two of you are married and you have a child to think of. The past is past and it's time to move forward."

Elizabeth glanced away, blinking against the sting of tears. "He won't forgive me. I told you that before we were married."

"Poppycock! The man loves you. Always has, always will."

He might have loved her once, Elizabeth thought. Not anymore. She stiffened her spine. "Reese doesn't . . . he no longer comes to my bed."

The old woman pondered that, then she grinned. "My nephew loves you even more than I thought."

"What are you talking about?"

"Reese loves you desperately and it frightens him to death. My nephew is a very virile man — all the Bransford men are — and certainly not one to ignore the physical needs of his body."

Elizabeth said nothing. She had no idea how Reese felt about her. Or even if he might be satisfying his desires with another woman. She only knew that he had abandoned her as she had once abandoned him.

"So what about you, Elizabeth? How do you feel about Reese?"

The tears she had been fighting welled in her eyes. There was no use lying and certainly not to a woman as perceptive as the dowager countess. "I thought I loved him when I was a girl. And I suppose in a way, I did. But I am a woman now and for the first time, I truly know what love is. I love Reese, and I would do anything to make him love me in return."

The old lady flashed a satisfied smile. "And so you shall."

"But how, my lady? Reese doesn't trust me. He's built a wall around his heart and he's afraid that if he lets me in, I'll only betray him again."

"But we both know you would never do that."

Elizabeth brushed the wetness from her cheeks. "No. I would die before I would ever do anything to hurt him again."

The dowager seemed pleased. "Then you will win his love. You will do what every woman has done for a thousand years. You will seduce him into loving you."

Elizabeth straightened. "Good heavens, I

couldn't possibly do that! I wouldn't even know how to begin."

Aunt Agatha eyed her shrewdly. "You are no longer the naïve young girl you once were. You know something of a man's physical likes and dislikes. I imagine with Reese as your husband, you know a great deal about what he enjoys. Instead of waiting for him to come to you — you, my girl, will simply go to him."

For several long moments, Elizabeth just sat there. Could she do it? Could she actually seduce him? Was she willing to risk herself that way? But she would do anything for Reese, even risk his rejection.

She felt an odd, tingling excitement rising inside her. Memories of Reese's heated lovemaking had the color rushing into her cheeks. A coil of desire tightened low in her belly at the thought of making love with him again.

Elizabeth looked over at the dowager and smiled. "I'll do it, my lady. I promise you I shall do my very best to win him."

"That's my girl!" The old woman's wrinkled face brightened with something like glee. She eyed Elizabeth shrewdly. "You know, 'tis bitterly cold outside. I think I've changed my mind. I would very much enjoy that cup of tea."

Elizabeth smiled, thinking that each time they talked, some of the old woman's enmity faded. Perhaps one day friendship would grow between them.

In the meantime, she had a seduction to plan.

"What is it?" Lily asked as the butler appeared at the door leading into the drawing room.

"Your friend, Lady Annabelle, Your Grace. She has asked to see you. She says that if you are busy, she will come back some other time."

Lily smiled, delighted at the prospect of company. "I am certainly not too busy for her. Ask her to come and join me."

The butler bowed. "Yes, Your Grace."

A few seconds later, Annabelle hurried through the drawing room door, her full, dark-blue silk skirts floating out around her. "Thank you for seeing me, Your Grace. I know I should have sent word, but . . ." Then Annabelle broke into tears.

Lily hurried toward her. "Good heavens, what in the world is the matter?" Slipping an arm around her friend, she urged her over to the sofa and Annabelle sank down heavily.

"I know I promised I wouldn't come here

and cry on your shoulder, but there is no one else I can talk to."

"You know you are always welcome here. Now . . . tell me what has happened."

Annabelle pulled a handkerchief from her reticule and dabbed it against her eyes. "It's Travis."

"Yes, well that much I guessed."

"I thought . . . I thought I was mature enough to deal with an affair. I thought I could see him on occasion, make love with him, and everything would be all right."

"But it isn't."

"No, it isn't. Every time I am with him, it is more wonderful than the time before. Until it's time for me to leave. The minute I walk out the door, I feel sick inside, and utterly and completely empty. I need him, Lily, and not just on occasion. I am so in love with him I am sick with it."

"Oh, Anna." Lily leaned over and hugged her, allowing the woman to rest her head for a moment on Lily's shoulder. "I know how much it hurts. Perhaps you would be better off to end the affair before it gets even more painful."

Annabelle straightened away. "That is what I have been thinking. I just . . . I don't know if I have the courage."

"Perhaps you should simply tell Captain

Greer the truth. That you love him and that it hurts too much to go on as you have been."

"I don't know, Lily. I . . . I think he was afraid something like this would happen. He tried to protect me. He tried to warn me away but I wouldn't listen." Fresh tears welled and Annabelle wiped them away. "This is my fault, not his. I don't want him to blame himself or feel guilty for what we have done."

"Poor Anna. Your heart is broken and yet you worry about Captain Greer's feelings instead of your own. You truly do love him," Lily said softly.

"I have always loved him. Now that we've been together, I love him more than ever." Anna reached for Lily's hand. "Tell me what to do."

Lily shook her head, moving the silver-blond curls on her shoulders. "I can't tell you that. Only your heart can tell you. But you must choose some course, Anna. If you wait, you will only wind up hurting each other more."

Annabelle nodded. She released a weary breath. "You're right, Lily. I have to do something — for both of our sakes."

"Indeed, you must. Doing something is always better than simply worrying and doing nothing."

Annabelle blew her nose and rose from the sofa. "Thank you, Lily. You are a very dear friend."

Lily's heart felt heavy as she watched Annabelle leave the drawing room. She knew exactly how it felt to lose the man you loved. She rested a hand protectively over her stomach, where Royal's child nestled peacefully inside her. She hadn't told Anna. She didn't want to cause the poor woman more grief. Unlike Anna, she had been lucky. In the end, Royal had discovered that he loved her, too.

Lily said a silent prayer for Anna and Travis. She hoped God would help them find a way to be together.

TWENTY-SIX

Elizabeth stood still as Gilda pinned the last of her heavy curls in place, letting the shiny black strands nestle softly against her shoulder.

"Ye look lovely, milady." Gilda gave her a wistful smile. "His lordship will be on fire for ye tonight."

Elizabeth fought a blush and prayed that Gilda was right.

She smoothed the skirt of the scarlet velvet gown Reese had chosen, the bodice cut low, exposing a portion of her bosom and the deep cleavage between. Gilda had corseted her waist so tightly Reese's long-fingered hands could fit round it. Which meant, Elizabeth could barely breathe.

It didn't matter. If her seduction worked, the price would be worth it.

"Gor, such a sight ye are," Gilda said, reaching out to touch the folds of heavy red velvet. "The color is perfect with milady's black hair and gray eyes."

Elizabeth smiled. "I hope Lord Reese likes it as much as you do."

"Oh, milady, he'll be over the top for ye."

Elizabeth hoped so. She had gone to great lengths to please her husband tonight. She wanted him to see past the hurt she had dealt him, see her as the woman he had married, the woman he desired.

Earlier, she had asked him if he would be home for supper and he had promised that he would. He was down there now, she knew, waiting to escort her into the dining room. And the extravagant meal she had planned included his favorite dishes — some of which, thanks to Lady Tavistock, Elizabeth now knew, along with an accompaniment of fine French wine.

She took a deep breath and opened the door, walked out into the hall. Reese stood at the bottom of the staircase, incredibly handsome in fitted gray trousers, a black, velvet-collared tailcoat, and snowy white cravat. Against his dark features, his eyes looked as blue as the sky over Briarwood, his hair as black as sin.

Her heart beat faster, began to pound against her ribs. Inside her lacy, front-closing corset, her nipples stiffened into tight little buds. She thought of the night ahead, of seducing Reese into making love to her, and damp heat slid into her core.

She flattened a hand against her abdomen, took a deep breath, and started down the stairs. Reese stood military-straight in front of her as she reached the bottom, and for the first time in days, his blue eyes burned with heat. They made a slow perusal of her body and came to rest on the soft mounds above the low cut bodice of the gown.

"You're looking particularly lovely tonight, Elizabeth."

She could feel the warmth of his gaze as if he touched her and her breasts swelled inside the lacy corset cups. She managed a smile. "Thank you. You're looking very handsome tonight yourself."

His mouth edged up. She took the arm he offered, let him lead her into the dining room, toward a seat at the long, polished mahogany table. With a low-burning crystal-prismed gas lamp overhead, twelve ornate high-backed chairs, and candles flickering in the silver candelabra in the center of the table, it was the most elegant room in the house.

Tonight the table was elaborately set with silver-rimmed porcelain plates, gleaming silverware, and long-stemmed cut crystal goblets.

One of Reese's black eyebrows cocked up. "Have I missed something? I would have dressed more formally had I known this was a special occasion."

"We are celebrating the news you brought this afternoon — that your friend, Captain Greer, has been cleared of all charges."

It was as good an excuse as she could come up with and certainly reason to celebrate. She couldn't help wondering if the captain hadn't so desperately needed his help at the same time as she and Jared, whether Reese would have married her.

"I'm happy for him," Reese said. "And of course it is one less problem to deal with." Moving behind her, he pulled out her chair and waited until she was seated, his gaze dropping down to the deep cleavage the gown exposed. Elizabeth's heartbeat quickened.

She drew her white linen napkin across her lap, giving her time to compose herself, hoping he wouldn't notice her hands were trembling. "Do you . . . do you think Colonel Thomas will press charges against Lord Sandhurst and the other men involved in the spying?"

One of the servants came forward and poured wine into their goblets before Reese had time to answer. "I'm sure of it," he said as the man left the dining room. "The more the colonel digs, the more evidence he is going to find, and that is going to be Sandhurst's undoing. Then the others will get what they deserve, as well."

"I suppose I should feel sorry for them," she said, "but considering the soldiers who lost their lives because of what they did, I'm afraid I cannot."

"The lad, perhaps, deserves your pity," Reese said. "For falling prey to his sexual appetites."

She lowered her eyes. "At one time or another, we are all guilty of that."

His eyes locked with hers, hotter than before. "Even you, Beth?"

The name washed over her, filling her with hope. "You showed me desire, Reese. You turned me into a woman, with a woman's wants and needs."

His nostrils flared. He might have risen at that very moment and led her upstairs if the first course hadn't arrived just then. He picked up his spoon and began to eat, but she noticed he consumed even less than she, though the soup, a creamy asparagus and lobster, was one of his favorites and quite delicious.

"Travis has been seeing Lady Annabelle Townsend," he remarked as a servant removed their bowls and another course was set in front of them. "Though I am not sure if it is supposed to be a secret."

"I shan't say a word." She took a bite of the turbot in lemon sauce they had just been served. "I like Lady Annabelle a great deal. I think they would make a very fine couple."

Reese took a sip of his wine. "Travis claims he is not the sort to marry."

"What does Annabelle say?"

"She's a widow. According to Travis, she claims she also has no interest in marriage."

Elizabeth's gaze found his. "That is what I thought before we were wed."

Reese didn't look away, just kept those penetrating blue eyes on her over the rim of his goblet. "And now?"

"Now, I have discovered a number of benefits to the wedded state. Particularly being wedded to you."

His mouth took on a sensual curve. "And what, if I may ask, would those benefits be?"

Elizabeth sipped her wine. Her heart was beating so hard she wondered if he could hear it. "To begin with, there is a certain security one finds in being married. And companionship, of course. But the greatest benefit is passion."

The silver fork in his hand paused halfway to his lips. Just looking at them, remembering the feel of them moving hotly over hers, sent a curl of heat into her stomach.

Reese swallowed the bite he had taken. "When we were first wed, you were afraid of passion."

"Yes, but you taught me not to be frightened but to enjoy it."

His eyes darkened to nearly black. "And would you enjoy it tonight?"

Her stomach contracted. She purposely moistened her lips, then wiped them delicately with her napkin, drawing out the moment. "I'm certain I would."

She could read the hunger in his expression. He was breathing more rapidly, and so was she. And yet she could see he was enjoying the moment, the heightened sexual awareness sparking between them. "And what, exactly, would you have me do?"

She hadn't planned for the conversation to go so far and yet she refused to back down from the challenge she read in his face. Elizabeth tilted her head, as if she pondered the notion.

"First I would have you kiss me . . . not just once, of course, but over and over again. I would want you to use your tongue, as it always feels so good when you kiss me in the French fashion."

His jaw clenched so tight a muscle

bunched in his cheek. He slid back his chair and started to rise just as a servant arrived to remove the second course and set another plate down in front of him.

He returned his chair to the table and waited for the servant to leave. When he spoke, his voice came out husky. "What else would you have me do?"

Elizabeth took a breath. She couldn't imagine herself speaking as boldly as she was, but it seemed to be working. She forced her embarrassment away. "I would want you to kiss my breasts. Even now my nipples are hard inside my corset, aching for you to taste them."

He stood up so swiftly, his chair toppled over. "If it weren't for my bloody leg, madam, I would sweep you into my arms, cart you upstairs, and do exactly what you require of me. As it is, I would have you take my hand and we shall make the climb together. What say you, my lady?"

She felt strangely giddy. "I should be delighted to join you . . . unless of course, you would rather stay here and finish the meal."

His jaw flexed. She had never seen such blatant hunger on his face. "I believe I would rather dine on you, my lady."

Her breath caught and a sharp pulsing

began between her legs.

In minutes, they were upstairs in his bedroom, a place she had never been before. In the past, he had always come to her, unwilling, she imagined, to allow her into his private sanctuary.

It should have taken longer for him to undress her, since he kissed and fondled each part of her body he exposed. But soon both of them were naked. Elizabeth had only moments to admire his lean, powerful build, the width of his shoulders, the bands of muscle across his chest. Ridges of sinew rippled across his flat stomach, and a powerful erection rode high and hard between his long legs, promising the pleasure she craved.

Standing next to the bed, Reese kissed her deeply, then lifted her into his arms and settled her on the deep feather mattress. It occurred to her that none of the old fear remained. Reese had banished them entirely. He was her husband. Her lover. The man that she loved.

The bed was wide and the mattress soft, the sheets of fine spun cotton and the pillows filled with pure white goose down. A fire burned in the hearth to keep out the chill, while outside the windows, a light rain had begun to fall, pattering gently against the panes.

The sound was far softer than the patter of her heart against her ribs, the gentle breeze mild in comparison to the storm of passion raging inside her. Reese kissed her deeply, again and again, nibbled and tasted and took her with his tongue, just as she had commanded. His mouth moved to the side of her neck, then lower, ministering to each of her breasts.

He cupped them, laved and suckled until she was writhing beneath him, her nipples aching, her body on fire for him.

"Reese, please . . ."

"Not yet, love. There is more about passion that I wish to teach you."

She knew enough, she thought desperately, aching to feel him inside her, eager to reach the pinnacle of fulfillment he had brought her to before.

Instead, he continued to kiss his way down her body, over her rib cage to her navel, whirling his tongue round the small indentation and making her quiver. Settling himself between her legs, he drew a finger through the tight black curls above her sex, parted the slick folds, and set his mouth there.

Elizabeth cried out as pleasure shot through her, unlike any she had known. She laced her fingers in Reese's silky hair and arched upward at the feel of his tongue gliding over her most sensitive place. Sensation rocked her. Heat and need burned through her. Her bottom lip trembled and she bit down to stifle a scream.

"Reese . . . !" she cried out as the first climax shook her, her body quaking with the force of her pleasure. Another swiftly followed, then a third.

She was languid and pliant as Reese rose above her, his hard length brushing the entrance to her sex. In a single deep thrust, he filled her and fresh need spiraled out through her limbs.

Dear God!

Desire rose swiftly. Heavy strokes stirred the banked fires to life. Deep, penetrating strokes had her writhing beneath him. Hard, driving thrusts had her begging for more. Elizabeth locked her legs around his, taking him deeper still, giving herself up to the fierce, pounding rhythm, the thrust and drag of his potent erection.

Release hit her, shattering her senses, spinning her out of control. Her body clenched around his hard length, and the muscles in Reese's shoulders tightened as he reached a powerful climax, his head falling back, his teeth gritted as if he were in pain.

For several long moments they remained

joined together, breathing heavily, their bodies covered with a fine sheen of perspiration. Reese kissed her softly one last time. Lifting himself away, he lay down on the mattress beside her.

Groggy and sweetly fulfilled, Elizabeth traced a finger through the black curls on his chest. "Will you . . . will you stay with me tonight?" she asked, praying he would say yes.

Reese chuckled softly. "I don't have much choice. The bed is mine. And I would like nothing more than to share it with you." He came up on an elbow, bent his head and softly kissed her. "Besides, now that I know your fondness for passion, I have a good deal more to show you."

She braced a hand on his chest. "I want you, Reese. But I won't . . . I won't share you with another woman."

Reese tenderly kissed her. "You're my wife, Beth, the only woman I want or ever will."

Relief trickled through her. Reese was a man of his word. He would remain true to his wedding vows. And clearly, whether he loved her or not, he still desired her.

Elizabeth gave herself up to the passions he stirred and told herself that it would be enough.

TWENTY-SEVEN

Reese walked toward Hyde Park, his small son gamboling along beside him. Mr. Gillespie accompanied them, a few paces to the rear. Jared loved to watch the fancy carriages roll past, along with the riders on their expensive, high-stepping, blooded horses.

Reese wished the horses they were watching were his own. He wished they were back at Briarwood, where Jared could ride Dusty and Reese could ride Warrior.

Absently, he rubbed his leg. He and Timothy had continued working the muscles, and the leg pained him less and less. Once they got home, he would attempt to ride again and this time he would not fail. Soon there would be crops to plant, barley to grow and harvest. There were tenants to manage and a score of other responsibilities he needed to handle. He needed to be able to ride into the fields, to survey his property and what needed to be done, and horseback was the best way to see it done.

He might have been forced into becoming a gentleman farmer, but now that he was, he intended to be a good one.

Somewhat grudgingly, he admitted that country life had changed him. The hustle and bustle of a crowded city had never appealed to him the way it did his younger brother. But he hadn't found city life distasteful, as he did now. After spending time at Briarwood, he chafed for the fresh air and sunshine, the sight of the rolling green landscape stretching around him.

Only a few more days, he told himself.

In a few more days, Pinkard had assured him, the courts would make their decision to grant the abdication.

Then Jared would be truly safe and they could go home.

They stopped at the edge of the gravel path to watch the daily procession of expensive carriages, flashy horses and elegantly dressed riders moving round the park. It was cold today, but the sun was out and people were dressed warmly.

"Look, Papa! See that big white horse? Isn't he beautiful? If he had a horn, he would look just like a unicorn."

Reese chuckled softly. The big, powerful

stallion with its white coat blending to gray along its strong legs was, indeed, magnificent. One of the finest animals Reese had ever seen.

He settled a hand on the little boy's shoulder. "He's something, all right, son. Not just showy, but powerfully built in all the right places. You've a good eye for horseflesh, lad."

Jared beamed at the compliment. It took so little to make the child happy, Reese thought. Just a kind word here and there. It angered him to think how little kindness the boy had been shown by the man who had raised him.

He thought of Elizabeth and expected the familiar rush of anger, but surprisingly none came. All of them had suffered. And lately he had begun to see that part of the blame belonged to him. If he had been more settled, less determined to seek adventure, Elizabeth might have come to him instead of running into the arms of another man.

Whatever had happened, it was all in the past. It was time for healing, not recrimination.

The stallion grew closer and Reese could make out the faint gray dapples beneath the horse's sleek white coat. Standing at least seventeen hands, the horse drew the eye of everyone in the park.

Watching the stallion approach, Reese felt the sudden tension in Jared's slim shoulders as the child backed a little behind him. Reese looked up to see Mason Holloway seated on the magnificent stallion's back.

"Nice morning for a ride," Holloway said, the breeze ruffling his thick mustache and the brown hair beneath his tall beaver hat.

"Fine animal," Reese replied, his features hard. "I didn't know you were interested in horses."

"Mostly I just like watching them race, but this one I couldn't resist."

"Planning to pay for him with Aldridge's money?"

Mason's lips thinned. "The horse and a whole lot more. And I'm getting tired of waiting."

"If I had my way, you wouldn't be waiting, Holloway. And you wouldn't need the money. You would be dead."

Mason's whole body stiffened. The stallion's nostrils flared and he started to dance, sensing the tension between the two men.

Turning his back on Holloway, Reese led Jared away from horse and rider. He didn't look back, he knew the man was livid. Perhaps Mason would call him out and Reese would have an excuse to kill him.

Reese scoffed. The man was a coward. Reese wouldn't be that lucky.

A gust of wind blew leaves across the street and rattled the branches of the huge sycamore in front of the rented town house. Walking next to Jared, Reese paused on the porch as he spotted a familiar conveyance bowling down the street, and Travis's carriage rolled up in front of the house.

Reese turned to his son. "You and Mr. Gillespie go on upstairs. I'm sure Mr. Connelly is here by now and eager for you to get on with your studies."

Jared looked up at him with dark, solemn eyes. "You don't like my uncle Mason."

There was no use lying. "No, I don't."

"I don't either," Jared said.

Reese's jaw tightened. The bastard had made his wife and son's life miserable. All those years and Reese hadn't been there. It made him feel powerless in a way he never had before. He settled a hand on Jared's shoulder and returned his attention to the street.

Travis strode up the walkway to the porch. "Good morning, Major."

"Morning, Trav." He looked down at Jared's dark head. "You remember my son, don't you?" He couldn't keep a note of

444

pride out of his voice. "You met him out at the stable at Briarwood."

"Of course." Travis went down on one knee, putting him eye to eye with the child. "It's good to see you, Jared."

Jared eyed the empty sleeve of Travis's coat. "What happened to your arm?"

Reese's grip tightened on Jared's shoulder. "It isn't polite to ask those kinds of questions, son." And in the past, the boy had been too withdrawn to ever ask. Perhaps it wasn't such a bad thing.

Travis just smiled. "It's all right." He looked down at the boy. "The same thing happened to me that happened to your father. We were wounded in the war. Your father's leg got hurt and I lost my arm."

"You were heroes. My mama said so."

Travis grinned. "Did she now? Well, I don't know about that. We mostly just did what we were expected to do when we joined the army."

Jared's dark eyes swung to Reese. "Maybe I'll join the army some day."

"And maybe you'll go to university and learn to be a doctor or something," Reese grumbled.

Jared made a face and Reese laughed. "All right, maybe you'll be something else. Whatever it is, you had better go on inside and get to work or your tutor will be assigning you extra lessons."

Grinning, Jared raced into the house, and Reese felt a tug at his heart. He had a son. It was the most wonderful feeling he had ever known.

Jared was gone from sight by the time Reese led Travis down the hall to the study. "Drink?" he offered, moving toward the sideboard.

All the energy seemed to drain from Travis's body. He blew out a breath. "I could use one."

Reese poured his friend a glass but refrained from pouring one for himself. Travis accepted the brandy and sank down heavily on the sofa.

"I have a feeling this visit has nothing to do with Sandhurst or Colonel Thomas," Reese said.

Travis took a long swallow of his drink. "As far as I'm concerned, that problem is over. In fact, I start my job at the *Times* in the morning."

"Congratulations."

Travis sipped his drink, and for the first time Reese noticed the dark circles behind his spectacles, the weary lines across his forehead.

"You like you've just come off a thirty-day

march."

"Yeah, well, that's just about the way I feel."

"Then your visit must have something to do with a woman and that woman could only be Annabelle Townsend."

Travis leaned back wearily against the sofa. "She ended the affair."

Reese cocked an eyebrow. "Did she tell you why?"

"She says she loves me too much." He sat forward and raked a hand through his hair. "You ever heard anything so insane? She doesn't want to be with me because she loves me too much."

Reese sat down on the corner of his desk. "You said she wasn't the sort for an affair. I guess you were right."

Travis shook his head. "I tried to tell her. I tried to warn her away, but she wouldn't listen."

"Women are like that."

Travis sighed. "The thing of it is, I didn't realize how much I would miss her. I mean, I can't sleep at night. I can hardly eat. I considered paying a visit to Madame Lefon's, but the thought of actually taking one of her women to bed made my stomach turn. Anna's the only woman I want and I can't have her."

"Why, exactly, is that?"

"You know why. Because I'm not the kind of man to settle down. Anna's sweet and loving. She's strong and determined and loyal. She deserves a lot better man than I am."

"I think she's made it pretty clear she doesn't want another man."

Travis looked up at him. "In time she'll change her mind."

"Will she? She was married before. She ought to know what she wants. And if she does change her mind, how will you feel? Are you ready to give her to someone else? Are you willing to stand by and let another man take your place in her bed?"

Travis's face went pale. "I'll kill the first bastard who touches her."

Reese laughed. "You're doomed, my friend. Why don't you just go ahead and marry her?"

Travis grunted. "You're as mad as she is."

"Am I? You're in love and you don't even know it."

Travis shot back his drink. "I told you, I'm not husband material." He rose from the sofa, set the glass on the sideboard and started for the door.

"Give it some thought, Captain."

Travis just shook his head, opened the

door, and walked out of the study.

Reese felt sorry for him. But he wasn't in a much better place himself. He was bedding his wife on a more than regular basis, but it always felt as if something were missing.

Elizabeth was withholding some part of herself from him, just as he withheld some part of himself from her.

He didn't know what to do about it. He told himself it wasn't important. All that mattered was their son and keeping him safe and providing a solid, loving home for him.

Love. Somehow that was the key.

Reese had no idea how to turn the rusty lock that would open the door to his heart.

It was late afternoon, an icy wind blowing outside, a weak sun threading its way through the clouds. In the drawing room, Elizabeth sat on the sofa next to Jared, helping him read a children's story called *The Little Gray Mouse*. After luncheon, Reese had received a note from his solicitor, Mr. Pinkard. The note hadn't mentioned why the man wished to see him. Elizabeth wouldn't stop worrying until her husband returned.

She pasted on a smile, hiding her worry

from her son. "Go ahead, read the last page."

Jared did so only a bit haltingly. "And so the little . . . little mouse lif . . . lif . . .'"

"Lifted."

"Lifted his nose and sniffed the air. 'I'm hungry,' he said. 'And I smell a sli . . . ce . . .'"

"Slice," Elizabeth gently corrected.

" 'And I smell a slice of cheese.' " Jared laughed, the sweet sound rolling over her.

"Go on," Elizabeth urged.

"Smil..ing, the little mouse . . . raced off . . . to join his . . . friends . . . and they . . . lived hap-happily ever after."

"Very good! You are getting to be a marvelous reader."

Jared beamed.

It was true. His reading was improving every day. She thought it might have something to do with how much more comfortable he was in his surroundings, no longer accountable to Edmund or Mason for his every move.

Elizabeth urged him up off the sofa. "I think that's enough for today. Why don't you run upstairs and play for a while?"

He looked up at her with his big dark eyes. "What are we having for supper?"

"Roasted partridge." She smiled. "And

almond pudding for dessert."

Jared grinned, raced across the room and out the door. Almond pudding was one of his favorites.

Elizabeth's heart tugged softly. He was such a dear little boy. Picking up the embroidery she had been working on before her son arrived, she tried to focus on the stitches. She wished Reese would come home. She hoped whatever news Pinkard had to tell him would be good.

A noise sounded down the hall and Elizabeth glanced up. In the entry, she heard Jack Montague's voice, then the sound of Reese's familiar, masculine, uneven gait as he walked toward the drawing room. An instant later, he stood in the open doorway.

Elizabeth looked at him and the bottom of her stomach dropped out. Reese's jaw was set, his expression so grim fear sliced through her. She shot to her feet, her embroidery hoop tumbling to the floor.

"Reese, what is it?"

"Our petition was denied. The court wouldn't even agree to a hearing. They said the boy was too young to be divested of such an important and honorable title. They said it wasn't fair to the late earl to deny the Aldridge title to his rightful heir."

She could feel the blood draining from

451

her face. "But . . . but if Mr. Pinkard were to tell them the truth, tell them Edmund wasn't Jared's real father —"

"It wouldn't matter. By law, Jared is the late earl's son, with the right to all that entails. The judges on the bench say once Jared is old enough to understand the ramifications of giving up the earldom, if he still wishes to abdicate, they will review his petition. Until that time, Jared is to retain the title of earl."

Elizabeth's hand came up to her trembling lips. "Dear God." The floor seemed to rush toward her an instant before Reese's strong arm went round her waist. He guided her over to the sofa and helped her sit down.

Elizabeth looked up at him. "Mason will stop at nothing to get what he wants. Our son . . . our son will never be safe. Reese, what . . . what shall we do?"

But she saw by the set of his jaw, exactly what he intended. "No!" She gripped his arm and refused to let go. "You mustn't go after him. You mustn't try to kill him! I refuse to save my son by losing my husband. I . . ." *Love you both too much for that.* "I won't let him take either of you from me."

For an instant, Reese's hard blue gaze softened. He reached out and gently cupped her cheek. "I should have done this long ago. It's the only way we can keep our son safe. You know I'm right, Elizabeth."

She swallowed past the thick lump in her throat. "You're . . . you're going to call him out?"

"He's left me no choice."

"But dueling . . . dueling is against the law. If you kill him, you'll hang."

"My brother is a duke. The authorities have been known to close their eyes to such matters on more than one occasion."

Perhaps. But if the magistrates discovered what Reese planned, he could be sentenced to three years' hard labor or transportation for fifteen years, just for making the attempt.

"What about the reports we've filed?" she pressed, desperate for some other solution. "The opium Mason and Frances gave me, the shooting at Briarwood, the threats he made against Jared, the attempted abduction?"

"The reports will certainly be a factor in whatever occurs. It doesn't change what has to happen."

Her hands were shaking. "Mason is a crack shot."

The edge of Reese's mouth grimly curved. "So am I."

She watched him turn and start for the

door, found her courage and ran after him. She caught him before he could leave.

"Please, Reese . . . I just found you again. I don't want to lose you. Jared needs a father who loves him. And I need you, Reese." She didn't realize there were tears in her eyes until they slipped onto her cheeks.

Reese gently kissed her. "I need you, too, Beth. And I'm not going to let a coward like Holloway ruin our lives."

She watched as he turned away, her heart pounding in her throat. Mason was a cruel, vicious man with entirely no scruples. He would not duel with honor. He would do whatever it took to win.

Dear God, she prayed, *don't let Mason destroy my family.*

But she had prayed to God before and He hadn't heard her. Lately, she had begun to believe that had changed. One thing she knew — the Lord helped those who helped themselves. Elizabeth didn't intend to stand by and do nothing.

She glanced up at the clock. If Reese had his way, at dawn on the morrow, he and Mason would face each other on Green's Hill, pistols drawn. In minutes, one of them would be dead.

Her throat ached. There had to be a way

to change the dangerous course Reese was taking, to protect him and their son.

Elizabeth intended to find it.

Twenty-Eight

Lifting her heavy skirts out of the way, Elizabeth hurried out of the drawing room toward the stairs. She would go to Royal, see if there was a way the duke could stop his brother from challenging Mason and, instead, help him find another way to protect their son.

She had just reached the entry when a knock at the door brought her to a jarring halt.

Standing guard along the wall, Jack Montague sauntered over and pulled open the door.

"My name is Chase Morgan," the man on the front porch said. "I'm here to see Lord Reese Dewar."

Chase Morgan. Elizabeth knew the name. He was the investigator Reese had hired.

"I'm afraid his lordship isn't in," the guard replied. "If you'd like to come back —"

"It's all right, Mr. Montague," Elizabeth

interrupted. "I'll speak to Mr. Morgan."

The man strode in, lean and hard, dark hair and rugged features.

Elizabeth managed a smile. "I'm Lord Reese's wife. My husband has told me a great deal about you. If you will please follow me . . ."

She didn't give him time to argue, just turned and led him down the hall into the drawing room. Once inside, Elizabeth closed the door.

"I think it would be better if I came back when your husband is home," Morgan said.

"I think it would be better if you told me why you are here. Then we can both decide what is best."

A faint smile curved his lips. He gave a curt nod of his head. "As you wish, my lady."

Morgan waited for her to be seated, then settled his tall frame in a chair across from her. "How much do you know about the murder investigation we've been conducting in the death of Ansel Van Meer?"

"My husband has kept me informed. From what I understand, it is likely my brother-in-law, Mason Holloway, was involved in the murder."

"Highly likely. In fact, that is the reason I am here. You see, I've uncovered information that suggests Van Meer's son, Bartel, was a witness to the murder. I think another man may have also been there that night, a close friend of Bartel's. Unfortunately, I haven't been able to find out the second man's name or convince Van Meer to come forward. I was hoping your husband might be willing to talk to him."

"I'm sure he will be eager to do just that. Since he isn't here and I am not certain exactly when to expect him, why don't you give me the pertinent details and I'll see that my husband gets them. Where does the younger Van Meer live?"

Morgan hesitated as if he weren't sure a woman should be entrusted with such valuable information. Elizabeth lifted her head and eyed him directly. "Mr. Morgan?"

His lips curved with a hint of admiration. "Bartel Van Meer lives in Lambeth, just off Kennington Lane. Number 8 Worring Street. His wife's name is Elsie. They have two children, one eight and one ten. Van Meer takes great pride in his reputation as a cargo broker. His father's activities were an embarrassment he would like to forget. And perhaps he is afraid of Mason Holloway."

"As well he should be."

Morgan handed her a note with the information written down on it. "Speak to your husband. Convince him to speak to Van Meer. If the son will testify as to what happened that night and if there was indeed a second witness, it would go a long way in convincing the authorities that Mason committed the murder."

"I'll talk to Reese as soon as he returns. I'm certain he'll wish to follow up on the matter as quickly as possible." Elizabeth rose from her chair and Morgan did the same.

"Thank you, Countess."

"You are the one, Mr. Morgan, who deserves the thanks. I'm sure my husband will be in touch in a day or two."

If he is still alive.

Elizabeth's chest felt tight as she stood at the window and watched Chase Morgan leave the house. Reese would be busy speaking to his brothers, asking them to act as his seconds. He would be going to the Aldridge town house to confront Mason Holloway and challenge him to a bloody duel in the morning.

But Morgan had brought news that might stop him.

If Van Meer could be convinced to stand witness against Mason.

Elizabeth paced in front of the fire, praying desperately that Reese would return. There wasn't much time. Someone had to speak to Bartel Van Meer this very night.

She glanced at the clock. Time was running out for all of them.

Mason strode into the blue drawing room of the Aldridge town house, his jaw set, his expression grim. "The bloody court denied Dewar's petition."

Frances shot up from the sofa. "What!" She moved toward him, her narrow face contorted by lines of anger.

"You heard me. The boy retains the title."

"That isn't possible."

"I'm afraid, my dear, it is."

Frances paced over to the hearth, but she didn't feel the warmth. She was cold inside, and angry. She and Mason had worked too hard, gone through too much to be denied the power and wealth they deserved.

"We have to get rid of the boy," she said flatly. "We don't have any other choice."

He nodded grimly. "It gets worse."

She turned to face him. "Worse? What could possibly be worse than losing everything we've worked for?"

"We could lose our lives, Frances. Apparently, Dewar hired an investigator when all of this started. A man named Morgan. He's good, Frannie. Very good. He's been asking around, trying to find out what happened to Ansel Van Meer."

Her face paled. "My God."

"Exactly. We can't afford to let him discover the truth."

Frances paced away from him then back to where he stood. "You're talking about Van Meer's son . . . Barton or Burton or whatever his name is."

"Bartel. I thought I heard something in the back room that night. I figured it could have been Van Meer's son, but I wasn't sure. When he didn't come forward, I thought we were safe. It looks like I was wrong."

"Even if Van Meer's son was there, he's kept silent for years. What makes you think he'll talk now?"

"I don't know that he will. But Morgan has been dogging him relentlessly, and Dewar is sure to be after him, as well. We can't afford to take the chance."

"What do you propose we do?"

"Silence Van Meer."

Frances took a breath and let it out slowly. "We must do whatever we must."

Mason's lips curled. "You always were a sensible woman, Frances."

Frances just smiled.

461

Reese stood across from his brother in the study of the Bransford town house.

"Are you mad! Have you completely and utterly lost your senses?" Royal stalked out from behind his desk like a big golden lion. "If you kill him, they'll hang you, sure as bloody hell. Being a Dewar won't protect you. Dueling is clearly unlawful and the authorities are ruthlessly enforcing the law." He cocked a blond eyebrow. "Of course, Holloway might kill you, instead. Then he would be the one to hang — which would also solve your problem."

Reese just grunted. "Can't you see, I have to do this. I don't have any other choice. My boy won't be safe until Holloway is dead." And he would have seen to it long ago, except he'd had enough of killing, enough of bleeding and dying.

And he couldn't just shoot the man in cold blood. He wasn't a murderer and never would be. A duel was his only option.

Royal's hard look softened. "I can only begin to imagine how you must feel." He smiled slightly. "I'm about to become a father myself, you know."

Reese nodded. "Elizabeth told me. Congratulations."

"I'm excited, I can tell you. And as I said, I can only imagine how frightening it must be to have your child's life in danger." A lengthy breath whispered out. "But maybe there's another way."

"What do you mean?"

"Chase Morgan dropped by to see me. He left just before you arrived. Apparently, he stopped by your place first. You weren't home so he spoke to your wife."

"My wife?"

Royal grinned. "Apparently, she gave him no choice."

Imagining his small wife confronting the hardened investigator, Reese almost smiled. "What did Morgan have to say?"

"He's found Van Meer's son. He thinks Bartel Van Meer may have witnessed the murder. There is even a chance he was in the back room of the office with a friend when it happened. Morgan wants you to talk to him, convince him to tell the authorities what he saw the night his father was killed. He left the information with Elizabeth."

"He must have arrived just after I left. I've been gone a while. I had some errands to run. And I stopped by to see Rule, but he wasn't at home." His younger brother had moved into the town house their grand-father had left to him. Instead of a country manor like Briarwood, the town house was perfect for a city dweller like Rule.

"Our brother's out carousing, no doubt," Royal said with a hint of irritation. "It's never too early to begin the night for Rule."

"He's got a good head on his shoulders. Eventually he'll change."

Royal just scoffed, not completely sure. "The point is, there may be another way to stop Holloway. Hold off on the duel — at least until you talk to Van Meer, see what he knows. If he was witness to the crime, see if you can convince him to come forward."

Reese nodded. It was a last desperate hope, but one he would grasp. "I'll talk to Van Meer tonight." He stared hard at his brother. "If the conversation leads nowhere, will you second me?"

Royal glanced down for a moment, then looked back up at Reese. "You know I will. So will Rule. Let's just pray it doesn't come to that."

And so Reese left his brother's house pray-ing Bartel Van Meer would have the answers that would save his son's life.

Elizabeth wasn't sure how much time

passed. She only knew that dusk had begun to fall and she couldn't wait for Reese any longer. She had to do something before it was too late.

As she moved toward the drawing room door, she caught a glimpse of herself in the mirror above the fireplace. Pausing for an instant, she noticed the straight set of her shoulders, the firm tilt of her chin.

She was a woman now, with a child to care for and a husband she loved. Over the years, she had changed, become the strong, independent woman she was today.

Resolve filtered through her, strengthening her spine and filling her with courage. As the clock struck the hour, she hurried out of the drawing room and walked down the hall toward the staircase in the entry.

"I shall be gone for a while," she said to Jack Montague. "You and Mr. Gillespie will make certain my son is safe?"

"Of course, my lady." The beefy guard, a powerfully built man Reese trusted, straightened to his full height. "You needn't worry about the boy."

She nodded. "When my husband returns, please give him this." She handed the folded piece of paper to Montague. If something should happen, at least Reese would know where to find her.

Lifting her skirts, she hurried up the stairs. "Gilda!" she called out to her maid as she walked into her bedroom. "Have my carriage brought round front, then come back and help me change."

"Aye, milady." Gilda curtseyed and raced away.

Elizabeth hurried toward the armoire in the corner and threw open the doors. Searching for more simple garments, she pulled out a soft gray woolen gown and a warm woolen pelisse and began to change. Outside the window, the sky had darkened to a pinkish purple. Soon it would be dark, but the hour didn't matter.

She was on her way to number eight Worring Street, on her way to see Bartel Van Meer and convince him to tell the truth about the night of his father's murder.

Determined to see Mason arrested and avert the duel that might get her husband killed.

Reese made a quick search of the town house, but found no sign of Elizabeth. "Have you seen my wife?" he asked the guard who stood in the entry.

"I'm sorry, my lord, but your wife isn't here."

"What do you mean she isn't here? It's

466

nearly time for supper. Where the bloody hell did she go?"

Montague shifted away from the wall. "She left this for you."

Reese scanned the note. Inside were written the names *Bartel* and *Elsie Van Meer* and an address in Worring Street, Lambeth.

"This is where she went?" His voice climbed an octave. Surely Elizabeth wouldn't go to Van Meer by herself.

"She didn't make a point of it, but I believe it is. I would have gone with her, but she wanted me to stay and watch after the boy."

Of course she would. She loved their son. And the threat was greater to Jared than ever before. "How long ago did she leave?"

"Not more than half an hour. She did take one of the footmen."

Reese felt little more than mild relief. He had no idea whether or not Bartel Van Meer had witnessed a murder or even the sort of man he might be. He only knew his instincts were screaming that something might go wrong and Elizabeth could be in danger.

He set his jaw as he stalked down the hall to the study and opened the bottom drawer of his desk. Ignoring the heavy Adams revolver he had carried when he was in the army, he took out a small, five-shot pocket pistol and shoved it into his pocket.

Instead of returning to his carriage, still parked in front, he headed for the stables at the rear of the house. He could make better time traveling on horseback. His leg felt stronger every day, and though there was a certain amount of risk, he believed his best option was to ride.

"Saddle a horse," he told the groom as he reached the stable. "Whichever one is the least cantankerous." There were carriage horses, of course, but also a couple of saddle horses, there for the servants' use.

"Yes, my lord." The groom took off to do his bidding and a few minutes later, returned with a placid-looking sorrel gelding. Reese took a leg up from the groom and settled himself in the saddle.

Damn, it felt good to be astride a horse again. He flexed his leg, felt his thigh muscles respond, felt a sense of control that had been missing when he had tried to ride the first time. Ducking his head as he rode out through the stable door, he urged the horse a little faster and the animal clattered onto the cobbled path.

He took every shortcut he knew to cut down the distance from Mayfair to Vauxhall Bridge, the route that would carry him to Lambeth and ultimately the house in Worring Street that belonged to Bartel Van Meer. Still, the place was a goodly distance away and Elizabeth had a considerable head start.

His heart beat dully as he thought of her. By now she might have reached Van Meer and there was no telling what sort of man he was.

He worried what the Dutchman would do when his foolhardy, brave little wife appeared at his front door.

TWENTY-NINE

With the coachman losing his way for a bit, it took longer to reach Lambeth than Elizabeth had expected, but finally she was arrived.

Some of the area along the route was run-down and a bit worrisome, but the houses in Worring Street were well-cared for, built mostly of brick and tidily kept. The carriage rolled to a halt in front of a two-story residence with lamplight spilling out through the mullioned window, and the footman at the rear of the coach jumped down and opened the door.

"Wait for me here," Elizabeth instructed as she departed the carriage. "If I am not returned within half an hour, go back and fetch his lordship."

The young blond footman eagerly nodded. "As you wish, my lady."

She left him there, grateful to know he and the coach waited outside the house yet uncertain what good they might be if trouble actually arose.

Steeling herself, she took a deep breath and knocked firmly on the front door. A few moments later, a matronly, mob-capped housekeeper pulled the door open and stared down at her from inside the house.

"May I help you?"

"My name is Elizabeth Dewar," she said, not wanting her title to intimidate the man she had come to see. "I should like to speak to Mr. Van Meer."

The housekeeper eyed her top to bottom, taking in the expensive garments that were simply cut but made of the finest quality fabric. The silver fox trim at the neck of her woolen cloak seemed to convince her.

"I'll see if he is in." The stout woman left her standing on the stoop and went hurrying off to speak to Van Meer.

Through the crack in the door, Elizabeth spotted two young children, a boy and a girl, laughing as they darted up the staircase. A petite woman, apparently their mother, smiled as she trailed along behind them.

Elizabeth's heart pinched. Jared was almost the same age as the boy, who seemed to have none of the cares her own son had suffered.

The housekeeper returned just then. "Mr.

Van Meer will see you in the parlor." The woman stepped back to let her pass then began to guide her in that direction.

Elizabeth flicked a last glance up the stairs, but the threesome had disappeared behind one of the doors. They were a happy family, she thought, for contentment seemed to shine in the children's faces.

They reached the parlor, which was modestly done in shades of deep blue fabric and heavy oak furniture. It was cluttered with bric-a-brac: small hand-painted ceramic pieces of a variety of animals and birds, silhouette portraits of the children, a pair of small knitted stockings, items that made her even more certain that this wasn't just a house but truly a home.

Van Meer rose as Elizabeth walked in, a small man perhaps in his late thirties, with sandy hair and warm hazel eyes. A nondescript sort of man, except for the intelligence stamped into his features and the wariness he exuded as she walked toward him.

"You wished to see me, Mrs. Dewar?"

She didn't correct him. She was Reese's wife and Jared's mother and that was all that mattered. "I came to speak to you about your father."

The warmth faded from his face, making

472

him look older and harder.

"My father is a subject I do not discuss."

"You have a son of your own. He is nearly the same age as my own boy. I am here to ask you to help save my son's life."

The hard lines faded. Clearly, he was a man who loved children.

He motioned her toward the sofa. "Why don't you sit down and tell me why you are here."

"Thank you." She took the offered seat gratefully. She had only so much courage and she needed to conserve every ounce she possessed. "Mason Holloway is my brother-in-law. Or at least, he was before my husband died. I believe you may know him."

Van Meer made no reply.

"Mason believes he should have been the one to inherit the Aldridge title when his brother died. He is willing to go to any lengths to get it — even if it means murdering my son."

Van Meer hissed in a breath. "You're the Countess of Aldridge?"

"I retain the position, but I am remarried. Now I am merely a mother trying to protect her child."

"I see. Holloway is next in line for the title, then, after your son?"

"Yes."

"And you believe he would go as far as murder to get it?"

"Do you?"

Van Meer's shoulders sagged. He walked over and sank down in the chair across from her, his features pale and strained. "I know he will. He and his wife will do anything for money. Murder included."

Elizabeth's heart filled with hope. "You saw him that night, didn't you? You saw him kill your father. Will you come forward and speak the truth?"

Van Meer shook his head. "That I cannot do. I have my family to consider. You, more than anyone, ought to understand that."

"I do understand. But I believe if we stand together, we can see justice done. The Duke of Bransford is my husband's brother. He and my husband have very powerful friends. If you will tell the truth, we can put Mason Holloway where he belongs and save the life of my boy."

Van Meer drew an uneasy breath. "It's taken me years to build the life I share with my wife and children. I don't want what my father did dragged out in the open again. I don't want the scandal to harm my family's future."

"What exactly did your father do?"

He hesitated for several long moments,

deciding how much to reveal. Then a sigh of resignation whispered past his lips. "My father made a mistake. An awful, dreadful mistake. He was a good man, but he let the Holloways convince him to take the easy road. Just one time, they said, and he would make enough money to provide his family with all the things they deserved. But the Holloways were greedy. They didn't want to share the unholy profits their swindle earned. My father is dead because Mason wanted it all."

Elizabeth's heart was pounding, thudding wildly inside her chest. "Will you tell the authorities the truth about the murder? Tell them you saw Mason Holloway kill your father that night? It's the only chance I have to save my son."

Van Meer's expression turned bleak. He shook his head. "You don't understand. Mason Holloway didn't kill my father. Frances Holloway murdered him."

Elizabeth's eyes widened in shock. Of all the things she might have expected Van Meer to say, this wasn't one of them.

Her mind spun. If Mason didn't kill Van Meer, the law could not save them from him. She was trying to form some sort of reply when the window shattered at the rear of the parlor and the sound of a gunshot exploded in the air. Van Meer slammed back in his chair, groaning softly and clutching his shoulder, which blossomed red with blood.

Elizabeth leapt to her feet as the parlor door slid open and Van Meer's petite wife rushed in. "Bartel!"

"He's been shot!"

Elsie Van Meer raced to her husband's side and Elizabeth ran to the window to see if the man was still outside the house. On the ground below, two men struggled in hand-to-hand combat, fighting for control of the weapon that had fired the shot.

"Dear God!" One of the men was Mason Holloway. The other man was Reese.

Elizabeth bolted for the door. Behind her, Elsie Van Meer worked madly to staunch the flow of blood from the wound in her husband's shoulder.

Elizabeth raced down the hall and out the back door, desperate to help Reese before Mason managed to kill him.

"Reese!"

The sound of Elizabeth's voice, high-pitched and filled with fear, distracted him. For an instant, Reese's gaze darted in her direction and Holloway seized the moment to land a blow to Reese's jaw, knocking him backward. The gun they fought for went flying into the air and landed in the grass a few feet away.

Reese cursed himself as another solid blow landed, stepped back and threw a vicious right to Holloway's middle, doubling him over, then punched him squarely in the face. Reese glanced round for the weapon. His own pistol had flown from out of his pocket when he had slammed his full weight against Holloway to prevent a second shot through the window.

Reese punched Mason again and blood spouted from his nose. The instant before he hit the ground, Mason's beefy hand snaked around and grabbed Reese's weak leg, twisted, and jerked him onto the grass. Reese bit back a hiss of pain as Holloway's heavy body slammed down on top of him. Rising up, Mason swung a series of blows; some of them landing, some Reese avoided.

Lurching upward, Reese threw Holloway off balance, knocking him over then coming up above the heavier man, jabbing blow after blow into Holloway's face. The men fought back and forth, first one on top and then the other.

From the corner of his eye, Reese saw Elizabeth moving closer. "Stay back!" he shouted, praying she wouldn't put herself in danger.

"You bastard, I'll kill you!" Holloway rolled on top a second time, frantically searching the ground beside Reese's head until his blunt fingers closed over the grip of his pistol. Reese locked a hand around Holloway's thick wrist and the struggle began anew.

Mason cocked the hammer and tried to turn the barrel toward Reese. He was strong as a bull and Reese felt his hold begin to slip. In that instant, he spotted Elizabeth rushing toward Mason, and his heart squeezed so hard he couldn't breathe. He saw her swing her reticule back, watched it fly through the air and slam into Holloway's hand, changing the direction of the barrel, and the gun went off with a roar that echoed across the backyard.

Reese looked down to see blood on his coat and for a moment he thought he had been hit. Rolling Holloway's heavy weight off him, he gazed down to see the lead ball had torn into Mason's body, instead, directly into his heart. Holloway's eyes were open and staring up at the black night sky, but his lifeless form saw nothing.

"Reese!" Elizabeth raced toward him. Swaying a little on his feet, his leg fiercely throbbing, he caught her as she hurled herself into his arms. "Reese!"

He cradled her cheek in his hand. "I'm all right. Holloway's dead, but I am fine."

"He — he shot Van Meer. He was going . . . going to kill you."

His arms tightened around her. "He might have done it, my love, if it hadn't been for you."

"Montague gave you my note?"

He nodded.

"H-how did you know Mason was here?"

"I spotted him ahead of me on the road. I saw him ride into the alley behind the house and I followed him. I didn't catch up with him fast enough to prevent the shot." He felt her body shaking with the remnants of fear and held her even closer.

"Everything's going to be all right," he soothed, not wanting to let her go. He needed her there, needed to be sure she was safe.

He took a deep breath and eased her a little away. "Everything is all right, but we need to see about Van Meer."

She nodded. Reese looked down to see tears on her lovely pale cheeks.

"I was so frightened. I — I was afraid he would kill you." A fresh tear rolled toward her trembling chin. "I love you, Reese."

The chest contracted so sharply it felt like pain. His heart throbbed fiercely and for an instant, he pulled her back into his arms. He had ached to hear those words. He wanted to say those same words to her.

He knew they were true.

The moment he had seen her standing mere inches from the barrel of Holloway's pistol, as he had watched her risk herself to save him, he had known the truth.

He loved her. Just as he always had.

But his battered heart refused to open and the words remained locked in his throat. Instead, he leaned down and very softly kissed her.

"Everything is going to be all right, love, I promise you." Ignoring the disappointment he read in her face, he guided her toward the porch and into a house full of chaos.

Elizabeth's gaze lit on the two crying children, the housekeeper, the cook, and a chambermaid who stood outside the parlor.

"I'll send the footman to fetch the authorities," she said, turning toward the front door while Reese made his way toward Van Meer.

The man still sat in his chair, his wife hovering over him, but his shirt was off and there were bandages round his torso.

"How is he?" Reese asked, striding toward them.

"The ball went all the way through," Elsie Van Meer said. "That is good, right?"

"That's very good," Reese answered.

"I have sent for a physician."

Reese nodded.

"Who are you?"

"My name is Reese Dewar. Your husband was talking to my wife when Mason Holloway shot him."

Bartel Van Meer roused himself a little. "Where is Holloway now?"

"He's dead. We've sent for the police."

"He's dead? Are you sure?"

Reese's mouth edged up. "Holloway managed to find justice on his own. My wife deflected the gun he was pointing at me and it killed him instead."

Van Meer slumped back in his chair.

Elizabeth walked into the parlor, over to Van Meer's chair. "Now will you tell the police the truth when they get here, tell them Frances is the one who killed your father?"

Reese's head came up. He had arrived in time to stop Holloway but he had no idea what Van Meer had told Elizabeth about the night of the murder.

"Perhaps, as your husband says, it is time justice was served. I'll tell the truth about the murder. And my friend, Christian

481

Brinkman, will also come forward. He was there that night, as well. Holloway was with his wife. I don't think either of them actually saw us, but he must have been afraid I would speak out against him."

"He must have found out Morgan was trying to convince you to talk to the police."

Van Meer smiled. "It was your wife, sir, who convinced me."

Reese slid an arm around Elizabeth's waist. "You shouldn't have come but I'm glad you did. Soon this will all be over and our son will at last be safe."

She gave him a weary smile, then returned her attention to the Dutchman. "Thank you, Mr. Van Meer. Thank you for everything. If you ever need help of any kind, I hope you will come to us."

"My wife is right. If you ever need anything at all, come to us at Briarwood. You can count on our help."

"Rest now, dearest," the man's wife said. "The doctor should be here any moment."

Van Meer closed his eyes and Reese urged Elizabeth out into the hall, giving the couple a moment of privacy. The police would arrive any moment. Once Mason's attempt to kill Van Meer was revealed and all of their statements taken, Frances Holloway would be arrested. Jared and the Van Meers would be safe. Justice would be served and Reese could take his beloved family home.

He looked down at his wife. He wished he could speak his heart as she had done.

But if he did, he would no longer be able to protect himself as he had for so many years.

Reese wasn't sure he could ever find that kind of courage.

THIRTY

Annabelle Townsend was holding a ball. She was famous in society for the elaborate parties she threw at her elegant town mansion, and people had begun to speculate as to why she no longer seemed interested in her friends.

It was Travis, of course. Loving him. Missing him. She no longer cared for the fickle social whirl. She would rather be spending her evenings with Travis, playing cards in his drawing room, or simply talking before passion overcame them and they made love.

Anna missed him and she would never stop loving him, but she had come to accept that she had a life to live and Travis would never be a part of it. He wasn't interested in marriage and she had discovered she couldn't be happy with anything less.

Travis was her weakness, but she had lived without him since she was a girl. She could certainly do it again.

"Fetch my jewelry box, will you, Sadie?"

Her ladies' maid hurried over to the dresser and plucked the inlaid rosewood box off the top. The girl returned and held open the lid. "Here you are, my lady."

"Thank you." Choosing a simple strand of pearls with a lovely pearl-and-diamond pendant suspended in the middle, Annabelle waited while Sadie draped the jewelry round her throat, then placed the matching earbobs in her ears.

Rising from the tapestry stool, she stood for a moment in front of the mirror.

"You look very fetching, my lady."

"I must say, the gown is lovely." Smoothing the deep blue velvet fabric, she adjusted her light brown curls against her shoulder then started for the door. It was time she got over Travis.

Or at least got on with her life.

Whatever it took, tonight she would be bright and gay, the belle of the ball, just as she always had been.

She wouldn't think of Travis Greer and how handsome he was and how he could make her heartbeat quicken with a single glance. She wouldn't think of his incredible lovemaking.

Not tonight.

Not even once.

Mustering a smile, Annabelle followed the sound of the orchestra tuning up in the ballroom and sailed out of her bedroom.

Travis stood just inside the ballroom door. Reese stood next to him, Elizabeth a few feet away in conversation with the duke and duchess of Bransford and Reese's aunt, Lady Tavistock.

"So what are you still doing in London?" Travis asked Reese. "I thought you'd be on your way home by now."

"The magistrates have a few more questions. We thought we'd enjoy a last evening with friends. We're leaving for Holiday House day after the morrow, then on to Briarwood."

"From what I read in the *Times*, Frances Holloway will be locked away for a very long while."

"So it would seem." Reese cocked an eyebrow. "What about you? What are you doing here? I thought you and Anna weren't seeing each other anymore."

"We aren't. I'm crashing the party."

"Tell me you are jesting."

"I didn't get invited. I wanted to see her so I came."

Reese's mouth edged up in amusement.

"Interesting."

Travis grunted. "Yes, well, I'm glad you think so." He stalked off toward the punch bowl, his mood grim. For the past half hour, he had been watching Anna float round the ballroom in the arms of one man after another. He knew she had seen him. Every once in a while, her gaze would drift in his direction but immediately slice away.

Instead, she danced and laughed and fluttered her damnable fan, obviously enjoying herself. And the men were lapping it up.

Anna was a beautiful woman, and incredibly desirable.

Travis knew *exactly* how desirable. Inside his trousers, his shaft hardened as a memory arose of them together in his big bed, of her soft little cries as he moved inside her.

He clamped his jaw. Walking over to the liquor table, he asked a servant to pour him a brandy and tossed it back in a single swallow. Another half hour passed while Anna continued to avoid him. For a woman who was supposed to love him, she had an odd way of showing it.

She was waltzing with that blackguard, Jonathan Savage, when Travis had finally had enough.

Pushing away from the wall, he strode toward the dance floor. He waited until the music came to an end and walked up to her before she had time to escape.

"I believe the next dance is mine," he said, casting Savage the darkest look he could muster.

The rogue just smiled. "Is that so?" He pressed Anna's hand into his and stepped away, playing the gentleman as Travis had rarely seen him.

"This isn't your dance," she said, lifting her little nose in the air. "You don't dance anymore."

Many of them were nearly impossible to do with only one arm. "No, I don't, so unless you wish to make a scene, you had better come with me."

Her feet didn't move. "Why are you here?"

"I wanted to see you."

"You could have come to the house."

"I could have, but I didn't." The music began, a lively schottische, which he ignored. He wanted to get her alone and he finally had the chance.

It was too cold to go outside. Instead, he ushered her out of the ballroom and down the hall to the long gallery, a narrow, multi-windowed chamber at the back of the house where the crowd had thinned to just a few couples.

With a hand at her waist, he guided her

toward a quiet corner next to a leafy potted plant.

"You seem to be enjoying yourself," he said, still a little piqued that she could so easily forget him, forget all they had shared.

Her chin came up and her soft mouth turned pouty. It made him want to kiss her. "Why shouldn't I enjoy myself?"

"I rather hoped you would be pining away for your lost love, namely me. That is what you said, isn't it? That you loved me?"

Some of her bravado faded. "Sometimes love isn't enough."

"I need to know if you meant it, Anna. I need to know if you love me, the way you said."

Amazement widened her pretty blue eyes. "You think I would lie about something like that?"

"Just tell me the truth."

For the first time she seemed to realize how important the question was to him. "I love you, Travis. I've loved you for years. I suppose I always will."

His chest ached. "Enough to marry me?"

She stared up at him. "Are you . . . are you asking me to marry you?"

"Will you, Anna? Do you love me enough to marry me?"

"But you don't want to get married. You

told me that yourself."

"You said the same thing."

"I didn't . . . didn't realize how I would feel after . . . after . . ."

"After we made love?"

"Yes."

"I was wrong, sweetheart. After you left, I realized the sort of life I was living. How empty it was until you came along. How lonely it was without you. Say you will marry me."

Tears brimmed in her eyes. "Do you love me, Travis?"

"Desperately."

Anna laughed, the sound filling his heart. "Then there is nothing in this world that I would like more than to marry you."

Relief hit him so hard he felt weak. Sliding his arm around her tiny waist, he hauled her against him, bent his head and very thoroughly kissed her. Both of them were breathing too fast when he finally let her go.

"Come on." He tugged on her hand.

"Where are we going?"

Uncertainty trickled through him. "You don't mean to keep it a secret, do you?"

"Heavens, no."

Travis grinned and tugged her forward, back into the ballroom and up onto the stage where the orchestra was playing. The music stopped. The guests in the ballroom began to fall silent.

"If I could have your attention," Travis said, "I have an announcement to make."

The last of the murmurs died away and attention focused on the stage.

"Lady Annabelle has consented to marry me. Since I am madly in love with her, I am the happiest man on earth."

Cheers went up.

"And you are all invited to the wedding," Anna added with a grin.

There were whoops of joy and shouts of congratulations. Travis was smiling — until he looked over at his best friend. Reese looked like a man who had been kicked in the stomach. And even from a distance, he could see the glitter of tears in Elizabeth's eyes.

He wasn't sure what was wrong. For his friend's sake, he hoped Reese would recognize the love he felt for his wife and not make the same mistake Travis had made.

Reese just stood there. He still couldn't believe it. His best friend had just offered marriage to Annabelle Townsend and declared his love for her in front of half of London. If he hadn't seen it for himself, he never would have believed it.

Why had Travis found it so easy to speak his feelings when Reese found it so unbearably hard?

He pondered the notion as he sat next to Elizabeth on the carriage ride back to the town house, and later that night after they had made love and he had curled her against his side as she had fallen asleep.

For Reese, sleep did not come.

He loved Elizabeth and he loved his son. Why didn't he tell them? He knew how much it would mean to both of them and yet he kept silent, afraid to open his heart.

Dawn came and still he lay awake, his mind in turmoil. Easing quietly from the bed, he dressed and went out to the stable, saddled the sorrel gelding he had ridden to Van Meer's and headed for the park.

His leg was still a little sore from his fight with Holloway but as he eased the horse into an easy canter around the gravel track, the muscles loosened and the leg gave him no problem. The brisk November air beat against his face as he increased the horse's pace, but it was more exhilarating than cold and it seemed to clear his head.

Just three small words, he thought.

I love you.

How could they be so hard to say?

The others were easy. *I need you. I want*

you. He'd had no trouble with those.

But those were not nearly so important. They didn't put your heart at risk. The very essence of your being.

Reese looked up through the trees at the sunlight filtering down on the glistening morning dew. As he gazed up at the sky, sunlight seemed to penetrate his skin and warm his insides. Courage filled him, seemed to expand until it pushed all his old fears away. With it came determination.

Whirling the sorrel, he rode back to the town house, where fires had been lit and chimney smoke drifted over the gray slate roof. He handed the reins to a groom and made his way inside to find Elizabeth just entering the breakfast room.

"Good morning," she said, but there was something missing in her voice, an emptiness that had been there since she had told him she loved him and he had said nothing in return.

"Before you sit down, I'd like a word with you in my study, if you don't mind."

She managed a nod. "Of course."

Reese strode on down the hall, sent a maid up to fetch Jared, then headed for his study.

He was waiting when his wife and son arrived a few minutes later, Elizabeth looking nervous, Jared downright wary. The child hurried over and grabbed onto his mother's skirt.

"Is . . . is something wrong?" Elizabeth asked anxiously.

Reese forced himself to smile. "Actually, there is. But the error is mine, not either of yours." He continued to smile though his insides were trembling and his heart was squeezing so hard he could barely breathe. "You see, in the past few days, I've realized the wrong I've done you both."

"What . . . what do you mean? You have been nothing but generous and caring since we first came to your home."

"Generous and caring? I hope I have been those things. But there is something more. Something I feel for both of you that I have not said." He knelt a few feet away from Jared. "Come here, son."

The boy came shyly, still a little uncertain.

"I asked you to come in here so I could tell you how much I love you. I haven't said that before, but it's true. I'm so proud of you, Jared. You are my joy and my hopes for the future and I love you more than my own life."

The little boy looked up at him, his dark eyes shining with some deep emotion. He reached out and touched Reese's cheek. "I love you, too, Papa."

His heart twisted. He leaned over and kissed the child's forehead, then rose to his feet. "And I love your mother." His gaze shifted toward her, standing there in front of the fire, her eyes glistening with tears. "She is my heart and my soul. I have loved her since she was a girl and I love her still."

Elizabeth made a strangled sound in her throat. "Reese . . ." She started toward him across the study and he met her halfway, swept her into his arms.

He pressed his cheek against hers. "I love you, Beth. Your strength and your determination, the wonderful mother you are to our son. I loved the girl you were, but even more, I love the woman you have become."

She smiled up at him through her tears. "My darling, Reese, I love you so much."

And then he was kissing her and he had never felt so free, so entirely happy.

Laughter rang out behind him and when he turned, he saw that Jared was grinning. Reese motioned for his son to join them, lifted him up against his shoulder, and the three of them stood together, arms locked around each other.

A lightness filled him, the way the sun had that morning, shining down into his heart. Joy expanded inside him. For the first time, the pieces of his life all fit together.

"I love you, Beth," he said, the words coming easy this time. "I love you both so very much." He smiled. "And I can't wait to take my beautiful family home."

EPILOGUE

Three months later

Elizabeth stood next to Aunt Agatha at Briarwood, behind the house on the brick path leading down to the stable. Reese and Jared were preparing their horses, getting ready for their morning ride.

"I knew he would be a good father," the frail old woman said. "I think it was that same caring that made him a good leader of men."

"Yes, perhaps that was it." For Reese was both of those things. A marvelous father and respected leader. Amazingly, a very good landlord and gentleman farmer. His tenants admired him and worked hard to please him. They were getting ready to plow, preparing to plant a very large barley crop, which Royal had assured them he would purchase for his extremely successful brewery business.

And Reese seemed to enjoy the work. She

497

hadn't been certain he would be happy giving up his military career and the life of adventure he once seemed to love, but she could see the satisfaction in his face whenever he looked out over the fields. He was happy at Briarwood.

And the knowledge made her happy, too.

"I heard they locked up that dreadful Holloway woman for half a century," Aunt Agatha said. Over the past few months, she and Elizabeth had moved beyond the old animosity into a steady sort of friendship. Elizabeth believed their mutual love for Reese and Jared was the underlying cause and hoped their relationship over the years might grow even deeper.

She had lost her mother far too young. She appreciated the old woman's counsel and hoped she could win her affections.

"Mr. Morgan personally brought the news of her sentence," Elizabeth said, "though it was in all of the newspapers."

The old woman nodded. "I heard, also, that scoundrel, Travis Greer, outdid himself and married the lovely widow, Annabelle Townsend."

The word *scoundrel* was said with a twinkle in the old woman's eyes. Elizabeth knew the dowager had always had a soft spot for Reese's best friend.

"Once they tried Sandhurst and his co-horts for treason and found them guilty," Elizabeth said, "the captain's complete innocence was proved. He has become a man of some celebrity in the journalistic community."

"I am sorry I was unwell the day of the wedding."

"It was lovely. I think he and Lady Annabelle make a very good match."

The old woman sniffed. "Indeed."

They looked out toward the barn, watched as Reese lifted Jared up on Dusty, the dapple gray pony, then swung himself up into the saddle of his big black gelding. Warrior snorted and danced, but Reese handled him easily. His leg rarely bothered him. He would always carry a scar and walk with a bit of a limp, but he no longer required the use of his cane, though on occasion he still carried it.

Elizabeth imagined he liked the protection the implement offered, with its hidden six-inch blade.

"Rule, that wicked boy, has probably arrived by now in the colonies. Perhaps all that hard work will straighten him out."

The colonies being America. Rule had promised his father he would strengthen the family's position by working to build ties with the Americans, though he was planning to return to England as soon as he could. One thing Elizabeth had learned, the Dewars were men who kept their word.

"Rule is a good man," she said. "He is young yet. In time, he'll know better what he wants."

Aunt Agatha grunted. "He wants under the skirt of every pretty girl he sees. He needs a wife, that boy. A woman who will bring his reckless nature under control."

"As I said, once he is older . . ."

"I suppose you're right. None of the Dewar men marry young. I doubt Rule will be any different. But mark my words, one day that boy will meet his match. I hope I am still around when that happens."

Elizabeth laughed. "I think you will outlive all of us, my lady."

The dowager just smiled.

Father and son urged their horses into a canter and rode off toward the fields, and Elizabeth's heart went with them. She could feel it beating, throbbing softly with love for her men.

Aunt Agatha's gaze followed hers. "I told you it would all work out."

And it had. Reese loved her and she loved him and they both loved their son. The old woman had an uncanny way of predicting the future.

"You have a lot to look forward to," the dowager said as if she had read Elizabeth's thoughts. "Reese is certain to give you more children, and the two of you will live a long and happy life together."

Elizabeth had learned to trust the old woman's instincts. As she watched her husband and son, she thought of the passionate night she had spent in Reese's arms and her odd feeling of contentment this morning. Gently, her hand settled protectively over the curve of her stomach.

This time Elizabeth was the one who smiled.

AUTHOR'S NOTE

I hope you enjoyed *Reese's Bride,* the second in the trilogy that began with *Royal's Bride,* a series about the handsome Dewar brothers and the feisty women they come to love.

Rule's Bride is the final book in the trilogy. Rule, the youngest Dewar, is now head of a highly successful London manufacturing company. To honor a promise he made his dying father, Rule entered into an arranged marriage three years earlier with the sixteen-year-old daughter of wealthy American Howard Griffin. Rule hasn't seen Violet since the day they were wed.

Since actually becoming a husband is the last thing Rule wants, he is stunned to find his grown-up child bride standing on his front door. Violet Griffin Dewar has matured into a beauty, he discovers, and he is eager to claim his husbandly rights.

Unfortunately, the only thing Violet wants

503

from Rule is to end their unconsummated sham of a marriage.

I hope you'll watch for *Rule's Bride* and that you enjoy all three books in the trilogy.

Warmest wishes,

Kat